Reviewers L

"Melissa Brayden has become ... . popular novelists of the genre, writing hit after hit of funny, relatable, and very sexy stories for women who love women."—*Afterellen.com*

When You Smile

"Taryn and Charlie's story strikes a perfect balance between emotional depth and lighthearted sweetness. The combination of warmth, honesty, vulnerability, and smiles makes their journey incredibly relatable and heartwarming. Grab your copy, settle into your comfy reading spot, and enjoy the ride."—*The Lesbian Review*

You Had Me at Merlot

"Sweet and delicious…Melissa has packed this story full of quirky characters who are all unforgettable and contributing in their own way to making the story memorable."—*LESBIReviewed*

The Forever Factor

"Melissa Brayden never fails to impress. I read this in one day and had a smile on my face throughout. An easy read filled with the snappy banter and heartfelt longing that Melissa writes so effortlessly."—*Sapphic Book Review*

The Last Lavender Sister

"It's also a slow burn, with some gorgeous writing. I've had to take some breaks while reading to delight in a turn of phrase here and there, and that's the best feeling."—*Jude in the Stars*

Exclusive

"Melissa Brayden's books have always been a source of comfort, like seeing a friend you've lost touch with but can pick right up where you left off. They have always made my heart happy, and this one does the same."—*Sapphic Book Review*

Marry Me

"A bride-to-be falls for her wedding planner in this smoking hot, emotionally mature romance from Brayden…Brayden is remarkably generous to her characters, allowing them space for self-exploration and growth."—*Publishers Weekly*

To the Moon and Back

"*To the Moon and Back* is all about Brayden's love of theatre, onstage and backstage, and she does a delightful job of sharing that love… Brayden set the scene so well I knew what was coming, not because it's unimaginative but because she made it obvious it was the only way things could go. She leads the reader exactly where she wants to take them, with brilliant writing as usual. Also, not everyone can make office supplies sound sexy."—*Jude in the Stars*

Back to September

"You can't go wrong with a Melissa Brayden romance. Seriously, you can't. Buy all of her books. Brayden sure has a way of creating an emotional type of compatibility between her leads, making you root for them against all odds. Great settings, cute interactions, and realistic dialogue."—*Bookvark*

What a Tangled Web

"[T]he happiest ending to the most amazing trilogy. Melissa Brayden pulled all of the elements together, wrapped them up in a bow, and presented the reader with Happily Ever After to the max!"—*Kitty Kat's Book Review Blog*

Beautiful Dreamer

"I love this book. I want to kiss it on its face…I'm going to stick *Beautiful Dreamer* on my to-reread-when-everything-sucks pile, because it's sure to make me happy again and again."—*Smart Bitches Trashy Books*

Two to Tangle

"Melissa Brayden does it again with a sweet and sexy romance that leaves you feeling content and full of happiness. As always, the book is full of smiles, fabulous dialogue, and characters you wish were your best friends."—*The Romantic Reader*

Entangled

"Ms. Brayden has a definite winner with this first book of the new series, and I can't wait to read the next one. If you love a great enemies-to-lovers, feel-good romance, then this is the book for you."—*Rainbow Reflections*

"*Entangled* is a simmering slow burn romance, but I also fully believe it would be appealing for lovers of women's fiction. The friendships between Joey, Maddie, and Gabriella are well developed and engaging as well as incredibly entertaining…All that topped off with a deeply fulfilling happily ever after that gives all the happy sighs long after you flip the final page."—*Lily Michaels: Sassy Characters, Sizzling Romance, Sweet Endings*

Love Like This

"Brayden upped her game. The characters are remarkably distinct from one another. The secondary characters are rich and wonderfully integrated into the story. The dialogue is crisp and witty."—*Frivolous Reviews*

Sparks Like Ours

"Brayden sets up a flirtatious tit-for-tat that's honest, relatable, and passionate. The women's fears are real, but the loving support from the supporting cast helps them find their way to a happy future. This enjoyable romance is sure to interest readers in the other stories from Seven Shores."—*Publishers Weekly*

Hearts Like Hers

"Once again Melissa Brayden stands at the top. She unequivocally is the queen of romance."—*Front Porch Romance*

Eyes Like Those

"Brayden's story of blossoming love behind the Hollywood scenes provides the right amount of warmth, camaraderie, and drama." —*RT Book Reviews*

Strawberry Summer

"This small-town second-chance romance is full of tenderness and heart. The 10 Best Romance Books of 2017."—*Vulture*

"*Strawberry Summer* is a tribute to first love and soulmates and growing into the person you're meant to be. I feel like I say this each time I read a new Melissa Brayden offering, but I loved this book so much that I cannot wait to see what she delivers next."—*Smart Bitches, Trashy Books*

First Position

"Brayden aptly develops the growing relationship between Ana and Natalie, making the emotional payoff that much sweeter. This ably plotted, moving offering will earn its place deep in readers' hearts." —*Publishers Weekly*

By the Author

Romances

Waiting in the Wings

Heart Block

How Sweet It Is

First Position

Strawberry Summer

Beautiful Dreamer

Back to September

To the Moon and Back

Marry Me

Exclusive

The Last Lavender Sister

The Forever Factor

Lucky in Lace

Marigold

You Had Me at Merlot

When You Smile

Dream a Little Dream

Soho Loft Romances:

Kiss the Girl

Just Three Words

Ready or Not

Seven Shores Romances:

Eyes Like Those

Hearts Like Hers

Sparks Like Ours

Love Like This

Tangle Valley Romances:

Entangled

Two to Tangle

What a Tangled Web

Visit us at www.boldstrokesbooks.com

DREAM
A LITTLE DREAM

by
Melissa Brayden

2025

DREAM A LITTLE DREAM
© 2025 BY MELISSA BRAYDEN. ALL RIGHTS RESERVED.

ISBN 13: 978-1-63679-839-4

THIS TRADE PAPERBACK ORIGINAL IS PUBLISHED BY
BOLD STROKES BOOKS, INC.
P.O. BOX 249
VALLEY FALLS, NY 12185

FIRST EDITION: MAY 2025

CREDITS
EDITORS: LYNDA SANDOVAL AND STACIA SEAMAN
PRODUCTION DESIGN: STACIA SEAMAN
COVER DESIGN BY INKSPIRAL DESIGN

Acknowledgments

I wrote *Beautiful Dreamer* nearly seven years ago, and even then, I knew I'd return to Dreamer's Bay someday—I was just waiting for the right story to bring me back. When Savanna and Kyle's romance came to me last year, I couldn't have been more excited to revisit the Bay and the characters who make it feel like home. It's my hope that you'll enjoy your stay for *Dream a Little Dream* and relish the chance to reconnect with some familiar faces and places.

I'd like to thank my editor, Lynda Sandoval, for the gentle nudges that reassured me I was on the right path and the insightful advice that proved spot-on. Would you believe that the last book we worked on together was *Beautiful Dreamer*? Pure coincidence—or maybe not. I believe in signs, and some things are simply meant to be.

As always, my deepest gratitude to everyone at Bold Strokes Books—from the top down—for the dedication and detail that bring our stories to life. A heartfelt thank you to Radclyffe, Sandy Lowe, Ruth Sternglantz, Toni Whitaker, Stacia Seaman, Inkspiral Design, and the proofreaders who catch what I miss. Your hard work does not go unnoticed.

To the reviewers—your work is invaluable across all genres. You amplify our voices in ways we never could on our own, and I'm endlessly grateful for your passion and dedication.

And to my readers—you mean more to me than you'll ever know. You're always in my thoughts, pushing me to be a better writer. Keep reaching out, sharing your impressions, and journeying through these stories with me.

For those who follow the signs.
They'll lead you to where you're supposed to be.

CHAPTER ONE

The Attic

I was an orphan again. Despite my best efforts, somehow, that kept happening. I was also a thirty-four-year-old redhead who lived alone and hadn't kissed a woman in a year and a half. But who was counting? Apparently, me. There was also a grocery store I was in charge of that was losing money, and I had my aunt's entire attic to clean out, full of all of her prized possessions and mementos I'd been too grief stricken to sort through until now.

The familiar grief swooped and settled. My Aunt Lindy was gone. It had been three weeks since her heart attack, and the reality was only now starting to settle. Lindy had been my rock after I'd lost my parents at eleven years old, the person who'd shown up to every school function and snuggled with me in my bed on the nights I was scared of jarring claps of thunder or was missing my old life.

Lindsay Renee Bright, my mother's sister, had been one of the good ones, and I vowed to be one, too. I'd make her proud and always try to mirror her kindness, her warmth, and her unwavering belief that the world was a wonderful place. I also hoped to stay a little silly in her honor and not take things like "stupid trash day" too seriously. I'd celebrate it instead with the little rhyming song that she'd sashay her hips to as she pulled the cans down the drive.

In the meantime, I had to figure out what to do with her things, all left to me. The volume overwhelmed, accumulated from over sixty years of experiences and memories made. Her crowded little home three blocks from the bay was just as she'd left it, and up here in this attic were all the keepsakes and important signposts from her life's journey. The certificate for volunteer hours she'd put in at the hospital. The old fishing pole my grandfather had used to teach his kids to fish. The jar of playing cards, each pack collected from a different city she'd visited. I smiled at the impact she'd made not just on me but on everyone she'd come in contact with. Each person was better for having known Lindy, and that was the best possible legacy. I hadn't had it in me to do much with her home until now. But the time had come to pull myself together and blink back the tears.

But grief, for me, wasn't new.

My parents were killed in a head-on collision twenty-two years ago while returning home from their anniversary weekend away. They'd splurged on an ocean view room at a fancy hotel my mother had been dying to stay in. Before she left, she told me the restaurant there was known for their amazing lobster. I never found out if she'd enjoyed it.

It had apparently been instant, their deaths. Everyone acted like that information should serve as a great comfort, but it didn't ever take away the fact that I didn't have parents anymore. And they'd been great parents for every year of the eleven and half we'd spent together. I still had very vivid memories. My mother loved chocolate ice cream and early evening game shows. My father was a sports guy who'd taken me to games every chance he got. Baseball had been his favorite, but honestly, any sport would do. He'd never been much of an athlete himself, so he'd made it a point to learn absolutely everything he possibly could about the sport, the players, the league, and the season as a form of compensation. Losing them both had been the tragedy of my life. How was I now losing Lindy, too?

I leaned back against the structurally necessary wooden post smack in the middle of the musty room. My Aunt Lindy's attic, as always, was warm and damp, one of the reasons I generally avoided it. The box in my lap held a twine-bound bundle of my mother's cards, letters, and pressed flowers, all of which had been a joy to sift through after so many years. I'd taken the afternoon and just absorbed the words she'd saved from her friends, relatives, and my mother herself. Distractedly, and as I still sorted through my feelings of panic and shock and who knew what else, I still clutched an old to-do list of my mom's that included picking up a cake topper for my parents' wedding. I blinked down at the faded swoops and dips of her penmanship. She'd had beautiful handwriting, even better than my own, which I took pride in. I ran my thumb across the blue ink, a time capsule transporting me back to a happier time. Memories flew by in fragments. Dance parties in the living room when I'd brought home As and Bs on my report card. Watching TV all together on the couch when I was scared of the howling winds in the middle of the night. My mom crying when our cat, Figgy Pudding, went missing, only to have her come wandering home a week later.

My life was definitely divided in two parts: before the accident, and after. I wondered if this loss would do the same. Who would I be now that I was completely without family? I wondered about starting one of my own someday. It was a momentary consolation.

"I'm here!" I heard the sound of the front door below, and it jarred me into the here and now. Jonathan had arrived, thank God, my best friend and other half. He'd planned to give me some time to sort through the attic on my own before meeting me here and helping where he could—from both the emotional and logistical standpoints. I needed him now more than ever.

"Hey, Savvy. Did you hear me?" Jonathan called.

"Down in a sec!" I called back.

As I gathered the haphazardly strewn cards and letters and placed them back in their twine binding, I reflected on my own trajectory. My life was certainly feeling battered these days.

My doctor felt strongly that I needed a vacation or outlet for all the pent-up stress I carried with me, but I preferred to press on and try to see the good in life. Because there had to be an infinite amount of joy out there if others were scooping it up and making it their own. I just needed some time to catch up with the rest of the world.

"Hey. Just checking in on you." Jonathan, with his soulful brown eyes and dark hair neatly styled with tea tree oil pomade, blinked at me with the tenderness of a good friend on a hard day. He'd somehow made his way up the ladder without me hearing him, which could have easily led to a fall.

Concern struck. "You should have asked for my help. Now I have to murder you." I was protective of him, always would be.

He shrugged, leaning on the forearm crutch that had aided his climb. "And ruin the surprise? Never. I live to shock and impress. Just look at you. You can't take it, murderer that you aspire to be."

He was attempting levity on what he knew was an emotionally charged afternoon. I attempted a smile for him. Our relationship was laced evenly with one part humor and one part sincerity. We leapt back and forth without notice, which I loved about us.

"Results are pending."

He shrugged as if to say *you can't win 'em all*. But there must have been something about the look on my face that alerted him to my new level of stress. He tilted his head. "What's going on?"

"I'm emotional. My heart hurts and my aunt is gone." I offered a halfhearted shrug.

"Fuck a duck."

"I know." Silence hit and we shared a laugh. Lindy would have loved that comment.

Jonathan chewed the inside of his lip and leaned more fully on his crutch. I could tell he was uncomfortable, which meant sincerity was on the way. "Savvy, I want you to know that I'm going to have the perfect words for you, but they're as of this moment, not yet assembled. I'm in the deep end with you, though." He opened his mouth and closed it. "I'm sorry for what you're going through. Let's start there."

Jonathan and I had been inseparable ever since the day he'd organized a Gay-Straight Alliance our freshman year of high school and I'd been the only other person to attend the first meeting. I firmly believe it was meant to be just us. We'd come out to each other that day, discontinued the less than successful club, and become best friends instead. With a graduating class of only a hundred and sixty students, we'd been the only gay kids in the mix until Lorelei Newman brought home a wife from college years later. Damn her for stealing the spotlight—and marrying first, too. But that had done it. Next, James Garza and Brett Lunsford were miraculously a couple and not just teammates on the town's recreational softball team. Devyn Winters and Elizabeth Draper, the most opposites attract story ever, were now living a few streets away in absolute bliss. The list didn't end there. We now had an *actual gay population* in little Dreamer's Bay, South Carolina. Who'd have ever predicted *that*? Jonathan and I had simply been ahead of our time. A trendsetting duo.

"Okay." He paused as if trying to keep up with the organization happening in front of him. "Tell me. What is your plan for all this?"

The shift in topic was the reprieve I needed. I could breathe again. "Simple. I go through each box, each belonging, each greeting card, and figure out what to keep and what to get rid of." I turned to him, the finality of it all weighing on me. "Isn't it interesting how it comes down to this? A bunch of things and furniture trapped here instead of with her. They're all just sitting around alone in boxes without their person."

"It is. But don't lose sight of the memories, Sentimental Sandy. We had a lot of fun here," he said with a gleam.

God, we had. Movie marathons. Disastrous cooking lessons where Aunt Lindy had done her best to teach us both a few staple dishes to catastrophic results on our part. We were too busy tossing the cheese we'd grated at each other to actually pay attention. There'd been birthday parties in the backyard that were decently attended by our more popular friends and classmates. It was a testament to the warm environment my aunt had always created for us, a safe but cool place for the teenagers of Dreamer's Bay to gather. Now it was up to me to figure out how to transition the now quiet space to something new and special.

I had one prominent idea.

But before expressing it, I blinked, wishing I had water. My throat was sandpaper, and my head now ached. Why did raw emotion always make me so thirsty? "I think I might hold on to this place," I croaked.

Jonathan's jaw dropped. His eyes went to saucers. "Stop. The house? Do you think you'll move in? This is better than a bottomless brunch at a Beyoncé concert."

I'd considered it. But I loved my own little house too much to let it go. It had taken so long to save up enough for a down payment, and once I had, my friend Devyn Winters, a real estate agent here in town, had brokered an amazing deal. That house was purely me and, now, my biggest accomplishment. I'd taken time to decorate it in my own random style. Framed magazine covers on the walls. Several seating nooks for reading or working, rather than just one central living room conglomeration. I'd gone with more pastels than the average person, leaning into blues and greens. Comfortable and bright, that was my place. I'd even constructed a garden in front and a second, more expansive one in the backyard, where I could sit on the patio, drink my milky-white coffee, and look out at the Carolina roses as they bloomed in the spring. I just couldn't imagine leaving my home, nor could I part with Lindy's house.

I took a deep breath. "Devyn thinks I can list it and take advantage of the market, but I don't think I can say goodbye to this place. To all of the memories here." My heart squeezed uncomfortably imagining that moment: locking the door for the last time and handing over the key to what had been my safe place. As for the idea I'd had percolating, I decided to just go ahead and say it out loud. Band-Aids were best ripped off. "I want to rent it out to visitors to Dreamer's Bay." There. It was out there now. I was giving the idea wings and hoping it flew.

"Yeah?" He squinted, quirking his head. "Like an Airbnb?"

"Exactly that." I could feel myself ready to explode with detail. "I already have a few ideas on how I can modernize the décor, change the paint colors, and make the study into an extra bedroom. I also want to put together a whole welcome packet for my guests, telling them all about the Bay and where they should head."

"And avoid," Jonathan supplied. "Ma's Café has given me food poisoning three times in three years."

I winced. "Yeah, Ma likes her chicken on the pink side. We'll tell the guests." Holding on to my excitement with all that I had, I made a headline gesture. "Tips and tricks from Savanna Potter, your honored host. Oh! Maybe I'll send a dozen donuts on their first morning."

"Maybe," Jonathan said with a nod.

I ignored his reserved chime. My thoughts took over like a boulder down the soft side of a hill. "Oh, and maybe even a basket of snacks and bottle of wine when they arrive." Honestly, I needed the distraction from whatever number this grief thing was going to do to me once I let it sink in. Maybe the goal was avoiding that moment altogether.

Jonathan tilted his head from side to side as he weighed the concept. "That's a lot. Are you trying to make money or new friends?"

It was rhetorical and I understood his point. I needed to slow my roll and not reinvest all my potential profits in perks. It was hard not to want to do all the things for my imaginary tenants. I wanted to spoil them, wow them, until they couldn't imagine staying anywhere as wonderful. They'd tell their grandchildren about my service.

"Okay, so maybe no donuts. But on the whole, what do you think?" I rolled my shoulders like a boxer heading into the ring. "Hit me with the Jonathan Parsons realism. Dash my dreams. Spit on my goals. I'll see if I can hold my own."

He nodded, absorbing. I very much valued Jonathan's opinion. He tended to see things from angles I hadn't examined, which was why our friendship was superior to all others ever invented. I was pie in the sky. He was practical and down to earth. His gift. He had no problem telling me that I was ridiculous when I good and *was*.

"I like it," he said, finally. "The potential is there. It's a lower risk investment. I say run with it."

I waited. "Where's the other shoe? Isn't there one you're about to lob at my head?" I raised a suspicious brow. I'd honestly believed he'd play the too risky card, and I'd have to lay out all the pros to his list of cons.

"Going barefoot today," he said with a very Jonathan-like smirk and shrug. "And avoiding that beautiful head. Plus, it's the first day all week your hair has slayed. The deep red works in an attic." He was so cute that I ignored the backhanded compliment. Why had no wonderful man snatched his snarky ass up yet? It made no sense to me.

"Oh, I like it. You called me beautiful."

"Well, everyone else does. I'm loosening up. It's the new me." He pretended to ease a strand of nonexistent long hair behind his ear.

"Say more words."

"About your venture? I will recommend your place on my wildly popular gay men's Discord group, Ocarina of Crime," Jonathan said, smiling more widely now.

"Is that a play on words I would get if I played *Zelda*?" His favorite. I made my way toward the ladder. The longer I stayed, the greater the chance that the past would swallow me whole.

"It is, and you've failed. You insult the honorable people of Hyrule. But I digress. Here's the nitty-gritty. We live in an ever-growing tourist destination, and you've recently inherited a viable property just blocks from the beach. Let me repeat that. Blocks. From. The. Beach."

"All true. Knowing you, I'm surprised you didn't add *bitch* for the alliteration."

"I considered it. Now, you get this house into shape within a couple of months, and it'll be perfect for a family or small group of friends. Bonus"—he exhaled and offered a relieved smile—"we get to keep Lindy's house, and I'm not at all against doing that." He said that last part in a rush.

"Right? It's still ours." My heart squeezed as I looked over a near mountain of boxes that had belonged to the wonderful woman who'd raised me. She was now with my parents in whatever comes after this life, probably drinking margaritas and whipping something up on a heavenly stove while the rest of them gabbed. God, I was jealous.

"And the Airbnb gives me the motivation to go through Lindy's things." I gave Jonathan a shake. "A new beginning to latch onto."

"A reason to look forward and not just back."

"Fair point. Now what? I gotta get moving on a plan to make it happen."

"That's all you. You're the idea-girl-that-could and will. However," he tossed his dark hair as if it would move, "I'd be happy to consult on the numbers since you tend to be the dreamer in our duo. No pun intended, ma'am."

"You nailed it all the same."

Not the first time I'd heard that one. Living in quaint little Dreamer's Bay did fit my personality like a marker to its cap. And Jonathan's numbers prowess was what made him the hottest financial planner in our adorable city. People scheduled sessions with him months out because he knew money management and had a unique vision for how to protect and grow accounts. "I will definitely take you up on that option. I may have already put together a small budget for your perusal. Was just waiting for this conversation to hit send."

I descended the four short steps of the ladder first and waited at the bottom, accepting the crutch he handed off so he could climb down easier, a system we didn't even have to speak about, it was so second nature.

"Well, hit send already," he said, reclaiming the crutch. "We're not getting any younger. Speaking of old things, are we going to the Chaplin marathon next weekend? I need a popcorn slash sticky floor fix."

"I can't. There's a seminar in Charleston for new rental hosts. It covers a lot of the basics, and I thought I might make it a weekend in the city. Want to come? Say yes. I can promise espresso martinis and gentle galivanting. We can even find a western bar so you can cowboy flirt."

His eyes lit up with delight. "Cowboys are such trouble."

"You tell me daily."

He thought on it. I could already predict his reservations. "Not keen on passing up a good galivant-cowboy gaze session, but…" Jonathan hesitated. As much fun as he could be, he was also cautious about being away from his built-in remedies should his arthritis flare. As someone who lived with chronic pain, some of it quite debilitating, he had to plan well in advance for the worst and be ready to sideline himself. He didn't like to stray too far from home. "I think I'm gonna let you grab all the big-city fun for both of us. Have an extra martini in my honor." The light behind his eyes had dimmed slightly, a reminder of his limitations. *Ah, fuck.* I didn't care for this at all. My chest squeezed uncomfortably. Jonathan came with an adventurous heart and less than cooperative body. It didn't seem fair.

I sighed but, of course, understood. "Are you sure? There might be a very handsome man in Charleston looking for a cute, numbers-minded man from a small town."

"From your bare lips."

"Who needs lip gloss for attic sorting?"

He exhaled, seeming to hang on to the daydream an extra beat. "Even so, the Charleston Man may need to come to me."

"Fair enough, Jon-Bon." That old high school nickname would never get old. I slung an arm around his shoulders and kissed his cheek with a smack, which inspired a blush. He wasn't the most touchy-feely guy, but I forced him to indulge me once every few months. He needed the practice. "Until then, you're stuck with me. For I'm a lonely sap."

"You're a *picky* sap," he corrected. "You get hit on way more than me on dating apps. I'm jealous with an extra shot of jealous. But I'm never speaking about it again because I hate giving compliments. There."

I stood taller. "I accept your jealousy and would like to thank the academy of queer women for their online attention." I shrugged, considering why I never seemed to connect with any of them. "I just want to make sure that I'm investing my time in the right person. That's all." And, yes, I could admit to having a more discerning palate when it came to women I'd consider dating. Too important not to.

Jonathan frowned. "Right. And what exactly would make her most worthy of your person? I mean, this week."

"Smart, driven, funny, and attractive, at least to me." I waved four fingers. "Those are the ones."

"The quadfecta," he said.

"That's a word?"

Scorn rippled off him. His signature. "It's like your father wasn't a compulsive gambler who took you to the track on his weekends."

"Well, I love the word. Thank you for the introduction."

He walked slowly toward the living room, the crutch moving in time with his right leg. "The quad is a good list. And I believe you're gonna find her one day, Savvy, and have a glorious ride off into the sunset. Maybe there'll be some lip gloss there waiting for you. But I'm going to need you to keep your mind open and flirt a little more. Sway your hips. Toss your hair like you own the room and find everything downright funny. Women like that."

"Do they, though? I've decided that I'm not sure what women like." I scoffed, my own signature, and led the way into the dim, dormant kitchen. Memories from the past played out all around me like an old film reel. The nostalgia grabbed me by my throat and squeezed, stealing my focus. I used to lounge on top of that kitchen counter, chatting away about the girls I admired—translation: crushed on— while Lindy layered her amazing chicken lasagna with the precision of a renaissance sculptor.

"I flirt," I said quietly, attempting to pull myself back into the conversation, an anchor to the here and now.

"You think you flirt." Jonathan placed the crutch against the counter and a hand on his hip. "But you refuse to fully commit to the act because it means you'll be vulnerable to whatever comes back. You're good at eye contact. But I have the unfortunate job of informing you that that's about it."

"I'm wounded and won't recover," I said flatly, turning to him, fully involved now. I sighed, giving in. "Fine. What am I doing wrong? Prove your expert status."

"I *am* an expert because I'm a noteworthy observer of people. The successful flirters *do* more. You have to give signals. Hold that eye contact you're so good at for longer than necessary. Laugh more openly. Like this." He demonstrated an enthusiastic feminine giggle I would never attempt, nor should anyone. "Oh, and shoulder bumping is big. I've watched women do that often." He bumped mine. "To be playful. To bond. To stir up a little heat."

"I flirt in my own way, okay? I just don't feel compelled to do so unless I'm interested, and that hasn't happened in a long time."

"Well, the good news is that Dreamer's Bay has been welcoming new people from far and wide since that special aired on the Travel Channel. More queer women are surely marching into town in curvy little lines as we speak."

One year ago, our very own small city had been featured on *Small Towns of America*, in which seven towns were heavily showcased and explored. They'd included visits to Amazin' Glazin', the donut shop, Bountiful Park, and even the grocery store I proudly managed: Festive Foods. Since then, people had arrived in seasonally driven spurts from all over. Some to buy and put down roots, driving up property values. But the majority were short-term visitors, staying for a week at a time to soak up the small-town culture before heading back to their big-city lives. The infusion of new people had been fortuitous and profitable for everyone, and the influx showed no signs of slowing down.

I glanced at my watch and grinned. "Any time now, right? Cue the lesbian stampede. Please, God?" And then I went still, struck by one of my fruitless moments of genius. " 'The Lesbian Stampede' sounds like a great title for a folk song."

Jonathan nodded. "I'll tell Linda the Lesbian from the movie theater. She loves a good open mic night."

"Not sure anything will top her last song, 'Sinfully Sapphic Stephanie.'"

"God. Nor should it," he said seriously. "Stephanie and her sinful ways will always haunt me." He leveled a gaze and sighed. "And I do mean *haunt*."

Jonathan was dry in his judgment, also known as wonderful. The best kind of friend.

"I can affirm that it was quite the night at Ronnie Roo's. I'm not sure we want to feed Linda any more titles."

I ran a fingertip across the gray and white marble counter, coated in a notable layer of dust. Time for a house-wide scrub down. I'd call Elizabeth Draper at On the Spot, the odd jobs company, and see if she had any part-timers who could tackle a deep clean. There were two housecleaning businesses in town, but Elizabeth was a good friend, and I liked using her services whenever possible. We were three years apart in high school, and I'd spent much of my freshman year looking up to Elizabeth, a senior then, and wanting to be as much of a go-getter as she was. It was impossible, but I tried anyway. In fact, I owed a lot of my successes to role models like her. I harnessed ambition like a lifeline and usually figured out how to achieve my goals as I went, which in hindsight seemed out of order. But I preferred to be self-taught and relied on myself as much as possible. There were no guarantees in life. I'd learned at eleven years old to not count on tomorrow being the same as today. Jonathan thought I had trust issues because of losing my parents so young. He was often accurate, but there was no need to encourage him.

"Charleston, huh? Savanna in the City."

I scrunched my shoulders to my ears. "I have a feeling this trip is going to make a big difference. I don't know what it is, but it feels like an important step on my way to...something."

"Then it will be."

CHAPTER TWO

The City

As much as I loved small-town life, the big city got my blood going. The constant movement most anywhere you looked, the hum of conversation, the angry traffic, the amazing aromas wafting from restaurants, and the idea that something important was happening around every corner made me feel like I was on the edge of my seat for a really amazing show.

The seminar turned out to be more of a conference with an entire day's worth of classes on various topics. I soaked up information in sessions covering: amenities that will set your property apart from the competition, knowing your rights as host, and pricing your property for maximum earnings. I was a happy little sponge, taking notes down the side of my pages, energized by the collective vibe of the room. I'd always thrived at the hospitality side of my job, greeting customers, learning their buying preferences, and developing relationships that made them want to come back time and time again. Now I had the chance to apply those same skills to this new venture, and that made me want to dance on top of one of those cocktail tables at the back of the room.

After eight long hours, separated only by a quick half turkey sandwich and a shaken espresso with oat milk (okay, two), I headed up to my room for a quick shower before dinner somewhere downtown. I had a couple of restaurants in mind, having researched the surrounding area like a burglar planning a job. I loved food in all forms and was not about to miss out on the opportunity to sample some of Charleston's most talked about options. Give me the little plates of all the things, a craft cocktail, and a view of something unique and I'm as happy as a penguin with a personal iceberg. It's one of the reasons I loved working for the grocery store. Surrounded by all of that fresh produce, interesting ingredients, and a variety of interesting customers to study made me thrilled to get to work each day.

After selecting a pair of dark blue jeans and a long-sleeved red blouse that set off the highlights in my hair, I made one quick change to my outfit. I dumped my standard brown boots for off-red pumps because I was in a big city, and why not? Tonight should feel special after such a successful day.

Currently, my mouth watered. There was a much-regaled restaurant just three blocks away, known for their handmade pastas and creative desserts. I was hoping to unwind with a dirty martini and the short rib pappardelle at the bar. Maybe I'd partake in a little people watching between noodles. Woot! I was on a high just thinking about the carb buzz when I caught the flowy side of my blouse in the hotel room door as I exited my room. I paused and stared, unable to move forward. That was a new one. Okay, okay, not a problem. I'd just grab it and give it a pull. Except it didn't budge, and I certainly didn't want to rip my new favorite top, purchased for the trip specifically and out of my normal price range of under $40. I turned to my crossbody bag for my keycard only to find that in my haste to get to the pasta, my crossbody bag had been woefully forgotten inside. *Crimson and clover!* I exhaled loudly and peered down the empty hallway for any benevolent human who might be willing to assist a trapped, carb-starved woman. When a door somewhere behind me opened as if hearing my thoughts, I jumped in happy surprise.

"Thank God. Hello? Excuse me," I said to the brunette with the thick ponytail and long bangs swept to the side. Impressive, the finesse of that swoop, but I didn't have time to get into it. My expensive top and martini-evening hung in the balance.

"Hi," she said, breaking into a smile that came with a question mark. She scanned the scene as she moved closer. "Well, this is certainly interesting. Are you...stuck?" She squinted trying to make sense of me, the door, and our Velcro status.

"Yes. Woefully." This was now embarrassing. Did my happenstance savior have to be beautiful? What were the odds that the one person to witness me in this predicament would look like her? My face went hot. *Stop that now.* I shoved my thoughts to the side and focused on my mission, not the gorgeous dimple on her right cheek. "Would you have a phone I could borrow to call the front desk?" I asked.

"Sure, but do you have your key?" This brunette was astute. She also had big aquamarine eyes that could lean either green or blue depending on interpretation. Taller than me. Not important. But God, yes, it *was*. I could wrap my arms around her neck and go up on my tiptoes and— *Cease and desist.*

"No. That's the additional dilemma." I indicated the room behind me with a toss of my head. "I left my bag inside, probably scared and alone."

"Well, that's the most tragic thing." She crossed her arms in thought. It was a leisurely move that I liked very much. Her, leisurely. Me, watching. "So, you were sitting here, stuck and stranded, hoping someone would come along."

"Yes. And just like magic, you have."

She lifted her shoulders and a remarkable smile blossomed. "That's me. Tada." She pulled her phone from her bag and scrolled. "Now, let's see if we can get you good and saved." She offered her phone. "I pulled up the number. Just activate the call."

I accepted the phone with the sleek blue case and connected with the front desk, explained my predicament, and requested help as if this was the most casual occurrence in the world. I could pretend if I wanted to. After a sympathetic apology and muffled laugh, the front desk attendant assured me someone was on the way. "All will be well soon, Ms. Potter. I'm sending someone with a key."

"Thank you so much," I said serenely, slid off the call, and handed the phone back to my attractive savior. "They're on their way."

"Great. So, besides the obvious snag, how's your day been?"

Uh-oh. I realized she planned to hang out and make conversation until I was free, and while that was incredibly considerate, it wasn't her obligation. "You don't have to wait with me. I fully release you to enjoy your Saturday night. They'll be here soon."

The woman surveyed the empty hallway, hesitating. "But if they drop the ball or forget, you have no recourse. I'm obligated, as a citizen, to see this through." She tilted her head, which caused her ponytail to cascade downward, half of it brushing her shoulder. I wanted to rewind the video. "Your day?"

"Well, just know that I appreciate the neighborly gesture. And my day was going amazingly well until the door ate my shirt. I attended the conference downstairs. Learned a lot. Now I'm here."

She looked thoughtful. "Something hospitality related, right? I saw the sign."

"Exactly." A pause hit that I decided to fill with more detail. Why not? We had a moment or two. "I'm opening up an Airbnb. My first." Just hearing the words sent a heady hit of exhilaration. I just loved a good project.

"Oh, yeah? Here in Charleston?"

"No. I'm from a little town along the water. Couple hours from here. Dreamer's Bay. Heard of it?"

"I have not, but with a name like that one, I now feel driven to look it up."

"Don't blink or you'll miss it." I grinned proudly. "That's somewhat of a saying we locals apply to our town. I'll have you know that we were on the Travel Channel." I offered her a wide-eyed look. "That's right." I sat back and waited, as if I'd dropped the most impressive bomb ever.

She laughed, picking up on my attempt at humor. It was captivating, and I couldn't look away. This just got better and better. *She did.* "Well, now I'm sold on a visit someday. You should have led with the Travel Channel."

"I'll know for next time."

We stared at each other for an extended moment I didn't want to end. A welcome tingle slithered its way up my spine. *Oh, hello.* When was the last time that had happened? A physical reaction. Maybe I didn't want to be rescued from the clutches of this door after all. Unfortunately, the elevator dinged a few yards away and my hopes and dreams came falling down like rain on prom night.

"Someone called for assistance?" a younger man in a blue dress shirt asked, jogging over.

No, thank you, I said, in my imagination.

Upon seeing me, he attempted to smother his smile, which meant they'd likely been taking bets about whether this had been a prank call. I couldn't blame them.

"I'm afraid I've imprisoned myself unintentionally," I told him with a wince. The embarrassment towered over me, but there was no escaping this moment. I needed this kid and his key card if I wanted to live a free life again.

He slid the key into the electronic lock and my new sexy friend from across the hall smiled supportively. I met her gaze. "He's here now. You've done your good deed for the day. I release you from noble duty."

She straightened and eyed me. "Only if you're sure."

"As can be." The lock clicked, the door opened, and I was able to move freely. I'd never take it for granted again. "And this is what I look like when able to move as I wish." I tossed my arms around fluidly like a marionette, which in hindsight was a ridiculous thing to do. And why would I even say that? I shrugged off the shame. Luckily, my hallmate seemed to find me amusing, which I latched onto like a wayward log in a dicey current.

"Who knew an upgrade was even possible?" she asked. "Enjoy your night."

You could have knocked me over with a feather. Had she really just said that out loud? If I'd had any doubt, the expression on the guest services agent dispelled it. His eyebrows rose to his hairline, and he passed me a congratulatory smirk.

"You heard that, too, right?" I whispered once the woman disappeared around the corner.

"Oh, yeah," he said. He nodded several times. We were bros now. "And I saw her check you out."

"You did?" I asked in a squeak. "There was checking?" I rolled around in the concept, luxuriating, basking like the queen of Egypt regaled by all.

"I thought you two were together at first."

"You're my favorite person now." Then a thought descended. I turned to him, now realizing the missed opportunity. Panic quickly replaced my excitement. "I don't even know her name and now she's gone. That seems like a mistake now." That woman, beyond her picture-perfect appearance, seemed smart, funny, and kind. Three of the four on the quadfecta. That combination was hard to come by. I wanted to peel her like an orange and write a memoir about it later. Sadly, that would likely never happen.

The young man lifted one shoulder. "Well, you know where she's staying. At least for tonight." I could tell he wanted to wink but refrained. Work decorum and all. We were still bros.

"I know she's that direction on this hallway," I offered weakly. But the truth was I wouldn't be acting on that information. I didn't have the kind of blind ambition required to hunt down a ridiculously hot woman to see if she wanted to hang out. Jonathan was right. I needed to sharpen the tools in my flirtatious toolbox so I'd be prepped and ready for scenarios like this one. "But I think, on second thought, that I'm going to enjoy the moment for what it was."

"Totally your call," my wingman said. "But I'm telling you, you got a shot."

I let myself enjoy that knowledge. "Thank you for saying that. Bless your extended family." I pointed at the door that ate me. "And I appreciate your assistance."

"Anytime."

I slid him a five for his trouble, high roller that I was.

What an eventful fifteen minutes that had been. Once alone, I gave my head a slow shake and grinned my way back inside the room to retrieve my bag and see a man about some pasta.

CHAPTER THREE

That Night

If noodles could be friends, these homemade pappardelle and I would be galivanting on girls' trips for life. The thick savory flat noodles and short rib lived up to every review I'd read about When in Rome. The restaurant had quite the fan base on Yelp. As I slid another savory bite into my mouth, it occurred to me that I should take a lap and visit all the noteworthy restaurants in Dreamer's Bay so I could provide updated reviews for my future guests.

"How's the food?" the bartender asked. He was one of those people who sounded entirely interested without looking that way in the slightest.

"I don't know my name anymore," I told him. I offered a chef's kiss and closed my eyes lost in flavorful bliss. God, I loved food. Working in a grocery store all day had certainly confirmed my affection.

He grinned and placed his palms flat on the bar in front of me. I had a feeling he was a fellow foodie himself. "Now we're talking. What else can I get you?" My martini was on its way out. "Maybe another one of these in five minutes?"

"I'm buying that one," a smooth voice said from down the bar. It gave me goose bumps. Who in the world?

I turned to see none other than my supremely hot hotel neighbor taking a seat down the bar along with another woman. She wiggled four fingers at me in hello. It wasn't an organically sexy move, but she made it one.

"Hi," I said, absorbing being in her presence again. The Fates were working in my favor. While this was a second opportunity to get to know her better, I was very aware of the fact that she seemed to have a date at her side. That was okay. I shouldered the disappointment and pressed on. "So you don't just exist between the walls of the hotel."

"Did you think I was the hotel fairy? I get that a lot." She turned to her date. "Jocelyn, this woman was recently swallowed by a door."

"It's true." I tossed in a grimace. "But I was luckily saved by…" I didn't have a name.

"Kyle," my new friend supplied. I tried it on. She was *Kyle*. I liked it.

Jocelyn leaned over. "Her full name is Alexandra Kyle Remington. Kind of unforgettable, am I right? I don't think we should leave the rest out."

Kyle smiled. "It's true. I have a superhero's name. But please, just call me Kyle, and don't mind my cape."

"It's a very nice name. Kyle Remington."

"Thank you."

"We don't have enough epic ones."

Her friend knocked Kyle in the arm with the back of her hand. "See? Our new friend gets it."

There was a noticeable familiarity between them. If they were a couple, they were a striking one, seizing on the yin and yang dynamic nicely. The other woman had shiny blond hair that contrasted with Kyle's dark brown like something out of a clichéd sapphic romance novel. I'd buy that book. Hell, I *had* dozens of times. So, it seemed Kyle was, in fact, interested in women, which was a huge score for women everywhere, but was likely already dating this one.

"And your name?" Kyle asked. Her lips pulled into a perfect smile. They were full and hard to look away from. Did she use liner? Hard to tell. No one had the right to have lips like Kyle's. Damn her, but also *thank you.* "I can't believe we went this far without learning each other's."

"I'm Savanna Potter. Also known as She Who Gets Stuck in Doors. Nice to meet you officially."

Kyle laughed, which maybe meant she appreciated my silly sense of humor. She had one, too, but it was dryer and more sophisticated. That made sense because so was she. I was taking notes for fun. "Nice to meet you, too. This is Jocelyn, by the way. We work together."

Colleagues, too. I wondered about their story. "And what do you both do?" I was being nosy, but my second dirty martini had arrived, and that meant I was way more comfortable running my mouth. Two Drink Savanna was in the building.

"We're doctors," Jocelyn said, and I about fell off my stool. This was a soap opera. I'd walked into an actual TV show and was one of the awestruck day players.

Of course Kyle was a doctor. She was living proof that they could be every bit as hot as the medical dramas I binged on weekends with Jonathan. I needed to text him ASAP. It also only upped Kyle's qualifications for the role of Savanna's Personal Dream Woman. Had Kyle been crafted from the literal list of desirable traits in my head, like a torn-up piece of paper, reassembled for this very moment? God was an eavesdropper, stealing details and producing them. But why was he or she taunting me with women off the table? And was Kyle for sure in that category?

"That's impressive," I said as serenely as possible. No big deal, just gorgeous gay doctors down the bar a bit. "Do you practice here in Charleston?"

"Yes," Kyle said. "I've been here just over two years."

"Two and a half for me," Jocelyn said.

"Oh." Confusion arrived. "But you're staying in a hotel?"

They exchanged what seemed to be a private smile. I felt like I'd overstepped. Jonathan would have shot me wide eyes that meant *behave*. "You know what? No explanation needed," I said with a smile and a wave of my hand. I sipped my martini as if I'd politely moved on from my query about them. *Them*.

Who was I kidding? *Her*.

Kyle turned fully on her stool. There were two empty ones between us. "My apartment is under construction, so I grabbed a few nights in the hotel so I didn't have to live among the colossal chaos during my time off. Joss just joined me for a night out. We're rarely off work at the same time, so tonight's a novelty."

"Resident life," Jocelyn said, glaring at the empty space in front of her, drink on its way to her lips.

I squinted. "And help me, but a resident is the portion of a doctor's career when they're…"

"Still building our skills within a specialty," Kyle said, picking up the slack. "But we're nearing the end."

"And did you always want to be a doctor?" I asked.

"Yes and no." She seemed to decide to tell me more. "I'm a former financial adviser who hated my job, ran away to medical school to reclaim my childhood dream, and now I'm in my last year of residency in emergency medicine."

"Look at you," I said too loudly, my brain forgetting to censor itself. "That's impressive," I amended in a more conservative tone.

Jocelyn pulled out a pager, an actual one, turned it around, and showed Kyle. "Looks like we're going to have to raincheck our little gathering."

"Paged?" I asked, having not seen one of those except on doctor shows and nineties movies.

"Joss is on call," Kyle informed me. "That's why her drink's a mocktail."

"Ah," I said, taking it all in. There was some kind of medical emergency, and Jocelyn would swoop in and help. I liked being on the fringes.

"I've got your drink," Kyle told her. "I hope it's an easy one."

"From your lips." Jocelyn leaned in. My cue to look away. That did not stop me from hearing the soft sound of a lip smack. I waved to Jocelyn as she gathered her belongings. "Nice meeting you, Savanna."

"You, too. I hope it's an easy night, as well."

Kyle said something to her quietly as I returned to my drink.

A couple moments later, Kyle tilted her head dramatically to catch my eye. "Do you mind if I...?" Kyle pointed at the barstool next to mine as the bartender poured a bright pink Cosmo from his shaker. I liked tonight. It shimmied with the sheen of something special. I was out and about making very cool friends in a city I didn't know.

"Not at all. I'd love company, actually." Attraction aside, I was genuinely enjoying getting to know Kyle and finding out more about her life, what she was like. Our sustained eye contact left me wanting more. Her energy had me excited, yet comfortable. I hadn't yet figured out how she managed to make me feel so important with so few words. "Sorry Jocelyn had to leave."

"Me, too," Kyle said, and stirred her drink once. "This was supposed to be our catch-up night. At least we got to have a nice dinner." She sighed. "Honestly, I could have predicted she'd get called in."

"It must be hard balancing your schedules."

Kyle tapped the rim of her rocks glass. Some kind of whisky drink with a large cube of ice in the center and a metal swizzle stick resting against the side. She looked sexy as fuck as she tilted it toward her, surveying the contents of the glass. "Yeah, but we knew what we signed up for. This stretch of time is not meant for anything but eating, drinking, and sleeping medicine."

"Speaking of, you must not be on call," I said, gesturing to the drink.

She smiled at me blissfully. "I have four straight days off. Rare, but I saved up and called in a few favors." She shook her head. "Time to myself is the most glorious thing. The only downside was the whole apartment debacle." She studied me. "But I have to say, I think it worked out for the best."

A warm shiver danced across my skin. What did that mean? She had definitely directed that comment toward me with no attempt to hide it. I was so very into direct communication patterns like that one. I might have been falling in love if it wasn't for the girlfriend situation she had going on. I glanced at the doorway Jocelyn had vacated. "How long have you two been together?"

Her brows rose. "Who two?"

"You two. You and Jocelyn."

"You thought we were…? Nope." She eased into a relaxed smile. "Joss is my best friend. I adore her but there's definitely no romance." She shook her head as if incapable of imagining such a thing.

"Didn't she just kiss you goodbye?" Was the world upside down?

"Definitely. She kissed my cheek. Her six-foot-two boyfriend probably wouldn't like anything more intimate." Kyle smiled into her glass, and I felt foolish first and then victorious.

She looked over at me, hitting me with that Kyle brand of sexy eye contact. "I'm entirely single. What about you?"

"You should know you're looking at a single who doesn't often mingle. At least not enough. My friend Jonathan is working on me like I'm his fall break project." Why was I confessing more than I should, and why did I start in rhyme? I blinked and pretended the moment hadn't happened.

"You have made me smile about eight times since we met. And how is it that you don't mingle, as you say, much? You're very pretty. You have these big brown eyes with these gold flecks that just… captivate." She sat back in her chair. "Is that okay to say? I would hate to make you feel objectified and should probably have smoother moves than remarking on your appearance. Like I said, I work a lot."

"Objectification is welcome," I said too loudly, and then leaned my chin in my hand. I made the give-me-more gesture, and she laughed again. I felt powerful and wanted to hear the sound as much as possible.

"That's nine times. You've very cute, too. I love the auburn. Or is it red?"

I made a show of twisting it around my finger. "Left to interpretation."

"And what about my earlier question?"

"I don't date a lot," I said sincerely, "because I don't love putting myself out there. There's a vulnerability that comes with dating, wouldn't you say?"

"I would. So, no boyfriend in the picture, then. Got it." She was fishing. It was glorious.

"No *girlfriend*, you mean." That was the information she wanted, and I knew it. I sipped my martini delicately as I reveled in the give-and-take.

"Oh, really?" Kyle said loudly and turned on her stool in dramatic fashion. "You don't say." Her overly enthusiastic delivery ushered in my turn to laugh.

"I do."

She touched her glass to mine. "What are the chances that you get stuck in a door, I leave my hotel room in the exact right moment to discover you, we both end up at the same bar several blocks away."

"We're both single," I supplied.

"Both date women."

"Both love wiener dogs."

She laughed. "I never said that part."

"You don't love wiener dogs? I don't know that I can continue talking to you."

"Except I adore them. My neighbor had one when I was a kid. Herman. He was a gentleman."

"Thank God for Herman. That was close."

She pressed on. "I'd say the chances of all of those things aligning are pretty slim." We shared an extended moment of what Lindy used to describe as soul-infused nonverbal connection. She'd shown me demonstrations on *General Hospital*.

"Want to take a walk with me?" Kyle asked. What I wanted to do was sweep the hair from her ponytail off her shoulder just so I could find out if it was as soft as it looked. A walk was a good second place option.

"I do," I answered without looking away. What was happening right now? It felt like every little detail had just clicked into place. There was attraction, a conversational rhythm, and the stars all aligning. This was a giant arrow sign designed for me, me, me. It had to be.

Kyle signaled the bartender and took care of both checks, which included my meal. "Thank you so much, but you didn't have to do that," I told her as we walked out. "Though you are a rich doctor."

She laughed. "I wish I was. Residents aren't exactly at the high end of the pay grade." She shrugged. "Maybe one day I'll climb the ladder, buy a nice car."

"You'll get there, Soap Opera Doctor that you are."

"And are you full-time with the rentals?"

"No. The Airbnb is a new side venture. I'm the manager of a small-town grocery store where everybody knows your name." I paused. "Well, at least I do. I take pride in greeting my customers personally."

Kyle stopped walking. "Wait. So you're saying you know all the shoppers' names? Surely that's hyperbole. How small is this town?"

I tilted my head from side to side. "Within the category of small towns, we're not the smallest, but not the biggest. However, I must say—"

"Please do."

"I will. Our tourist population is rapidly multiplying. We're becoming a player in the vacation game."

"Helpful for your new venture."

"Entirely the reason for it. The tourists' names are harder to pin down, though, especially if they're only in town for a week."

"Wait. Are you saying you try and learn their names, too? The one weekers?"

"Oh, yes. That kind of thing matters."

Kyle shook her head in amazement. I already had a major thing for her hair. The dark color, its thickness, and the way it fell haphazardly into perfection. "You get bonus points for tourists' names. That store is lucky to have you."

I absorbed the compliment, feeling taller and consequential. A foreign state. "What are you? Five nine?" I asked. Height now at the forefront of my thoughts. Would I go up on my tiptoes to kiss someone her height? Innocent inquiring minds.

"Close. Five eight. And you're…five six."

"Wow. Impressive and correct."

She nodded. "Just part of the job. Like knowing your customers' names." She gestured ahead of us with her chin. "The park two blocks that way is lit up at night. It even has a little suspension bridge over the pond. Want to check it out?"

"Definitely." I really did. I also would have gone with her to watch a haircut on Mars. "I'll follow you." *Anywhere.*

"Tell me what you think about this," she asked as we landed on the sidewalk in front of When in Rome.

"All right."

She paused dramatically, as if to say *wait for it.* I braced for whatever it might be.

"Can I take your hand?"

I smiled, melting. Not only would I welcome the opportunity to hold her hand, but the fact that she'd *asked* with such respect in her voice left me hovering happily, my feet surely not anywhere near the cement. "I'd like that. Yes."

Our fingers intertwined loosely as we strolled the sidewalk lined from above with twinkly lights, benches every ten feet or so. It was an area meant to be welcoming at night, and the people of Charleston seemed to know it. The park was bustling. I pulled my jacket tighter around my body as the wind rustled by. Several couples walked their dogs ahead of us. Another read by the warm illumination of the curvy streetlamp above their bench, warm beverages cradled in their hands. God, give me a curvy streetlamp to read beneath. I loved everything about this park. "What's this place called?"

"Nightingale Plaza."

The name was perfect. "You know what? They did it justice." Just then, the heavenly aroma of cinnamon pecans wafted over like a holiday sweater you didn't know you wanted but secretly loved. Cozy, a little bit over the top, but hard to pass up. "Okay. That smells too good to ignore."

Kyle gestured to the cart a few yards ahead. "I think we have to." She didn't wait for a response before dropping my hand and hurrying over to the vendor. I followed slowly, unable to pull the grin off my face. My pseudo date was attentive and thoughtful. When she returned moments later with a small bag of warm almonds, pecans, and cashews, I smiled up at her. "Thank you. Somehow, my night keeps improving."

"You had a hard day. Anyone attacked by a door deserves a nice bag of nuts." She froze, probably playing that back.

"Yeah, maybe I'm not so hungry," I said with a laugh and held up a hand.

"I will spend the rest of my life apologizing for that line."

"Well, in that case..." I made the gimme gesture and accepted the bag.

"By the way, I've decided I like you." She grinned and promptly walked on, leaving me there staring after her, heart thudding. A sexy hit-and-run. The kind they put in the movies, but it was happening to me in real time with no one around to notice. I had to prompt my brain to keep up with my heart and memorize every detail about tonight.

I hurried the handful of yards required to catch her, now wishing I'd gone with the other shoes. "You like me, huh? That's a nice thing to say to another person. That you like them." I was staring straight ahead, surely matching her grin.

"Did I say like? I mean, you're *okay*." She offered me a wink.

I liked the sapphic ping-pong match we had going very much.

"What do you think of *me*?"

"Your hair could be better."

She stopped walking, mouth agape, and turned to me.

My laughter crept in because her brows pulled down in utter offense, reminding me of a cartoon character. There was no way she'd been told anything but glowing affirmations about the gloriousness of her hair.

"Stop it. You definitely know I'm teasing you."

"I know no such thing." She straightened, pulled back her shock, but made no move to walk on, waiting for an explanation or apology. "I'm wounded." However, the tone of her voice never once deviated from self-assured.

"You seem it."

"This is my wounded face."

It hadn't changed at all. I was beginning to adore this person. "The sorrow there is unmatched."

She blinked. "I know."

I stared her down. The wind lifted her hair slightly, a look I liked very much. "You happen to have A-plus hair and know it."

"I mean, I'm no redhead, but..." She gave her hair a toss, satisfied. "You decimate me one minute. Flatter me the next. You're going to keep me on my toes, aren't you?" She passed a wink over her shoulder, and it sent a shiver from my head to my wrists. I was on a high because it sounded like she was alluding to times ahead. Was it possible we'd have those? *Too soon. Reverse course.* I shelved the speculation and decided to live in the present instead, which happened to be pretty great.

"Are you an ice cream person?" I asked, catching up to her. There was a stationary truck ahead, and I had trouble saying no to treats when I ran into them in the wild.

"Are there non ice cream people? The audacity."

"We're on the same page." I reached for my wallet. "I'm buying this time. What's your pleasure?"

She paused and turned. "Anything with strawberry."

Strawberry fit what I knew of Kyle. Sweet, shapely, universally adored. I'd seen her charm in action. "Coming right up."

I found her a few yards away on a bench on a circular section of the sidewalk that reminded me of a roundabout for foot traffic. "How's this?" she asked.

"You found a nook. I love it."

She smiled. "Me, too. I thought we could sit and people watch. It's a decompressor for me, especially on harder days."

I remembered her job. "I imagine there are a lot of high stress days in emergency medicine."

The playful smile dimmed, and I'd realized I'd taken her somewhere more serious than the lighthearted territory we'd been flirting in. "I always knew it would be a stressful job, and it is."

"But?"

"It's not the long hours that zap me, or the lack of sleep when things pick up. It's the heavy heart I go home with." She watched a little boy chase after his older sister, who'd stolen his ball. "I wasn't prepared for the effect the difficult cases have on me. I thought I'd be emotionally…stronger."

The disappointment in herself was shocking, especially when I looked at people like Kyle as the heroes of our society. "I don't think you should do that to yourself." I couldn't imagine the things she had to see on a daily basis, the emotions she had to hold. "You're human. You can't just shut off your feelings. In fact, they probably help guide you."

She turned and found my eyes. Everything about her seemed different with just the shift in conversation. It was startling but also made me want to know more about her, somehow make it better. How odd to be so invested in someone so soon. "I try to, though. Realistic or not." We sat in silence for a few moments, watching a couple of loud college guys razz each other. They'd certainly had a few.

"It offers me a lot of perspective, though. The time off this week. It's a reminder there are other aspects of life I'm missing out on, living in the bubble of the hospital. Other people, for one."

I nodded. "Does that mean you don't date either?"

"Not very often. I'd like to someday, but until I'm through this crazy year, I don't have the time. Or the energy to move after a trying shift. None of that would be fair to her."

It made sense. Kyle was a work machine and likely didn't have the capacity for much else. "Maybe it helps to remind yourself that everything is temporary. There'll come a time for you to leap into all the other wonderful things life has to offer."

"Yeah." Her eyes danced, almost as if she was imagining that time now. "I really look forward to it." She looked over at me. "Spending time with people like you. Just not this year."

My heart sank. I was a realistic person and understood that the likelihood of Kyle showing up in my life beyond tonight was slim. Yet I hadn't stopped myself from wondering *what if?* in the recesses of my mind. This conversation had put the period at the end of our short sentence. Kyle wasn't looking for a girlfriend. And that was okay.

"Totally understandable."

She took a deep breath and looked around. If I had to guess, I'd say she was trying to distract herself away from the entire topic. "What prompted you to the Airbnb world?"

Yep, a big leap in subject matter. I could certainly help distract. "Well, my aunt died not too long ago. She left the house to me, and though I don't want to move into it, I can't stand the thought of selling it. Too many memories there."

"I'm sorry. It sounds like she was an important person in your life."

"She raised me after I lost my parents. Did I mention I was an orphan?" I nodded along. "I often lead with that bit of trivia. So, my aunt and me? We're very much a duo." My heart hung heavy when I realized the tense I'd just applied. "Well, we *were*."

Her eyes went wide. "That's a lot of loss. How old were you when you lost your parents?"

"Almost twelve. Car accident."

She placed a palm on her cheek and winced.

The quick shake of my head in response to her expression was meant to convey a *no, don't be sad* vibe, strangely enough. It seemed whenever I talked to new people about my unfortunate past, I wound up trying to make them feel better about it. Not an easy habit to undo.

I placed my hand on her knee in reassurance. "Hey, I'm okay. Promise. I definitely wonder what life would have been like with my parents around to sign my report cards, but my aunt was honestly a godsend. Warm, wonderful, everything you'd want in a substitute parent."

"And now you've lost her, too." Kyle's voice was a gentle caress. I opened my mouth and closed it, startled by the emotion that swarmed beneath her stare. My ice cream was melting, so I took a swipe. The words had disappeared as a slash of grief hit. I'd become astute at blocking those waves, so this one caught me off guard.

"I think, um...I'm still processing it all." I swallowed the uncomfortable lump and ordered the incoming tears to stand down.

"Give yourself time and all the grace you need. I'm serious."

Her incredibly blue eyes were soft, a cushion to my fall. I nodded and hauled in air, lots of it. "I did not mean to infuse our evening with any of that."

"Why not?" She tilted her head to the side and waited. The question suddenly made perfect sense. It was my story, and there was no good reason to bury it.

"I don't know. You're right, though. Nothing to apologize for." The conversation was an unexpected salve. "Why am I able to be myself around you? We just met." My voice was quiet and reflective.

"I don't know," she said, mirroring my tone, "but I'm experiencing something eerily similar. Who are you, Savanna Potter?" I enjoyed my ice cream and considered the question. "Rhetorical," she informed me and turned to her right as if checking out something in the distance. "You want to walk over to the suspension bridge? It extends over a beautiful pond."

"Ducks?"

"It's possible. Do they have a curfew?"

"I don't think so."

She nodded. "Then probably ducks."

"Sold."

She took a last lick of her ice cream. "You're quick-witted."

"Aww, you noticed. It's from hanging out with my gay judgmental friend, Jonathan." After a beat, I slid into sincerity. "Sometimes I think I overdo it. Reaching for the clever answer also helps mask my anxious side."

Kyle passed me a look as we walked toward the sliver of bridge that had slid into view. "I can relate in many ways."

"No way I'm buying that. You don't strike me as the type to get rattled even when humans are stuck in doors."

"You should have seen me the first time I had to cut into a dead body."

I winced.

"Too much?" she asked. "I never know the line."

I gave my head a shake, eyes wide. "No. Just trying to imagine myself in your shoes. Being tasked with taking care of the love of someone's life. Or their child, saving their life."

She nodded. "Trying to, anyway."

"That part has to weigh heavy, too. Losing a patient. I don't know how you come back from that and do it all again the next day."

She stared ahead, reflective. "I always want to be able to say that I did everything I possibly could have done."

"And that's not always the case, I take it?"

She went quiet for a bit, and I gave her that space. Then finally, "I'll say this. There's a lot of second-guessing, wondering if I'd played it more conservative, or some cases, taken the bigger risk, would the outcome have been different? It's not a perfect science. That part's been harder than I ever expected." She regarded the sky.

That's when I noticed how clear the sky was, the stars pinpricks of light tossed and scattered.

"I don't often talk about this stuff."

"Maybe it's easier because I'm a stranger."

"You're not a stranger. You're Potter."

It was the best answer she could have come up with, and before crafting a reply, I let the warm comment land, blossom, and spread out. "I know you said you have a rough *year* ahead of you, but what are you doing for the *rest* of your life?" I was only half kidding.

"Everything is up for discussion," she said in a breezy tone.

Another stellar answer. We shared a smile as we approached the suspension bridge. It was larger than I'd imagined. Quaint and gorgeous, stretching across the pond. The rustic charm accentuated the quiet beauty of the park all around it, causing visitors to pause and snap a photo.

"Isn't it beautiful? I ran into it one night on a decompression walk and just stopped and stared."

"Look at it. Just sitting here, so close to the hustle and bustle of the city."

"I thought the same thing. A hidden gem tucked between cement and metal chaos."

I marveled, realizing it was the bridge's lighting scheme that stole the show. "Look at that," I breathed. Every one of the cables was individually illuminated, isolating each vertical extension as it stretched down from the towers to the bridge itself. "There's a theatrical quality to these lines that would be hard to capture in a photo."

"Which is why we should just enjoy the view. Let's walk across," Kyle said and slid her fingers between mine again, intertwining them. We were holding hands, and my heart sang. She turned, checking in on me, on us. I sent her a smile back, because I very much enjoyed the feel of her hand in mine. I felt protected, valued. Her advice was also sound: *enjoy.* I could do that.

"If you could travel to anywhere in the world, where would you choose?" I asked. I turned and leaned against the railing of the bridge, facing her. The sizzle I'd felt since the moment we first spoke intensified now that we stood so utterly close. I could feel the heat from her body.

"Dreamer's Bay." She smiled serenely, proud of herself.

"Funny. But truthfully."

"Truthfully, it's on the list. You sold it really well. I want to get groceries and be greeted by name. And it's on the water. Even better." She slid a strand of hair behind my ear, in a flawless execution. I was waiting for a stumble, a misspoken word, or an awkward comment. Nothing yet. She caught me staring and grinned.

"Visit anytime."

"I'm going to hold you to that."

"Where else, Kyle? Where would you go?"

"Somewhere in Greece. I want to eat a giant salad and watch the giant waves roll in from atop a giant cliff."

"Well, you've finally done it." I straightened.

"What did I do?"

"I was waiting for you to have some sort of social misstep, and it's happened. You've gone and tried to romanticize salad, and Kyle? That simply won't work. There's nothing about a salad that should make someone wistful. I'm sorry you've been led to think that."

Her eyes narrowed. She was ready to fight. "What? Salads, I'll have you know, are remarkable not only in their ability to please a palate but in their versatility. A salad can mean so many things. You're being judgey, Potter. Back away from the salad."

I shook my head slowly, infusing sadness over my features. "Our first disagreement. It's finally here."

Kyle shrugged. "It happens to the best of couples."

I shrugged back, matching her energy. "What can you do?"

"We could find a way to make up."

The silence hung in the air as we stared each other down, two magnets resisting the pull. The electricity zipped and zapped. Heat danced across my skin from my cheeks to my neck to my shoulders and downward. The attraction, which had been PG-13 up until now, slid decidedly into the R column. I was turned on. I felt her all over. My breasts tingled and ached in response to the look on her face.

"I mean, I could show you my room," she said. *Well, well.* The invitation was clear as the sky overhead. I didn't do things like this, meeting strangers and following them to hotels, but this felt markedly different. *She* felt markedly different.

"I could compare it to mine." *That's right, Savanna, play it innocent.* Might help send home a few of the butterflies that fluttered around my midsection at the thought of anything physical happening with Kyle. Correction. Dr. Kyle of the Hot People.

She slid a hand onto my waist and stepped forward, making this conversation a tad more private. To anyone strolling by, we were lovers lost in a moment, enjoying our evening in one of the more beautiful locations ever created. I liked the fiction and allowed myself to believe in it for a few wonderful stretches. "Shall we head back or do you want to linger a bit?"

The answer was both, but with each second that passed, closing a door behind us and seeing what happened next was harder and harder to put off. "Let's go," I whispered, boldly reaching for what I wanted. She smiled down at me, touched my cheek, and led the way.

CHAPTER FOUR

The Pact

Her room was much, much bigger than mine, but of course it was. A spacious suite that dwarfed my double queen considerably. On the way in, we passed a sitting area made up of two royal blue sofas with sculpted backs and bronze turned-up feet. She dropped her bag onto one, and the strap landed across the armrest as if choreographed. When I turned, I saw the bedroom door had framed Kyle like a memorable painting. She sat on her king-sized bed with about eighteen pillows behind her. The lights had been dimmed but not extinguished.

Good God. She was a present to unwrap.

Before moving a timid muscle, my mind took a picture, because I didn't want to ever forget what I was looking at. That self-assured stare, the aqua blue of her eyes, the way her hair, now down, swept past her shoulders as the city lights twinkled through the oversized window to her right. I wondered if I could catch a glimpse of the bridge from here.

I entered the bedroom slowly, aware of each of my footsteps. I wanted to be quiet, but it was not to be. We shared a quiet laugh that helped to break some of the tension. When I reached her, I didn't think. I stopped doing that completely. Instead, I *felt*, allowed my instincts to lead, and placed my hand against her cheek. She pushed against it and offered a stare that said she good and wanted me.

I was gone.

Done.

I never made first moves. Ever.

Tonight would be markedly different.

I leaned down and took her whole face in my hands, cradling it, studying her features before angling my head and brushing her lips with mine. She smiled into the kiss, an actual smile. I loved everything about the kiss/smile combination. I went in for more, tasting a hint of strawberry ice cream and deepening the kiss. Our mouths moved together unhurriedly, a perfect dance until slow was no longer enough. Desperation rippled to the forefront, and need took over. Her hands went to my waist, and she pulled me down on top of her. When our bodies pressed together, I closed my eyes and swore. More of this. We were getting somewhere.

"You're fucking sexy, you know that?"

I didn't answer. I couldn't. My body was on fire, my skin extra sensitive to, literally, air, and my brain was on a one-way mission to remove every piece of clothing Kyle had put on that night (and possibly everything she had in her closet). She touched her tongue to my bottom lip, a request I could not deny. I parted my lips and whimpered quietly at the welcome feeling of her tongue in my mouth. In response, she raised her thigh upward until it pressed firmly between mine. Startling pinpricks of pleasure radiated from my center out to my entire body. I'd never experienced anything as intense. She consumed my mind and body so fully that there was room for nothing else but that moment. *This. Her. Us. Help. Except, don't.*

My shirt was pushed up and the cup of my bra was briskly pulled down, freeing my left breast. Her mouth, God her mouth, found my nipple and devoured it like she'd been studying for this her whole life. I moaned, my hands in her hair. She sucked and swirled the nipple unabashedly with her tongue. Damn, she was good at this. No surprise at all. I distantly realized I was rocking against her thigh, sending the pressure between my legs up, up, and up to a near breaking point.

When she pulled her leg away from mine, I nearly begged her to reconsider. But my zipper was on its way down, her doing, and that made up for the loss. She found my gaze and held it, her eyes darker than I'd seen them all night. That was desire. Kyle was turned the hell on, which made this all the sexier. When her hand dipped into my underwear and began to caress, I saw stars and began to inch closer and closer. The pressure between my legs was torturously wonderful. It climbed with each small touch. It doubled with each more direct press of her fingers. She was pulling responses from my body that I'd only read about. My already rocking hips picked up pace. My body skated to the edge, already on the verge of careening.

"Oh, no, you don't," she whispered in my ear. Her lips were on my neck. I liked them there very much, the heat of breath entirely welcome and intoxicating. Her hand was gone, though, roaming my body, making it hard for me to breathe at a proper pace.

"What are you doing to me?" I managed to ask.

"What am I doing? I'm taking my time, that's what." She crawled down the bed and my stomach tightened, anticipating. I bit my lower lip hard as the discomfort between my legs begged for release. I wanted to ask, but I also didn't want this to ever end. That first touch of her tongue sent a shock wave of pleasure straight from my center and out to my limbs. Her hands slid beneath me and cradled my ass as she continued to work her magic. One swipe of her tongue, then another, a third. I whimpered, hanging on, lost in need. She paused and crawled up my body to my breasts, pulling a nipple into her mouth. *Damn it all.* My eyes slammed shut. She swirled her tongue and took her sweet time sucking. All the while, her hand had returned to its spot between my legs. With one motion, she entered me, which was maybe the most satisfying moment in my sexual life. When she began to move in and out, I writhed beneath her, holding on, the pressure building as her unhurried motion continued. As she kissed my breast, I realized that she'd matched the rhythm of her hand perfectly. When I came, it was white hot and shocking in its intensity, to the point that I cried out as I rode the wave of pleasure. Kyle was patient and stayed inside, allowing me to rock against her hand and come down at my own pace. "You're beautiful," she said quietly as I attempted to breathe normally again.

Once I relaxed against the pillow beneath me, she joined me there, sliding her body up against mine, not breaking that contact.

"It turns out we're really good at that," Kyle said. "Wow." She smiled against my cheek and placed a kiss there. I turned to face her, finding her eyes.

"This whole night came out of nowhere. You did. I'm still in shock."

"Listen, I was just walking down the hall. You're the one who shut yourself in the door and changed the course of my whole night."

"I'm just really awkward. Who else gets trapped in doors?"

Kyle pulled her face back. "Let me just tell you that there is nothing awkward about you. In fact, you have some highly impressive moves." Her gaze dipped to my chest. "And your body backs them up. It's amazing."

"No, yours is. Your breasts are…" I shook my head. "There aren't words."

"Yeah? I have it on good authority that they like you right back."

I grinned, marveling. "It's not just me, right? I mean, we fit really well together, don't we?"

She nodded, eyebrows raised, and eased a strand of hair off my forehead. "Can you stay? Say yes. Your place is literally yards away. You don't need it." Her blue eyes carried hope as she traced the outline of my breast.

"I can stay," I said, honored that she wanted me to.

But we didn't sleep. In fact, we spent much of the night talking and kissing and having sex another two times. We were already well on our way to learning each other's bodies and minds. When the morning came, a sadness nestled in my chest. I didn't want to say goodbye to Kyle, and wasn't sure what to do about that. The circumstances kind of dictated that this was a hookup, even if the way we treated each other didn't.

"It's not a hookup," Kyle said, when I indicated as much.

"Isn't it? You can be straight with me." I was sitting on the side of the bed, searching the floor for my clothes.

She eased me back into bed beside her and kissed my neck, lingering as if she belonged there. "Nothing about us is straight."

"That's a good point," I said, sliding my fingers into her hair. I pulled back and met her gaze. This was too important. "But I'm all about realistic expectations. I don't want to set myself up for one thing, and then it turns out to be quite another. We had a great night. Maybe that's all this was." My heart thudded because as nonchalant as I was attempting to be, I was desperately wishing that our story didn't end today.

"I don't look at it that way."

"Okay," I said, trying to understand. "How do you look at it?"

"Maybe we're just ahead of our time."

I nodded. "If we'd met a year later, maybe."

"Can't we?"

I tried to follow. "What do you have in mind?"

She sat up, taking the sheet pressed to her chest with her. "Let's press pause and find each other in a year. Do this thing right. My last gasp of residency will be over. We can see what's here. I have a feeling it's a lot, Potter."

I let her words wash over me. "You realize this is kind of romantic. 'Meet me in a year.' It's what all romantic movies say."

"I like romance, and I like you. Meet me on the suspension bridge in a year. The anniversary of last night. I'm asking you on a date, just with a little bit of lead time."

"So, to summarize: Am I free *a year* from now?"

"That's the question at hand, yes. I have to see you on that day. I'll be desperate to." She fell back in bed, pleased with herself, and rested the side of her head in her palm, the sheet still draped across her body as if she'd been posed by one of the greats.

"What's going to happen then?" I asked, so ridiculously curious about this plan.

"We are. Because I refuse to accept this is it." She moved closer and softly twisted my hair around her finger. "How are you this beautiful in the morning? I didn't even know I have a thing for redheads, but trust me, I do now."

"Don't distract me with flattery." I batted my lashes.

"Fine. But it's true."

"Then I'm forced to forgive you." I stole a kiss, luxuriating in that newfound liberty. I loved her lips, the way she kissed, and the way she tasted.

She sighed happily when we came up for air. "So, the bridge. We're doing it? Say yes."

I paused, dropping the playfully flirtatious tone we'd been tossing back and forth because this was my real life. "You're serious about this? Honestly." I studied her for clues. All I saw was determination.

"About you? Very." These were the most gratifying and unexpected words. "We click. We have amazing chemistry. You make me laugh. You're fucking sexy. I've never met someone I can just be myself around so easily, so quickly." A pause. "But the timing is horrendous. I don't have an ounce of extra energy or a spare minute in my day as long as I'm in the midst of this residency." She leaned in, so incredibly intentional, which I found captivating. "I'm a smart woman, Savanna. I go after what I want. I'm not going to let you get away just because of what season it is."

I propped my head up on my hand, mirroring her. "Keep talking."

"We have our whole lives to live, and what if..." She held up a finger. "What if we're eventually supposed to do that together? Shouldn't we at least find out?" She tilted her head. "Not that I'm getting ahead of myself."

The line sent a ripple through my midsection. "You know what I say?"

"Tell me."

"Get ahead of yourself. I am." I stole a kiss and slid on top. We truly did fit together in all the different ways. I also enjoyed this unexpected sexual freedom, the newly discovered bedroom confidence I had with Kyle. I wasn't overthinking or concerned with minor details. Kyle made me *feel*, and the rest took care of itself. I could really get used to our dynamic. I'd only read about this kind of thing, and there I was...living the fantasy.

"Verdict?" she asked, staring up at me.

These were such uncharted waters for me: explosive chemistry and mutual admiration. And I knew one thing for certain. I didn't want to walk away from Kyle and have that be it. I didn't want this fairy tale to end. I met her blue eyes and went soft. "The bridge? Count on me. I'm there."

That inspired the biggest smile, the kind that made her eyes crinkle at the sides. She pulled me to her and kissed me, my hair falling against her bare shoulders, her skin pressed to mine. The sheet was abandoned and her hands were on my breasts. The shot of arousal pulled a quiet murmur. I sank into the warmth of her mouth, the soft feel of her lips moving with mine, perfection. The rush of need became my lifeline; the urge to touch her and be touched was all consuming. There was a moan. Someone's. My body craved, my head spun, and I didn't want to ever go back.

"We're doing this," she whispered.

I kissed her with everything I had, my promise to her. "I'll set an alarm for one year from today."

She smiled against my mouth. "The bridge or bust."

CHAPTER FIVE

(Almost) One Year Later

Festive Foods was bustling, which was typical for a Monday morning at a grocery store. People liked to start their week off with a full pantry full of food, a symptom of our hunter-gatherer instincts. New week, fresh groceries, and it was our job to make sure their experience was a fantastic one. I was in my fifth year as store manager and at this point knew the store and my job like the back of my hand. I made a point to be on the floor as much as possible on busy days, to lend my staff an extra hand, but also for that valuable one-on-one time with our customers. That kind of relationship building went a long way.

"Mrs. Martinelli, how is Henry?" I asked one of the Monday regulars. Her dachshund had had knee surgery weeks ago and hadn't been allowed to run or jump since. Last we'd chatted, he was going stir crazy, and as a result, so was she.

Mrs. Martinelli immediately directed her cart my way, already launching into it. Her face said it had been a saga, and with Henry Higgins, as she called him, it always was. "He's just had it with me, Savanna, and I don't blame him. He's ready to get out there and terrorize the squirrels, but I've explained to him that patience is a virtue. He scoffs."

"I bet. Are there any distractions?"

"I've gotten him a few busy toys, and that's helped occupy some of his energy. Thank you for asking, by the way. Not many people remember Henry's struggles."

"Well, I'd been wondering. Oh, and we received a whole new shipment of those dried pineapple rings you love."

"It's a good day, then. Gonna grab some right away. I saw Linda Robinson on aisle four and she always hoards those rings. I'm gonna beat her to it and skip all the way there."

"Aisle ten," I said.

She whirled back, a thought hitting. "And I have to tell you, those rosemary crackers you recommended for my charcuterie party were such a hit."

"Perfect. They're a well-kept secret that shouldn't be, you know? I buy a box every time I think about it."

"You're a gem, Savanna. Have a good day. Off to fight the pineapple ring battle. Linda better look out."

"Linda's feisty. Be careful. Let me know if you need anything."

"Will do." She returned to her pineapple ring mission. "Woman with a cart! Coming through!"

I spent another half hour on the floor, greeting guests and checking in with my employees. Three full-time and a handful of part-timers. Morale seemed to be high, which was always nice to see. I wanted the store to be a bright spot in the day for everyone who came through, not just the customers, and did what I could to be present and a good listener.

Maya, one of my full-timers, was the youngest on staff and also taking classes twice a week at the local college. "Jason asked me to dinner when I was swiping his eggs."

Anywhere else and that would have been a weird sentence. In a grocery store, and with Maya, it made all the sense. I folded my arms and grinned. Jason was the mayor's son, and she'd obsessed about him for months. I knew Jason's favorite shirt. The different versions of his smile. I was aware of how often he was absent on Thursdays. The two of them had a chemistry class together and apparently had a little of their own.

"You could be Mrs. Mayor's Son, Maya. I love that for you. Is this dinner happening?" We were in the midst of a lull and stood near the registers where we most often would shoot the small-town breeze.

"I don't know. That's the problem. I froze," she said, green eyes wide. "I told him I'd have to check my work schedule."

"No, you don't. I clear you to dine with Jason. Tell me when and we'll cover your shift if you're on."

"Yeah, we will," Henrietta called from her register. As the senior cashier and a woman in her sixties, Henrietta had been with the store for over two decades and had seen it all and wanted you to know it. "I'm not busy that night. I'll put in the time in the name of young lust."

"We haven't scheduled anything yet," Maya pointed out.

Henrietta shrugged. "I'm not busy any night. It's just my life to not be busy."

"Text him and tell him you're in," I said, with a soft touch to her shoulder.

She stared me down with fiery intensity. "You really think I should take this leap?"

"Maya, he's all you talk about. What Jason wore to class. How maybe, when he smiled at you, it meant he really wanted to kiss you. This is your chance to find out." I knew a little something about longing to find out and used it to usher young Maya forward on her quest to find love.

"Okay, okay. I'm gonna do it. But"—she held up an emphatic finger—"I'm gonna wait an hour."

"That's fair," I said. "Whatever you feel most comfortable with. You be super vibey. Low key. Isn't that what the kids do these days instead of chill?" I wasn't low key. I had no rizz. I barely understood what the words meant.

"Eager is not your friend, sweet girl." Henrietta nodded in agreement. She was the romance novel reader in our group, with an ever-changing stack in her employee locker at any given point. The saucy kind, too. "Wait two. Make him squirm. I just read a book by Genevieve Haughton and her heroine played hard to get half the book and it paid off in really hot spades." She fanned herself. "As in naked spades."

"No, I think we translated," I told Henrietta. I knew nothing about the games dating people played, preferring to be more of a straight shooter myself. Maybe my naïveté was why I hadn't seen a ton of success in my own love life. Well, *yet*. I brought my shoulders to my ears at the prospect of that possibly changing with a very certain date approaching on the calendar very soon.

"Okay," Maya said tentatively. "I think I'm gonna do it. But you're gonna have to look at my outfit choices and tell me which is giving happy to be here but also don't get too comfortable."

"Easy enough," I said with a smile. "I'm such an outfit pro. God, I wish people would stop pointing out how I excel at all things fashion. I mean, look at these brown boots whose brand I don't remember."

"They slay," Maya offered.

I really liked these people. My friends. "I think that's good. Gonna pretend, either way, because my ego demands it."

I spent my lunch hour at my desk in the small office on the back wall of the store. I went over last week's inventory shifts and put in the order for the following week. Tracking buying trends, especially how they related to weather patterns and changing seasons, was the most fascinating part of my job. For example, our lemonades and cold drink mixes sold much faster in the summer than in the colder months, and my ordering tendencies would always reflect that. In the midst of numbers, apps, spreadsheets, and orders, I tried not to hyper-fixate on the weekend ahead. When I did allow myself to imagine meeting Kyle on that bridge, it sent me on a daydream tangent, smashing my productivity like a gnat with no chance. Nope. I certainly wouldn't think about the snacks I'd purchased for the roadtrip to Charleston, or the playlist I'd curated with the general thesis *Good things are coming.* No reason to dwell on the room I'd booked at the very same hotel where I'd met Kyle the year before. Or the suspension bridge we were scheduled to meet in the middle of in just five short days. But I was apparently powerless, because the excitement infiltrated my system anyway, elevating my heart rate and making me squirm in my chair with bonus, happy energy.

Kyle was near all I'd thought about for twelve straight months, and the possibility that maybe my own happily ever after was finally on its way.

"C'mon. You're legit telling me that you've both kept your word and haven't contacted each other even once?" Jonathan had asked the night before from the corner seat of my new perfectly beige sectional. It was too big for one person living alone. But you know what? Maybe that wouldn't always be the case. At the very least, I could entertain more, now that I was embracing the space.

"No. I promise. There's been zero reaching out either direction, which I admit was hard at first, but then I started to appreciate the romance in waiting."

"It's certainly a unique approach." He squinted. "Not even a DM?"

I shook my head, enjoying his skepticism. "She has one social media account and doesn't touch it." I shrugged sheepishly. "I mean, I had to at least look."

"Well, yeah, you did." He sat forward, still incredulous. His hair, which he'd grown longer this year, flopped onto his forehead. I liked the way he used it to express himself. "How could you not? This whole thing is very hard to wrap my mind around. Guys would never do this. We don't have the patience for delayed gratification. Kudos to lesbiankind."

I laughed. "On behalf of the others, thank you for the nod. I happen to think good things are worth waiting for."

He eased his feet to the side so I could take my customary seat.

"If this all works out, it might be a great story to tell one day."

"It's Instagram gold. You need a camera crew."

"We're not like that."

"And if it doesn't work out?" He was making a gentle point. I sighed. I tried not to think about the answer to his question too often, but the reality was a lot could go wrong. After a glorious weekend with Kyle a year ago, I knew we had the *potential* to be fantastic together. But that's all I knew. A lot could have changed between then and now, and when I saw her, she might not be the same person. I hated that possibility and tried not to dwell on it. I'd waited too long, held on to so much hope.

When I'd returned home from Charleston last year, I wasn't the same. I saw the world differently and found light in the most mundane tasks, wondering why that lettuce suddenly looked incredibly leafy green and gorgeous. How lucky we were to have lettuce! Kyle had done that for me, flipped the world sunny side up. As a side effect, I'd become exponentially more aware of the calendar, watching one day fold into the next as we rounded one holiday after another. But I also feared the moment I'd head to Charleston. The moratorium would be up and we'd see, once and for all, if Kyle and I were meant to be. In my heart of hearts, I was hopeful. Lies. I was way beyond hopeful. I'd clung to nothing but unaltered hope since the moment we said goodbye and held on to each other for far too long, my face pressed into her watermelon-scented hair. I'd not allowed myself to live in the memory of that weekend entirely, but I did take it out on occasion and revisit glimpses.

This week was different, however.

We were scheduled to meet up on that bridge on Saturday, and now that the time was here, I allowed myself the luxury of uninhibited revisits to that time and what it meant to me. My heart squeezed when I thought about Kyle, how much I liked her, how worthy she'd made me feel. I wondered what her year had been like, how difficult the final throes of residency had been for her. Had she been looking forward to this weekend, too? Did she think of me? I entertained short fantasies about walking straight to her and kissing her again, holding hands in the park, spending long mornings in bed, discussing the headlines and getting to know each other at a slower, more luxurious pace. To my credit, happily ever after was a thought I reserved for down the line, but only because I wanted to be conservative in my expectations. The easiest way not to get hurt, after all. Because it was wholly possible she'd say she still wasn't in a place to get involved with someone, or worse, she was *already* involved with an amazing woman she'd unexpectedly met. Her name was probably Ella and they would get married in France beneath the Eiffel Tower with plans to live the most exciting life. I had to be ready to hear her out and also realize I might not like the words.

I met Jonathan's solemn brown eyes. He was worried for me, which was what Jonathan did. Neither of us had been dealt the best hand in life, and we looked out for each other. I swallowed and faced him. "Well, if it doesn't work out, I'll wish her well."

"It's a risky move, but I'm proud of you for going there and making it."

I shrugged. "Kyle and I are just two people trying to make our way in the world. Maybe she's already in love, maybe she has no room on her plate, maybe she's a different person now. Who knows?" I sucked in air and pretended to check in on something on my phone. The stakes felt incredibly high, and it was so much easier to deflect.

Now, sitting in my office staring at inventory, I had only four days between me and my journey to that suspension bridge. I needed to keep my head down and focus on the here and now. The rest would sort itself out sooner rather than later. Who was I kidding? I threw myself back in my leatherette executive chair and grinned the happy sigh of someone with birds and hearts flying in a circle above their head. *Four short days.*

❖

On Thursday morning, I let myself into Lindy's house, correction, *my Airbnb.* I was still getting used to the sound of that. Wow. I did a casual walk-through a few hours before my next set of guests was scheduled to arrive. The complimentary bottle of cabernet was out, and I added my handwritten note. A small platter of assorted cheeses was nestled in the fridge with a welcome sign on a toothpick. Elizabeth and her odd jobs company were doing a fantastic job turning the place over between guests, even picking up the cheese from my deli. We'd struck up a reasonable deal, and the whole thing was now functioning like a well-oiled machine. I quickly checked the guest book I kept on the end table and saw that my recently departed tenants had left a wonderful note of thanks with some recommendations for future visitors.

Do not, I repeat, do not miss the oversized glazed donuts at Amazin' Glazin'.

I grinned, because it was sound advice. With donuts bigger than my hand and a wonderfully messy glaze, no one would forget the little shop that could. They'd recently expanded their space, overtaking the dry cleaning business next door when it went out of business.

I climbed the pull-down ladder up to the attic, which was now only a quarter full of Lindy's belongings, a work in progress. Each time I stopped by the house, I made it a goal to take one box with me to sort through. Today's box had the word *Rachel* written in faded black marker. Lindy's handwriting. I'd been sidestepping that box for weeks, unsure if I was in the right headspace to open it and handle and explore items that had once been my mother's. Her hands had touched, if not treasured, the things in that box. My stomach flip-flopped with nervous excitement. Today felt like the right day. I scooped up the box and carefully carried it down the ladder, protective of the contents inside and how sacred they felt.

I waited until after dinner, a huge blackened chicken salad, to explore the box. "All right, Mom. You and me," I said quietly, as I placed it on the table in my kitchen. There were so many odds and ends crammed inside that I took my time, to not overwhelm myself. A small makeup bag, still with a few lipsticks inside. Surreal. A couple of romance novels that looked like they'd been read multiple times. I smiled and pressed one of the paperbacks to my chest—a girl after my own heart. This was fun, getting to know my mom in a whole new way. Several trophies and certificates she'd won over the years. One for entrepreneurship in high school, making me wish Lindy was here so I could ask for more details. My mom was a businesswoman at seventeen? I loved it. At the bottom of the box, I found several basic-looking file folders. The first one contained a hodgepodge of paperwork: her birth certificate, greeting cards from my grandparents and Lindy, as well as a handful of photos from her college years. I loved going through them, my eyes welling with wistful tears as I took in her youthful, smiling face. Everything in me wished I'd had the opportunity to know her at the age I was now, that she'd know me, as well. What would she think of my job? Of Jonathan? Would she attend Pride parades at my side? There was no question. I knew she would have.

I opened the second folder and dropped my brows. The papers inside were all the same. A thick stack of handwritten letters she'd saved from what looked to be my dad. I skimmed the first. They were figuring out their summer schedules, apparently, during their college years. I flipped through the thick stack of pages, paragraphs upon paragraphs from him, pouring his heart out. He was telling her he loved her. I felt the warmth spread out in my chest. I snuggled into the soft part of the chair. He wanted to be there for her. He'd raise her child as if it was his own. Record scratch. I sat up. Rocked. *Hold on.* What child? I set the page on the table and blinked at the wall with my framed daisy photos. A whoosh of nausea descended like a lightning strike. I swallowed and rushed back to the page, infused with adrenaline, my eyes searching the words, but the letters failed to make sense in their order. Nothing did. "Okay, just hold on a second," I said to the empty kitchen. "Pause. Breathe. Look at the dates." The sound of my own voice helped center me and calm my scattered thoughts. I went back to the letter and found the date, which was just seven months before I was born. I didn't have a long lost sibling. They were talking about *me*. The letters were one hundred percent from my dad, which meant only one thing. "He wasn't my biological father," I murmured. The colors I'd meticulously picked out for my home began to fade from the edges. The panic was replaced by a strange, and almost welcome, numbing sensation. The buzzing sound in my ears was less helpful.

"I think I need wine," I said, continuing my streak of speaking out loud to no one. It's apparently what I did now. "And maybe a pet so I don't have to launch into soliloquy to an empty room. A sweet puppy to lick my face and tell me that this didn't exactly change anything. Fuck." I slid my hand into my hair and gripped as hard as I could, the physical pain taking center stage over the mental anguish for a much-needed moment. "He was still my dad. Right? Dammit. He still raised me for every second we were together on this Earth." I poured a hearty glass of cab, stared at it, thought better and added even more.

"Hell, in the letters, he was an absolute supportive gem. So, what's the problem?" I took a long swallow of wine. "Except that you're not at all who you thought you were." I stalked back to the table, harnessing new determination. A fire stirred within, born of a need to know and a sense of betrayal at having not been told. Had Lindy known? I couldn't imagine her keeping something this important from me. I was up again and moving. My father was not related to me by blood, which ushered in a question I had yet to consider: Then who the hell was? Who was the man I shared DNA with? The idea that I potentially had a living parent out there about knocked me over. I was an orphan. In fact, that status had become an integral portion of my identity, my plight in this world. But it wasn't necessarily the case? No. Another gulp of wine. I put on loud music, whatever Alexa picked out for me, and walked circular laps around my kitchen. My watch notified me astutely that I'd hit my steps for the day and more. Damn right I had. "Thank you," I said pointedly to it, because it felt like the only friend I had nearby.

Now what?

I was scheduled to drive to Charleston in two days to meet up with the potential love of my life, and my place on this Earth was just run over by a Mack truck. What was I supposed to do now? I wanted to call Jonathan but I also didn't want to say all of the words out loud because doing so might make them real. With a deep breath, I returned to my kitchen table once again and started reading, consuming every detail. If I knew everything, I could figure this thing out and put myself back together again. If desperation had a name, it would have been Savanna. There had to be a hundred letters, all one-sided, of course. I'd never know for sure what my mother wrote back, but there were clues. She wanted to move away from Dreamer's Bay and start somewhere fresh, and he'd agreed. That made sense. They'd apparently gotten married several months before my birth and were planning on getting jobs and making a go of it. They'd sorted out the details back and forth, professing their love and excitement for a time they could fully be together. It was actually incredibly romantic, and I took comfort in that part, using it to soothe what felt like a gut punch. I headed to their wedding album that I'd stashed in the drawer of my end table. I exhaled in satisfaction when the dates on the back of their smiling, happy wedding photos confirmed the timeline I'd established from the exchanges. After they'd married, the letters stopped, which made sense. After poring over every word, I sat back on the couch and blinked at the empty room, floating back to the present. My eyes were full of gravel. It was after midnight, and I needed to be back at the store before the sun was up. The thought nearly made me weep.

I didn't waste time with pajamas, allowing the cool sheets to press against my skin as I let go of my thoughts, hoping, somehow, someway I'd wake up to discover this was all a dream.

CHAPTER SIX

The Bridge

It was the day I'd been waiting for, and yet it didn't feel real. The idea that I was going to lay eyes on Kyle for the first time in twelve months hadn't fully hit me yet. I sat at the outdoor café around the corner from the park, unable to touch the chicken salad sandwich I'd ordered for dinner and instead had requested a cappuccino. The heat radiating from the white ceramic mug in my hands helped anchor me in the moment. I smiled at the couple at the table adjacent to mine, enjoying how in love they seemed and wondering if that just might be me someday. I could admit to feeling rattled after what I'd learned two days ago, and I very much needed today. I needed to see Kyle and I needed to anchor myself in the here and now. Focus on the future like a lifeline and press pause on the past. Today was a bright spot.

I checked my watch.

Ten minutes.

Butterflies swarmed, but my smile could not be dimmed. I signed the credit card slip and stood. I'd selected a green and white dress and added a cropped denim jacket because the combination felt very much me. With my heart pounding rapid fire in my chest, I took the short walk to the park, hyperaware of every human, pet, insect, and breeze that came my way. I just needed to relax and remember how at home I felt around Kyle.

The park was everything I'd remembered and more. Even the ice cream truck was tucked in its same spot. I took a minute just to soak it all in. Finally, I found my way to the suspension bridge with two to three minutes to spare. A quick scan up and down told me Kyle wasn't on the bridge yet. I was first and that was okay. It would give me a moment to catch my breath, smooth my dress, and run my fingers through my likely windblown hair that I'd had trimmed the day before. I found a spot midway from one side to the other, as close to where I remembered us standing together as I could manage. Not sure which direction she might come from, though, every few moments, I scanned both, looking extra closely anytime a brunette appeared in the distance. We'd agreed on eight p.m. because the sun would be going down. Watching the brilliant colors on display now, it had been a good call. Wow. I took a breath as I saw a woman about her height walk toward the bridge from between the trees. She paused. Hugged someone. *Oh, God. Here we go.* Deep breath. Then the woman turned and went back the other way. Not Kyle.

Ten more minutes passed. Twenty. I didn't understand. Maybe she'd been called into the hospital. She'd made it clear that that kind of thing happened all the time. Thirty minutes. I walked to the end of the bridge and back again, still searching the faces of everyone I passed. An hour. I pulled the jacket tighter around me as a sense of dread began to settle. Ninety minutes. She hadn't been called into the hospital. Somehow, I knew that much. I stayed on that bridge anyway, quietly trying to understand. My feet were hurting because the shoes were new. I wasn't sure why I stayed, except I needed to see this thing through, to bear witness and understand without any doubt that Kyle stood me up and left me there alone.

Dusk eased gradually into night. The stunning lights illuminated the bridge's suspension wires in such a striking manner that a painful lump formed in my throat at the stark contrast of the beauty in front of me and the sadness within. I was supposed to be swimming in happiness tonight, anticipating all that was to come. I didn't want to take any of this personally, but honestly, it was the most personal thing ever, being stood up, especially for something as big as this was. I flashed on myself singing happily in the car on the way here, searching down the hall for my hotel room. The stupid café in which I practically vibrated with excitement. I laughed quietly, shook my head, and stared down at my fingers as they grasped the railing. My legs ached. I needed to get the hell off this bridge.

"Did you have a nice evening?" the doorman asked as I approached the entrance to the hotel.

"Not really," I said flatly. "But I hope you did."

I stayed that night, checked out the next morning, and drove straight home.

My parents had lied to me. I had no idea who my biological father was. And I'd just wasted a year of my life on a woman who didn't even have the decency to tell me it was over in person. I felt betrayed on so many levels that I didn't quite know how to move through the world as myself. The one-two punch had done a number on me, and when I looked in the mirror I saw someone looking back at me who was apparently very easy to let down.

CHAPTER SEVEN

Turning the Page

"I just never imagined I'd feel so many different things for someone." Maya sat across from me at the circular table in the break room. "When Jason walks in a room, the temperature changes and the planets hug each other or something. Like, the planets are just as in love as we are. It's like they're these beings with hearts."

"Wow. Planets with hearts." I nodded along, as much support as I could manufacture, which wasn't an impressive amount.

Maya didn't seem to mind the complete lack of enthusiasm in my voice. Hell, she didn't even seem to need me here for this conversation. She plowed forward like a homesick horse that saw the barn in the distance. "My skin gets sensitive in the best way, and I just want to stop whatever I'm doing and stare into his dreamy hazel eyes until the world goes away forever. Has that ever happened to you?" She laughed.

I didn't. I blinked and set down my half-consumed carton of blueberry yogurt. "No."

She waited for more. There wasn't any. I was a failure at romantic cheerleading these days.

"No? Savanna, that breaks my heart. You more than anyone else are deserving of the most wonderful love on Earth." Maya had been noticeably different since she and Jason had become an item. Starry eyes and overly talkative, just positive that romance was the be-all and end-all. She threw herself back in the chair and let it roll a few feet. She was hardcore in love with Jason and convinced everyone should join her in the land of the gaga.

I hated it.

Yep. That's who I'd become in the last few months, the founding member of Dreamer's Bay's very own Love Can Kick Rocks Club. Boo to hearts. Screw attraction. Forget romantic meet-ups on bridges and doctors who snapped your hope in half like a twig. I couldn't exactly say that to lovestruck Maya, however, so instead I slipped into smile mode and shrugged. "That's me, deserving of wonderful, happy love during my time on this planet." I made a show of catching the time. "Oh, look. I better take a lap around the floor. After that, I'll be in my office for the next fifty years if anyone needs me."

"I know you're probably still upset about the woman from Charleston, but there are plenty of awesome women out there."

"Yep. Just everywhere." I didn't feel the need to correct her.

On the way to my office, I made a mental note to change aisle seven at the store into the Lonely Hearts aisle. It would feature Kleenex bulk packs, lots of chocolate, and wine. I predicted it would be the most popular aisle in the store inside of a week. Not that I needed any more help in that department, personally. I was well over Rejection on the Bridge, as I liked to call it. It had taken a couple of months for me to wallow in my sadness and absorb the lost future I'd sold myself on, not to mention recover from the blow to my ego. But I was there now, and happily jaded. And maybe jaded was so much better than sad. I was a realist these days, no longer romanticizing a concept that didn't deserve the boost. Let the Hallmark TV movies brainwash *other* people for a while. Life was too short to get caught up in fantasy. I actually preferred the new enlightened me.

"I don't like this Bitter Betty version of you," Jonathan said over drinks that evening at Ronnie Roo's. Martinis were on special for five dollars, and I wasn't about to miss.

"Why exactly are you jaded now?" Elizabeth asked with a curious squint. She didn't relish martinis and opted for a Blue Moon. As much as I loved Elizabeth Draper and valued her friendship, she was a forever optimist who was, of course, in a wonderful relationship. Thereby, her outlook couldn't be trusted.

I shrugged. "I just think that true love is a high bar that only a few attain. I'm not opposed to finding it, but I'm also just fine with it never happening, the more likely scenario. It feels so much better to just accept that. Sex? Sure. Love? No longer needed, thanks. I'm good."

Jonathan hooked a thumb. "See? Bitter. The worst. And all because that doctor in Charleston ghosted her. We hate her."

"No, we don't," I said, placing a hand on his wrist. "She had her reasons and I have to respect them. Whatever they are."

Elizabeth watched us, her gaze moving from Jonathan to me as if piecing together the puzzle. "I don't know this story. I'm woefully behind."

"It was a whole thing that happened. I don't broadcast it," I said. "Who wants to tell people they were stood up in dramatic fashion?"

"It was dramatic?" Her eyes were wide as she leaned in. "Oh, no. I'm so sorry. Now I need details."

Jonathan took the reins. "Highlight reel. Savanna met Dr. Kyle, a gorgeous brunette, in Charleston. They spent a hot and heavy weekend together in the big city. There was lust. There were feelings flying like witches on broomsticks." I tried not to roll my eyes as he pressed on. Or worse, allow myself to remember the details of that weekend too vividly. "They wanted more of each other. But the timing was extra bad, so the fancy doctor suggested they meet on the suspension bridge in," he held up a finger, "wait for it. One year's time."

"No," Elizabeth said, wide eyed.

"Oh, yes."

"You anticipated this for a year?" Elizabeth's brow creased with worry. "And Dr. Kyle didn't show up?"

"She did not," I said, and stirred my second martini. Going for two was maybe not the best idea on a weeknight, but here we sat.

Elizabeth blinked, trying to reconcile the information with her overly large heart that was probably bleeding for me this very second. "Savvy, I'm so sorry. I can't believe I didn't know any of this."

I covered her hand. "Don't take it personally. I didn't tell anyone but Jonathan and a few of my coworkers."

"And you didn't even have your sweet Lindy when you came home." She shifted into her feisty mode. I'd seen it before during cornhole tournaments and Tuesday night bowling. Her team, the Ballbusters, didn't mess around. "You should have come to me with this. We could have eaten popcorn all night. Downed a bottle of red wine while we cursed out medical dramas on the TV."

I realized she was right, but I was someone who had trouble asking for help. After a life filled with grief, I'd learned to carry my sadness on my own. People got tired of feeling bad for you. "I've always been a pull myself up by the bootstraps kind of person," I confessed. "I think that's what I was doing."

"Childhood trauma," Jonathan said, nodding along. "Abandonment issues, which I'm sure this didn't help."

"Don't therapize me while I'm having martinis. Besides, it's all good now," I added. "Speaking of childhood, I should probably tell you both that I don't know who my biological father is." Damn, those second drinks sure did loosen lips. Where had that sprouted from? Possibly because Elizabeth's kind offer had softened my heart. Eating popcorn all night and cursing at fake doctors sounded downright wonderful.

The table went still. My two friends exchanged a fully shocked look and my cheeks went warm with embarrassment. My blurt was out there now. No going back. "Yeah. Not a big deal. But, *yeah.*"

"What are you talking about?" Elizabeth said gently. "You're wondering if your dad was actually...*your biological parent?*"

I took a beat. "He wasn't. I read the firsthand correspondence between them that confirmed it." I raised a shoulder. "Maybe they were waiting for me to get a little older to break the news. Maybe they were never planning to. I'll never know." My gaze immediately dropped to my drink, emotion welling and threatening to take over. I fought hard against it. Jonathan had yet to speak.

"Why do I feel like a loser twice over now in this conversation?" I added a laugh to ease the tension. Before I could continue my train of thought a moment longer, two arms were around me. Jonathan's. The warmth and tightness of his squeeze sent a wash of calm through my entire body. God, I needed that. I relaxed into him, my safe friend, aware that there were tears in my eyes, obscuring my vision. He had me. These two people truly did care. Wordlessly, I covered his arms with mine and held on, this time not running from the emotion.

"It's okay," Elizabeth said. I met her gaze across the table and offered a wobbly smile. She'd gone all misty, too. "We have you. You don't have to keep up any of those walls, okay?" I reached for her hand, and she gave it a squeeze, her words making me want to sob. After months of holding it all in, this was the first time I'd confessed the truth about my parents to anyone.

"Thank you," I managed in a rasp before sucking in oxygen. Not my prettiest moment. I caught the tear that fell with the back of my hand, realizing my entire cheek was wet. "I don't know where any of that came from. Pardon my public waterworks."

"Well, I know," Elizabeth said. "You've been carrying a heavy load and you just laid down a portion of it to your friends. It's exactly what you should be doing. In fact, do it more, okay? Bad day at work? Call me. Call Jon."

"Okay," I said, reaching for a napkin to dry apparently my entire face.

Jonathan nodded and returned to his stool. "Tell us what you read."

"Oh, the letters." I recounted the story of my parents' courtship piece by piece, including my dad's pledge to love and raise me as his own. At the end, I placed my empty drink on the table. "So, the remaining question is, if Bradley Potter wasn't my father, who is?"

My friends, who'd scarcely moved a muscle as I recounted the story, came alive at my question. "You have to find him," Elizabeth said emphatically.

"Only if that's something you're interested in," Jonathan said cautiously. He always had looked both ways before crossing a street. "But it is, right? I mean, you want to know?"

"I'm not sure I do. Why go asking the universe for trouble?"

They exchanged a look, as if checking in with each other, likely out of their depth. Couldn't blame them. I was, too.

"I think you play it by ear," Elizabeth said. "Doesn't have to be today."

"Good point," I said. "I can start that search any time I want or not at all."

"Exactly," Elizabeth said. "And this doesn't change a single thing about you. You're the same person you always were."

But was I?

As I walked home that night, it felt like something had been unleashed that I couldn't rein back in. Just as I'd feared, saying the words out loud forced me to look at my situation head-on. Maybe for the first time. I turned right onto Lonesome Dove Lane and laughed at the irony. "Won't be staying long," I told the houses I passed. Canary Park was a much happier street, and I was glad I'd chosen to call it home. In between, I couldn't stop thinking about who my father might be. Was he right here in town? Across the country? Had we ever met? Did he even know about me?

I had a sneaking suspicion I was going to deal with all these swirling questions sooner rather than later. "Oh, please be later," I mumbled as I arrived in my driveway. "I just need calm waters for a while. Can we do that?" I asked, peering up at the darkened sky. "No more ripples. Thank you! Plate is full. Gonna rest now!"

I stared at the stars and nodded with finality. Yep. That should do it.

❖

I hated having to rush. The chaotic fury that descended on me when time was of the essence was perhaps my least favorite state of being. I added cushions to travel times, sat in parking lots in advance of any given appointment to ensure I dodged the pressure-filled drive to the venue. However, Elizabeth called to report that Eileen, who usually handled the turnovers for me at the Airbnb, had called in sick with the flu.

"I'm so sorry," Elizabeth explained. "I'd do it myself, but I'm booked driving Mrs. Gray to her cardiology appointment."

"Mrs. Gray is more important," I told her. "I'll handle the turnover. Thanks for letting me know, Lizzie."

"I will find a way to make this up to you."

I smiled into the phone. "A skydiver writing my name for all the town to see? I've always wanted to see *Savanna Rocks* in the sky."

"We can work out the details later."

"Don't let me down."

After we slid off the call, I assessed my schedule. Check-in time at the Airbnb was any time after ten, which meant I needed to sashay my ass on over there and get to work. The booking was for three nights, taking us into the long Indigenous Peoples' Day weekend. With most folks off on Monday, the grocery store would be overrun with customers on the hunt for burgers, barbecue sauce, chips, and snack foods of all varieties. Luckily, we were stocked and ready for 'em. I checked my watch, which made me sprint like a maniac to the Airbnb. In record time, I changed the sheets, scrubbed down the kitchen and bathrooms, placed my welcome bottle of wine on the marble countertop, and personalized my welcome card. The coffee carousel was fully stocked, and the remotes were neatly lined up for use in the living room. I placed the keys in the lockbox on the doorknob, leapt into my car, and headed for the market, only ninety minutes late. Not bad, all things considered. I was determined to survive this day. Hell, maybe I'd even turn it around in overtime.

I sang along to my anti-romance playlist that was full of songs about strength and empowerment, with hints of accusation. I was quite proud of myself for leaping into action when Elizabeth called. I carried that same triumphant energy with me to work, moving about the floor like a seasoned politician among the masses. Smiling, chatting, helping direct our customers to the aisle where they'd locate the cookout foods they sought. "You'll find the marshmallows on eight," I told Brandon, my old lab partner from high school. "Grab the ones in the bright blue packaging. They plump better and I'm not even kidding."

"Hot tip. Swing by the garage soon. I'll give ya twenty percent off an oil change."

I actually needed one of those. Brandon was a helpful guy who never forgot that I used to slip him the answers on our weekly bio quiz. "In that case, I'm bringing my car by this week."

He tipped his Clemson ballcap, which hid the fact that he was losing his hair. Man, time was marching on and dragging us all with it. At least Brandon was married with a family. No. *Stop that*. I refused to pay attention to that little clock in my head anymore and took pleasure in smashing it to hell with my imaginary baseball bat.

I smiled after Brandon and turned, moving with purpose toward the front of the store, and smacked right into a woman carrying a bag of mandarins in each hand. To my horror, they both split on impact, sending tiny balls of citrus scurrying in all directions like cockroaches when the lights were turned on.

She looked down in surprise, her eyebrows dashing to her hairline.

"I am so incredibly sorry," I said, dropping to my knees. Maya, who was returning from her break, was immediately at my side, helping to coral the wayward produce. The woman joined us and I realized I'd never seen her before. She had shoulder length blond hair and brown eyes, and seemed to be around my age.

"No," she said. "All my fault. I was lost in my own world and left the oranges vulnerable to attack. When will I fucking learn?"

I laughed. "Admittedly, I have to stop attacking the produce."

Once we had the mandarins assembled and wrangled back in their bags, we stood. "I can swap these out for you," Maya said, taking the busted bags and dashing off toward produce.

"I don't think we've met. Are you in town for the long weekend?" I asked. Maybe this was my new house guest.

"Actually no, I moved to town a little over a month ago, but I've been using a grocery delivery service." She smiled at me. That was meaningful eye contact if I'd ever seen it, and love sucks club or not, I didn't mind. "I'm realizing my mistake now."

Well, well. Did that mean what I think it meant? I stood a little taller and noticed we were about the same height.

"In that case, welcome to town. I'm Savanna. The store manager."
I extended my hand, keeping it professional.

She closed her hand over mind. Firm but not too firm. "Nice to
meet you, Savanna. I'm Mary Jane, but everyone calls me MJ."

"MJ it is. What brings you to the Bay?"

"I handle commercial real estate and a friend offered me a job. Did
a really great sales pitch on all this little place has to offer."

A thought dawned on me. "Does that mean you work with Devyn
Winters?" I remembered Elizabeth saying Devyn had been working to
expand the business when we had martinis the other night at Ronnie
Roo's. Maybe MJ was part of the new team.

"Exactly. Wow. You know Devyn? Small world."

"Small *town*," I corrected. "Same high school. Her wife, Elizabeth,
is a good friend of mine."

"Perfect." Her eyes shone bright. "Then we should all get together
sometime."

"Definitely."

She passed me a winsome smile. MJ was pretty and appraising me
in a manner that pinged my gaydar. Interesting. "I'm serious, though.
I'm not just making conversation to be polite. It's not who I am." She
slid a strand of blond hair behind her ear. I liked her subtle pink gloss.
"I'd love to, I don't know, hang out. Get to know you. Hear more about
the store." She was staring at me happily, both confident and wistful.
What in the world was happening? Women didn't often walk into town
and pay this kind of overt attention to me. Then again, we didn't have a
million gay or bisexual women roaming the streets, and straight women
didn't look at me the way MJ was.

I was now aware that Maya had returned and was watching the
exchange like the last few points of a tennis match, clutching two bags
of mandarins like her life depended on it. "Shall I carry these to the
front?" she finally asked, leaping in when I'd let the conversation drop.
The problem was my brain was trying to process the fact that I was
being hit on in my very store, and my mouth was lagging behind.

"That would be so helpful," MJ said, breaking our eye contact and
turning fully to Maya. "I'll follow you to checkout."

I raised a hand, returning to manager status. "I'll be sure to tell
Elizabeth that I ran into you."

"Take care, Savanna. Watch out for the fruit. Seriously." She
shook her head in annoyance and then broke into a playful smile. I had
a feeling she was a lot of fun.

"Good advice." I watched the very attractive woman who'd kinda sorta hit on me round the corner and head to the front of the store. I didn't leap with excitement at the very viable dating prospect who'd just moved to town and shown actual interest. That would have been the old me. But I did smile pleasantly, my spirits a tad higher, as I wondered if anything would actually come of it. Who knew? Maybe love wouldn't suck forever, a thought I hadn't actually considered until this moment. Maybe I just needed the right person to waltz in with their bags of mandarins and make everything feel a little lighter.

Maybe all hope wasn't lost.

A short time later, Maya appeared at my side as I straightened the mess the sweet snacks aisle had become. People really went crazy when they arrived in the middle of their favorite snacks, like toddlers at a cookie buffet.

"She was so nice, right?" Maya said, sliding her hand into the pockets of her store apron and executing a perfect heel to toe rock.

"Mm-hmm. She was." I picked up a package. "Did you see that a new batch of seasonal Oreos arrived? Grab 'em while you can."

"She was really pretty, too. Did you notice that?"

"Who?"

Maya blinked patiently. "MJ. The woman with the mandarins who you shoulder checked. I think she liked it."

"Oh, right! Yes. She was pretty." I could admit that much.

"You should take her up on that offer and get together with your friends."

"I might."

"When?" Maya sighed. She wanted everyone to be in love because she was, and I was ruining her fun by not playing along. I could throw her a bone.

"Not sure, but maybe I'll keep an eye out for the next time she's in the store."

You would have thought I'd just hit her happy switch, as an enthusiastic smile took over her face and sparks of light practically shot from her head. She pointed at me, backing up. "I will keep an eye out, too, and let you know the very next time she's here." She clapped like a sorority girl at a rosé brunch. "This is gonna be awesome. Just wait. I feel like we had an important discovery today, and I'm gonna keep an eye on this situation for you, Savanna. I'm your wing woman."

I nodded along passively. "Thank you for that. I've not had one of those."

A little fun never hurt anyone. It wasn't like I was emotionally invested in this working out, which was kind of the glory in the scenario. More shoppers came and went as Friday coasted into Friday night. I finished my workday making the schedule for later in the month so my employees could make plans. The day had been mundane, outside of mandarin-gate, but as I moved through it, I allowed the memory of my run-in with the newest resident of Dreamer's Bay to bring a smile to my face…and I kinda liked it.

❖

Though the store was open seven days a week, I personally had Saturday off, which allowed me to marinate in the sheer excitement of having absolutely zero plans. I could call Jonathan and see if he wanted to grab food on the boardwalk. I could stay home and read an entire novel on the couch, uninterrupted. Maybe I'd scoot over to Ronnie's and see who was watching a game at the bar and join them. There was likely a cornhole tournament of some kind I could sign up for. However, most of those things couldn't happen without my phone charger, which I couldn't seem to locate. A quick retrace of my steps told me that the last time I'd seen it was when I'd turned over the Airbnb. I closed my eyes, realizing that I'd definitely left it in the kitchen, likely still plugged into the socket. Sadly, my phone was moments from dying completely. Surely I could message the Alexandra woman staying there, apologize profusely for the interruption, grab it, and go.

An hour later and I'd done just that: messaged my guest, grabbed a shower, fluffed my hair, and applied lip gloss. I planned to swing by Ronnie's before a round of cornhole.

"How would you feel if we invited MJ, Devyn's new associate, to play with us?" Elizabeth asked on the call as I drove to Lindy's place. I could hear the smile she was likely trying to hide even through the phone.

"I'm fine if you want to bring MJ." The truth was the idea sent a small shiver up my spine, which was alarming and pleasant at the same time.

"Fantastic! You know this is gonna be a great day, right? We are going to slam this town at cornhole and then enjoy the best celebratory drink at Ronnie's. Go, team, go!"

I allowed Elizabeth her small celebration, because like Maya, she was in love and hell-bent on the world joining her.

"Yes," I said smiling. "We will do all of those things, but I better run because this phone is not long for this charge."

"I can't believe we're going on a double date. This is fabulous!"

"Wait. A date. Is that—" But the sound cut out because the phone was now dead. "Dammit." I dropped my phone onto the passenger's seat and hurried up the walk, wondering how I was going to maneuver a date I had no original intention of going on.

I knocked and placed my hands on my hips, ordering myself to relax and embrace the opportunity to get to know MJ. She was beautiful, funny, and actually my type in a lot of ways.

The door swung open and I stared at who I presumed to be Alexandra, the guest for the weekend. Only it wasn't. Kyle stared back at me, her eyes big, luminous and searching mine before she broke into a tentative smile. "Hey." She held up a hand. "I realize you're probably surprised to see me. Also, maybe not thrilled."

Silence hung in the air, untouched and still. I stared. I blinked. I tried to catch up, but my heart had stopped beating, or maybe it hammered so forcefully that I couldn't decipher the individual beats. "Hey?" I said back. It sounded like a question because it was. My skin prickled uncomfortably.

"Sorry. That feels informal. It's good to see you, Potter."

"Please don't call me that." The name jolted me back to a different time, a different me. I held up a finger. "You also don't get to smile at me, okay?" There was a hushed quality to my tone that I didn't have full control over. At least I didn't sound welcoming. It would be just like me to allow my duties as host to supersede my own damn feelings.

She nodded and stood at full height, removing her hand from the doorjamb. This time I was less impressed with the two inches she had on me. "I understand, and you have every right to be unhappy with me." She placed a hand back on the doorframe. Apparently, we were both uncomfortable. I refused to allow my brain to absorb the details of her appearance. I was already aware that she looked just as attractive as I'd remembered, if not more, so I abstained from analyzing the details. I needed to remain on course. "I was unhappy with me, too."

Every part of me wanted to ask why she'd left me alone on that bridge and why, if she had a good reason, she hadn't contacted me to explain. I wasn't hard to track down. I'd made sure of that. I was also a good listener and generally a compassionate human being. She hadn't taken advantage of either. And offering her a platform to explain *now*, all these months later, would hijack my brain just when I'd started to get it back. "It's all good," I said coolly. Go, me, not backing down.

"It's not all good. It wasn't okay. That's part of the reason I'm here."

"What's the other part?" I placed a hand on my hip and waited.

"I wanted to see this place. I've thought about it a lot since…that weekend." She brightened. "The town is honestly every bit as beautiful as you'd described."

"I can't argue with that. And you just happened to book *my* Airbnb?"

"That part was definitely on purpose. But I did need a place to stay."

The anger I'd kept tamped down began to bubble. "You can't just waltz in like this and expect me to be happy to see you."

"No. I don't."

"Great. And wait a second. My notes said Alexandra." I peered behind Kyle. "Where is she?"

"Alexandra is my legal first name."

I remembered that now.

"It's also my mother's name and my grandmother's." She swallowed. She was nervous. "Family tradition. We all go by our middle names."

"Very convenient." There was no reason to poke at her family, but I was grasping at any pebble I could throw.

"Do you want to come in?" Kyle asked. The sunlight slanted onto the porch and made her eyes shine bright blue. I hated the sun. And nature. I even loathed this porch all of a sudden, and it was an innocent porch! "I have your charger all ready for you."

"Yep. I'll just grab it and go." I barreled my way forward, forcing her to flatten against the side of the door to give me room to pass.

"Oh," she said in surprise at the clumsy shuffle I'd forced us into, chest-to-chest. The second problem with that little maneuver was that it put us in extra close proximity, and the instant smell of her watermelon shampoo, lotion, or whatever the hell it was sent me spiraling back in time to the hours we'd spent in bed, talking, laughing, and well, everything else. My face buried in her hair, my hands at her waist, moving upward. And now here she was, smelling…*like her*, which nearly brought me to my knees. Damn Dr. Alexandra Kyle.

"Sorry," I mumbled and moved away from her as fast as I could, heading down the hall, making a left into the kitchen, snatching up my charger, and stalking right back to the door. She met me in the hall and followed me.

"Savanna."

"What?"

"Do you think we could find some time to talk?"

"Today? No. I have a date," I called over my shoulder. "Lots of potential, too."

"Okay," she said, drawing the word out. "Maybe tomorrow, then. I'm here for a bit."

"You're only booked through Monday at ten a.m. I'm a stickler for a prompt checkout."

"Right. But I saw the house was open next week. I'd love to extend now that I'm here."

"No."

"No?"

"No room at the inn." I was being petty. Kyle hadn't murdered anyone. She hadn't lied or cheated on me. But she had destroyed my feelings without a word, embarrassed me, broken my heart, and now wanted to stay in Lindy's house on extension? Some people might have bounced back easily from what had happened between us, but I wasn't one of them. My heart had been battered too many times in my life to give her a second shot to land another blow.

"Surely you can find another place. Any other place."

"Yeah, it's just the holiday weekend—"

Indigenous Peoples' Day; I hadn't forgotten.

"—might make it difficult."

I briefly met her eyes as we arrived at the door and, just as quickly, looked away again. That moment of connection felt too personal, and I didn't want to give her even that small piece of me. The problem was I'd caught the concern in her eyes and hated the thought of someone with nowhere to stay, even if it was Kyle Remington, of love 'em and leave 'em fame.

"Fine. You can stay, but this is not some kind of agreement between friends. Fill out the official online paperwork and reserve the place formally. And no discounts." I folded my arms, pleased with my stern delivery.

She held up her hands. "Easy enough. I'll do it right now."

I paused, still letting my thoughts assemble like a torn-up piece of paper seeking repair. "What are you going to do for a week?" The question had flown from my brain to my lips before I could intercept it. I didn't need Kyle erroneously thinking that I cared about her itinerary. I didn't. I was simply confused as to why she'd stick around.

"Well, first of all, I'm planning on getting a tan."

"Summer's pretty much gone," I said, even though that wasn't the best argument.

"The beach here is still gorgeous, and I plan to use it. After that," she shrugged, "the sky's the limit. I heard there's a pretty cool pub in town. Ron the Rooster?"

"Ronnie Roo's." Kyle was planning to hang out at Ronnie's? *My* Ronnie's. What was happening right now?

"Right. That is exactly the one." She seemed thrilled I knew of it. "Thought I might check it out. Catch a college game and a beer."

"You do you." Look at me. So unaffected. So over it. Not at all wondering what she was like when screaming for her favorite team at a bar.

"Okay." She exhaled. "I'd still welcome a conversation, though. In fact, I'm putting in a formal request."

I shrugged one shoulder. "Let's just put that on ice for now. You should explore Dreamer's Bay and all it has to offer." I slipped into host mode, which was so much easier. "Hopefully, you found the binder I made with all the tips and recommendations for restaurants and outings. Bountiful Park is beautiful. Mature trees. Walking trails."

"I read the binder back to front as soon as I arrived." She was staring at me unabashedly. I remembered now that she did that. Eye contact was her strong suit. It was how Kyle moved through time and space, like she owned them. I'd found that ridiculously attractive once upon a time. Right now, it just annoyed me. "You look really great, Savanna."

"I hope my date thinks so."

"She will," Kyle said softly. "What's her name?"

"MJ."

She nodded but said nothing.

I refused to feel guilty. "Anyway. Enjoy your stay. Send me a message through the app if you have any questions or concerns."

"What if I want to ask you for a friendly drink? We can catch up."

I froze. I had so many questions, and the invitation was likely harmless. But then I remembered my last few months, the changes in me, the disdain for romance, feeling like such an unwanted little fool. No. I couldn't be dragged backward again. Not when I was just now poking my head out from the hole I'd burrowed into.

"I'd rather keep it professional. Guest and host."

"That's fair. Well, I hope you have a nice time on your date with MJ." She sounded sincere. That was something.

"Thank you. I hope you enjoy Dreamer's Bay."

"I'm truly looking forward to exploring all the best spots. The boardwalk alone sounds like somewhere one could spend a lot of time."

"It is." I deflated against my will. She'd be exploring my town, and I wasn't going to be a part of it. Why did I feel completely off balance by all this? I knew why. Because she'd blindsided me. Again. That's what Kyle did, apparently. "It's the perfect day for it," I said in my most serene tone. "Have a nice time."

I didn't look back. Everything in me longed to stalk to my car, but I made a point to glide. She would not win whatever game she was playing. I had a beautiful woman fresh into town who was interested in getting to know me, and nothing made me want to get to know her more than Kyle's appearance in Dreamer's Bay.

CHAPTER EIGHT

First Dates and Bars

"I just think you should be required by law to tell someone if you're the returning cornhole champions," MJ said, beer halfway to her lips. Ronnie Roo's was the perfect unwind for the four of us after MJ and I had lost epically to the resident sharks in town. "There should be a firm declaration."

"Define champion," Elizabeth said, in earnest. "We won last week. But not the week before. So by that token, do we declare forever or only right after a win?" Both of these women were ultra-competitive, and I was here for the watch party.

Devyn threaded her fingers through Elizabeth's at the high-top table we occupied in the bar. She had her blond hair in a ponytail, the picture of sporty and cute. It reminded me of her head cheerleader days. "Elizabeth's right," Devyn said. "We're merely trying to make our way in this big cornhole universe." She blinked her eyes in innocence that nobody bought. She was a former big-city wheeler and dealer in the corporate real estate world, taking no prisoners. When Devyn went after something, she generally achieved it. Elizabeth had a way of turning her into a warm puddle, however, which was fun to watch in real time.

"I feel like we were hustled tonight," MJ said to me. We'd teamed up in the weekly tournament and hadn't had the best showing. Devyn and Elizabeth smoked us easily in round one, followed by an apologetic Maya and Jason for our final elimination.

I touched my glass of Sav Blanc to her pint glass of some local IPA. "I don't disagree. I'm fairly confident they practice in their backyard while the rest of us sleep."

Elizabeth nodded solemnly. "You've figured us out."

Devyn shook her head, grinning. "Another round?"

MJ waved her off. "I have an early round of showings in the morning."

"What about you, Savanna?" Devyn asked.

I was enjoying myself, so why not? "I'm in."

"Awesome. Be right back." Devyn disappeared to the bar, and Elizabeth merged into a conversation at the next high-top over with her friend, Dexter, and his fiancée, Amber. Dexter was my strong, bald occasional gym friend who didn't take any prisoners. When I needed a spotter, Dex was always there. I was surprised when Amber had managed to land him in a forever, head-over-heels relationship. He hadn't seemed the type until she'd shown up. But that's what love did, it changed everything you knew about yourself.

MJ met my gaze. "Hey."

"Hey, back."

"Today was great," she said, covering my hand with hers. "I had fun being on your team and listening to you trash talk."

"It's the only part of the game I'm good at. I'm sorry about that last round." I tossed in a wince. "I feel personally responsible for this tragic loss in the parking lot of the hardware store."

"It's probably something we'll never forget. I really wish you'd tried harder." She leaned in as she broke into a smile and we laughed together. It was nice, enjoying a moment with her. I was comfortable around her and at ease. I also liked the way she teased me. "Want to get together again sometime? Just us?"

The insinuation was clear. A second date. Bam. I was all for it. "Yes. Let's do dinner," I said, feeling confident in the decision. "There's a new little seafood place just outside of town I've been meaning to try. It was reviewed by Alexis Wakefield on her blog, so everyone around here's been feeling a little famous."

"Oh, I like her. She's funny in her reviews. Decided. We have to go." She glanced at her phone. "Speaking of going, I'm getting concerned about the amount of prep I have to do tonight for my appointment tomorrow. I usually have comps pulled and figures ready to go, and I'm behind."

"Then get out of here already. I'll be heading out soon, too. Working in the morning."

She stood and slid her bag onto her arm. "I'm jealous of your job. The grocery store seems like such a cheerful place."

"Most people don't get that," I said, standing up, too.

She ran a hand from my shoulder to my hand and gave it a squeeze. "I wish I could stay longer."

I smiled and threaded our fingers. It wasn't a good night kiss, but it was a step. "Me, too. I'll reach out about that dinner."

"I can't wait," she said, backing away and waving with both hands.

MJ dashed off to say goodbye to Devyn and Elizabeth as I exhaled, alone at the table and catching my breath. The second half of the day had been a much-needed reprieve from my own thoughts. I'd redirected them back to the friends I was with anytime they tried to drift…elsewhere. I'd just have to keep doing that. It was that simple.

Devyn arrived back at the table, placed a drink in front me, and leaned across the table, her palms flat. "So, who do we think the mysterious brunette is at the bar? She's pulling an audience. The men are tickled, but I'm getting the vibe she's not into them."

My stomach went tight. I had a feeling I knew exactly who she was describing. "Oh. Damn."

"What?" Devyn asked, an eyebrow arched. She turned back to the bar, attempting to see what had pulled my response.

I threw a glance behind me and confirmed the suspicion. "That's… Kyle." The sound of her laugh hit, and I closed my eyes briefly at the familiar sound. She had her hair down. The thick, dark strands fell halfway down her back with a hint of a wave. She wore a forest green sweater and what looked to be dark jeans or pants from what I could see. The bartender laughed at something she said, and Frazier Jeffries, who seemed to own his barstool, watched her in utter fascination, probably thinking it was his lucky night. He was single these days and let everyone know how wonderful a pot of chili he made. I grimaced. She turned to him and offered a full wattage smile as my stomach roiled. I had prepared myself to see her in the wild, but I wasn't prepared for it to happen so soon and with Frazier smiling like a happy cat about to have dinner. Deep breath. Nothing to see there.

Elizabeth, mid conversation, whirled around. "Did you just say *Kyle*? Surely not *the* Kyle."

"The Kyle," I said simply.

"Who is The Kyle?" Devyn asked in full squint. "And how do you both know her?"

Elizabeth was immediately at her side. "Last year, Savanna had this sexy whirlwind weekend with The Kyle and they made a pledge to meet a year later on this suspension bridge in Charleston. Crazy romantic, right? Guess who didn't show?"

I couldn't hear this story again. "I'll speed this along. Not me."

Heat flooded my cheeks. One of the most humiliating things that had ever happened to me was becoming a wider known story, and it pained me.

"Why is she here?" Elizabeth asked, whirling back to me. "Is she trying for a second chance?"

"She said she's always wanted to see the Bay," I said, using the local shorthand. I caught them up on the rest of my conversation with Kyle, including her invitation to talk at some point. "I don't think I'm interested in that conversation anymore," I said, just in time for another round of Kyle's laughter to float across our conversation like a freezing cold blanket.

"You just winced," Elizabeth pointed out. "She's getting under your skin. Do you want to go?"

"No," I said emphatically.

"Who cares about her?" Devyn said with a dismissive shrug. "You have things starting to cook with MJ, who is awesome and smart, and very pretty, by the way." Devyn was practical, and in that moment, made a ton of sense. In fact, I longed to be more like her. Devyn owned every situation she walked into like the calm, cool, and collected corporate badass she was. With, of course, the exception of Elizabeth Draper, who'd turned her life upside down and dismantled everything she thought she knew about herself. It had been amazing, the way the two of them had fallen desperately in love when Devyn had returned to town. If love had been my goal, these two would be the blueprint. Luckily, it wasn't. If anything, getting to know MJ might be a recipe for sexy fun, and I could certainly use a little of that in my life.

"Good point. Bring on more MJ." I tossed back some wine like it was a shot. See, look how carefree! This wasn't Kyle's bar. It was great she was there, the more the merrier. I wasn't about to lose another moment's thought over the situation. We'd all moved on from the events in Charleston. There was a period at the end of that sentence.

"In fact…" I smiled with confidence at my friends. "Be right back."

"Um, Savanna," Elizabeth called from behind me. "Are you sure you wanna…?"

I waved her off, determined to make my presence known and

extinguish anything awkward. I arrived at the bar and paused two seats down from Kyle, placing my forearms on the polished oak surface. "Hey, Sean. We'll take an order of mozzarella sticks at table four when you have a chance."

Sean began typing on his mobile screen. "You got it, Savanna."

At the mention of my name, Kyle turned mid-conversation. When her gaze found mine, everything about her softened. Her shoulders. Her eyes. Her entire demeanor. I blinked, caught off guard. I'd spent months constructing her villain persona. She couldn't come in here and *soften at my presence*, torpedoing the whole project. That wasn't how this worked. I needed her to behave like a self-centered bitch. Why wasn't that happening?

"Hi, Savanna."

I wished her voice wasn't butter smooth. "Hi." I flashed a brief smile and then faced the front, waiting for Sean to run my card for the food I didn't actually want. We'd grabbed tacos from the truck on the beach after cornhole, making this whole exercise now feel manipulative and like a big ole staged show. For what?

"How was your date?"

"My date?" I blanked. That's right. I'd had one of those. I took a minute to remember the details, off balance. "You know, it was nice." That needed more. "*Fabulous*, actually. We lost the cornhole tournament, but what are you gonna do? There was so much laughter, though." I nodded eight times. "Which is what you want. At a tournament." A nod. A shoulder lift. "On a date or whatever." I was awful at playing it cool. I struggled with aloof. I needed lessons, I realized, as my heart hammered endlessly.

"I don't have a clue what cornhole is, but I'm sorry you weren't victorious. Laughing is my favorite, too."

Damn her and her serenity. She *didn't* need lessons.

Kyle gestured to an empty stool. "Do you want to join us?"

My gaze moved from Frazier to Kyle to Sean. All eyes were on me. "No, no," I said, springing back into animation. I hooked a thumb behind me. "My friends are waiting for me." Kyle turned, so I did, too, just in time to see Devyn and Elizabeth instantly look away, feigning exaggerated interest in the décor, the table, and each other. Zero points awarded for believability.

"Ah, I see. No worries at all." She sipped her drink, which I recognized as Sean's Old Fashioned. He was pretty proud of that recipe.

Something about walnut bitters. I wondered what she thought of the bar. Apparently, I wouldn't find out because Frazier had launched into a speech about tax season and what a bitch it was this year. His amazing pot of chili was surely next. I closed out the check and returned to my table, off center and feeling unsatisfied by the whole exchange.

"How'd that go?" Devyn asked.

"She's really pretty, isn't she?" Elizabeth said, risking another glance back.

"Um, I'm not exactly sure how it went. Fine, I guess?" I told Devyn. My mind raced. "She was nice. Again." I turned to Elizabeth and nodded. "And hot, which she has no right being, because this is my town. I should get to be the hot one."

"Maybe she thinks you are," Devyn said.

"Not helping," Elizabeth said quietly.

"It's fine," I said, waving the whole thing off. "Totally fine."

"Which is what all fine people say," Devyn pointed out.

They exchanged a look. I was confident they saw how rattled I'd been on the return.

"It's okay to be thrown for a loop," Elizabeth said softly. "It was pretty bold of her to show up in *your* hometown, in *your* Airbnb of all places. She could have reached out first. Seen how you felt about her coming to stay."

"That's true. A thoughtful person would have done just that."

"She's a doctor, you know," Elizabeth said quietly to Devyn, whose eyebrows hit her hairline.

"Lots of people are doctors," I said automatically, refusing to hand out the credit. "Anyway, MJ and I are going to dinner soon. It's like the stars aligned and sent her at the exact right time."

An order of mozzarella sticks was placed in the center of our table. I lifted my gaze to thank Sean only to see that Kyle had delivered them. She shrugged. "He seemed busy and I wanted to introduce myself to your friends."

"Why?" I should have maybe said that in a nicer tone, but my mouth had lost its filter in Kyle's presence, apparently.

"Because I'm friendly and nosy and wanted you all to have your mozzarella before it got cold sitting on that bar waiting for Steve to walk it over." That shut me up.

"That's friendly of you," Elizabeth said conservatively. "I'm Elizabeth and this is Devyn, who I'm desperately in love with."

Kyle nodded. "It's awesome to meet you both. I'm Kyle, a friend of Savanna's."

"Oh, we know," Devyn said with pointed eye contact. She was so good at this.

Kyle shifted her aqua blue eyes to me, her brow furrowed. "At least, I hope we're still friends. I suppose time will tell."

"Sean," I said.

"I'm sorry?"

"His name is Sean, the bartender. You called him Steve. He's a friend of ours, so just wanted to set that straight."

Kyle's mouth formed the shape of an O and she placed a hand on her chest. "That's on me. I'm so sorry. Sean, from now on."

"And that rhymes," Elizabeth said with an uneasy smile. She never was one for tension and would do anything in her power to make choppy waters calm.

Kyle offered her a smile and tapped the table. "Well, I'll let you get back to your evening and the cheese sticks."

Once she was out of earshot, Elizabeth's eyes went wide. "Wow. So that's Kyle. Wow. Wow. Wow. I get it."

I closed my eyes, knowing exactly what she meant. Kyle was gorgeous up close and had presence for days, more so than my memory had even allowed for. "That's her," I said with a sigh.

"And you're certain we can't forgive her?" Elizabeth asked, having totally changed her tune. The Kyle effect, I realized.

I leaned forward. "Do not get weak on me just because she's friendly and has impressive lips. She's a no-call, no-show variety."

"You're totally right," Elizabeth said weakly, her eyes darting toward the bar and back. "She's tricky, though," she whispered. "Because she seems human and nice."

I touched my forefinger to the table. "We will not fall for her smile, her hair, or her charisma."

Devyn looked between us. "I'm Team Savanna. But I need marching orders. Are we icing her out? I'm the best at that."

Elizabeth's eyebrows dipped with concern. "Icing is hard, but I can do it." She folded her arms as if closing herself off. I felt awful, because that actually wasn't what I wanted for anyone. Plus, I wasn't sure what the hell I was doing. I simply knew that I was feeling defensive and not sure which end was up.

"No. No icing. I'm going to be myself and you should be

yourselves, too." I sighed. "It's such a unique situation." I lowered my voice in case it carried to the bar. "We were never in a relationship. It was one weekend, but it affected me."

"It would affect anyone," Devyn said quietly. "You waited a year, anticipated the meetup, and were ghosted."

I shook my head. "I don't hate her, though. I just don't want to get mixed up with her again. I'll be nice and ride out her short stay in town. It's just a few days. How hard can it be?"

Devyn raised an eyebrow.

"Pshh." Elizabeth reached across the table and covered my hand. "If anyone is capable of being the bigger person, it's you, Savanna. I have all the faith in your ability to protect yourself and hold your head high with grace."

I exhaled slowly, feeling better just having a plan. "This town may be small, but it is definitely big enough for the both of us."

CHAPTER NINE

Spring Sprouts

When I headed off for two years of business school after completing my bachelor's, I'd dreamed of small business ownership. Starting something of my own, developing a relationship with my customers, and watching that business grow and grow under my watchful gaze. I wasn't talking about global domination, just a little carved out piece of this world that was mine to nurture and develop with all the knowledge I'd gained through my studies. When I was hired by Donald Faber, the owner of Festive Foods, to take the reins of the grocery store I'd been shopping in with Lindy since I was eleven, it was meant to be temporary. A management position that would season my skills while I got my ducks in a row to start my own venture. But that little store had grabbed hold of my heart and held on, derailing my entrepreneurial plans, or at least delaying them.

The Airbnb was a nice way to scratch the still existing itch, but I also knew I was capable of so much more. I had ideas, ambition, and the work ethic to make big changes at Festive, if only given the proper leeway to do it. Mr. Faber's arrogance, however, was an obstacle at every turn. He was a man in his late sixties with way too much money. Sadly, his ego knew no limit, and his stubborn refusal to get out of my way at the store was a problem I was still very much working on.

I coasted through the first part of the weekend at work, enjoying my customers and putting the finishing touches on the newest promotion I'd been developing for next year's spring months at Festive Foods. Planning ahead was my specialty. I was calling the promotion Spring Sprouts, which essentially entailed shining a spotlight on a different produce item every week throughout spring, offering education, fun facts, and trivia. Hopefully, Spring Sprouts would remind our shoppers of items they hadn't picked up in a while or at all. Cantaloupe, for example, was a favorite that a lot of people forgot about. I was all for championing its cause and had it lined up to kick off the program once March rolled around. All I needed was for Mr. Faber to sign off on the project when he was in the store this afternoon, and I'd get the marketing graphics commissioned, which would leave us plenty of time to get to print. I had a fantastic display idea and was itching to get started.

"I love it," Buster said as he peered at my screen in the office. He was the employee in our store who knew the most about produce. A true star, and the people loved him. He could talk about not only the optimal season for each fruit and vegetable but what soil was best, what climate they thrived in, and ultimately how to best prepare each one. If there was anyone's input I valued, it was his.

He pointed at my computer screen. "On that list of interesting facts, there, you could also include that the plural of cantaloupe is *cantaloupes*. You would be surprised how many people tell me they're looking for several cantaloupe to take home." He met my gaze, his brow furrowed as if the crime was too great for him. "It's honestly rampant and just plain wrong. This is our chance to make a difference."

I nodded, smothering a smile, and earnestly typed a note. "Good tip, Buster. That's why I always consult with you on anything in the produce section."

He inflated. "I'd be happy to answer any questions about the spring sprout of the week. I could make sure I lap through produce more often. Maybe three times an hour. Or even four. Would that be good?"

"I think it's a great plan. I love the idea of you as our ambassador and was hoping for your help on this."

He beamed and clapped his hands once loudly like a football coach. I could tell I'd made his day and was happy to recognize him and his expertise. He was already standing two inches taller. You'd have thought it was his birthday. "I hope you know how much I value your contribution."

He beamed. "I'm just so thr—"

"All right," a loud voice said—no, *bellowed*. "I'm here, Savanna. What in hell do you need?" I turned. Faber. He wore a blue windbreaker track suit like it was the eighties, fighting wind harder than anyone had ever fought. I truly disliked this man but knew that without his approval, my project would be dead in the water. He required me to run any marketing expenses by him personally, and it was rare he listened for more than thirty seconds before expressing his usually off-base opinion. Exhausting.

I forced myself to send him an enthusiastic smile. More bees with honey and all that. "Perfect. Hi, Mr. Faber. Come on in." I offered my most confident smile. He was a businessman, and I needed him to see me as someone who had the best interest of the store in mind. "I asked you to swing by because we don't have anything special planned for spring just yet and I wanted to show you the new promo I'd like to roll out in March." Buster offered me a nod and secret thumbs-up sign behind Faber's back before fleeing my small office. None of the employees were fond of him. Faber had never been kind to any of them, treating them like cattle who happened to be in his way at every turn, which made them feel underappreciated. I worked double-time to convince them otherwise.

"All right. All right. Show me." He had the courtesy to take the toothpick out of his mouth as he strolled to my laptop. He frowned at the screen. "What? You're saying it's a little fruit stand-up thing? What am I looking at? I don't get it." He seemed really bothered by the whole inconvenience.

"Physically, it's a display, yes," I said, hoping my enthusiasm might be contagious. "An opportunity to spotlight a new item each week in the produce section. I really think that—"

"No. I don't want people thinking we're simple. BeLeaf would never have anything like that in the store." BeLeaf, the corporate grocery store giant, continued to be the meter stick to which Faber compared everything Festive Foods did. If I never heard the word *BeLeaf* again in my life, it would be too soon.

I held up a patient finger. "I agree. But BeLeaf isn't attempting to capitalize on a small-town vibe. They're a national chain. That's how we're different, and we should embrace it." I attempted to explain, feeling like I was treading water in a dicey current. "We thrive when we offer personal attention, and a promotion like this one is a great conversation starter. I guarantee it will result in moving more product out the door. Isn't that the goal?" Had he forgotten that I saw the weekly numbers before he did? I was well aware of the fact that with delivery services gaining popularity and forcing a discount, we were in a revenue decline.

"Savanna. What is it you think you're telling me about my own business, huh? I'm a grocery king in this town. I have a boat."

I stared at him trying to translate the non-sequitur, a hallmark of his. Sometimes I truly thought we spoke different languages. "And it's a nice boat, but if we could—"

"Do you have one?"

"A boat? No. I don't. I still think we need to come up with a few new ideas to get the store back in good financial shape. Every bit helps."

He waved off the topic and leaned in, clearly on a mission of his own. "Have you seen Harlowe in the store lately?"

I sighed at the mention of Harlowe Tranton, his thirty-six-year-old personal assistant. The whole town knew it was more than just professional between them. Apparently, they'd had a fight the week before, and she wasn't taking his calls. Likely on purpose; when she went quiet, he threw more money at her. It was a messy situation that I tried to stay clear of. A year prior, he'd tried to make her my assistant manager when she convinced him that she should be calling the shots for one of his businesses. The only problem was she had zero experience. When I threatened to walk, he'd relented and bought her a condo instead.

"Um, it's been a few days since I've seen Harlowe."

He stared at me with determination. "Did she ask about me?"

"I can't exactly remember. I don't think so."

"She'll come around." He leaned in like we were pals. We were not. "She gets all bent out of shape when I show a little attention to other girls. I hired Mandy from the salon to tidy up my place a few times a week, and we like to hang out after. Big deal."

"Got it," I said, still hoping to convince him my produce promotion was worthwhile.

"Harlowe will come crawling back. I'll spoil her a little, buy her something nice, and we'll be just fine. Just might not tell her the next time Mandy comes over, you know?" He bounced his eyebrows and a part of me died.

"Okay." I nodded and closed my eyes briefly. "But about the promotion? I know it will be a hit with our customers. Let's lean into who we are and embrace our charm. Can I proceed?"

"No promotion. We don't need it. What we do need is for you to sell more groceries. Can you handle that simple task?"

I stared at him, leveled. This man refused to let me do my job, and I was frustrated and angry. "I will certainly try with what few tools I've been given." My voice was low and even. He didn't care or notice the change.

"Well, do better than that." He tapped the doorframe as he passed. "I got a pickleball match in an hour. Tell that guy that was in here earlier not to look so creepy. Customers don't like it. Maybe he needs a new haircut or something. You'll figure it out."

I dug my nails into my palms to keep myself from lashing out in defense of Buster, who was the most wonderful human being, and the best employee this store could have. Faber had no idea about Festive Foods or the fantastic qualities of the people who worked in it.

As I passed Buster sweeping aisle twelve a few minutes later, he grinned and sent me a questioning thumbs-up. He'd been just so excited about a produce promotion. His time to shine.

"No go," I told him quietly as I passed, feeling as though I'd failed him. "Faber wasn't a fan."

He paused mid-sweep. His face fell. "He said no?"

"Yeah," I said, hating breaking his heart after getting his hopes up. I shouldn't have even mentioned the project until I'd dealt with Faber. Lesson for next time. Self-recrimination and utter frustration bubbled steadily as I walked, threatening to overflow. Feeling the dam of my emotions threatening to burst, I sought out space to have that moment on my own. Tears burned hot in my eyes, obstructing my vision as I walked quickly to the back of the store, where I was least likely to see many people. Dammit. Leaving the office so soon had been a mistake. Why had I done that? I launched into a full-on retreat, walking faster, hearing the sound of my low heels on the linoleum. I'd worn them today instead of my comfy tennis shoes, hoping to look more professional when I pitched Faber. Dumb. I'd head back, pull my sneakers out of my drawer and— My thoughts were sideswiped when I was hit with the warm smell of freshly fried donuts, the power of which nearly brought me to my sweet, dear knees. I was no amateur and quickly surmised that I was standing eighteen inches from the fan favorites bag from Amazin' Glazin'. I raised my gaze to the lucky donut owner, only to hijack my poor brain further. Kyle's bright blue eyes met mine, and yep, my pesky knees lost strength a second time, confirming her presence.

"There you are," she said. She looked dreamy. Jeans and a white top with cap sleeves. Low heeled brown booties of some kind. I wasn't cool enough to know the actual name of the style, but smart enough to know they had one.

"Me?" I blinked. Her presence was incredibly soothing and I

resented everything about that, prompting the tears to multiply and spill because I'd apparently lost all control of myself. Just wonderful and not at all embarrassing.

"Oh no. Savanna, what's wrong?"

That was new. She hadn't called me Potter. I was Savanna in this very vulnerable moment, and the intimacy made me crumple all the more. "Just one of those days, you know?" A woman walked past eyeing me. Tourist. Maybe I wouldn't have to see her again.

Kyle set down her donuts and opened her now free arms without hesitation. I immediately moved into them, a cold person to a warm blanket, without considering my actions. When we came together, the world went quiet. It hadn't been a novelty between us a year ago, or a memory I had exaggerated. The effects when we came together were that powerful, almost like two important pieces of a hard-to-work puzzle. Kyle held on to me firmly, and just for a moment, I allowed the feeling of her holding me to calm my seas. Comfort in the storm. I didn't want to let go, but I did. I had to. Regrouping, I wiped my face with windshield wiper hands.

"So sorry about that," I said. "On-the-job hazard." I heard my words and remembered Kyle's actual job in an emergency room, where real things went horribly wrong. "I want to take that back. I realize that grocery store stress doesn't compare to what you and your colleagues must face in an ER."

"I don't think there's a copyright on stress. We all know it when we feel it." She tilted her head as she watched me. "And yours is every bit as valid as mine or anyone else's."

"Do you still work at the same hospital?"

She hesitated as if the answer wasn't cut and dry. "I finished my residency and am taking some time off to catch my breath before next steps."

"Good for you, Kyle." She was smart and driven, and I had zero doubt that she was a fantastic doctor. "And great taste in donuts, too." Not sure what to do now, I gestured to the front of the store. "I better get back."

"Right. Of course." She leapt into motion and retrieved the donuts from the shelf next to us. "But these are for you."

"Me? Why?"

"Because I wanted your day to be better."

I eyed her as I accepted the wonderfully grease-stained bag, which was still warm on the sides. "But you had no way of knowing it was bad."

"Didn't matter. Whatever it was, I wanted to make it better." She walked backward a few steps, heading out. "And I love the house, by the way. All the little touches. The personality. The pot holders hanging on the side of the fridge with the little sayings might be my favorite. Especially the one that says *Don't drop it like it's hot.* You knocked it out of the park with the place."

"Thank you." I had to admit it was nice that she'd noticed. Not everyone did. "Jeannie LeRoy made those pot holders for the fall festival in Bountiful Park as a way to pay for her kitchen remodel. You should have seen the line, but while I was waiting, I made eye contact, and since I always save the best filets for her on Monday mornings, she set aside a few pot holders for me just in case."

"You are very much the businesswoman. It's impressive."

I pocketed the compliment, unsure if I would examine it again later. A lie. I totally would. We stood a good twelve feet apart when her features softened to sincerity. "I don't know what happened today to make you sad, but," she shrugged, "you have someone who cares. Hit me up if you ever want to have that talk."

There it was again. *The Talk.* It should come with its own theme music. I continued to put the day on that bridge out of my mind, but maybe that was a knee-jerk reaction. Maybe I did need to hear what Kyle had to say about it, or maybe that was a whole can of worms best left on the shelf entirely.

Conflicted, I shoved the entire concept to the side and focused on regaining control of my workday. I didn't want to admit that running into Kyle had been a helpful reset when I desperately needed it. Nor did I want to acknowledge that I was wildly attracted to her in spite of the caution tape. It wouldn't be long until she rode off into the sunset again, and all I had to do was stay steady on my course until then. I stared down at the bag of donuts in my hand with reluctance draped across my heart. I'd put them in the break room for the employees. Polite but firm, I reminded myself. No eating enemy donuts.

Okay, so I grabbed a maple bacon for myself first. It didn't mean a damn thing!

CHAPTER TEN

Library Day

One thing I knew about Jonathan was that his father was not an active participant in his life, and that had been a sore spot. His dad had moved out on his mom once it was clear Jonathan would be a child with special needs. It had taken several surgeries to get his mobility to the point it was today, but his dad hadn't stuck around to see that part. An occasional stressful visit, and sometimes not even those, was all he remembered of his dad from childhood. He didn't talk about him much, but these days, given my own recent discovery, it had me thinking.

"Do you ever think about reaching out to your dad?" I ran my hand along the long line of book spines.

Jonathan paused in the middle of the mystery section, a Felice Picano novel in his hands. "You're asking about my father *right now*? I just told you I wanted to read something sexy, gay, and mysterious, and you ask about my loser of a father? What's going on?" He closed the book, his brows pulled together above his nose. "It's *library* time, Savvy." Code for sacred. I knew this. He knew this.

We both loved a good read and had made a pact years ago to become weekly reading buddies and never look back. Nerds united by a good story. In fact, the library pact was one of the best parts about us.

I shrugged apologetically. "I've been wondering about mine is all. This is a new set of feelings that I'm trying to navigate. Beyond examining my own identity, there's a parent out there in the wild."

He pulled the book to his chest and moved toward me. It must have been a good day for him pain wise since he'd opted for just his cane. To his credit, he'd had it painted a vibrant purple, which made him look fabulous or like an eccentric millionaire. He was all about embracing his disability, rather than downplaying it. "Parent in the wild is certainly in my wheelhouse. To the reading nooks, sweetie. They should be empty at this time of morning."

"Now you're talking my language. Lead the way."

I happily followed Jonathan through the fiction shelves, saying hello to comedy, intrigue, and of course, my favorite, romance. I glared at the newest Parker Bristow novel as I passed. I still hadn't forgiven her for killing off the brother in that small-town book that grabbed my heart. I'd absolve her one day, but for now, the breakup stood.

"Don't you throw sass at Parker. She was just doing her job and you know it," Jonathan stated as we cruised by.

"There's no defense there. Dead to me."

The reading room was empty just as Jonathan had predicted. I loved the reading nooks and their creative/comfortable offerings. They were these adult-sized pods with overly soft chairs and a mass of artificial vines and tree branches covering the tops of each one, giving the illusion that you were reading in the plushest forest that ever existed. The library even piped in sounds of nature capable of erasing the present, allowing the reader to float away. Something about the serenity quickly made every muscle in my body unclench.

"So, your biological dad is likely out there somewhere," Jonathan said, taking a seat inside the treehouse-themed pod.

I slid into the chair in the black bear nook that faced his leopard version. "Why am I so curious? I want, more than anything, to leave well enough alone."

He nodded thoughtfully and tossed a strand of brown hair out of his eye. "Because it's natural to want to know one's own villain origin story. But if I may?"

"Certainly."

"Sometimes what you find when you go looking isn't helpful. Cue my asshole of a dad, for a real-life example. I would've been better off if he'd remained a mysterious figure rather than the letdown he turned out to be."

"But maybe that would make this whole thing easier. If I found him and he was a garbage human, I could just move on."

"I'm not sure it's that easy."

He had a point. I sighed. "At least I'd know."

I watched as his wheels turned. Jonathan was a demonstrative thinker, and he seemed to be mulling something over. "Valid, to a degree," he finally concluded. "But knowledge isn't an instant cure for all that's bothering you. I just want you to understand what you might be unleashing."

I blinked, asking myself if that's what I was doing. "Keep talking."

Jonathan scooted to the edge of his soft green cushion. "You grieve for your parents and now your aunt."

"Quite true."

"But finding your bio father, even if he's the greatest human on Earth, isn't going to magically fix any of that." A pause. "Or the feelings you're wrestling with for the hot doctor."

"Kyle? I'm not interested in my dad because Dr. Soap Opera showed up in town with an unknown agenda." A pause. "She brought me donuts two days ago."

His eyes went wide.

"The fan favorites collection."

His eyes went even wider. "Stop."

"I *know*."

"Did you make out with her?" he asked in his saucy voice.

"Jon-Bon. No! May God smack you. It's like you don't even know me. I have strength. I come with conviction."

"Shove all of that to the side. The fan favorites box might be worth a little lip action in frozen foods. Second base was calling your name." He touched his imaginary boobs. "Not even on top of the shirt?"

"Stop that." The idea made my stomach free-fall, and the room was suddenly way too warm. Did I flash to a topless Kyle from our weekend together? No comment. "I did cry in her arms, though."

If looks could kill. "You always bury the lede."

I waved him off. "Faber struck in typical fashion, and she was there at the exact right moment. Not that exciting."

"I don't believe coincidences for one damn second." He gave me a stern look. "She was meant to be there in that moment."

"For a numbers guy, you sure invest in the concept of destiny a lot."

"There's no way we're on this Earth just wandering around randomly. It's like you don't know *Zelda* at all."

"I don't. I keep telling you."

"A crime." He used his right hand like a knife on the palm of his left. "Link is destined to save Zelda, which perhaps brings me to what I have to tell you."

I frowned, my interest more than piqued. "That sounds more than ominous."

"As your best friend, I'm charged with looking out for you."
Jonathan looked at the ceiling and then back at me. "So here goes."

I braced, watching his face intently.

"I did hear something interesting at Ronnie Roo's once upon a time that might play into the DNA discovery of yours. But I can't say for sure."

I sat back in my nook. "And you're just now telling me? What the hell, Jonathan?"

"I wanted to be sure you were interested in pursuing this thing before upending your peace. This conversation tells me that you are."

I shook my head. "What did you hear?" My heart was a drum in my ears.

"It might be nothing. But I was sitting near those bridge club women one afternoon drinking a macchiato by the window, as I do."

"You mean Deena Haney and the visor brigade?" The sixty-year-old women were known around town for their trendy sportswear, whether they'd participated in anything athletic that day or not. It was their brand and they owned it.

"That's them. They were just back from a tennis match or something, sipping iced tea and shooting the breeze."

This was certainly interesting. "What did Deena and crew have to say that made you go pale when you mentioned it?"

"It's not awful. I promise." He exhaled and slid a little closer, as if to be sure this stayed between us. Not that there was a soul within earshot. "They were talking about a hot and heavy romance between Rachel Bright and," he hesitated, "someone older than her from back in the day. How they were magnets for each other, couldn't keep their hands to themselves at some beach party, and how sad it was when it never went anywhere."

"Who was it? The older guy." I didn't mean to hold my breath but realized I was doing it anyway.

"Jake Kielbasa."

I knew the name. "The retired police officer who dates Peggy from the donut shop?" I touched my chin. "Wears a little scruff here but not a full beard."

Jonathan nodded. "That's him. If it helps, he's kind. Bought me a beer once so I didn't have to walk back to my car on a high pain day."

The world went quiet. We were in a library, so that wasn't hard, but it was a unique quiet, as if something key had just clicked into place, silencing the chaos in my brain. Was that a sign that I'd just discovered the missing piece of the puzzle? "It's him," I said. "I don't know how I know, but I do. Sometimes you just have an innate feeling about something."

"I think so, too," Jonathan said.

Then another detail hit me. "He's *Charlie's* father. From the liquor store." Charlie was a good guy. A few years older than me. He'd been in a long-time relationship with Devyn's older sister, Jill, for years. I scanned my brain for every detail I had on Charlie. He sported spiky hair and plaid shirts on the regular. He knew his liquor business like the back of his hand and had a tendency to be shy until you got to know him. Had I been buying Grey Goose from my half brother for years and not realizing it?

A lightbulb went on above Jonathan. "There is some resemblance there, now that I consider it. You have the same big brown eyes, though yours are the long-lashed version of his."

"I look like Liquor Store Charlie?" I asked, using Devyn's nickname for him. This was all happening fast. "Jonathan, I've never had a sibling before. My whole identity of orphaned only child is crumbling more and more with each new discovery."

A pause. "What are you going to do about all this?"

With this new information, I didn't see any path except forward. It didn't matter if I was afraid, nervous, or shy. There was no way I was going to be able to live my life without turning over this very important stone. "I think I need to talk to Jake."

I was pretty confident that the average person doesn't know that strawberries strewn across a grocery store floor can make a person dance. They can, especially if one tries to avoid them. They'll send you right down the road to funkytown until you succumb to gravity and find yourself flat on your ass in the middle of aisle one in front of everyone. Unfortunately, I found out firsthand.

"Oh, no. Savanna?" Mrs. Martinelli said, approaching with one arm outstretched. "Are you okay?" She knelt next to me, and I began to answer that I was fine. Embarrassment always trumped pain. But I paused because something *was* really wrong. It was my foot. I couldn't exactly feel it, and that was likely because it was underneath me in the most interesting configuration.

"Um, I think I'm a pretzel." It wasn't the most helpful sentence, but it was the only way to describe my current predicament.

"Oh, help, please!" Mrs. Martinelli yelled. "She fell on strawberries. Henrietta?"

It was Maya who appeared first and was quick to act. "Backup to produce," she said into her walkie before joining me on the ground. Only, the way she sat made it seem like we were about to have a strawberry picnic. "Are you hurt?"

The words seemed to prompt my body to answer in the worst manner possible: a burst of red-hot pain that shot from my right foot straight to my calf. "I think I might be." I looked around to see who might have witnessed all of this. I wanted off the ground immediately. And yep, a small group had gathered, the small-town paps. I smiled and held up a hand. "Totally fine," I told them. "Just tripped on a strawberry. All part of a day's work in a grocery store." All the while the pain pulsed, and—dare I say—grew?

Buster appeared and offered two hands to pull me up. "I got you," he said, easing me to my feet, one of which reflexively lifted right back up again.

"Uh-oh," I said. "This one seems angry."

"We should get that looked at," Maya said, eying me dubiously.

"Dammit," I said. Could there be one uneventful day in Dreamer's Bay this week? Just one? While my employees couldn't exactly abandon the store because I'd gone and banged up my foot, Elizabeth Draper had no problem dropping whatever she had going and taking me to the ER. I didn't even have to call her. Apparently multiple shoppers had beaten me to the punch, knowing she and I were friends.

"Now, don't stress at all about this," Elizabeth told me on the drive. "I know you're doing that thing where you're imagining your next few weeks without mobility, but the truth is you're going to be fine either way. We've got you."

"Who's we?" I asked, with a grateful grin. For someone without any family at all these days, my friends sure knew how to come through.

"Literally everyone." She looked over at me as we passed the park. The hospital was a mile and a half up the road just on the perimeter of town. "Do you not realize how universally adored you are in this town? Every single human sings the praises about all you've done to make Festive Foods a kickass place to shop. I head there the second I need something because of how cheerful that place is. And you're there to smile and talk with anyone and everyone. So yeah. If you're immobilized for a bit, I'm confident your friends and neighbors are gonna have your back."

"Well, damn." My smile went wobbly and I was a misty mess of vulnerability when I hobbled, my arm draped around Elizabeth, into the ER.

Tasha Wilhite stood up as soon as we came through the double sliding doors. "We heard you were on the way, Savanna. Didn't think your day was interesting enough or something? Had to stir up some drama."

"Apparently, I wanted to see you. How's Tim Jr.?" Her eight-year-old son was a bundle of mischievous energy who once took down a whole display of microwave popcorn while I watched.

"Lives in his treehouse and pretends he's Spider-Man. About gives me a heart attack every time I walk into the kitchen and find him perched on the counter like a statue. Follow me." Tasha opened a door to one of their small, uninteresting, and uncomfortable looking exam rooms that could really take a page from the library's book, no pun intended. She gingerly helped me onto the bed with the glamorous tissue paper covering and gave my knee an affectionate tap. "You make yourself comfy for a few and fill out this paperwork. Then we'll get you all fixed up."

"Will do," I said, trying to ignore the throbbing from smack in the middle of my foot. I hadn't yet revisited the semi-dramatic scene I'd caused at the store. I knew there would be an onslaught of inquiries about how I was doing for the next four years. I would now be remembered for being taken down by a wayward berry brigade. A shame I'd have to live with. I turned dutifully to the clipboard Tasha had handed me and went to work.

"How's the pain?" Elizabeth asked, offering a sympathetic wince. Her perfectly messy ponytail showed off the intermingling shades of brown and blond unique to Elizabeth. She even had a few auburn additions if you looked closely enough. I'd always been a fan of her hair-of-many-hues.

"It's significant and infuriating. Of all the things I truly didn't need."

She quirked her head. "Hey, look at me. Sometimes you just have to surrender to what the world has in store for you. Today, you're supposed to be right here in this very room for reasons we're not even aware of. So, make friends with this room and let go."

"I should be at work right now, not—" *Staring into the eyes of a gorgeous woman who makes me hot every time she walks into a room.* Kyle Remington, soap opera doctor and bridge ditcher, stood right there in our very exam room, wearing a lab coat and hitting me with the vibrance of those aqua eyes. Did the universe just have it out for me?

"I hear there was a fall," Kyle said, an iPad pressed to her side like a boss. "You okay?" She dropped her brows in concern.

"Why is it you again?" I blurted, taking a beat to look at the door behind her as if *it* had made a mistake. They'd sent the wrong person in, surely. I took a breath and tried the word thing again. "I don't understand. You don't work here."

"I do. Temporarily." She smiled and hooked a thumb behind her. "I met Dr. Collette at the duck pond in the park. He and his son were feeding the little guys and we got to swapping stories. He told me how short-staffed they were this season and wondered if I'd be interested in jumping in."

I honestly couldn't believe this.

"I said okay, and what do you know? They extended me privileges."

Of course they did. I was more than floored. I wasn't rolling well with this particular punch, and my foot throbbed so much I could scarcely work my busy brain. Wasn't I due for some sort of hiatus from plot twists? "Wait. Aren't you leaving tomorrow? I have you down for checkout and another booking for the house right behind it. Unfortunately, I can't cancel it." That should do it. Back to Charleston she'd have to go.

"Not exactly," Kyle said, brightening. "I thought I'd stick around a little bit. I like the town, and Dan set me up with a place on the beach for a little while."

Dammit, Dan. I stared her down with white hot intensity. "Fabulous," I bit out. "That's so, so great." I apparently found it important to emphasize each word.

"Well, we can always use more doctors," Elizabeth said. "I, for one, always say the more doctors, the safer we all are."

"You've never said that." Then a thought struck. KC Colette was her best friend in all of life, and Dan was KC's husband. "You knew about this."

I watched the blood drain from her face. "I heard a little bit in KC's kitchen."

"Traitor," I mouthed as Kyle worked on her iPad. Apparently, my week on this planet had pushed me too damn far.

Caught, Elizabeth's eyes went wide and she stood looking fearful.

"I'm going to give you two a minute or eighteen."

"You don't have to do that." I pointed at the chair she'd just vacated.

"Do, too."

I watched her scurry away, realizing Kyle and I were about to be alone.

Kyle watched me, brow arched in interest, but seemingly unaffected. She always managed to project happy and collected, which made me wonder all the more about what went on inside her head. What did Kyle actually *think* about things? I felt like there had been a time when I knew. It wasn't today.

"So, tell me what happened to your foot."

I sighed. "Damn strawberry attacked me."

"With a weapon or without?" she asked without delay, now fully engaged with the iPad. She was too good at this.

"Without. I was walking through the produce section, technically aisle one, and knocked a carton of those suckers with my elbow. The assailant and his group of friends tumbled to the floor. I did my best to avoid."

"And failed," she said like it was the most unfortunate story, all the while typing away.

"Yes."

She paused and met my gaze. "Let me take a look."

I hadn't been prepared for an exam, but I supposed it was standard. What wasn't standard at all was the feel of her hands on my skin as she softly lifted my injured foot. She examined it visually first, before pressing gently on various parts of the foot, taking care not to hurt me. "Yeah, look at this. Already have some bruising on the bottom. Did you hear any sounds? The dreaded pop?"

"No. Just my pride screaming in protest."

The look of concentration on her face as her thumbs moved to the top of my foot sent a shiver I hadn't expected in the midst of this crisis. She looked really good in that lab coat, too. Her hands were still on me, so my stupid cheeks went hot. God, I hoped she hadn't noticed.

"Can you wiggle your toes for me?" Kyle asked. There was a soft quality to her voice I'd not heard before. Tender, even, and it made me forget what her words actually were.

"Hmm? Can I do what now?" I asked, my eyes locked on hers. I was feeling a little drunk. Must be a pain response and not the vibrancy of her eyes.

"Your toes," she said, gesturing. "Are you able to wiggle them?"

"Oh." I gave it a shot to some very slight wiggling. "Hurts, though."

"Yeah, I can tell. You're dealing with a lot of swelling."

"I'm dealing with swelling?" Focus. "No. You're right. I am."

She stepped back, releasing my foot. I felt a little sad about that part. "I'm thinking you have a bad sprain on your hands, but let's grab an X-ray to be sure there's not a fracture hiding out."

"Okay. If you don't think it's any trouble. I can just go, also."

The corners of her mouth tugged. I remembered what her lips tasted like. Sweet like the strawberry ice cream, which seemed appropriate now. "No, Savanna. I promise you, administering medical attention is no trouble at all." She dropped the iPad to her side. "We'll wheel you over in a few. In the meantime, would you like something for the pain?"

"No," I said automatically and with too much conviction. Projecting strength was my default, but my foot ached so bad, I wasn't sure what I was going to do.

"Hey, look at me." The familiarity in her tone made me snap to attention. "This isn't the time to put up a brave front. I'm a doctor."

"You're *Kyle*." She knew exactly what I meant, too.

"And both of us want you pain free, okay? I happen to care about your well-being."

"Do you, though?" I asked before thinking better of it.

She didn't falter. "Yes, very much."

I exhaled slowly while she waited. "Fine. I'll take the pain meds."

She nodded, pleased. Gorgeous. Smart. And the source of a lot of my anxiety these days. "Coming right up."

Ninety minutes later, we had our answer. Kyle returned once the films were read, turned her screen to face me, and showed me my foot. "You're in luck. No breaks. No fractures. Just a no-fun sprain that's going to get in the way of your life for a bit."

"That's great news," Elizabeth said in the chair she'd reclaimed.

I squinted. "Define get in the way. I have a job where I'm on my feet a lot."

"Not for the next few weeks, okay? We'll get you outfitted with a pair of crutches, but the more you're on that foot, the longer it's going to take to heal. Do yourself a favor and rest it as much as possible so you can put this in your rearview." She sounded so intelligent and authoritative. I couldn't help but appreciate the impressive doctor persona. And the coat. Let's be honest. She was *fantastic* looking in the lab coat, which served as a nice contrast to the dark of her hair, in a ponytail today. In a surprise, I even allowed myself to admire her appearance freely for a moment or two. Objectification activated.

"You okay?" Kyle asked with a squint.

"What? I'm fine."

"You looked a little weak. I don't want you passing out."

"I'm completely fine," I said, probably too emphatically. "Hey, when are you going back to the hospital in Charleston?" I'd just grabbed that question out of the sky. Anything to get the focus off myself.

Her gaze went dim. "Uh…I'm actually not."

"Oh."

"It's a whole thing. For another time." She flashed a smile that didn't feel authentic. It also didn't give anything away. For a moment, I ached for the connection I used to feel to her. I also wanted her smile right back in place where it had been moments before.

"Oh. Again." I blinked, my mind trying to fill in the blanks because this was wholly unexpected. I'd always imagined Kyle hard at work at the hospital back in Charleston, happy and possibly in love. Frolicking in the fields with her gorgeous fiancée, tossing glitter in the air and laughing at my humiliation. A stark reminder that sometimes my imagination was my own worst enemy. The real Kyle was nothing like the bitter fantasy. "Kyle." I heard the softness in my voice. "Do I get to know more?"

She paused, holding eye contact with me before snapping out of whatever memory she'd been lost in. "Sure. But I have another patient to get to now. Let's grab that drink sometime, and I'll tell you all about it."

Bait on a hook. What was a girl to do? "I'll check my schedule and get back to you." It was a lay-up that allowed me to figure it out later.

She shook her head. "No. Not good enough. Are we going to talk or not? Just be straight with me."

"Well, if you're going to hold my feet to the fire."

Her eye contact was unwavering, bright blue burning a trail. "I am."

I swallowed, affected by her in so many ways. "Okay, I don't have anything on Tuesday night."

"I'm free Tuesday."

"I'd say I'll pick you up, but I have no idea where you'll be living at that point."

She nodded. A strand of hair had escaped her ponytail and framed her face. Maybe by design. "Good point. My temporary landlord is giving me the boot, so I have new, not quite as quaint lodging." She walked to the door and held it open. "Let's meet at Ronnie's at seven on Tuesday." Elizabeth was watching this exchange like it was the most exciting tennis match.

I paused. "Okay, but that's a really public venue."

"You're afraid to be seen with me?"

"Not in the slightest, but we will be interrupted about eighteen times, and quite possibly joined by whoever decides to pull up a chair and shoot the breeze."

"People do shoot the breeze a lot in this town," Elizabeth interjected. "It really is something."

I lifted a shoulder. "So maybe somewhere that doesn't resemble the town square with alcohol." I hated admitting that if we were going to really talk, I'd prefer a more private exchange. But it was true. Whether I was happy about it or not, I did have a vested interest in hearing what Kyle had to say. Closure was apparently a very helpful accessory.

Elizabeth raised a finger, apparently sensing the personal direction this conversation was heading. "I'm just gonna wait out here. See what Tasha is up to."

Kyle allowed Elizabeth to pass and walked back toward me, letting the door close behind her. "Do you know a quieter venue?" The doctor cap was off. It was Kyle the woman addressing me now. The quieter, more intimate tone in her voice sent a shiver. I'd heard it before.

"Salvador's. It's a really great Italian restaurant about seven minutes outside of town." What in the world was I getting myself into? Salvador's was quiet and cozy. Under the right circumstances, it would easily feel romantic. I didn't want to confuse myself. At the same time, it was the most privacy we were likely to encounter in a town like this one unless I invited Kyle over to my place. But the idea of introducing her to my home felt too personal, a part of my life I didn't want to share.

"I love pasta."

"You gotta try Sal's." I kept my tone light, though my hands were tingling.

"I'll be coming straight over from a shift, so why don't we meet there?"

"You're actually working here, then? Not just today." This was feeling like a real job. What was I going to do if it was? I refused to panic.

"I'm helping to fill a few gaps in their schedule, but it's going well."

How well? I wanted to ask. The last thing in the world I needed was for Kyle to move to Dreamer's Bay and parade through the grocery store on a weekly basis looking beautiful, dropping off donuts, and projecting success. Or maybe I wanted that very much. Dammit. What was wrong with me? My head was all over the place.

"Me, too," I said. "The going well part. Just everything is. For me." What was I saying? I had a sprained foot, a mystery parent, a self-centered boss, and a semi-ex I couldn't/didn't want to shake.

"Fantastic to hear. And things with the woman you're dating? I'm sorry, was it Myrtle?" That had to have been on purpose.

"Her name is MJ."

"Right."

Dating was a strong word for the one date I'd gone on with MJ, but Kyle didn't need to know that. "It's early, but she's...everything." I was so awful at this.

"Is she now?" Kyle asked. Yep. She saw right through me. "I'll see you at Sal's." She turned back pointedly. "Don't bring MJ."

I blinked at her parting words as I watched her disappear through the door to my room. No, there would certainly be no MJ in attendance. I would have to brace myself for this meeting, wondering what excuse she planned to cough up. Kyle had a way of making everything seem understandable, and I would be smart to remember that.

Tasha and Elizabeth popped in looking eager for some kind of update. "How are things?" Elizabeth asked in an overeager voice.

Tasha was carrying a pair of cellophane-encased crutches, which she promptly began to unwrap. "Dr. Remington is such a gem. We're lucky to have her. Did you two...have a good chat?" she asked, exchanging a look with Elizabeth.

"You told her everything, didn't you?" I asked, swiveling to Elizabeth.

"What?" She balked. "It was literally a number of hours before someone else did. You know that's true. I merely helped it along and made sure the details were accurate."

As true as that probably was, I planned to huff and puff about it, which was my right as today's small-town gossip victim. "Still, Lizzie. Still." I turned to Tasha. "Dr. Soap—ington was very helpful regarding my foot." The two of them nodded silently. But I wasn't great at withholding, so quickly ended with "And we're having dinner on Tuesday."

"Tuesday is a great night," Tasha said. "Not too early in the week, not too late. I have pj's with the word *Tuesday* all over 'em. It's a good day to get a little action, if you know what I mean." She was beaming like Christmas morning. I raised my eyebrows.

Elizabeth wasn't fazed. "And you'll still be rested from the weekend," Elizabeth pointed out. "Too much fun Tuesday, I hear they call it."

"They don't," I said. "And the two of you need hobbies."

"Tiger Tuesday?" Elizabeth asked and then added a roar and paw swipe.

"No." I shot her a stare.

"Let's give these a try," Tasha said, extending the crutches with a twinkle in her eyes. "Tits out Tuesday?"

"Tasha!"

"Sorry."

CHAPTER ELEVEN

The Truth

True to my character, I arrived at Sal's twelve and half minutes before my designated meeting time with Kyle. Necessary? No, but my fear of being late always trumped rational thought. Plus, my parents died in a car accident, so I lived my life obeying each and every speed limit. Reckless driving, even when late, would never be my thing.

"Would you like to order a drink while you wait?"

"Maybe eight," I said, surveying their small cocktail menu. I'd been nervous about this meeting-not-a-date all day and wondered why I'd agreed. The restaurant was half full, with soft music underscoring the quiet conversation. An oak bar across the room sat apart from the kitchen, which I thought was an odd setup.

"What are you contemplating right now?"

I looked up and my bar to kitchen relationship query flew right out of my brain. Kyle wore a black sweater dress and another messy ponytail. This one was even more perfectly messy than the last. She did it to me again with the ponytail! It's like she knew how I felt about her in them. More likely she knew how everybody felt about her in them. She was Kyle, after all, and had to know that.

"Why are you here so early? We're not supposed to meet for five more minutes."

"You can't answer a question with a question," she said, sliding into the chair across from mine. "And anyway, you're even earlier than me."

"Don't point things out," I said, doubling down on my own non-sense.

"Never again." An amused grin graced her features. She brushed a strand of that dark hair from her eyes. "What are we drinking? Dirty martini for you and a Manhattan for me?"

Because I had decided to be perpetually grumpy in her presence, which went against every normal behavior pattern I had, I pretended to peruse the menu further. "Probably going to try something else."

"What are we having?" our server asked, returning. I was pretty sure he was Lana and Simon's son, Preston, who'd gone off to law school before coming home, horrified by the study load.

"Dirty martini for me," I said, refusing to look at Kyle.

"I'll have a Manhattan." Kyle placed the cocktail menu on the table, signaling we might need it later. "And can we order your calamari to start? Is that okay?"

"Yes," I said. Sal's calamari was a favorite of mine. How had she known? She hadn't. We were just really good at meshing together. I'd known that part from the start.

Possibly-Preston took down the request and flashed a smile. "On it. And I'll be right back with those drinks."

"How was the ER today?"

Kyle shook her head. "There's nothing like it, Potter. In my most dramatic case of the day, I removed three porcupine quills. That would never have happened in Charleston. The pace and style of care is entirely different."

I nodded. "That makes sense. And I'm guessing it was one of the Martins? Porcupines aren't native to South Carolina, but the Martinettes have that little wildlife rescue on about six acres and take rehab cases from all over."

"I can confirm that the animal was not a local. Didn't even know what a Jessamine was."

"Hence his displaced anger and those lodged quills."

"I still can't believe that this is what living out here is like."

I laughed. "Don't say out here. We're not another planet."

"Feels like it." She covered my hand. "In a really good way." Only she didn't take it away right off and I stared at our point of contact, my skin running hot beneath her touch. Catching my surprise, she slowly withdrew it just as our drinks were placed in front of us.

"Are you the new doctor?" Preston asked.

"I think so?" Kyle answered. "I certainly am both of those things."

"My mom pointed you out at the Grinder." Don't even get me started on the name of our town's coffee shop. It was equally horrifying and hysterical at the same time. "She thought I should get your number."

My eyes narrowed. Was Preston the law school dropout hitting on my date? I shook my head at my own brain's error. At my *dinner companion*.

"She sounds very sweet." Kyle peeked over at me. "We might be ready to order when you are."

I stared at Preston hard. "I'll take Sal's Chicken Penne," I said to the tune of *I've got my eye on you, buddy.*

"Make it two," Kyle said in a much more serene delivery.

Once we were alone, she turned her focus back to me. "Everyone is so friendly here."

"One word for what that was."

She sat back in her chair and eyed me. "Wait a minute. Are you a little jealous?"

"Not in the slightest," I said, and sipped my drink, ready to speed things along. The strong taste of vodka and olive juice offered me the mix I needed to take us there. "So, you'll never believe this, but four months ago, I showed up on this adorable bridge in Charleston and waited."

Kyle nodded, the smile slipping right off her face. Rightfully so.

"And waited. But no one ever showed up."

"That must have been an awful day."

I didn't like to revisit those memories, for fear of being swallowed up whole by them all over again. "It was. So...what happened?"

For a moment, I thought I saw a flash of panic behind her eyes followed by a look of resignation. "No matter what I say, it's not going to be good enough. But I'll do my best." She swallowed and met my gaze. "It wasn't a good day for me either, mainly because I knew you were there waiting for me and I was paralyzed. I wish I'd handled it differently."

"Why were you paralyzed?" I could barely move waiting for her response.

"I lost a young patient at the hospital about a month before the day we were set to meet. I lose patients on occasion, and it's not that you ever get *used to it*, but you do learn to cope. This time was different." She sat back as if transported. "He was just a kid who'd been in a pretty bad bike riding accident, multiple injuries, several systems affected. Every step of the way there was a new obstacle I wasn't expecting. But he should have pulled through." She paused. "And didn't, possibly because of a decision I made."

"Oh," I said, absorbing.

"It was one of those moments as a physician where you're standing at a crossroads, and you have to make the best call possible in a short amount of time and with no information. Yet the center of someone's entire world, their kid, is in your hands."

"I'm sure you did the best job you could."

"I don't know that I did. I never will. I think about that day a lot. Replay each small moment wondering what would have happened if I had made a different choice for him. I pushed for surgery. That's what it came down to. I pushed, and he wasn't stable enough." She shook her head almost imperceptibly, seemingly swimming in self-recrimination. My heart tugged uncomfortably as I searched for any words that might help. The reality was, I was out of my depth.

"Kyle. You can't do this. You can't second-guess yourself over something you can't change now."

"I'm not the only one who did. That's the next part. I was placed on leave while the hospital investigated after the family brought a lawsuit. It got very ugly very fast, and I found myself, I don't know…" She paused as our water glasses were refilled. "Grief stricken and lost. Questioning everything. My ability to practice medicine, my place in the world, who I was meant to be. And I couldn't stop thinking about that family losing their son and brother. This twelve-year-old kid who had his whole life ahead of him. Who would he have been and what would he have contributed to this world if I hadn't been the doctor on call that day?" Her focus fell to the white table cloth as if looking for refuge. "I wanted to be there, Savanna. I'd been looking forward to that day since the moment I said goodbye to you." She raised her eyes to me. They were brimming with fresh tears. "But when the time came, I couldn't face you when I could barely face myself." She whispered that last part, the emotion strangling her voice.

For a few moments, neither of us spoke.

Finally, I asked the second question I'd been carrying with me for months. "Why didn't you reach out? Tell me what happened. Maybe I could have been there for you."

"I didn't know what to say or how to explain. I was lost in every sense of the word. I doubted everything, but most of all myself. I don't know if you've ever been in that situation, but it's the worst." She looked away, embarrassed, and used her napkin to dab at the tears before they could escape. "So I just sat there that evening, alone in my apartment, watching the time crawl by until you were surely gone forever."

My heart tore witnessing the anguish that washed over Kyle's face. I'd never seen her look so broken, so completely devoid of her signature confidence. I forgot about my own feelings, unclenching the resentment I'd been hauling around for months. "And now?"

"I've had time to pick up the pieces. The lawsuit was settled. I was invited back to work, but it didn't feel like the right fit anymore." Her eye contact was unwavering. "And now I'm here for you."

The sentence about knocked me out of my seat. I wrestled for the talking points I'd been handing myself and anyone else who asked about Kyle. "I put us behind me." The words hung in the air, unconvincingly. A mirage.

"I don't think our story's over, Savanna."

"I know, but I think it has to be."

She slid her hand forward on the table and her pinkie touched mine. That little bit of contact left me without my next inhale.

"I don't think I can take another bridge." I pulled my hand away and into my lap.

"You won't have to. I'm not asking you to marry me."

I leaned in. "You'd leave me standing there at the altar."

She closed her eyes and took a moment. "I deserve that."

"Maybe you don't. I'm just a little off my game, okay? I'm sorry if that was a low blow."

She gestured as if wiping a dry erase board clean. "All I'm asking for is a chance to get to know you again. Cards on the table this time. And I'm going to start with a confession."

"Okay." My heart thudded. I felt like I was a passenger in a car moving way too fast.

"I never should have let you go after that weekend. Not for a year, not for a day. I'm not a perfect person, but I don't make the same mistakes twice."

The imaginary car slowed down. I took a breath. Because what if? What if the bridge was only a symptom of the season in Kyle's life, not at all indicative of her true tendencies? I'd sworn off love. I'd sworn off risks. I'd sworn off Kyle. Was I ready to undo all of those?

"I don't know."

"That's a perfectly legitimate answer." Our food arrived and we smiled at Preston.

"It was looking serious over here for a second. Another round?"

"No," I said.

In the same moment Kyle said, "Sure." I swiveled back, and she flashed me a smile. "C'mon. For old time's sake."

"Fine. But that's it." Getting drunk with Kyle was not on my agenda. But the food was beyond excellent, and I was pretty sure Sal had stepped up his game in the sauce department.

"You look like you're hovering in the land of the happy," Kyle said, gesturing with her fork.

"I'm never eating again. A, Because this experience can never be matched. B, I don't want this food to feel jealous in any way. C, I'll be too full to attempt it."

Kyle nodded. "It's big of you to care about the food's feelings."

"Well, it deserves and has earned every ounce of my consideration. How's yours?" I peered at her plate. She'd done an impressive job. My kind of dinner companion.

"Just as wonderful. I think it might be in my interest to order what you order everywhere I go."

"That might be the best compliment I've had all year."

"I can do so much better." Kyle went back to her plate as a flutter moved through my entire midsection. I knew acutely how she could make me feel.

"Dessert?" Probably-Preston asked.

"No," we said in unison, sitting back in our chairs. That prompted a moment of shared laughter, and I couldn't help but relish the true happiness behind her eyes, a welcome sight after her anguish earlier. I realized something key in that moment. I didn't want to punish Kyle or see her unhappy in any way. I was simply protecting my heart, maybe a little more fiercely than the average person, given the loss I'd experienced in my life.

"I'll take the check," Kyle said.

"I think that's fair for the whole bridge incident," I said and sipped the last of martini #2, already in full effect. I'd be picking my car up later. Praise the wonders of Uber and whoever thought to invent it.

"We're near the water. Want to walk down to the beach?" She looked down at my foot, which was better than she'd last seen it, but still achy. I was down to one crutch. "Or in your case, hobble?"

"Okay, but don't think I'm going to magically find a beach the perfect setting for romance and stars and hearts."

"I would never think that about you." She stood. "You're cold like ice and prickly." She shivered.

"Yikes. Ow."

With that, she turned and headed for the door, leaving me hurrying after her.

"I'm just checking in because my martini-influenced ears thought they overheard you call me cold like ice."

"I did say that."

"You think I'm prickly and cold?"

"I don't. I do, however, think you're fun to tease. Your face is so red right now. I feel a little guilty about that."

I opened my mouth and closed it again. A squeak escaping.

"What was that? Do you want to say it again for emphasis?" she asked, along with an arch of her right brow, the expressive one. I knew it well. Oh, she was enjoying this a great deal.

"You talk a lot. Are you ready to go to the beach or not?"

Kyle relaxed into a lazy grin. "I thought you'd never ask."

CHAPTER TWELVE

Dreamers and Schemers

Waves have a way of whispering. I didn't know a better way to describe the effect, the way the crashes and breaks tickled my ears and reminded me how big the universe really is. The vastness of the ocean really did help put my own personal struggles in proper perspective, one of the things I loved about living near the water. Lindy used to bring me to the beach anytime I was having a bad day or missing my parents so much I couldn't breathe.

But I've always noticed the whispers more at night, when the waves cresting with the foam on top were less visible, stripping me of one of my senses and forcing me to rely on the ones that remained. It was one of the things I loved most about nights on the shore, mysterious and calm.

"Cold tonight," Kyle said. She'd grabbed a jacket from her car before we'd headed down. I'd done the same, also draping my favorite green and blue plaid blanket over my crutch from the stash of beach supplies I kept in my trunk for such an occasion. You never knew when you would need a little beach sitting to clear your head or just to take in the beauty of the shoreline.

"The breeze off the water." I looked over at her, shrugged into a maroon cargo jacket. "Good color on you." I found a spot, then tossed the blanket, letting the air spread it evenly.

"A compliment? Didn't see that coming." She took a seat next to me facing the dark sea.

"See? Not entirely closed and unfeeling." I bumped her shoulder. I didn't know if it was the vulnerable moment she'd shared with me earlier or the two martinis that made me feel closer to Kyle, but that familiar connection hovered somewhere close by. I was afraid to look at it head-on.

"No, I'd say you're kind for saying so. Thank you." She looked down at her jacket. "This one's seen me through a lot." We sat in silence for a moment.

"What was his name? The boy."

She stared out at the water. "Jacob."

"His name was Jacob." I went still. "Jacob's a good name." I was someone who believed in coincidences. But the story that changed her year and the story that had changed mine were linked by the same name, and it felt too important to be just that.

"He liked outdoor sports and playing video games with his friends and was counting the days until his family's annual camping trip to the state park at Myrtle Beach."

"He sounds like a great kid." I watched her profile. "And I think he knows you did everything you could."

She nodded. "I hope so. More than anything."

"I lost my parents when I was almost twelve."

"I remember. I can't imagine what that must have been like for you."

"The world was upside down. There's no other way to describe something like that year. When I was in school, after they'd passed, I used to imagine my mom watching my day. I'd imagine her reacting in heaven to how I did on a test or what new friend I'd made. I hoped that she was proud of me, but at some point, I had to stop wishing the accident had never happened and play the hand I'd been dealt."

She nodded. "I hear the advice coming my way. And you're right. I can't change what happened to Jake. That's what his friends and family called him. But I'm trying to figure out how to be me again."

"How much more damage are you going to allow that day to do?"

"That's an interesting way of framing it. I don't think I've come at it from that angle before. It feels unending."

"It can. But the potential to do good is still right there stretched out in front of you. Don't deprive the world or yourself of all that's still left. What do you need to make that happen?"

The wind swept in and flipped up the side of the blanket. It also lifted the strands of hair that framed Kyle's face. "I want to get past the crippling doubt. I want to get back to medicine as I once knew it."

"If it helps at all, you seemed to be doing just fine when you treated me."

"The hospital here is different. The pace. The types of cases. I think it's been good for me. I like the time I spend there."

I turned to her fully. "Are you saying you haven't been back to work until now?"

She winced. "That's exactly what I'm saying. I resigned from the hospital after I was cleared in the investigation. I just didn't trust myself. I was a wreck." She dropped her head back and watched what we could see of the stars. "I have you to partly thank for taking the first step."

"What do I have to do with any of it?"

"You make me want to be better," she said without hesitation, lifting her head and looking over at me. "Being around you again, even in short spurts, has given me the kick in the ass to try again. This place turned out to be exactly what I needed."

"We definitely move at a slower pace around here. I imagine the ER is less exciting."

"But no less important. And maybe the change is the perfect reentry point for me. So, thank you. How's the foot?"

"It didn't love the short walk down here."

"Maybe I should have carried you." The concept short-circuited my brain. Dr. Remington carrying me down to the beach, protective and in charge. I could live in that kind of fantasy for a long time.

"Maybe you should have." I met her gaze, and a familiar spark crackled. She didn't have an answer for that. I'd clearly caught her off guard, which I kind of liked. I didn't have a map for handling the Kyle and me situation. I knew what she'd done had hurt me, but it wasn't the worst thing a person could do by any means. Her explanation actually resonated. The problem? It didn't make me any less afraid. Part of that was on me. My fear of losing, of picking up my heart and figuring out a way to move forward. I was way too familiar with loss and the damage it could do.

"I can forgive you, Kyle. But I'm not sure I can let you back in again. Even if I want to."

Kyle nodded, solemn and thoughtful. "I completely understand." We stared out at the mysteries of the ocean. "And do you want to?"

"I don't think I want to answer that. I'm allowed to plead the Fifth."

"I'm noting that you didn't say can't."

"No. I didn't." A couple walked by, their hands loosely intertwined in that casual, relaxed way people in love often traveled. They looked like they'd been together for some time, comfortable and happy. They probably alternated who cooked dinner on weeknights and planned vacations for the holidays. Two weeks ago, I would have rolled my eyes. I didn't tonight. *Well, look at that.* They seemed kind of sweet, actually. Interesting development.

"Why don't we just see how it goes? You do your thing. I'll do mine. We'll see what takes shape. Or what doesn't."

"Diplomatic. Does that mean you're sticking around?" Hope flared. I couldn't deny it.

"For a while." She leaned in, and I could smell her watermelon shampoo. I was instantly transported in time. I'd spent a weekend nuzzled into that shampoo once upon a time, the scent burned into my memory for all time. It was all Kyle to me. "And just between us, the new rental doesn't compare to your place."

I sat taller, ordering myself into the present. "Yeah? That might be the nicest thing you've ever said to me."

"It won't be. I promise."

This was getting entirely too dangerous. I made a show of hugging myself, tossing in a shiver for good measure. "We should probably get out of here before the temperature drops any lower."

"C'mon. It's autumn on this beach. It's supposed to be chilly."

"Maybe so, but it's also a weeknight." I began the process of standing up with a wrapped foot and crutches, which took way more effort than I would have imagined a week ago. Kyle was quickly on her feet assisting me.

"There you go," she said, gathering our belongings and the blanket. "Looking like a champ with those things."

"Crutches are from Satan. He invented them." I paused. "Does that make you Satan's helper?"

"That's a little harsh, but I admit crutches are a pain. Piggyback ride?"

I was already walking. Correction, *hobbling.* "I'm good, thank you."

"My car's a little closer. I can drive you to yours."

"Again, I'm all right."

"Why won't you let me help?" she asked from my right. She'd caught up easily, because I moved like a sloth on these things.

"Because I don't want…"

"Me to get the wrong idea?" she asked resolutely.

"Yeah," I said, hating the look I'd just put in her eye.

"Yeah. No. Trust me. I won't." She shoved her hands into her pockets. "Thank you for listening to me tonight."

I paused and turned to her. "Thank you for the insight into your last year. I realize you didn't have to tell me everything that you did."

"I wanted to." She tilted her head. "Anyway. Have a nice night, Savanna."

"You, too."

Kyle remained on the curb near her black Audi while I covered the fifty extra yards to my car. I felt silly, realizing she was watching me lose steam as my tired arms turned to jelly. This really was a brutal workout, and I regretted my stubbornness fairly quickly. Maybe it was time I learned how to loosen my grip a little bit, and try and accept the fact that the world was not out to get me.

"Tall order," I mumbled. I slid into the driver's seat side with a small thud. My foot throbbed. My ego was bruised. My heart hung confused as hell.

❖

Every bottle at Dreamers and Schemers, the town's only true liquor store, seemed to come with its own personality. Honey brown whiskeys in bottles of all shapes and sizes lined one wall, while tall crisp, clear spirits decorated the shelves across the way. Even the labels battled for attention, some in silvers, golds, or bright eye-catching colors. The wide variety made a striking display.

I knew all of this because I'd been perusing the aisles for much longer than the average customer. The impetus? Charlie Kielbasa managed the store, who, in all likelihood, was also my half brother. The idea of a sibling was still so strange. It toyed with the only-child identity I'd claimed my whole life, right along with orphan. Still reeling from the news that neither was entirely true had me wandering the store for the occasional glimpse of Charlie, a man I'd paid very little attention to beyond an occasional hello at town functions.

"Have you tried the Tennessee Honey?"

"Hmm?" I asked, swiveling, hands on my hips. "Oh, the whiskey drink? I mean the whiskey? The flavor right there? That one. Yep. I mean, no. No. Can't say I have. Do you, um, recommend it?" *This might be your brother. This might be your brother. This is likely your brother. He has your eye shape.*

"It depends on what you like. The honey flavor definitely softens the bite of the alcohol." He squinted as if trying to give me a read. "Are you more of a purist?"

"I'm more of a martini girl, but I'm open minded."

"My favorite kind of customer." Then Charlie did something remarkable. He leapt onto the nearby rolling ladder and rode it down the aisle à la Belle from *Beauty and the Beast*. I watched in amused captivation as he skated a good twenty feet. Charlie hopped off with more grace than I would have assigned him and grabbed a small bottle. "Apple Cinnamon Sipper. Perfect for fall, and fitting for a martini drinker looking to try the brown stuff, with a little bit of a buffer."

That actually didn't sound bad at all. I accepted the small bottle. "Sold! You know your stuff, Charlie."

"That's why they pay me such a very small salary around here." He added a laugh to what was a joke he'd likely told before.

I liked him. I really did. And our rapport was good. I wondered if he had any idea about our potential connection. Had he heard similar rumors about his dad and my mom? And even if he had, it didn't mean he'd imagine anything or anyone had come of their relationship.

"Anything else for you today?"

"I think you've got me all set up."

"I'll carry this to the front for you." Charlie gestured to the one crutch I was still using a week after the sprain. "And stay off that ladder. You look like you're not at full speed just yet. Was real sorry to hear about the fall."

I followed him to the cash register, my hands shaking. "You did? I had no idea it would be major news."

"Are you kidding? Folks around here love you and everything you've done with the grocery store."

"That's really nice to hear." I had received quite a few texts and calls checking in on my pain level and to see if I needed anything. Mrs. Martinelli had dropped a hash brown casserole on my doorstep with an adorable illustration of her dog, Henry. Maya brought me a stuffed animal that doubled as a heating pad when placed in the microwave. Even Kyle had sent multiple texts to check on my pain level.

"Hey, how's Jacob doing?"

"My dad? Oh, he refuses to get his eyes checked. I watch him squint at the TV, but he's too damn proud to go to the optometrist. I'm not done fighting, though."

I shifted my weight away from my sore foot, but I was smiling. That little detail made me imagine them bickering the way I likely would be with my parents if they were still alive. I missed out on that adult relationship. I wondered what it would be like to have them walk through the grocery store, wave, smile, and steal an update session before buying their weekly haul. Maybe I had a chance for something adjacent now.

"Well, I'm sure you'll get through to him somehow," I told Charlie. "Give Jill a hug for me."

"You got it. And let me know what you think of that whiskey sipper."

"You got it, Charlie."

I left the store still off balance, but a little lighter than when I'd gone in.

"And how are you doing after seeing him, knowing who he may be to you?" Jonathan asked from my kitchen. He'd recently got his hair trimmed, which always motivated him to toss it a great deal more and spend time in the kitchen, perfecting his stir-fry recipe. I'd never known anyone who got such invigoration from a haircut but was happy I was about to reap the benefits for dinner.

"He's a good guy. Our brief conversation just reinforced that. You know how you get a feeling from someone, often good or bad? I already liked him but left somehow reassured. If he is related to me, I could do a whole lot worse, you know? What's wrong?"

Jonathan's face had gone still as he stared at his phone. "It's the guy I've been talking to online."

"Calling you?"

He nodded. "He's too successful, attractive, and emotionally available to be interested in me."

"Answer the phone."

"I don't think I can do it." He dropped the phone on the counter like a scalding hot pan. I immediately picked it up, slid onto the call, and grinned. "Jon's phone. This is his friend, Savanna."

"Is he around? This is Christian."

I made a show of looking around the kitchen. "He's around here somewhere. Yes. Christian, you say? Sure, lemme see if I can grab him, Christian." I liked saying his name. I hit mute and grinned. "He sounds nice. Very rich voice. Pretty sure he's ripped." I gestured to my abs.

"He is both. Which is exactly why he's not going to be into me. I should avoid him and save myself the heartbreak when he realizes he's out of my league."

"Wrong. You're adorable, dashing, and smart. Now, use words in order." I offered him the phone, prepared to handle the call if he truly didn't want to speak.

Jonathan stared at me and then seemed to make a decision.

"You got this," I whispered and whacked him on the shoulder, imagining that's what guys did for each other, with no idea why I thought he needed that. But it worked! He took both the phone and a deep breath.

"Hi, it's me," he said. A grin took over his face until it reached his eyes, making them crinkle slightly on the sides. Perfect.

My heart went pitter-patter at the way he seemed to melt.

"Well, it's nice to hear your voice, too."

Then I watched him conduct the cutest, most thoughtful six-minute conversation while I stirred his veggies and mentally cheered him on. Jonathan's cheeks were pink as he walked in lazy circles around the kitchen, his forearm crutches abandoned because his pain was well managed today. I hoped to lose mine soon, as well.

When he clicked off the call, I whirled around. "That went well, I think."

His eyes were wide. "It did, right? Not just me."

"No. Not just you. You were *on*. Charming, even. What's the plan?"

"We're going to get together on Thursday. He lives about fifteen miles away in Miller's Point."

"That's close!" I was excited. Even in the midst of my own disdain for romance, Jonathan's news silenced every bitter thought I might have had. He was my best friend, and nothing would stop me cheerleading till the cows came home. "You have a red hot date."

He laughed. "I guess I do."

"An illicit meet-up."

"We'll see."

"A date-a-rooney."

He winced. "Really?"

I straightened. "No. Who says that?" I asked with an amused smile. "No one with an engagement to get to next week."

He sauced the meal and looked over at me, a gleam in his eye. "We're really out there doing it. Living our lives. Me, having a shot with Christian, and a gorgeous doctor sweeping into town to find you."

Fear flared as it always did at post-bridge Kyle mentions, but I smothered it. "And MJ. She wants a second date."

He turned to me with a frown. "Are you legit interested? I thought maybe Kyle would dim the shine on all others."

"Kyle made quite the impression. It's true. But don't laugh when I say it's got to be water under the bridge."

He leaned back against the counter and pointed at me with the spatula. "You said that she explained why she wasn't there, and that her reasoning resonated."

I nodded, found a large spoon in my drawer, and gestured back. "True. And I can forgive her for standing me up. But that doesn't mean I want to risk feeling that way all over again if things don't work out."

"That's a risk with any relationship."

"Which is maybe why I'm seeking out companionship that comes with lower stakes."

"This is pitiful, Savvy. You're choosing the MJ route because she doesn't make you feel anything. I know you've been dealt some hard knocks in your life, but I don't think I grasped the extent of their effects."

I handed him two plates for the food. "Yeah, well, tada." I offered one halfhearted jazz hand, probably as pitiful as my tale.

He plated the stir-fry in generous heaps and silently carried our meals to the couch, where we always ate. The table felt too regular. I regarded him over my dinner.

"What's on your mind?"

"This isn't who you are, dark and depressing."

I shrugged and took a bite. "Maybe it's who I am now. Do you realize you're literally the only person I've ever loved who I haven't lost?" Emotion in the form of a painful lump rose in my throat. "I'm not saying I was in love with Kyle after one weekend, but I've never had feelings like those, Jonathan. Nothing even close, and when it all went sideways, I was back to losing someone important to me all over again."

"And so recently after we lost Lindy," he said, as if the pieces were clicking into place. "She was always your soft place to fall."

"Now that's you. I love you, Jonathan, and this is me, falling."

He set his plate on the coffee table, pulled me in, and kissed the top of my head. "I love you, too," he said quietly. We sat like that for a few long moments before he looked down at me. "Just keep an open mind, okay? You don't have to leap if you don't want to leap. But don't close yourself off to the possibility of leaping someday."

I sniffled, feeling safe and protected. "I'll work on keeping an open mind."

"That-a-girl. Now, let's eat stir-fry and find some trash TV to make us feel better about ourselves."

"You're on." My happy place had been activated. Sitting next to my best friend, I let the world and all of its stresses fall away. If nothing else, I had a date with MJ to look forward to and a pair of crutches I was incredibly close to ditching. Then there was Jacob and Charlie Kielbasa. I could explore getting to know them. Or not. I had options. The soap opera doctor refused to be excluded from my brain, so I admitted that Kyle was also an option.

"You'll be very proud of me."

He paused our show and peered over at me. "Why is that?"

"My mind is open."

CHAPTER THIRTEEN

Meet Kyle

Leave it to the trees of Dreamer's Bay to trot out their gorgeous autumn colors early, just in time for Fall Flicks and Fun, held every year in Bountiful Park. I'd had a spring in my step all day just imagining the top-your-own hot chocolate and cider stands lining the sidewalk. Of course I'd be introducing MJ to the freshly popped popcorn drizzled with caramel. I'd asked her to accompany me, thinking it would be a nice way for her to meet more people. Was it a date? Maybe. Probably. I was waiting to see where the wind blew us.

"Wow. Everyone is here. This crowd is huge," MJ said, looking around.

"When there's an official event, the world comes out. You should see the Groundhog Day breakfast. People literally decorate their cars and come in full dress."

"I don't quite know what to say to that except that I'm intrigued."

"You're right to be. I get into it, though."

She squeezed my hand. The one she'd been holding since we'd taken our spot in chairs the town council had put out. Rows upon rows all facing the big screen. This year's film was *Little Women*. I'd seen this adaptation in the theater but looked forward to the revisit. I gestured to the ad on the screen. "Which sister are you?"

"Amy. In a heartbeat."

I turned to her. "Really? And you own it and everything."

"I'm a go-getter and I know it. There's something to be said for chasing after the things you want in life. I didn't hesitate when I met you at the grocery store, did I? I feel like Amy would have done the same."

"I think you're right about that."

"What about you?"

"I've always gravitated to Beth while longing to be Jo. Call me Bo."

"If you really want." She laughed. Her blond hair was a little shorter than it had been the last time I'd seen her, not quite touching her shoulders. I liked its thick layers. MJ had great hair along with a nice smile. Was I trying to convince myself of something? Why was I getting so specific? "Hey, isn't that Elizabeth's bestie over there? KC."

"Yep, KC and Dan Collette. KC works with Elizabeth at her odd jobs company and Dan's an ER doctor." I smiled because he was hand in hand with their son, Gray. The seven-year-old tried to buy me out of fruit rollups whenever he had the chance. I enjoyed his affinity for sweets and high fives. Plus, who could resist that mop of curls and his toothless grin? "And that's little Gray."

"Oh, he's adorable. Who's his friend?"

I exhaled. "That's Kyle." Gray looked up at her in adoration as she chatted animatedly with him. Apparently, Dan and Kyle were getting along well at the hospital. KC gestured to a group of four seats diagonal from ours. They'd attended the fest together. How awesome. Even if I felt a little queasy.

"They'll just let anyone into this thing," I yelled playfully, deciding to get ahead of this thing. Kyle and I were in a good spot. There was no reason not to embrace this friendship without getting hung up on the past.

She turned at the sound of my voice and grinned. She went quickly to her knees, said something to Gray, and then made her way over. "Is this like Coachella for small towns? This place is packed."

"We do not slack when it comes to fall gatherings. Or the celebration of any season, for that matter. I was just explaining the small-town dynamics to MJ, who also happens to be new around here."

"Kyle Remington," Kyle said, extending her hand.

"With a name like that, you might think she's a TV character, but I assure you, she's not."

"MJ Wells. You're the one Raven has a crush on. I was showing her spaces for her beauty supply shop this week, and she mentioned Dr. Remington who she'd seen at Roo's."

My eyes narrowed. Raven had her sights set on Kyle? I relented, because what lesbian wouldn't?

Kyle laughed. "Yes, I know Raven. She's supposed to be here

somewhere." She looked around, to no avail. Did they have plans to meet up? Was Kyle on a date? Not that I could hold that against her, given that I was, too. The world felt so off balance. If you'd told me last year that Kyle and I would be sitting at Bountiful Park about to watch *Little Women*, I'd have been ecstatic but not shocked. If you'd tossed in that we'd be on dates with other people, I'd have fallen out of my chair. "Anyway, any snack recommendations? I was overwhelmed by all the booths on the way in."

"I definitely recommend the warm popcorn with melted caramel." Glancing down at our bag, I realized MJ and I were still holding hands. Kyle would have caught that, too. She was one who observed all the small details. I felt a little nauseous. I slid my hand out of MJ's and used it to hold up the popcorn, realizing how much I would have enjoyed introducing Kyle to all of my favorites. In fact, I would have loved it. But I'd chosen to invite MJ along for a reason, and it was up to me to not abandon that cause now.

"She's not wrong. We'll need a big bag." Raven. She'd surfaced, popping up behind Kyle. Her short bob haircut had been parted in the middle. The look fell somewhere between nerd and ahead-of-the-fashion-trends-supermodel, depending on what she wore. Supermodel was definitely winning tonight with her high waisted jeans and short waisted brown sweater. Watching them interact made me squint in annoyance. Kyle and Raven took a moment to small talk with MJ, and now that we were all best friends, I grinned at the group, firmly committed to focusing on the event at hand. It was, in fact, the star of the show, and I wasn't about to let Kyle on a date get to me.

"Well, I hope everyone has the best time. Tonight is one of my favorite nights of the year."

"You are easy to please and I like it," MJ said with a laugh and side hug. I laughed right along with her, not sure if that was a compliment for me or commentary on the film fest. The slight raise of Kyle's brow was not lost on me, however. She'd heard it, too.

"It's amazing. The whole setup. Even the weather is perfect."

"Right?" Raven said. "And this is an awesome jacket." She gave the sleeve of Kyle's green suede jacket a tug. It was fitted in the waist and looked killer on her. Raven could take her hand right back, though, and that would be fine.

"Thank you," Kyle said, meeting her gaze. She turned back to us. "We better go grab snacks before the movie. Enjoy the show, okay?"

The interaction shifted my entire mood. MJ talked a lot about work and the different clients she was juggling, but I had trouble focusing on our conversation. Kyle and Raven settled into their seats alongside the Collettes, and I found myself stealing glances. When the movie started, I wondered what Kyle was thinking of each impactful scene. I could see the side of her face and checked in on the funny parts, the sad ones, the joyful. Her hands were folded neatly in her lap. She occasionally reached for a bite of popcorn or a sip of the Octoberfest beer at her feet. I was jealous, plain and simple. I wanted to be sitting next to Kyle and experiencing all of this with her, and it was my own fault that I wasn't. I was frustrated and confused and seemingly unable to bench my fears long enough to be open to love.

Bringing MJ had, perhaps, been a mistake that was in no way her fault. It was time to face facts. Kyle had my head spinning, and I probably needed to deal with the fallout before involving someone else. I needed to be clear with MJ and myself about where I stood. I took a final look in Kyle's direction as the crowd filed out to the sound of the credits rolling. To my surprise, she was already looking over her shoulder right back at me. Only she wasn't smiling, and neither was I. That moment, the sizzle, the intention, the yearning, burned right through my chest and radiated downward. In just a four-second exchange, I could feel Kyle all over.

"That movie was so much better than I was expecting," MJ said on the drive back to my place.

"Wait a minute. Are you not a fan of the book?"

She held up a hand. "I love the book." She laughed. "Look at you getting all up in arms."

"It's my duty to protect *Little Women* at all costs. They're little, after all, and need my undying protection and loyalty." I smiled, signaling that my outrage was all in good fun.

"You're adorable." She looked over at me with clear affection. "I'm possessive of the original novel, too, and was really happy to see the characters as I knew them come to life."

"Now, that is a satisfying answer." I smiled and watched through the window as the sights of Main Street ambled by. I loved the Bay at night. The little shops all lit up and only a patch or two of people walking up and down the sidewalks, illuminated by the curvy lampposts the city council had installed for extra-quaint strolls. The drive home was short, but it definitely gave me time to decompress and relax out of the emotions that had fired and shook.

I really did like MJ. Everything seemed so much less terrifying when it came to her. We had decent enough chemistry. We had similar world views. Plus, the lack of fire and feeling was so incredibly... comfortable.

She killed the ignition and turned to me. "Can I come in?"

"You know, I'm a lot more tired than I'd planned on." *Tell her. Tell her. Tell her like a fucking adult.*

"Then I'll walk you up."

I'd gone without my crutch today, which made my pace a little slow. "Cool. Thank you. Tonight was great."

"When are we doing it again?" MJ didn't shy away from what she wanted. "I like you a lot."

"I like you, too, but I need to—"

I'm not sure she heard anything past those first four words because her lips were on mine so quickly I didn't have time to blink. In fact, I took a step back from the force at which the kiss had landed on my surprised lips.

"Sorry about that," MJ murmured before pulling back, adjusting, softening her lips and pressing them to mine a second time. It took me a moment to fully tune in, but I did. I kissed her back, closing my eyes. *Trying.* There was the problem: I already knew what it felt like to kiss someone who made my toes curl, who I craved, and who kissed me like we were born to do it. You couldn't unknow that feeling, and it sadly made all other experiences seem as mundane as the nightly dishes. MJ pulled back from the kiss and smiled, and for the first time since I met MJ, I saw a glimmer of self-doubt, which meant she saw straight through me and my reaction to our kiss.

"That was nice."

"Nice?" she said. "Ouch. See, I was hoping for more than *nice.*" She raised a shoulder. "We could try again."

I wasn't up for that and had to find a way to explain my situation. Honesty had always been my go-to, and today should be no different. "Here's the thing," I told her, meeting her gaze. Her soft brown eyes held mind attentively. "I don't think I'm at a place where I can leap into a relationship."

"Right. Okay." She seemed to mull this over, hands easing into the back pockets of her gray jeans. "I hear you. Let's have a nice time, then. We're adults. You could invite me in. We could see where things lead." Oh, MJ. Always the go-getter.

"A few weeks ago, I think I would have taken you up on that offer."

She frowned and rocked back on her heels. "I hear a *but* on the way."

"But I have some personal matters to sort through."

"The soap doctor?"

I narrowed my gaze. "What have you heard?"

"Well," she slid a hand through her hair, "I work with Devyn Winters, you know, and we spend a lot of hours in the office."

Devyn had dished on me. I should have considered the connection. "Aha. I see." Devyn was there when I spilled pretty much everything about Kyle and me, and her wife would have surely filled her in on the finer details. Couldn't blame Elizabeth and Devyn for being ridiculously close and cute. Plus, I hadn't wrapped the information in secret society tape.

"But I'd already heard something about you getting stood up by a woman from out of town."

"Why doesn't that surprise me? Nothing is sacred in these parts."

"Well, not at Ronnie Roo's anyway. People drink and talk. It was Cricket someone. Red hair. Lots of Botox and opinions."

"Cricket Johansson should be the villain on *Real Housewives of Dreamer's Bay*. In fact, I have it on good authority that her lifelong goal is to make fur coats out of Dalmatians."

"Hell, this place just gets more and more interesting all the time." She looked me in the eyes. "So, what you're saying is that your plate's a little full."

"My confused brain is."

"Well, that's a shame because you're a catch."

It was the nicest sentence, and I took a moment to turn over the compliment in my hand and absorb it. "That might be the nicest thing I've heard in a while." My ego had taken a hit in the romance department as of late, and hearing the words made a much larger impact than even I would have predicted.

MJ held up a hand. "I'm gonna say this, and I want you to hold on to it."

"Okay. I'm ready."

She stepped into my space. "There's always room to change your mind. And I'll be here if you do."

"I will remember that."

"Hey, and if nothing else, you have a cheerleader and friend. Because I happen to think you're really awesome." She walked down the sidewalk a few steps and turned back. "And also the hottest woman I know."

"You're good for my ego, MJ. And pretty awesome yourself."

"Stop!" she called without looking back this time.

Alone with just my porch light, I was overcome with the unmistakable desire to take control of my life in other ways. This exchange with MJ had given me a little burst of power I had apparently been missing. I'd said what I needed out loud and improved our situation. A little drunk with relief, I knew I needed even more. That meant addressing the loose ends. What was I going to do about Faber at work? The temptation that Kyle presented? Seeking out Jacob Kielbasa once and for all? Maybe I needed to make a list. Either way, I was prepared to reclaim my life for myself, and that meant taking the reins. Hell, maybe I'd even get a puppy.

CHAPTER FOURTEEN

Pepperoni and Regret

The following week, I was in luck. I'd agreed to a follow-up visit with Kyle at the clinic adjacent to the hospital. Dan had her set up with a small office next to his. To look my best, I'd only tried on about eight different outfits before settling on a pair of pale blue jeans and my navy and white checked sweater. I paired it with my short brown leather jacket even though I didn't quite need one, given the moderate temperature.

"Lesbians love outerwear," I remember Devyn saying once, over drinks at Ronnie Roo's, and as someone whose fashion sense I very much admired, I made a point to memorize that tip. I could outerwear the hell outta this season and planned on it. With a bounce in my still tender step, I made my way to the clinic without crutches.

Tasha clapped her hands when I arrived. "Look at you. Good as new." She stood and applauded louder, which prompted me to take a bow.

"You work at the clinic, too?" I asked, tilting my head in slight confusion.

"It's like you forgot you live in a small town. We're all one big family in the Dreamer's Bay medical community," Tasha said, waving me off. "Sometimes I'm here. Sometimes I'm there. They point and I go. It's just my destiny." She switched gears and craned her neck behind her. "Dr. Remington is finishing up with a patient, but she told me to get you set up in her office rather than an exam room."

Her office? It felt halfway like I was being called in to see the principal and half like I'd been granted access behind the Kyle curtain. Both ominous and exciting. I took a seat in a rather comfortable, expensive-looking green chair with a high back across from a very large desk that faced me. "Wow. Who knew doctors snuck away to places like this."

"They have a lot of paperwork and dictation, I've found."

"I'm learning so much."

"About what exactly?" Kyle stood in the doorway, trapping Tasha between us. She performed the signature eyebrow arch that only confirmed her soap opera status.

"The inner workings of small-town medicine culture," I informed her.

"Oh, well, I've learned a lot, too." She came into the room and deposited her laptop and stethoscope on the desk. An honest to goodness stethoscope. I refused to swoon. "First of all, people in small towns bring you food. You'd imagine maybe a few cookies, but it could be anything. I'm still working through a macaroni and cheese casserole. It has the most amazing crispy crust on top."

"Madeline Marks was here." She had the best mac and cheese casserole in South Carolina.

"See?" she deadpanned. "This place is so intertwined you know people by a two-sentence description of their *recipes*. That would never happen in the city."

"Nor should it," Tasha said.

"They can't be stealin' our shine."

Kyle laughed. "I've never thought of you as Southern, but there was a slight twang on that sentence."

I shrugged. "It comes out when I get protective," I said, now performing a full-on drawl.

"You stop that," Kyle said, eyes wide in the midst of laughter.

Tasha offered a fist bump that I accepted. "I'll let you two get at it."

I think we both raised our brows this time.

"To it, I meant. I'll let you get to it."

"Thank you, Tasha," Kyle said, and waited patiently for her to close the door as she left. She walked around her desk and took a seat in the black leather executive chair. Her hair was down today, with a handful falling neatly across her forehead. "So, how have you been?"

"My foot?"

"Exactly. Yes. Your foot." Her eyes were bright and inquisitive. What I'd learned about Kyle was that you could tell everything about her mood based on her very expressive eyes.

"It's actually doing a lot better. I only even remember it's injured when I'm on it for extended amounts of time."

"And you're giving yourself breaks at work? And using crutches when needed?"

"Yes, Doctor. I've followed all of your directions."

"Even elevation? It can make a big difference."

I laughed. "You're very thorough."

She met my gaze. The temperature shifted. "Thank you."

"You're welcome."

With a deep breath, she looked around her desk as if searching her brain for whether she had anything else to say. "I would encourage you to watch out for strawberries at the store and continue to pay attention to your pain level, okay? Pull back if the foot is giving you trouble, and feel free to call me directly with any questions."

Oh, no. That was it? We weren't going to flirt anymore? She wasn't going to attempt to pursue me and then I'd dodge the attention, when actually *this time*, I planned to meet it head-on? I wore my outerwear. I was ready to mix it up. It appeared I wouldn't be given the opportunity today. That was a shame and had me flustered.

"Yes, totally. I will do all of those things."

"A model patient. Take care, Potter."

I made my way quietly to the parking lot, shooting Tasha a wave as she chatted away on the phone. Well, that was a crash and burn if I'd seen one.

Apparently, meeting in her office didn't have any larger implications after all. Maybe the other exam rooms were just full and Kyle was squeezing me in somewhere. And then a horrible thought occurred. What if things had taken off with Raven? That had to be it. Just as I was coming around, Kyle was interested in someone else. My stomach turned, and I went cold and clammy. That was certainly telling, wasn't it? I drove home and made myself a frozen pizza for dinner, shutting the oven door extra hard because that's what a person with a wounded heart did.

So much for taking back control of my destiny.

Bring on the damn pepperoni and regret.

❖

I guarantee the devil was laughing the day he invented karaoke. When I'd agreed to meet up with my friends at Ronnie's to celebrate

Elizabeth's tenth year in business with On the Spot, I hadn't forgotten the once-a-month karaoke component and now watched in amusement as Cricket and her group of minion friends sang "Come and Get It" by Selena Gomez, to embarrassing results.

"But they believe they're good, though," Jonathan said, studying the stage as Cricket shook her hips and the microphone in unison. "And that takes a lot."

"A whole, whole lot," I answered earnestly.

"Bless their hearts," we mouthed in unison.

"I can't believe those women used to be my best friends in high school," Devyn said, squinting. "I'm rethinking so many choices right now." As the former captain of their mean-girls cheerleading squad, she'd come a long way since then.

"You've more than made up for it. Plus, you've moved forward with your life, grown, blossomed. Cricket is boycotting the school book fair just like she boycotted the blood drive in eleventh grade." I sat back with a smile. "So, the least I can do is enjoy the car crash onstage right now. Even Sean is cringing, and he's the most supportive bartender ever."

Elizabeth stared hard at the stage. "I feel like Heather practices that pouty face in the mirror." She inclined her head for an alternate view. "How does she get her lips to stick out that far? I'm so confused right now. But also a little bit impressed."

I laughed and shook my head, having dutifully forgiven Elizabeth for swallowing the Kyle-works-here-now headline. I was actually having a really good time. The karaoke was atrocious, but that had worked out in our favor. I owed Cricket and her crew a fruit basket, which I once proposed we assemble and sell at the store. Faber said no.

"Dr. Kyle's here."

Record scratch. My laughter faded. "She is?"

"Look at you perk right up," Devyn said. "Things must be better on that front than the last time we ran into her here. You looked like you wanted to throttle her." A pause and a wink. "And not in the fun way."

"We talked," I confessed to the table. These were my good friends, after all. I trusted them. "Cleared up a few things. And…we're friends."

"Friends," Jonathan said with tented hands. "You pick each other up from the airport? Pat each other's hand when you're proud? That kind of friend?"

"Or," said Devyn, looking me straight in the eyes, "the kind of friend you press up against the wall and—"

"Don't give away all our secrets," Elizabeth said.

"*Well, well.*" I swiveled to her like a lollipop on a turning mechanism. "Someone's feeling extra saucy tonight."

"Sometimes I surprise people. But which of those friends are you two?" she asked, turning straight back to me in playful challenge. Our table's friend energy was recharging me tonight. These were the kinds of nights that lifted me up and gave me life to face the rest of my workweek.

"The airport kind, I think."

"Boo," said Jonathan. "I was rooting for a comeback story."

"Maybe I was, too. But if it's not meant to be, it's simply not."

Devyn sat back. "What are you waiting for? She's right over there talking to Maya and Jeremy. If you're even a little bit interested, make it known," she said, as if going after what I wanted would be the most natural thing in the world. For her, it was. I sighed. I should take a page from Devyn's very successful book and collect my courage.

"You think?" I was asking Devyn specifically. Elizabeth and Jonathan swiveled from me to her like cats following a laser dot.

"I know."

I nodded. I turned. *I got this.* It would be easy enough to approach one of my valued employees. No big deal. I talked to Maya every day. And just because Kyle looked so very *Kyle* tonight, it still didn't alter my determination. She wore black jeans and a purple top with sleeves that came to just past her elbows. I really did enjoy her strong and feminine forearms. Use it, I told myself.

"What are we drinking tonight?" I asked, approaching Maya's table like the mayor of Ronnie Roo's. Jeremy sat across from Maya, engaged in conversation with Kyle.

"Hey," Maya said, her eyes lighting up. "We were just talking about you."

"Me?" I turned to Kyle. "Dare I ask?"

She raised her longneck and shrugged. "What can I say? Everyone wants to thank me for saving your life."

"You mean patching up my sprain?"

"Same thing."

She pressed her lips to the bottle for a drink mid smile. I couldn't look away. *God grant me strength in this bar.* When I finally did turn back to the table, I saw Maya and Jeremy exchanging a look. Was I about to become break room gossip? Probably. In this moment, I was willing to risk it.

"Hey, did you see Faber today?" Maya asked. "He let himself into your office and left with a bunch of file folders."

I frowned, lust session placed on hold. The filing cabinets contained our financial records. At least the hard copies. He wouldn't know how to access the digital if he wanted to. "Did he say anything to anyone?"

Maya laughed. "Not a word, just shuffled on out of there, his comb-over in full effect."

"An actual comb-over?" Jeremy asked, as my mind raced trying to figure out what he might be doing there. Surely this wasn't another attempt to teach Harlowe the business and install her at the store.

"Jare-Bear, this man is a walking crisis with more bank than God."

"He does have too much money for his own good," I mumbled. Kyle was watching me, her brow creased. Jeremy and Maya were laughing with their heads together, young kids in love. Kyle took the opportunity to check in. "Hey, are you okay? Want to talk it out?"

It was a good offer. She inclined her head to an open space next to the bar where we could have some space to ourselves. "I'll catch up with you later," I said, giving Maya's shoulder a squeeze. But lost in Jeremy's eyes, I wasn't sure she heard a word.

"I saw the look on your face when she mentioned your boss leaving with file folders. This is the same guy who made you cry that day in the store?"

"Same guy. I don't know what he's up to, but he's the stupidest bull in the china shop when he gets an idea in his head. If I didn't care so much about the store, I'd let him run it into the ground."

"But you do. You care a lot. You're Savanna." She leaned a casual shoulder against the brick wall, which left us standing fairly close together. I resisted the urge to wiggle my shoulders as the zap of energy moved straight through me. I didn't think I'd get used to the Kyle effect.

"I'm not sure I could turn it off if I tried."

"My advice? Don't let him think he can push you around, because he will. I speak from experience."

She was right. I let him get away with too much bad behavior in order to keep him off my back and as far away from the store as possible. "Right. But what if I've already done that?"

"Doesn't matter. You make the change starting now." The determination in her eyes was admirable. She and Devyn would surely get along. "Anyway."

"No. I appreciate the words of wisdom. Thank you."

"I hope I didn't overstep, but I saw the way your whole demeanor shifted."

She'd noticed? Not a lot of people knew my tells, those little details unique to me. "You didn't overstep."

She straightened. "Good. Well…let me know how it goes."

"That's it?" It sounded like the conversation was over, but to me, there was so much more I longed to say. I wanted to tell her how good she looked and how much I appreciated all the little things she'd done for me since coming to town. How I still remembered how much it had broken my heart to be stood up on that bridge, but I was healing because I understood *why* she'd done it. I wanted. I wanted. I wanted.

"Is there something—"

I went up on my tiptoes and silenced her lips with mine. Holy hell in a lust-filled handbasket. The ripple of desire that shot through me in the first second of contact reminded me why Kyle and I were incomparable in the chemistry department. I could get lost in these lips forever, soft and responsive. She didn't hesitate to kiss me back with the kind of soft determination I remembered from Charleston. What I also now remembered was how expertly she kissed. With heat surging, I wanted more. I was also acutely aware of our surroundings. A bar. We were kissing in a bar. With people.

I stepped back, searching for air and control of myself. My heart thudded, angry I'd ended the really nice kiss. I was one hundred percent in agreement.

"Where did that come from?" Kyle asked. There wasn't a lazy grin, or even a playful one. It was an earnest question, because the answer mattered to her.

That resonated with me, because it meant she cared.

My heart squeezed as her eyes searched mine for any kind of clue. "I think it was only a matter of time." I shrugged and sent her a small smile. "It's us, after all."

"After all," she said, returning the smile. "Can I see you soon?"

"I was hoping you'd ask. But—"

"I know there are details we need to address about the past, about what happened, and you probably still have a lot of feelings about it—"

"Yes, all of that. But I was just checking in on where things might stand with Raven."

She looked at me strangely. "Raven? What about her?"

"I didn't know if you were dating, and if you are, that's fine—"

"You think I came to Dreamer's Bay for you and then took up with some other woman? Not happening."

Warmth blossomed in my chest. Fear fluttered in my stomach. There was a lot going on, but none of it had to be figured out right now, and that realization left my spirits soaring. I could just enjoy letting go for a moment, enjoy this stolen moment when everything felt...perfect.

I turned to my left to see if she wanted to join the group at my table, only to find nearly every human in the bar and restaurant staring straight at us. Kyle must have noticed, too.

"Whoa," she said, quietly.

"Should have known," I said back. "Nothing here happens under the radar. Nothing." I looked at her. "We will be the headline tomorrow at every water cooler in town. Just how it is. I'm sorry. This is on me."

"Uh-uh, you don't get all the credit. Besides, this has been my favorite five minutes in a very long time. I wouldn't change a detail."

I smiled and probably blushed. "Do you want to sit with us and listen to some bad karaoke?"

She hesitated. "I'm actually on really early in the morning and should get a good night's sleep, and I happen to feel like this was a really nice end to the evening." She touched my cheek. "I'll call you soon. Or, you know, you call me."

"You got it," I said.

She set her beer on the bar, said goodbye to a few people on the way out, and disappeared into the night.

When I returned to my friends, I was met with three wide-eyed stares.

"What?" I asked, like it was no big deal to make out with doctors in bars.

"You know exactly what," Elizabeth said. "That was epic. That was iconic."

"I'm honestly shocked," Jonathan said. "And impressed. You really went for it."

"I took Devyn's advice and let my feelings be known."

"And how do you feel?" Devyn asked.

I exhaled and let the exhilaration, hope, and potential of all to come wash over me. "Like I'm ready to take on the whole world."

She grinned and touched her glass to mine. "You will, too."

CHAPTER FIFTEEN

A Gut Feeling

In a donut shop, life feels a whole lot sweeter. That's why I made a point of swinging in for a dozen for the break room at least once a week. And though I wouldn't say I'm the wisest person to ever live, there is one truth I stand by: There is nothing that can compete with the aroma of freshly fried dough, sugar, and spices. That's why I consumed more donuts than was probably advisable.

Amazin' Glazin' happened to be my very favorite business in all of Dreamer's Bay. Lulu and Peggy co-owned the place, trained their focus on one thing and did it really well. With artisan donut shops popping up all over the country, Amazin' stuck with the classics, capturing our hearts with their greasy glazed masterpieces.

I stood in the doorway and let the heavenly smell wash over me. I refused to rush, closing my eyes and enjoying that precious first moment. The dining room sounded half full, as the sounds of satisfied customers chatting quietly filled the space. "Savanna's here," I heard Peggy call to Lulu, who spent most mornings in the kitchen, making the goods. "And she's off the crutches."

"Is she off that new ER doctor, too?"

I opened my eyes and stalked to the counter to confront the two women who had become my friends over the years. They were too busy air-fiving to notice. Both Peggy and Lulu were in their sixties and a true comedy act, playing off each other and their customers in that effortless way not many could master. "I'd act offended, but I don't think it would bother you two."

"Nope. We're selling you donuts either way," Peggy said, hands on the back of her hips. She wore her customary white apron with the red lettering in line with the shop's cozy, classic vibes. I gazed at the display case in reverence. Their award-winning glazed, chocolate frosted, sprinkles, and the classic jelly donut were the stars of the show. The apple fritter was a star in its own right, and I'd be back for it next week. The coffee at the shop was standard coffee, served from a pot that offered a gentle hum. No giant espresso machine to be seen on the pristine countertops. The flour on Lulu's cheek was reserved for the kitchen, visible through a large square window where she slid trays of the freshly fried donuts through to Peggy.

"What'll it be, Little Miss Kisses Women in Bars?" Peggy asked with a smirk.

"You know too much."

"Just the important bits. Gossip is the jam on my toast." She slid a strand of imaginary hair behind her ear like some kind of a sugar-coated victory lap. She'd stopped dying her hair a few years back, and her now silvery locks were pulled back in a tight ponytail. Lulu kept hers short and curly.

"The higher the hair, the closer to God," Lulu would always say. Then she'd wink at you. "But I hang out with the devil more often. Don't tell my mama."

In response to Peggy's question, I studied the menu as if I didn't have it entirely memorized. Still riding the high of the night before at Ronnie Roo's, I decided to splurge a little. "A dozen glazed. A fan favorites bag. And a chocolate frosted for me to eat right here in this establishment like the sugar sinner I am."

"The warmer the better, I always say," Peggy quipped. "And these gentlemen are fresh. Prepare for your little piece of heaven in South Carolina."

As she rang me up, I shifted my weight, wondering if I was honestly about to go there. "Speaking of romance, how's your love life been lately?" Damn. I'd just gone and done it. Can of worms opened.

"Well, I'll tell you right off. Jake hasn't brought me flowers in over a year, but he visits me daily so we can argue about the best way to mow a lawn. If you feel like arguing, too, he's right over there sippin' on his coffee."

I turned automatically, and sure enough, there he sat. Jacob Kielbasa. Jake to everyone who knew him. My first time seeing him since learning the truth about my biology. I went still, unsure how to feel, what to do. He sat at a table by himself with a cup of coffee in front of him in a tan diner mug. A newspaper folded in half sat off to the side while he chatted with Chaz Schumacher from the garage and Tim Newton from the bait and tackle shop, both seated one table over. It was the most casual scene in the world. This was likely their standard morning, but nothing felt standard about it to me.

"Savanna, you've gone white as a sheet," Peggy said, handing over my two big bags and one smaller one. "You need some water or a chair?"

"No. I'm fine. I just"—I turned back to her absently—"need to do something. I think."

The joking between us set aside, Peggy regarded me sincerely. "Then you go on ahead and do it, sugar." Her words were quiet and encouraging. Did she know? Did *he*? I nodded and walked into the dining area like someone sleepwalking, pulled along on an invisible string toward Jake's table until I stood alongside it.

The three men, noticing me, paused their conversation. The world moved into slow motion and my senses went into overdrive. I was hugely aware of the soft clinking of silverware being gathered, the aroma of the fresh pot of coffee coming on, and the feel of my own nails digging into my palm. *Get it together.*

Jake turned, likely curious about the purpose of my presence. Other than occasional pleasantries, generally lasting ten seconds at the market or a town gathering, when had we ever had a true conversation? He offered a smile. "Hey there, Savanna. What's new?"

I didn't say anything because the three different sentences I had floating around in my brain all seemed inadequate. I was nervous and stripped of my traditional interpersonal skill set like one of those bad dreams where you realized you hadn't attended class all semester and knew nothing for the big test. I opened my mouth, hoping the words would take over. They didn't. I was nervous and humiliated.

"Why don't you sit down a minute?" Jake said, concern lacing his features. He had brown eyes like me. His were soft, which had to have served him well back in his days on the police force. I bet people trusted him. Right now, I did.

"Okay," I managed to say.

His gaze hadn't strayed, and Tim and Chaz had struck up a conversation at their own table, giving us privacy. "You doing all right today? Can I get you a cup of coffee to go with your donut?" That's right, I had my single donut, meant to be a treat to me this morning. Forgotten now, in favor of a bigger moment.

"I think you knew my mother," I said, barely above a whisper. It was almost as if I was afraid to say the words any louder for fear of shaking the very universe that was propping me up.

"I did," he said without hesitation, nodding, never breaking eye contact. His silver hair feathered back into neat layers, thick like mine. His eyes were brown and wrinkles creased his face, most prominently around his eyes. He was handsome, one of those men who wore his age well. "She was a great girl. *Woman*, I mean. I'm so sorry we lost her."

"I think she loved you once upon a time."

He took a moment before answering; a slight hesitation made him look away. "I like to think she did. We had a little something going at one point." He took a deep breath. "I was older than she was, and life was complicated at the time." His eyes were clouded with either sadness or regret.

"I understand." The next pause seemed to stretch on for ages as I gathered the confidence to ask the question that burned a hole in my heart all these months. Nothing would ever be the same again once I did. "Do you think it's possible that you're my father?"

His features seemed to freeze and the words settled. It took a few beats for Jake to gather himself and reanimate, paler now than when we'd started the conversation. I had, in fact, just tossed the grenade of the question his way without warning.

"Um…" His voice was hoarse. He cleared his throat and tried again, meeting my gaze. "I think it is."

"Oh." Where did I go from there? My hands went entirely numb, and the quiet chatter around us faded to the edges of my periphery until it eventually disappeared entirely. "Why didn't you tell me? I don't understand why no one did."

"For one, you had a real good dad. And I wasn't entirely sure until I was sitting with you here right now, looking into your eyes. Shit." He sat back, pulled a ballcap out of his back pocket, and gave the worn, blue bill a tight squeeze. "I wanted to ask her, your mom, but she was, well…with your dad, and I had my family, and it felt like a lot to undo. For a whole group of people who seemed real happy."

"The whole leaving well enough alone mentality." My ability to think was drifting back.

"I suppose that was it. Things were different thirty years ago than they are now."

"Thirty-five," I corrected.

"Then, too." We shared a short smile, anything to cut the heaviness of the moment.

I took a breath, feeling the need to explain my intentions. I didn't want the man on his heels thinking he was now expected to leap into my life and make up for lost time. I was realistic enough to know it didn't exactly work that way. "Hey, I didn't ask this question to upend your life or to ask for anything from you. I just needed to know the truth."

"I get it. I've always kept my distance out of respect, but wanted more than anything to get to know you some." Tears appeared in his eyes and he looked away, embarrassed.

I now wished I hadn't done this with his friends so close by.

"Maybe we could do just a hair of that here and there. I don't know."

"Yeah," I said, caught off guard. I honestly hadn't expected anything from Jake. "I'd love to hear more about your life sometime. Your time on the force."

"The good old days." He smiled. "The life I've led is nothing out of the ordinary, but I'd be happy to lay it all out there. And I could, maybe, hear more about yours, too."

"That'd be great." I stood, deciding to take this thing in small doses. The few words we'd exchanged left me feeling overwhelmed. My head was spinning and my emotions were firing in a lot of different directions. It was clear to me that I was going to have to manage this new discovery in small doses. There'd been no DNA test. Nothing was certain, and yet it was. Some things in life just came with a gut feeling so powerful, it couldn't be ignored. I'd just had a conversation with my biological father. I had a living parent, who'd lived and worked just blocks away from me most of my life. When I'd stood in line for pancakes at the firehouse breakfast as an orphaned twelve-year-old, I'd likely had a dad standing in line, too. A brother. How did my brain make sense of any of this? I was excited, invigorated, but also a little bit angry at the decisions that had been made on my behalf.

Donuts in hand, I headed to work in a daze. I went through the motions of my daily list of tasks, taking care not to cut any corners but aware of the fact that I was distracted. I smiled and laughed in all the right spots. I wondered about Kyle and how her afternoon was going, while letting Buster know that two jars of pickles had been dropped and shattered by a customer on aisle four. But I had a father who now knew I knew, and my life was never going to be the same again.

"What if this whole thing starts rumors about my mother? I would hate that," I asked Jonathan, taking my comfort cookies out of the oven. After I'd filled him in on my morning, he'd promptly come over to my place after his dinner date with the new guy, Christian. I'd needed someone to vent to, and Kyle had a shift in the ER until midnight. Plus, did I really want to drag her into the deep end so soon? We'd only just barely gotten off the ground again.

"It might," he said, locating the milk in the fridge. "But like every other rumor, it will run its short course until it's replaced with who's making out with Leon at the Laundromat."

"More like, who isn't making out with Leon? He's such a kissing bandit. I hope I have that kind of game when I'm eighty-three."

"Right? That man can sneak up on you. Or send the snake up on you, if you know what I mean." He bounced his eyebrows.

I stared at him. Hard. Arched brow and all.

"Not that I've experienced it!" he shouted in horror. "Damn, Sav. I'm not that hard up."

"I don't judge," I said primly.

He studied the warm little comfort cookies, lined up like dutiful soldiers on the sheet pan. "And after ten minutes, nor would the people of the Bay. That's my point about your lineage scandal."

"God, I've never been a scandal before. Maybe I should try to see it as some sort of badge of honor."

"You're racking those up," he said, popping a piece of the chocolate chunk cookie he'd selected. "First, hard launching you and Kyle in the middle of Ronnie's and now announcing your bio dad suspicions on a busy weekday at the donut version of town square. My, my. What a week."

"Well, when you put it that way…" I put three large cookies on my plate, stared, then added a fourth before heading to the couch. Comfort cookies were best enjoyed in generous quantities. Jonathan followed, sporting one arm-crutch today. I knew that meant his pain level was moderate.

"I want you to know, even though all of this may be scary, I'm proud of you, okay?"

I smiled up at him, a small lump emerging in my throat. We didn't get sentimental too often, living more comfortably in humor, so it mattered when one of us went there.

"You came right away when I called," I told him. "You had a hot date and everything."

"There will be plenty of opportunities for gazing dreamily at Christian." His smile dimmed. "But there's only one you, so of course I'm here. You can always count on me. Got it?"

He knew what I'd been through in my life, and the sentiment underscored his words tonight. "I love you."

"I love you right back."

CHAPTER SIXTEEN

Breasts (The Chicken Kind)

It had been a mistake to take Kyle to a cooking class for our first official date in Dreamer's Bay. I realized that now. Penalty flag thrown. However, twenty-two hours ago, when the idea had first occurred to me, I couldn't think of anything more fun than embarking on a culinary adventure together that might take our minds off nerves and stress. Plus, we both loved food. How perfect that Sandy Morrison, who owned her own catering company, had one of her monthly couples classes lined up. We could totally do this. We might even wind up the stars of the class. Did they have winners?

"We are the worst students ever," Kyle whispered too loudly.

"I think effort goes a long way," I told her, with a grin, as I pulled the thick chicken breast through the breadcrumbs as instructed.

"But we're five steps behind." More quiet laughter. Sandy sent us a patient, albeit tense look, and I made sure the smile fell off my face until she looked away again. We were the class cutups for sure. It wasn't my fault that instead of reading the instruction sheet, I'd gotten caught up watching Kyle's hands as they interacted with the ingredients. She had really good hands, too. And it wasn't exactly easy to concentrate on Sandra's verbal instructions when Kyle's gaze was purposefully dipping to the neckline of my blouse.

"You can't do that when I'm trying to listen," I said, refusing to pull my focus away from Sandy at the front of the room as she demonstrated how to arrange the breasts in the pan.

"She says *breasts* a whole lot," Kyle said under her breath. "Have you noticed that? What kind of class is this?"

She was on a roll tonight and taking me straight to hell with her.

Not that I wasn't a willing copilot with a lust-bolstered agenda. But it was clear our focus was on each other, and the class was unfortunately becoming collateral damage in our wake.

"Do you two think you can find your way back to the dish?" Sandy asked, when I playfully got a little extra flour on the front of Kyle's apron.

"Well, now you've gone and ruined my entire look," Kyle said, blinking those big blue eyes in innocence.

"Yes," I told Sandy. "The chicken. Such a great recipe. We just need to catch up on a few steps."

"No," Kyle said. "I'm afraid we're only going to ruin this poor food at this point."

I lifted my eyebrows in surprise, never one to buck up against authority.

"We should probably get out of your way." Kyle clearly had no problem asserting herself calmly.

Sandy raised her chin. If she weren't three inches shorter than I was, she'd have been looking down her nose at us. "Well. That's up to you, but I'm not refunding your fee."

The steep two-hundred-dollar ticket, which included the class and subsequent meal, seemed like a lot to let go of.

Kyle took out her credit card without missing a beat. God, she knew how to handle a room. "That won't be a problem at all. We had a great time."

"Maybe too good," Sandy said, stalking to her point-of-sale machine.

I made wide eyes at Kyle, a kid scolded in class, prompting her to give my chin a reassuring shake. Once we were squared away with a huffy Sandy, Kyle took my hand and pulled me to the door, the aroma of sizzling chicken our final farewell.

It was dark and chilly when we spilled out onto the sidewalk along the red brick building used for small events. We looked at each other and immediately burst into the laughter we'd held back for close to forty minutes. I would owe Sandy an apology email the next morning, but for now, I welcomed the chance to let go of the energy I'd buttoned up.

"We just got in so much trouble," I said in near disbelief.

"Please. I think we loosened the place up." She slid a strand of dark hair behind her ear. I watched her wrist, feminine and strong with a thin silver tennis bracelet. Did she play tennis? There was still so much about her I longed to know.

"Well. You certainly loosened *me* up," I said, realizing the truth of that statement. It was the first time since speaking with Jake that every part of me felt relaxed. Kyle had done that, like the drug I didn't know I needed. She stole my focus and made me crave more time together. I wanted to kiss her up against a wall until her toes curled and then talk about the highs and lows of her day. I fantasized about making her a cup of coffee on a lazy Saturday and watching as she blew on it and settled onto the couch for a book or a TV show. But God, I had to come back to that wall kissing moment, because that's where my longing pulled me tonight. To her. To those adept hands and highly kissable lips.

"You're looking at my mouth," she said from just two feet away. The low tone of her voice sent a ripple through my stomach. The sidewalk was dark and empty, the only illumination that of the event center's awning.

"Mm-hmm." My only reply.

She took a step closer, bringing us standing in each other's space.

Her proximity kicked my body out of its stasis.

Her hands went to either side of my waist and there was a possessive quality to the move that made me go still. My breathing went shallow, and the scent of her watermelon hair sent warmth to my cheeks.

"Hi."

"Hey," I whispered. I wanted her to kiss me so badly, but I also wanted to stand right there, living in the delicious anticipation, for as long as possible. A breeze hit, reminding me that a cold front had blown through earlier that afternoon. The wind lifted Kyle's hair, giving it a wild quality I didn't want to forget.

We moved at the same time. She dipped her head just as I went up on my toes, my arms around her neck. Perfection. This. All of it. The cooking class tension had been all the preamble we needed, and the kiss was hot and insistent from the second our lips touched.

"Where did you learn to kiss?" Kyle murmured into my lips.

"No talking," I said, going back in for more.

"No agreement." Another long, amazing kiss. "I have to know what you're thinking."

I pushed my tongue into her mouth and enjoyed her little hum of satisfaction. I thought what I was thinking was pretty clear. "I like kissing you," I whispered, prompting us to share a smile before our lips clashed again.

"Oh, whoops. Excuse us." Another couple from the class had apparently finished their assignment. "Weren't those the same women Lisa said were kissing at the bar?"

I waited until they'd made it a safe distance away. "We're getting a reputation."

"Trust me, there are worse things." The door opened a second time. "Wanna get outta here? You can see my new place."

"Your rival Airbnb?"

"Dan and KC's place on the water." She hauled me in closer. I loved it. I couldn't stop smiling. "Seven-minute drive."

"Is this a sleepover? Because I don't have any clothes."

"I'm sure we could figure something out," she said in my ear, instigating a full-on shiver. "C'mon." She gave my arm a tug, and hand in hand we walked down the block to her fancy black Audi.

"You realize I drive a very basic used Honda. I'm not glamorous like you."

She smiled at me. "It's very on brand for you to warn me how uncool you think you are. I, on the other hand, happen to think the exact opposite of you."

Well, that shut me up.

"And your car is cute and green and what could be more perfect?"

"I mean, an Audi."

"I have that part covered. Two would be boring. Don't you think? We have chemistry for a reason, and it's not because we're alike."

"I think you make me see a lot of things through a different lens."

She kissed the back of my hand. "To more of that."

We drove to the ocean and hung a left until we came to a row of white cottages just set back from the beach. I'd heard about KC and Dr. Dan's little getaway place but had never seen it in person. It was dark and windy when we drove into the small carport, but I could see the blue paint and the white shutters. Adorable. Quaint. Kyle killed the engine, which silenced the music she'd played much louder than I would have guessed.

"I realize how loud that was now that it's quiet in here." Her eyes were wide. "I always play it loud to pump myself up for the ER, and it's just become habit." She exhaled slowly. "And now, I'm a little embarrassed."

"Don't be. I'm getting a little glimpse behind the curtain right now."

The dome light above our heads allowed me to see the color enter Kyle's cheeks. I had to admit, it was so much easier to give in to the attraction, even if it did feel like the scariest free fall possible. There were no guarantees, but I was willing to give this thing a shot while simultaneously praying to the heavens that my heart survived whatever this might turn into. "I might be a little afraid of you."

Her face shifted and her smile dissolved, which told me she knew exactly what I was talking about. "Would it surprise you to hear that I feel the same way?"

It did actually, but I saw the flash of vulnerability of her face.

"I don't want to screw this up," Kyle said, "but I also realize I'm coming back from an experience that changed me."

I reached out and cradled her cheek, remembering all she'd told me. We were certainly a pair. "Then maybe we find a way to help each other be a little less scared."

She nodded and kissed the inside of my palm, causing a quiet rush of energy.

"Kyle," I whispered.

"Yes?"

"I think you should take me inside."

She smiled and I melted. "Follow me."

The wind was in full force, more noticeable off the water than in town. As we walked to the front door of the house, it whipped our hair around and riled up the waves as they crested to the shore not far away. It had only just started to rain when we pulled up, but the wind carried the drops sideways, pelting us as we laughed and scurried beneath the porch covering. "Get in here!" Kyle yelled.

"Where did this come from?" I shrieked, laughing, and joining her. She found her key, and moments later we were safe inside the house, the calm, quiet room a noticeable contrast.

"I could ask that same question about you." She could have taken that moment to give me the grand tour, offer me a beverage or a chance to tame my hair in the bathroom. Instead, she took my wrist and pulled me in until our bodies pressed together. The rain picked up, underscoring the rapid beating of my heart. A lamp glowed across the room, but the house remained mostly in shadow, creating the perfect romantic backdrop to what I knew we were about to do to each other. I pulled her face down, capturing her lips with mine. We tried to go slow, keep our pace measured, our hands still and chaste. It didn't last. Like a wildfire in a dry forest, the heat licked its way down my body, wrapping around us in a blaze.

"Yes?" she asked, kissing the underside of my jaw.

"God, yes," I said.

She took my hand and led me to the couch, where I slipped onto her lap, my knees on either side of her body. I loved the slight height advantage. "I could get used to this."

"Do." Kyle slid a strand of hair behind my ear. One side of her face was illuminated, the other side in mysterious shadow. I loved the lighting. I loved the warmth of our bodies pressed together. With one finger, she pulled my collar to the side and placed a kiss on the top of my chest. The rain picked up, and the sound of it pelting the roof both soothed and turned me on. She kissed the column of my neck, in no hurry at all, as my hips began to rock against her, slow and hypnotic. I was lost in the feel of Kyle beneath me, the ache between my legs growing stronger with each moment that passed. "I want you stretched out in my bed." A kiss to the underside of my jaw.

I could definitely get behind that suggestion. I smiled. "Where's your room?" I stood and allowed myself to be led to a room off the living area just as a loud clap of thunder hit, killing the small amount of illumination that lit our path.

"I think we just lost power."

I paused. "What do we do?" My brain flashed to flashlights or those little battery-powered lanterns. Candles were nice, but then you needed matches.

"This," Kyle said, cradling my face and kissing me tenderly.

As she laid me on her bed, my eyes adjusted to the room. Small, but with tall ceilings. The frequent lightning on the beach did a surprisingly nice job of illuminating our space in intermittent flashes that I found sexy as hell.

"Come here," I said, holding out my hand to her.

She easily slid on top of me, and the weight of her body was heaven on Earth. I lived in that wonder for an extended moment before giving the hem of her shirt a tug. She took the cue, sitting up and slowly pulling the shirt over her head as a clap of thunder shook the walls.

Fucking apropos.

Kyle wore what looked to be a low-cut black bra that you'd never imagine beneath your doctor's lab coat. "This too," I said, indicating the bra, eager to see her.

She nodded, eyes hooded, unclasped the hook from behind, and tossed the bra onto the floor.

Now the most gorgeous woman I'd ever seen was sitting on my stomach topless and ready to be touched. I sat up, hungry to kiss the full breasts I'd been thinking about for well over a year now. I caught a nipple in my mouth and tugged softly until it went hard, reveling in the murmur of appreciation from Kyle. I was immediately wet. As I moved to the other breast, she tossed her head back, and her hair tickled the arm I'd wrapped around her waist. "Why are you still wearing clothes?" I began to unbutton her pants. I wanted my hand between her legs, moving through folds, taking her to heights of pleasure until she broke.

"Why are you?" she asked, lifting her head back up. "Let's both get naked."

I'd forgotten how much fun she could be in the bedroom, all confident and present in addition to ridiculously sexy.

To oblige me, she stood next to the bed, slowly pulled her jeans down to her ankles, and stepped out. Before she could do the same with her underwear, I slid my hand down the front and watched as she closed her eyes and bit her lip. She was wet, more than I'd even been expecting. I stroked long and slow, pulling a quiet whimper from her lips. I slid the bikinis down her legs and eased back onto the bed where she watched me finish undressing.

"I've missed this view," she said, her blue eyes darker than normal with desire. She pushed herself up onto her knees, cradled my face, and kissed me good and long. I joined her on my knees on the bed and ran my hands down her bare sides, tracing the outline of her breasts as the rain pelted the windows.

"Lie down," I whispered and watched in reverence as she did. I took her in, the dark fan of hair on the pillow, the luminous eyes looking up at me, and those full lips I could never kiss enough no matter how many days I lived. She was naked, beautiful, and waiting. Without hesitation, I parted her thighs and settled between them. When I kissed her intimately, she groaned, so very wet and so very ready. I placed another slow, open-mouthed kiss on her center, the heaven that was her, and wrapped my arms around her legs to the sound of her murmuring in appreciation.

"I forgot how easily you take me there," she said, half into the pillow.

I licked her languidly, in no particular hurry, and instead enjoyed the ability I had to bring her pleasure. I wanted to live in this space for as long as possible, reminding myself of what kinds of touches affected her most, what combinations drove her wild. I wanted to know everything about Kyle and how her body liked to be touched.

I paused my attention and kneaded her breasts, watching as her eyes slammed shut. I kissed her neck, her collarbone, and back down to her stomach. There wasn't an inch of her I didn't explore. The noises she offered told me she was close, so I returned to where I knew she needed me most. I slid inside to moans of pleasure and began to take her higher and higher and higher, until the dam finally broke and she arched in stillness, her skin flushed and beautiful. As she rode out the waves of pleasure, she did something I hadn't expected: She locked her gaze to mine. I'd never experienced a connection like the one that clicked into place then and there. My heart swelled, and the feeling of warmth and fullness was beyond my current comprehension. There was something very special between us, and tonight had only confirmed it further. Tears welled in my eyes, and I had no real inclination to hide them. That was what she did for me.

Kyle allowed me to just be...me.

A flash of lightning lit up the room just before a loud clap of thunder shook the house. In a burst, Kyle's lips were on mine. For reasons we both seemed aware of, there was a desperation to come together, to consume each other, and fast. As we kissed, she cradled my breasts, pushing them against my body and releasing them. I was on my back and she kissed her way down my body on a mission that wouldn't be deterred. I parted my legs for her and she traced circles with the flat of her tongue. My hips reached for her, asking desperately for more. The room flashed bright, followed by a crash. She pushed inside and I cried out, clenching around her fingers, overwhelmed by sensations. I began to rock as she moved in and out again, in even rhythm. Her signature move.

"More," I pleaded. Her methodical motion was torturous and she damn well knew it. She made no move to alter it, a determined woman who owned me and knew so. The pressure between my legs steadily rose. I clawed at the sheets until I burst, seeing white behind my eyes and calling out probably too loudly. I bit my lip to quiet myself, but it didn't work in the slightest. Sex with this woman was too good to be allowed.

"I've missed you," she said in my ear as I returned to myself from an orgasm of the caliber I'd never forget. "I've missed this."

"What are you doing next week?" I asked, breathless and happy. I was met with a burst of laughter from Dr. Kyle, Soap Opera Doctor at Large.

CHAPTER SEVENTEEN

Elizabeth Damn Draper

Grocery stores seem unacceptably mundane after really great beach house sex. How was I supposed to concentrate on cauliflower ripeness and plentiful orders of Flamin' Hot Cheetos when I'd just come off a hot and steamy sexcapade weekend I'd not soon forget? As in, twisted-in-the-bedsheets good, laughing quietly in the early morning hours good, and making love until we couldn't hold our eyes open another minute. That good. I needed to process it all. First of all, I had to start with her breasts, because God in Heaven. Kyle's should win awards.

"Hi, Mr. Anderson. We just got some of those cherry tomatoes you love."

I flashed on the way she'd flipped me over like a pancake and done decadent things with her mouth while I'd gripped the sheets, totally at her mercy.

"Laura, your daughter looks more and more like you every day."

The way I'd orgasmed more in a twenty-four-hour period than any other time in my life.

"Ms. Dolly Lee, do you want me to grab an extra cart for you? We can swap this full one for an empty until you're ready to check out."

The way Kyle took her time with each little touch, paying thorough attention to every inch of my body.

"Hey Buster, there's a spill on twelve. Do you mind handling it?"

My skin was hot and extra sensitive. My brain moved too fast for its own good, always reverting back to the sexiest of thoughts, the kind no one should have in public. I needed a distraction in the form of an outlet. Finally, I spotted exactly what I needed to get myself through this afternoon. Elizabeth Damn Draper, who fell squarely in the confidante column these days. She was perusing the cake mixes, which was entirely on brand, when I hurried up on her. "Ma'am, I don't mean to interrupt your shopping, but could you come with me a moment?"

Elizabeth paused mid-marble-cake-box-inspection. "Savanna, am I in trouble at the grocery store? Did I break a covenant rule and someone sent the manager?"

"We can discuss that privately. Follow me to my office."

She frowned, placed the box back on the shelf, and followed dutifully behind me until we were in my office with the door closed. "Okay, what's going on? I've never been pulled into the principal's office before, but this is giving those vibes."

"I had a sexy weekend at KC's beach house."

"The bungalow? Stop it. Even I've never had a sexy weekend at the bungalow." She sat in the chair next to my desk as if preparing for story time. "So, it's on? You're a thing?"

I didn't exactly know. "We haven't defined the details of our relationship."

"Oh," she said, nodding supportively. "You totally have time for that down the road. I remember Devyn and me before we were official." She fanned herself. "That level of heat took some getting used to. I'm still not sure I'm fully there even now."

I took a seat across from her. We were bonding now. I loved Jonathan, but Elizabeth spoke my lesbian language. "Right? It's like I can't wrap my mind around the fact that our first weekend in Charleston wasn't a fluke. We matched it at the very least." I placed my hand on her forearm. "And Elizabeth, I'm pretty sure we surpassed it."

"Tell me more immediately."

"I most certainly will." The lid was off now. "Our Friday night together had to be the sexiest night of my life. Did you hear that? My life."

"Damn it." She said it in a good way.

"I know. I don't even know which detail to share."

She slammed her hand down on the desk. "All. You should always share all. Was there tension first? The pent-up kind that twists around you like a lusty vine you could cut with a knife? I love winding tension."

"There most certainly was that kind." I looked her dead in the eye and told her all about the cooking class foreplay. The street kissing. The arrival at the bungalow I hadn't even known was a bungalow until today. "It was amazing. The couch make-out session, the thunder, the flashes of lighting that lit up the room intermittently. Lizzie." I squeezed her wrist.

She nodded, her eyes wide as if she was hanging on every detail I offered.

"I couldn't imagine a night like that actually living in my memory bank, but it does now." I sat back in my chair and sighed with the smallest bit of regret.

"I hear a *but* coming on," Elizabeth said.

"There is one," I said. "In the midst of the downright sexy, there was also the sense that we were holding ourselves back from anything too serious. Is that bad?" I was pretty confident fear had been responsible. At least on my end. The mood had been light, fun, and memorable, and I certainly couldn't complain about that. But should I be reaching for more?

"I think I understand. The sex was good, but it wasn't necessarily charged with emotion," Elizabeth stated matter-of-factly.

"Yes." I was impressed. "You put that really well."

She raised a shoulder. "I was on the speech team. Ask Devyn which one of us most often wins our arguments." She made a gesture as if wiping the board clean. "But back to your life. I don't know Kyle's history, but it makes a lot of sense when I think about yours. You're in self-protection mode, and I think that's okay for now. Go at your own pace. Get your sexy on and don't feel bad about it."

"Yeah?" I rolled my shoulders. "Okay, I can get behind that. There's no reason to have everything all figured out."

"Yes. That's what dating is for."

"Valid point. We're *dating*. Easy breezy." I felt the muscles in my body already start to unbunch.

"I'm not claiming to be a highly regarded romantic expert, but here's my advice: Enjoy this for what it is and don't get ahead of yourself. Time will answer all questions, and you and Kyle will navigate your own course." She leaned forward, determined. "Love is tricky, unique, and there's no such thing as one size fits all."

I regarded Elizabeth very seriously, grateful for this friendship in my life, that it only seemed to grow stronger each day. "You are a lifesaver, and I'm thrilled I ran into you. However, I fear your ice cream might be melting, and we should get you a replacement."

She brightened. "I'm just so excited not to be in grocery store trouble. This was the best trip to Festive Foods ever."

Before I could answer, the door to my office was flung open. No knock. No warning. Nothing.

There stood Faber in a navy and orange Adidas track suit. His style was nothing if not predictable. "I don't know if you've heard, but I'm selling this place."

I froze in shock and played the words back, unsure I'd heard him correctly. He'd said many surprising things to me over the years, but this one toppled the rest. "You are? You're selling?" My voice was an octave higher than normal.

"Yes. I'm pivoting. Plan to focus on water sports and make a killing. Harlowe thinks that's where everything is heading."

I blinked. Harlowe again. This woman wiggled her pinkie finger and Faber leapt.

"Surfboards. Jet Skis. Banana rafts. Groceries are out these days." He said it like the store left a bad taste in his mouth, as though people would no longer need to purchase food because Harlowe said so. I was instantly concerned about what this would mean for the store, for my employees who depended on this place for their livelihoods. What about them?

It was all starting to make sense. "That's why you took the financials."

"Yep. Buyers needed to see the books." He surveyed my small office. "I'll be moving most of this stuff out, too. I don't plan to hand over anything not included in the nuts and bolts of the deal."

"What about us? The employees?" I asked, afraid of what he might say.

"Not my problem. Once the ink is dry, the new guys can decide who they keep. I need that," he said, pointing at the very chair Elizabeth sat in. "Now."

"Oh. Okay," she said, eyebrows raising. She looked just as amazed as I felt.

Faber didn't hesitate. As soon as she stood, he grabbed the chair and dragged it straight out of the office. "I'll be back later for more."

"What in the world is happening?" I said to the ether. I turned around in a daze.

"I think you just lost your awful boss, and maybe that's not such a bad thing?"

"Unless we also just lost our jobs." I tried to decide what to do next. "I better figure out what's going on. Will you be able to—"

"Replace my own ice cream? Absolutely." She clapped me hard

on the shoulder like a football coach. "You got this, okay? Go get 'em." That was a growl if I'd ever heard one.

I stared at her in surprise.

She straightened. "I was trying out a new technique."

"I see. Keep workshopping, though."

"Yep." Elizabeth flashed a killer smile. "You got it."

The week had been one to write home about if I didn't already live there. I'd fallen back into the hot and steamy with Dr. Kyle Remington of all people, spoken to my newly discovered father, and likely lost my job. I wasn't sure I'd be able to top the drama. I also didn't want to.

To find a way to decompress and find my bearings, I'd invited Kyle to eat-and-walk, one of my favorite pastimes in all of life. We needed time together to just…be. And what could be better than introducing her to the eat-and-walk Aunt Lindy and I had perfected?

"An eat-and walk? So how does this work?" she'd asked over the phone while on break at the ER. I could hear the hospital announcements through the call, reminding me how important her work world truly was. "I imagine there's eating. There's probably walking, too."

"Yes. Very astute. You grab a guilt-inducing snack, one you can't possibly indulge in without feeling at least a little bit bad, and hit the sidewalk for a scenic stroll. When paired together, those two things are a magical combination capable of making everything better."

"Even the headache from the drunk man hollering in exam room three?"

"Especially him. This exercise was designed for ridding the brain of angry drunk folks."

"Okay, if you're going to be there, sign me up."

"You're in such luck."

Tonight, we'd chosen strawberry ice cream cones from Jimbo's amazing homemade cart and paired them with a stroll through the center of town as the sun set. I looked out at the sky as we started our walk, humbled by the soft pinks and purples swirling on the horizon—as if the universe had paused to paint us a moment of calm. "Dusk is my favorite time of day. I'm not sure I've ever told you that."

"You definitely haven't."

"Not daytime anymore. Not yet night. Almost like we take a little break in between regularly scheduled programming." I took a minute just to soak in the quiet. Most people were home from work or getting ready to start dinner. It came much earlier in autumn, but it was the same old wonder. "It's this unique little stretch of time where everything is relaxed and beautiful."

"Is that why you chose this time for us to meet?"

I scrunched my shoulders, making sure I absorbed every beautiful nuance of our surroundings. To not be left out, Kyle's aqua eyes shone extra bright, caught by one of the last slanted rays of sunshine. "That's exactly why. It brings me peace, this thirty-minute window. Did you know that's how long it lasts? Much shorter than most people think."

"I did not know the metrics"—she studied the sky—"but I think you've just made me appreciate each of the thirty."

"Just like you've made me appreciate people with blue eyes." I gave my head an appreciative shake as I watched her.

"Thank you, Potter. You're good for my ego." She took a beautiful lick around the side of her cone. An ice cream endorsement or foreplay? Definitely both.

"Oh, and guess what happened today at the hospital? This one threw me for a loop."

I took a lick of my own and closed my eyes to savor. Jimbo had not skimped on the fresh strawberries. "Tell me."

"Well, I can't now. I'm too busy watching the show." When I opened my eyes, her gaze was fixed on my mouth, just as mine had been on her moments before. We were a pair, and I reveled in the flirtatious energy that pinged back and forth.

I offered her a smile. "Show's on pause. What happened?"

"I had a blast from the past in the form of the very guy my parents wanted me to settle down and marry one day."

I quirked my head. "Here in town? Get out."

"Yes. Small world. We were teenagers. His family was rich. My family was rich adjacent."

"Ooh la la."

"Don't get excited. I don't have my parents' money."

"Easy come, easy go." I pushed her back on track. "Tell me more of the young Kyle story."

"Well, our parents were just positive we'd be engaged by the time we were twenty-two." She shrugged. "I came out at eighteen and ruined everything."

"You bitch."

"I know."

"Anyway, Brent went on, got engaged, left at the altar."

"Ouch."

"It was horrible." Kyle winced. "I was there to see the whole thing. But he's good now. Found an amazing girlfriend, and they're still together."

"Good for him."

"Well, not today. He'd just finished up a business lunch, came outside to a flat tire, and smashed his hand changing it on an incline. Never smart."

I paused my ice cream enjoyment. "That gives me chills just thinking about. Gotta be careful around a jack. He's so lucky. Brent's his name?"

"Yes. Brent Carmichael."

I frowned and stopped walking. This was hitting too close to home. "This is a long shot, but he's not related to the Carmichael family who own BeLeaf Foods?"

"Yes, his dad does own a chain of stores, now that you mention it. That's something you two would have in common. Brent went into the family business."

"Which brings me to my big news. Faber, my boss, is selling my store."

"Oh, wow."

"He's selling a grocery store, and Brent, who works for a grocery store chain, is in town for business."

She turned to me, wide eyed.

"We're going to become a BeLeaf Foods." I blinked.

"I think you just might be."

I was absolutely floored. Never in my wildest dreams did I imagine we'd be acquired and turned into a national brand. The Bay was populated by mom-and-pop businesses. Recognizable corporations didn't like the conditions the city leveled on them and generally stayed away.

"They're going to come in here and install their own people." I suddenly didn't want the rest of my cone and tossed it in the nearby bin.

"We don't know that. But whatever does happen? You're going to be just fine."

"How do you know that?" I asked, but my brain was only halfway engaged in the conversation, having downshifted to despair.

"No. Look at me. I mean *really* look at me." She stopped us in front of the Miriam's Antiques and Fun Finds. I loved the fun finds, but it was hard to find joy in this moment. "You're smart and innovative and a go-getter. That conference you went to in Charleston was the perfect example. You now operate an amazing Airbnb, and I speak from experience."

"Maybe I need to open five more. Do you think your rich parents would finance my venture?" That earned a laugh that I sorely needed. I loved Kyle's laugh. The sound even helped lighten my spirits.

"I'll give them a call. See what I can do." She offered a playful wink and I was overcome with gratitude for the way she made a shitty situation feel manageable simply by proximity. She gave my chin a soft shake. "Do you want me to see what I can find out from Brent?"

Somehow that felt like cheating, and I didn't want to insert myself in the middle of a deal I wasn't supposed to know about or be factored into. Faber would have to tell all sooner or later, and now I had a good idea of what was coming. "No." I took her hand in mine and started walking. "Let the chips fall where they may. We'll know soon enough."

I had a little money put away from the Airbnb business, so I knew I'd be okay. But maybe it wouldn't be an awful idea to start looking for a job. Maybe Elizabeth Draper could use another dog walker. Maybe Sean could put me behind the bar at Ronnie Roo's. The shape of my life was definitely changing, and it was time to find a way to accept it.

I turned to Kyle, trying to do a better job of asking for what I needed rather than shying away from what scared me. "Want to come over tonight?"

She turned, arched brow signaling her intrigue. "I'd love to. I get to see your place?"

I smiled and held her gaze, shoving trepidation to the side. Baby steps. "I think it's time."

CHAPTER EIGHTEEN

A Friendly Place to Work

Dark hair fanned out across my pillow, and Kyle's bare shoulders on display beneath the white and purple plaid sheets brought me a sense of calm as I watched the morning arrive. This was what I would call more than a good start to my day, giving me hope that all would be okay. I sat next to where she lay, sheets still wrapped around me, my body still happily sore from the night before. I needed to get to the store by eight, but Kyle wasn't on at the hospital until noon. No reason to wake her. I took one last look at her peaceful features, placed a soft kiss on her temple, and hopped in the shower.

When I'd finished my cup of coffee before heading to the car, she emerged from my bedroom in nothing but a gray T-shirt that said *Soulmate* across the front in blue script. She kept an extra bag of clothes in her car for when she was on call at the hospital. It apparently also doubled as a handy overnight bag. I shook my head, peering at her from around my mug. "It's not at all fair that you look this good in the morning." Even her bedhead came off as tousled chic.

"I don't know what you're talking about." She walked toward me with purpose, all gorgeous legs and bright eyes. "But I wanted to be here to say goodbye. You sure it's okay if I stick around until work?"

I made a sweeping gesture to my living room. "Have a leisurely morning. The back patio is especially nice for watching Mrs. Watson garden, which she occasionally does in her underwear. Consider yourself warned."

She looked to the back door. "Frisky neighborhood."

"This isn't the big city. We put it all out there, Kyle. Think you can handle it?"

She wrapped one arm around my waist and pulled me close. "Are you kidding? You and I are going to give Mrs. Watson a naked run for her money. We should start soon."

"I think naked gardening might challenge my demure sense of self."

"Good thing I'm here to corrupt you." She brushed her lips across mine and then came back for more.

We didn't seem to be just one kiss kind of people, and holy hell that was okay with me. There weren't too many things that could make me agree to be late for work, but Kyle's lips topped that list—just as she'd topped me the night before. *Hey-o!*

"You sure you have to leave?" she asked, and kissed me softly just below my earlobe. "The groceries would probably understand. I could write you a doctor's note."

My skin tingled and a shiver ran through my body. "Oh, you can't play the sexy doctor card when I'm trying to save a grocery store."

"Now who's sexy? I have such a thing for female superheroes." She tugged softly on a strand of my hair. "God, Savanna. Why do you have to be so hot?" Her hands snuck beneath my blouse to the small of my back, sending me places I had no business going unless I wanted to scrap my entire morning. Tempting.

"I'm not. I'm hideous."

That earned a laugh. Kyle leaned back against the counter. "I really, really like you."

I pointed at her. "Okay, well, you have to like me from over there."

Kyle grinned and folded her arms. "I will do my best to exercise restraint so you can go about your workday."

I softened when I realized we were about to say goodbye. "Will I see you soon?"

"Yes. I will need groceries. Lots of them. More groceries than any human has ever required."

I liked the sound of that. "And I might sprain my other ankle. And then a few fingers."

"Maybe we can spare the fingers?" She tossed in a wink, and I decided that this was the way I wanted to start every morning from here to eternity. How did I make that happen?

I watched her, content, warm, and happy. "This is good."

"I agree," Kyle said, nodding. "This is really good. It's *us*."

We shared a smile that seemed to say we were actually on the same page. I'd never experienced that kind of shorthand with someone, nor the kind of physical synchronicity matched with a true emotional connection.

"I better go," I said softly.

"Are you going to tell them what you found out?"

I paused, bag on my shoulder, sack lunch in hand. "I think I have to." I shrugged. "They're family and I owe them that much."

❖

There are moments in time that I don't want to relive, and telling my employees that Festive Foods would no longer exist as we knew it was one of those times. I'd gathered everyone in the break room twenty minutes before opening, and took a breath as five sweet souls looked back at me with smiles on their faces. This really was such a friendly place to work, a testament to how much we all loved each other and the store.

"I probably don't have clearance to share this piece of information with you, but Mr. Faber informed me recently that he's selling Festive Foods."

Maya did something I hadn't expected. She touched her stomach, but not in a casual way. She touched her stomach in a protective sense, the way a mother would.

"Maya," I whispered and looked down at her hand.

Her eyes went wide and she dropped her hand. "Not the way I wanted to tell you. But yes." She looked at the others, who had all blossomed into warm smiles. "We're expecting this little one next summer. So I guess I'm wondering if I'll have health care. Or a job."

I swallowed as guilt descended. Maya was one of four full-time employees along with Buster, Henrietta, and myself. The rest were part-timers who filled in the gaps. Could we use more help? Sure, but Faber shot down my proposal to hire more staff a year ago.

"Congratulations!" I said enthusiastically.

Henrietta had already pulled her into a motherly hug, and the rest of the group looked like they were torn between being happy for Maya and concerned for their jobs.

"I wish I had more answers for you," I said to the group, though my eyes were on Maya, who I was now incredibly worried about. "I promise to do everything in my power to advocate for you with whoever the buyer is."

"Do you know who?" Henrietta asked. She held her hands together in a pose I recognized. Her nervous stance.

I hadn't planned on divulging anything yet. It wasn't what a good leader would do.

"Come on, Savanna. You know something. I can tell. You're biting the inside of your cheek. It's what you always do when you have a secret."

I instantly stopped the biting. "There's a rumor, but I have no way to verify its authenticity."

"What's the rumor, boss? We got you. No one's holding you to what you say."

"It's possible BeLeaf Foods is in the mix."

There was an audible gasp from Maya. "I love BeLeaf. Oh, my God. Yes. That means they're not going to bulldoze the place."

I held up my hand to slow her down. "I know. I know. Just rumor. But I can hope."

I had to admit, the enthusiastic grins of my employees relieved some of my concern. They seemed legitimately happy about the BeLeaf prospect, and that counted for something with me. I smiled right along with them.

"So, if this place stays a grocery store, they're gonna need people to work in it," said Faison, my favorite part-timer.

Henrietta nodded. "And with no Faber in the way, Savanna can do her job."

Faison smacked the table. "That sounds badass to me."

I didn't feel the need to point out that BeLeaf would likely install their own store manager, because I didn't want to kill their joy. No, it was best I quietly prepare myself for whatever came my way and be grateful for the time I'd been given at Festive Foods. If my staff was taken care of, I'd be just fine.

With the meeting behind me and having gone so well, I dove into my day, tackling one project after another until I found myself turning onto aisle eight and coming face-to-face with Charlie Kielbasa.

"Oh. Hey, Charlie." I shifted my weight from one foot to the other.

His eyes brushed the ground before settling back on me. The friendly vibe that always accompanied him was noticeably absent today. "I guess I'm supposed to say hi and make small talk, but the truth is I don't really want to."

"Okay." I said it quickly to reassure him that he didn't have to.

"I heard about what you said to my dad."

I looked around to see who might be listening. We were, after all, standing in the middle of my store, and maybe this wasn't the time to—

"I don't know what it is that you're after, but maybe you could back off a little, okay? I don't think that's asking too much."

There were circles under his eyes that I didn't remember seeing there before. His shoulders hung haggard, like maybe he'd had a hard night. Or week. Was this my doing? Had he talked to his dad and taken the news hard?

I swallowed, praying for the words to explain. "I'm not after anything, Charlie. I just wanted to know if—"

"My dad was sneaking around on my mom?"

The force of his words nearly made me step back. God, I hadn't really considered that angle, what the details might do to Charlie, to have others in town hear them. I braced against the recriminations that swarmed thick and heavy. I wasn't sure what to say, my brain having downshifted on me.

"We don't know exactly what happened."

He shrugged as if having given up. "I can check dates just as easily as the next guy. I would have been three. Four when you were born."

"Charlie, I didn't know any of that."

"Now you do, so could you not make our lives any harder with your public displays?"

He meant the donut shop. I should have talked to Jacob privately. This town was too damn small and gossipy for its own good. This wasn't the juicy details about who was kissing who at Ronnie's. This was people's lives.

"I promise." A pause as he studied the handle of his cart. "Charlie, I apologize. I most definitely didn't want to cause you, of all people, any pain or grief. I should have been…more careful. And I will be."

I wanted to ask him for coffee sometime or a meal. I wondered what he and Jill might be doing for the holidays. Somehow, that felt out of bounds now.

He nodded and continued past me down the aisle. "Right. Well… thanks."

That hadn't been how I'd hoped our first conversation would go. I stood between the jars of marinara like my feet were fused to the floor, dumbfounded and attempting to recover. I'd only wanted to know more about where I came from and maybe reach out to a portion of my family, the only portion left. Yet I'd screwed it all up, allowing my emotions to invite an impulsive conversation. Alone on the aisle, I closed my eyes and took a deep breath, hoping my heart rate would slow. I walked on, trying to remember what my day looked like and what I needed to accomplish next, but a heaviness wrapped itself around me. I went through the motions of the rest of my workday and sat quietly on my couch afterward, until Kyle arrived from her shift.

She kissed my cheek from behind the couch, and I smiled at the scent of her watermelon hair. "Don't move. You've had a hard day. I got dinner." It was after nine p.m., but I'd waited for Kyle to eat. Not that it had been hard. My appetite had apparently left to make room for exponential amounts of guilt.

"You don't have to do that," I said softly, turning as she walked to the kitchen with purpose. Her hair was piled on top of her head, more disheveled than I'd ever seen it. It made me think of her day and the variety of patients she'd taken care of. It made me want to rub the back of her neck and take the stress away.

"I'm making waffles." She smiled at me. "I saw this morning that you have a waffle maker and, well, I'm a pro."

"Waffles?" I asked. "I don't think I've ever had waffles for dinner."

She'd already found a mixing bowl and moved around my kitchen in blue scrubs like a damned professional. "Well, you're about to learn why they're considered comfort food. You have a bad day? You eat a waffle. That's just how my life works."

"I'm intrigued." I leaned over the back of the couch. "Do you take yours with syrup or no syrup?"

Her adept hands went still and she placed the measuring cup of flour on the counter. "This is the most heartbreaking question you've ever asked me. People don't eat dry waffles, Potter." The serious expression on her face said that she did not come to play when waffles were the subject.

"I'm sure some people do."

"The most menacing of individuals, maybe. Villains in superhero movies. People who hate dogs. No one likable."

"Thank God I have you, the waffle empress, to guide me."

She met my gaze. "Thank God. Now sit and relax. I got this."

I sat at one of the counter seats with the green cushions Lindy had made for my place by hand when I moved in. "I will sit, but it will be right here so I can ogle my—*you* while you create waffles in my kitchen." Whoops. Had she caught that little slip of the tongue? I did my best to play it off, smooth operator that I was not.

She lobbed me a curious side-eye. "What were you just about to say?"

"Nothing." Were my cheeks pink? They felt warm and were thereby traitors. Dead to me.

"You said *my*, which generally speaks to possession, if my English classes served their purpose."

I frowned, such an actress. "I'm confused. What was it I said again?" That's me. Lost as to what Kyle could possibly mean? Innocence abounded. *Don't mind me, ma'am, I'm new to this kitchen.*

Kyle placed a hand on her hip. "You almost said I was yours, and you know it."

"But I didn't finish the thought, so it's not out there."

She came around the counter, eyes wide. "It's definitely out here. You can't put syrup back in the bottle, Savanna."

"You're getting a lot of mileage out of that condiment tonight."

"Don't deflect. Do you want me to be yours?"

I was at a loss. I impulsively wanted to say yes and tie an official bow around this thing we had going, but impulsivity was what got me in the doghouse with Charlie. "I don't know what to say."

She relaxed. "Say you're hungry and that you can't wait to taste this amazing waffle about I'm about to make you." I loved the casual quality of her look tonight. Home from work after a busy day. Makeup faded, all but gone, still in her scrubs and tennis shoes. That weightless flutter in my chest hit that was unique to Kyle and the effect she had on me.

"I don't know whether it's the waffle or the show that has me more excited." I held up a hand. "That's a lie. I do know."

She reached over, found my hand, and pressed her lips to the back of it.

"What was that for?" I asked. Just being around her was the salve I needed tonight. I wasn't thinking about the confrontation with Charlie or what was going to happen at the store. Kyle had a way of whisking me away that had me grateful and surprised.

"I just like you," Kyle said, heading back to pour the batter. "And maybe one day I'll tell you my super-secret technique for the best waffles ever."

"I want to know now."

"No way," she said, waving my Teflon spatula. "There's an order to things. First, you have to try one."

It was only another three minutes until the entire kitchen smelled like a street fair in spring. My mouth watered and I realized I was much hungrier than I'd realized. My appetite was back and ready to break down the doors to get to that waffle. Two minutes after that, Kyle expertly plated mine, along with maple syrup in a small ramekin she must have found in the back of my cabinet.

I studied the fluffy waffle on the square blue plate. "I had no idea how hungry I was." I picked up the ramekin. "And the presentation is four stars."

"Who pours from the bottle?" she asked with a scoff. "Only the best for your first waffle à la Kyle."

We took a bite of our waffles at the same time. The warm crispy outside gave way to the soft, buttery middle while the sweetness of the syrup offered the perfect balance. I had to work to keep my eyes from rolling back in my head, but I did hold them closed a minute.

"And?" Kyle asked.

"Busy right now," I said with my mouth completely full. I didn't care. "Come back later. But leave more waffles."

"My work here is done," she said, and placed a kiss on the side of my head. I opened my eyes to see her head to the couch with her plate. "This okay?"

"Eating on the couch. I applaud it."

"I just don't want to break any house rules, or you may not invite me back."

"I think you found a surefire way through that door." I indicated the waffle on my plate, but it was honestly so much more. I followed her to the sitting area of my living room and took a seat close by. "You called this comfort food for my rough day. Is this the kind of late dinner you indulge in when you've had a rough shift?"

She looked thoughtful, her perfect brows dipping as she studied her plate. "I think that's safe to say. And for a while there, I had a lot of difficult shifts. Covid caused a lot of staffing shortages, and to this day, the big cities, especially, are doing everything they can to offer the same level of care. Nurses had it worse than us, but it was hard to be everywhere at once, and I often would come home feeling like I fell short."

"How do you not let that drag you down day after day?" I gave my head a mystified shake.

"If you find out, let me know. I used to be better about leaving it all at the hospital, but over time, it crept in. The grief, the second-guessing, the sleepless nights. I forgot all of my self-care in the midst of long hours and trying to keep my head above water." Her voice had lost some of its energy, as if she'd drifted off somewhere dark. "I allowed myself to feel all the things I'd held back, and they became this tidal wave that overtook me."

I let her words settle, causing my heart to squeeze uncomfortably. I couldn't imagine carrying that kind of burden over a decision I made at work. If I ordered too many watermelons, nobody died. If I had to let an employee go for cause, their family would recover. "And now?"

"It's a balance. I'm still climbing my way back from what happened. The lawsuit. The loss of my young patient. The obliteration of my confidence." She met my gaze. "It's been a true journey of self-discovery and repair."

"Kyle." I slid over close to her and took her hand. "So, what's the solution?"

She took a deep inhale. "I don't ever want to be an automaton. I've worked with a few of those. But I also can't let my emotions cloud my judgment. Every day, I'll search for the right mix of logic and humanity."

"You're a smart and brave person. I admire you."

She looked away, vulnerability peeking through. It was rare for her, but I was catching more and more glimpses of her softer side, which I liked very much. "Thank you. That means more to me than you will ever know."

"Now I'm going to scarf the rest of this waffle and probably crash. I was hoping you would crash with me."

She leaned her head back on the couch and turned it in my direction. "Now you're spoiling me. I can't remember a time I was this tired." She paused. "We've never just…slept."

I stared at her, finishing what was left on my plate. I would need another one of those someday soon. "No, no. We have to," I said, pointing at her with my fork.

"And we can." She savored the last bite of her waffle, then carried my empty plate to the sink. "Our first chaste night. Look at how grown up we are."

"Just don't get used to it."

"Have you met us?" she asked with a wink. I knew exactly what she was talking about.

The weight of the day settled. We moved wordlessly to the bedroom and slipped beneath cool sheets, sleep tugging gently. I turned off the lamp next to my bed and reached for Kyle, who wrapped her arms around me. "Tomorrow will be better," she said and kissed me softly.

I placed a hand on her cheek, searching her features in the pale pool of moonlight that crept in. "I think so, too." She'd swooped in and taken care of me that night, a foreign feeling, but one I could certainly get used to. Sleep must have claimed me shortly after. I remember my eyelids growing heavy, my thoughts sharpening then dulling, and the edges of the world spreading out until they were gone.

Peace.

With Kyle's arms around me, I slept in peace.

Comforted, cared for, and falling in love.

CHAPTER NINETEEN

Best Believe

When I arrived at the store the following Sunday morning, I turned on the lights to my office to find it empty of any and all furniture. My computer was gone. Just a few loose power cords left as evidence that it had ever been there. The filing cabinet had also been removed, right along with the framed pieces of grocery art on the wall, two of which I had purchased with my very own money.

"Well, damn."

I stood in shock with my hands on my hips, once again wondering what it was like to be someone as self-serving as Donald Fucking Faber. My ability to do my job had been stripped right out of the building, without any kind of notification of what was next. Even worse? When I attempted to call Mr. Faber, I was sent to voicemail each and every time.

"What now? Do we lock up and go home?" I asked Henrietta as she logged into to her checkout station. As my longest-standing employee, I looked to her for advice most often. We'd be opening our doors in thirty minutes, and though I still had access to our vendor accounts via my phone, I felt like we were operating this place with one hand tied behind our back.

Henrietta didn't hesitate. "I think we just take the reins and keep this place afloat until she sinks like the grocery store version of the *Titanic*. It's the least we can do." She finished her login and turned to me with soft eyes. "I love this place. I won't be the one to walk away when it needs me."

"I admire your loyalty, Hen. I'm just worried that the lights and water are going to be the next thing to go, and without evidence of a sale, we've been abandoned by our self-involved former leader."

"Excuse me."

Henrietta and I turned in surprise to see two men, one in a maroon sweater, one in a sport coat, both looking like they stepped out of a department store ad. Neither from the Bay. "So sorry. We're not open for another fifteen minutes." But I also hadn't unlocked the front doors, which left their presence a mystery. "How did you get inside, if you don't mind my asking?"

"Should have led with that. I'm Brent Carmichael," Sports Coat said. He held up a key. "We're from BeLeaf Foods, the new owners. We're scheduled to meet with Savanna Potter at eight a.m. We're a few minutes early."

I looked to Henrietta and back. "Um, I'm Savanna, but no one told me we had a meeting, or that you had officially bought the store. That's…wonderful news."

The two men looked at each other in confusion. "I apologize. Don told us when we signed the papers that he'd be transitioning the employees and the building, but then he stopped speaking to my office altogether, which I'll admit was…unusual."

"He probably got in a fight with his hussy girlfriend," Henrietta offered. "She has too many opinions and too tight an ass."

My eyes went wide. So did Brent's. I gestured behind me to move us forward. "We can head to my office for that meeting, but I have to warn you, Mr. Faber has removed all the furniture and office equipment."

Maroon nodded politely. Bless him.

"It looks like we've been burglarized, and I would hate for that to be your first impression." My heart hammered. "I promise you, we're a fantastic little store. You're going to love us." I was willing that to happen, hoping to keep my little grocery store family together. I needed these guys to like us.

Sweater held up a hand. "Why don't you walk us around the store, then? I'm Peter and I'll be overseeing operations. I'd love to hear your thoughts on what works around here and what could use a second look."

Well, if that wasn't music to my ears. I grinned at him.

"I have a lot of ideas. But mainly, I want you to know how much I love this place. I don't know what your plans are, but the people of

Dreamer's Bay are the heart and soul of this store, and that starts with my employees."

Brent nodded. "And you're worried we're going to come in and clean house."

"A little. Yes. If I'm being honest."

"Everything I've seen tells me that you're good at your job, Ms. Potter. The previous owner thought so, too. I think we have a place for you here, but we'll need to discuss terms and get you trained under the BeLeaf system."

"Well, I *beleaf* that's the best news I've heard in a while." I smiled at my own joke and waited for them to join me. Apparently, they'd heard it before. I swallowed. "And my employees?"

"The staff, as it stands on the books, looks a little thin," Peter said. "We might need to hire a few more folks to fill in the perceived gaps in service. We have incentives for full-timers."

"The benefits we offer are excellent," Brent said.

That was better news than I could have even hoped for. I wanted to leap into the air, high-five Peter, and backflip my way back to the front of the store to tell Henrietta that we just might be saved. Hell, I wanted to announce it over the intercom knowing I had two more employees working in the back storeroom who would appreciate the news. Instead, I smiled, thanked the new bosses, and took them on a more informative tour than I knew Faber would ever be capable of. I showed them the tricks we'd put in place to get the produce misters timed out perfectly.

"I have a lot of ideas for store promos, but I do realize that BeLeaf likely has their own."

"That's true. We do," Brent said. He was easy to talk to, which I appreciated. I could imagine him and Kyle shooting the breeze over a beer. "And you'll be oriented to all of them, but we're not one size fits all. We want this branch of BeLeaf to have that small-town vibe. It should be unique and stand on its own."

"I can definitely do unique. I once pitched a choir of singing pumpkins for our Halloween display. Sadly, it never saw the light of day."

"And maybe it should have. You know your customers. We welcome your ideas, and if they're a fit for your store and our brand, we'll be happy to green-light them." He offered me his hand and I shook it, noticing the bandage on the other. Kyle had done that, and my heart squeezed with pride. "Now, I'm going to let Peter get the lay of the land. He has a lot to go over with you once you get your morning kicked off right. I'll be in touch."

I watched as Brent Carmichael strode right out of my store, leaving it very different than when he'd arrived. I turned to Peter, who smiled at me warmly. I liked my new boss. I liked my new prospects. I adored the woman who'd slept in my bed the night before, and maybe, just maybe, I was on the path to getting my life right where I wanted it to be.

❖

With autumn in full effect and Thanksgiving now just around the corner, homes were beginning to smell like cinnamon and pumpkin. Turkeys were moving out of the store faster than we could stock them, and a general hum of excitement moved through the chilly air. My sweater drawer was getting tons of action, too.

"I love you in sweaters," Kyle said to me one morning before work. She stayed at my place more nights than she didn't during the week, and we floated over to the beach house on weekends for a dose of the fresh sea air.

I looked back at her, still lounging in bed in plaid pajama pants and a tank top I very much would have enjoyed removing. As I wrestled to get my earring secured, I sent her a smile. "I'm obsessed with sweaters. Especially the lightweight ones you can trot out when you don't necessarily need a jacket. There are sweater levels, you see. And I take full advantage."

Her mouth fell open. "I had no idea you were so opinionated about and well-versed on the topic. I'm more than a little attracted to you right now. Sweater me this. Oversized or fitted?"

"Both. Fitted for work. Oversized for movies on the couch, with an occasional crossover appearance."

"I like it. I like you. Take the sweater off." She was being playful. We'd gotten to the point where I could easily decode her looks. When she was serious about us blowing off our jobs to get naked, her posture moved to perfect and her eyes took on a dark and determined quality that sent a shiver through my body every damn time.

"Later. That's a promise." I tossed in a wink.

"That image will carry me through my day. You realize that, right?"

"Why I said it. Hey, did you ever hear what your Thanksgiving schedule looks like at the hospital?"

She fell onto her back and her hand went to her forehead in thought. "Yeah, I think I'm six to two."

"We can eat at three. BeLeaf is closing us entirely for the holiday, which is more than Faber ever allowed."

"But if we eat at three, then I won't be able to help. You can't feed all those people on your own." This would be my second Thanksgiving without my Aunt Lindy, and I'd since taken over her tradition of hosting. So far, I had Devyn and Elizabeth, Jonathan and Christian, and Kyle and me on the attendee list. Some of the others had two Thanksgivings to hit up that day, so I was juggling schedules.

I shrugged. "No need. Jonathan will help, Elizabeth and Devyn are bringing a green bean casserole, and I'll put a glass of wine in your hand as soon as you get here."

"What? No."

"Or you can jump in wherever you want. Your choice."

Kyle slid out of bed and stalked over to me, clearly on a mission.

"What?" I asked, watching her in curiosity.

She held me at my waist. "I need to be front and center when I say this."

"Okay." I ran my hands up and down her bare arms.

"I want us to be a partnership. Equals. You can bet that I will never kick back with a glass of wine and socialize with guests while you work to prepare an elaborate meal. That will never happen."

I melted a little at how much she seemed to care. "I hear you. And I love that." She'd used the word *partner*, and I couldn't help but wonder if she was taking that step in her head. Did it mean anything, her use of that word? "You said partnership. As in partner?"

"I did say that." She didn't hesitate, and she still had that spark of intensity behind her eyes. "And yes. Partner. Girlfriend. Significant other. Whatever you want to call it, I want to be it."

"No." I said it in disbelief rather than rejection.

"No?" She searched my eyes.

"No. I don't mean *no*. It was more like NO," I said, emphasizing the disbelief. "So, it's a yes. A hell yes."

"I'm trying to follow all of that."

I skipped the words, threw my arms around her neck, pressed my body to hers, and kissed her madly, passionately, and deeply until she came up for air with a smile. "Okay. That's a total yes. I happen to be brilliant when it comes to decoding your kisses. We'll work on the words."

"Mm-hmm," I said, stealing another kiss. "A double yes with a cherry affixed to the top."

"You're my girlfriend?" she asked, with a graze of her lips to the underside of my jaw. My midsection went all fluttery and my cheeks warmed. What a way to head into work. Didn't matter. I was on a high.

"Duh. That's my other name. Kyle's Girlfriend. Yours is Soap Opera Doctor."

She laughed. "I'll change my nameplate at work."

I felt lighter, but also like someone had just removed the net from below my trapeze walk. Exhilarating and risky. But this time it was okay. All of this was. I could face my fears if it meant I could settle into happiness with Kyle Remington, who occupied most of my thoughts and all of my dreams for the future. She had for a long time now, whether I'd wanted to admit it or not. But there was a steady momentum building in all aspects of my life, and I wasn't about to shy away now.

"Does that mean you're staying? In town, I mean." We hadn't discussed logistics because we'd been so careful about not defining our relationship just yet. Now that we were, it presented a few key questions. Namely, did she live here now? If so, would she be buying Dan's place? Moving in with me?

"Well, I like the town. I feel like the slower pace has taken a little bit of the stress off my job. That's been helpful in getting back into the swing of practicing again."

"But you're not sure."

"I wasn't letting myself go there just yet, but maybe I need to." She'd hesitated, and that was telling.

"I'm not saying long distance is off the table, but it would certainly be hard not seeing you every day."

"I'm not going anywhere," Kyle said. "We have a lot of Thanksgiving dinners to cook in our future, and I will wholeheartedly take on mashed potatoes, because I have a butter technique that will rock your world."

"Don't turn me on with butter in the morning."

She blinked. "A sentence I never thought I'd hear."

"Just another example of how unique we are. Thereby, awesome.

Okay, gotta run." I tapped her chest. "Save the people of Dreamer's Bay from the illnesses and injuries that plague them, all right?"

"On it. Kiss me?"

"Best request ever." We shared a dizzying kiss. We were so good at this, I thought, as our lips clung for an extra beat. *Happy sigh.*

"I hope your day is awesome." She took a step back and smiled, wearing pajamas in my kitchen. "We're going to have Thanksgiving together."

"It's my favorite holiday. And I'm going to spend it with my favorite person."

We shared the moment, smiling and reveling in this newfound domesticity. And then it occurred to me: These were all my friends. What about people she might want there? "Is there anyone you want to invite? The more the merrier."

"Not this year. I want to focus on you and life here." She lifted a shoulder. "I'll call my family. I'll FaceTime Jocelyn. We'll invite them next year, right?"

Next year. I closed my eyes and absorbed the meaning. Warmth hit and spread from my chest to my limbs. "Yeah, of course."

"Oh, and before you go…"

"Yeah?"

"Did you consider asking Jake? And maybe even Charlie?"

"Oh. I don't think Charlie's quite ready to break bread together, given our last conversation. Maybe he's another one for next year's list. But Jake is…trickier." I didn't know what to say. Because I had entertained the thought for all of three seconds before the intimidation factor had taken over and I'd shoved the concept to the side. "Might be too soon for that, too."

"Dessert then?" She held up a hand. "I don't want to push, but it might be nice for you to have…family there." She'd said the word delicately as if not sure it was allowed. I appreciated her sensitivity.

"Dessert," I repeated. Not nearly as big a time commitment, and dessert came with a come and go whenever casualness I could latch onto. "Maybe dessert. I'll think on it."

By the time my lunch break was over, I'd sent an invitation to Jake's fairly dormant-looking Facebook page inviting him and Peggy for coffee and dessert. He probably didn't even use the old account and wouldn't see the message, but at least I'd made the effort and could feel good about that. But by late afternoon, when I hung up my newly acquired BeLeaf apron for the day and headed into the parking lot—

now lit up with a bright green BeLeaf sign—I had a message in my inbox.

Yep. Would love it. Peggy says she'll bring her famous apple pie. See you then.

Well, hell. I stared down at my phone in surprise. It seemed we were doing this.

CHAPTER TWENTY

Homemade Pie

Thanksgiving was a day of simple pleasures. The air was crisp with an autumn chill, and colorful leaves had finally drifted to the ground just in time for the holiday. A blessing. The meal had come together just as I'd hoped, and we'd stuffed ourselves over wine and the best conversation.

Presently, the Lions and the Bears battled it out on the TV in the living room while Kyle, Devyn, and I finished putting away the last of the Thanksgiving dinner dishes, the ones that wouldn't fit in the now overflowing dishwasher. The day had been a memorable one. We'd all hugged and laughed and shared wine and all kinds of sweet and savory dishes across the long table in my formal dining room. This was only the second time I'd used it, having inherited it from Lindy. Everything seemed to have slowed down for us all to gather and celebrate the abundance we had in our lives, which very much included each other.

"It's ridiculous to go for it," Christian said, tossing his hand in the air. "This offensive coordinator needs to lose his job." He sat back and shook his head. One thing we'd learned about him today was that he cared a great deal about football.

I smiled from my spot at the sink as I scrubbed a serving dish. "You tell 'em, Christian. Who goes for it on fourth and nine?"

"It's honestly really hot," Jonathan whispered to me. "He's such a dude. I love it."

"I think he loves *you*," I said back quietly. "I've been watching. He smiles whenever you walk by and laughs the loudest at your jokes. Plus, he ate everything on his plate like a good little boy."

"Look at us. With people," Jonathan said, standing a little taller. "In relationships. I wish we could send their photos to our high school selves."

"Young Savanna's head would explode."

"Young Jonathan thought he'd die lonely and limping literally through life."

I turned to him. "God, he was so wrong. And don't you ever again think such negative things about my best friend, or I'll punch you in the face."

He gasped. "I'm on crutches, you bully." It was his favorite retort.

"Do I need to break you two up?" Kyle asked from her spot at the drying station. She tossed her hand towel onto her shoulder. The cream-colored sweater, jeans, and boots look was so catalogue perfect, it hurt to look at her. Cuddly and chic.

"Don't you listen in on our secret conversations," I said over my shoulder. "You could never keep us apart. We have too much dirt on each other."

"So true," Jonathan said with a shudder. He gave me a hip bump.

I couldn't remember a day when I'd smiled as much. Everything had been, quite simply, perfect. It almost helped me forget about the fact that I was hosting the dad-I-never-knew-I-had for the first time. I'd taken to calling him that for the truth of the nickname and the rhyming scheme.

"You ready?" Kyle asked quietly as I sank onto the couch next to her twenty minutes later. It was twenty to six and I thought I'd steal the time to relax. Enjoy the company of the room.

"Tackle him!" Elizabeth screamed at the top of her lungs and leapt to her feet, ready to bust through the screen and do it herself.

"She has a lot of feelings," Devyn said matter-of-factly and gently ushered Elizabeth back down to the love seat they occupied.

"Well, I have the pecan and the pumpkin set out. I mean, it's too early for the ice cream. But I guess I could soften it."

"I mean are *you* ready?"

Aha. She was checking on my anxiety level, which was moderate to I just googled *Can you die from overthinking?* "I'm going to be. Just my first official social event with…him."

She gave my knee a squeeze, and it instantly slowed my breathing. I didn't know how Kyle had such a centering effect on me, but I was grateful.

A short time later, the doorbell rang, and I opened the door with the smile I'd planned on, the one that said *Welcome to my home. It's Thanksgiving and I'm thankful for your presence.* Surely I'd nailed it.

"Savanna!" Peggy enthused. She wore fire-engine red lipstick and had her hair in a French braid. "I can't believe we've known each other all these years and never visited each other's homes. I'm so glad we're doing this."

"Me, too," I said. "Come in. Come in."

"Hi," Jake said from behind her. He wore a maroon sweater with a gray and maroon striped tie underneath it, which I found touching. I'd never seen him dressed so nice, which meant he cared about today. His cheeks were rosy, which told me he was nervous, too. More so than when I'd seen him at the donut house.

"Hi." I met his eyes, realizing they really weren't far off from my own. Trippy. "I'm so glad you're here."

He held up a covered dish. "We brought the pie. She made it. I just do the carrying." He laughed nervously and moved past me into the house.

"Both count!" I said back, just as nervous. I followed them in and stood off to the side as my friends greeted the newcomers.

"Ohhh, I've heard all about you," Peggy said, pulling Kyle into an embrace. "Everyone has a crush on you, ya know."

I raised an amused eyebrow at Kyle, who sent me a news-to-me face. "Really? Well, that's not something I was aware of."

"Half of those people who show up in that ER are not injured, I'll have you know. They confess all their sins to the donut ladies. Part of the job. Have you met Jake?" She hooked a thumb. "He spends too much time doing crossword whatevers, but other than that is a pretty good fella."

She turned to him. "I've heard a lot about you. I'm Kyle Remington."

I grinned. "What a name, right?"

"Real nice to meet you," Jake said, giving her hand a squeeze. "Brought some pie," he said to the room. Everyone exclaimed their excitement and gratitude, and I went about taking orders. Once everyone was squared away and in the midst of conversation, I turned to Jake, who'd joined me in the kitchen.

"I'm not quite sure what to say," he said, "but I think it's really nice of you to extend the invitation."

I raised one shoulder. "I thought it might be a nice way to get to know each other. Did you see Charlie today? I don't think he's happy with me."

"Ah, yep. He's on his heels. I should have been more up front with him all these years. Hell, I should have been more up front with myself."

"With me, too." I still wasn't over that part. No one had been honest with me. Not one person.

He nodded and sobered. "With you, too." A pause. "I like to think I'm a better man today than I was back then."

I nodded.

"As for Charlie, he needs time. He's a good guy."

"I know, and I wish I had considered his feelings before my less than discreet ambush at Amazin' Glazin'."

"Not your fault," he said, as a round of laughter erupted in the living room. They were giving us space to talk. No one had come in to refill a drink, grab a napkin, or drop off their plates and join the conversation. "People like to gossip. As soon as the next rumor rolls in, they'll be onto it and forget all about us." He shifted.

"I had a great dad," I blurted. "I loved him a lot. Still do. Always will." I don't know why I felt the need to get that out there right away, but it was important. I wasn't replacing my own father, in any capacity, by reaching out to Jake. Both things could exist.

My comments didn't seem to faze Jake. "He was a good guy. I liked him. You were lucky to have him as your dad. It was a terrible loss for the whole town. But especially you."

"That might have been the time to step forward, you know."

He went still for a moment. "Would have made sense. The version of me from twenty years ago was a chickenshit who drank beer, quaked in his boots, and put those feelings first. I wouldn't make that same decision again. I'd wring that guy's neck if I could. But I was a grown-ass adult who wasn't grown at all."

I did my best to see things from his perspective. "I imagine your family factored in."

He nodded. "I was married. She didn't know I'd fathered a child, and I was afraid to tell her."

"Right. I gathered that after talking to Charlie." I was absorbing as we went but knew I'd take the conversation out again, when I was alone, and examine it more fully, comb through each detail. "And you're fairly sure...that you fathered this particular child?"

"The timing matched. And you look so much like my mama, I can barely believe it. Yeah, I'm sure. But at some point, sure, maybe we—"

"Find out officially?" I finished. Kyle had already briefed me of the quickest way to test paternity.

"Just for your peace of mind."

"How's the pie?" I asked. He'd taken a couple of distracted bites.

"Oh. The fuckin' best. Peggy is a genius when it comes to this kind of thing. As you know." He knew I frequented the donut house. He'd had his eye on me all this time. While I still hadn't worked through the resentment of not being told, there was a surprising feeling of comfort in the thought of him watching out for me.

"This is still a lot to wrap my head around."

"I know. But I did some thinking, and the most important thing for you to hold on to is that everybody, you know, loved you." His voice had gone raspy. "Everybody." I watched as his face went pink with emotion just like mine so often did.

My throat ached with an uncomfortable lump and my eyes filled. Dammit. I didn't mean to get all sentimental, but there I was, fighting emotion as Christian and Elizabeth argued about whether a foot had been in bounds when the receiver caught the ball.

I smiled at myself and Jake returned it. "What a day," I said. "Thanksgiving might be my favorite holiday."

"I'm a big eater, so I'm right there with ya," he said with a laugh. "Wanna watch the game?"

"I definitely do."

We joined the others and sat around my living room, shooting the breeze and trading stories as the memorable day wound down. A peaceful calm settled over me while Kyle and I said our final goodbyes to Devyn and Elizabeth, the last couple to leave.

"You did an amazing job today," Kyle said.

"I don't know about *amazing*."

"Don't downplay." Her eyes were determined when she met my gaze. "You made the day wonderful for everyone. I don't know how you do it, but you have this welcoming spirit that makes people comfortable in their own skin."

"That's such a nice thing to say." I watched her. "The truth? Today was only what it was because I had you here with me." Now that the dust had settled, I thought about her trajectory and experienced immediate guilt. "And you must be so exhausted. You worked a full shift and then jumped right into the throes of preparing a huge meal with guests everywhere. You haven't had a break or any downtime."

"This wasn't work. I loved every minute of it." She paused. "But yes, every muscle in my body is screaming."

I laughed. "C'mon. I have an idea."

I used my fancy remote to turn on my gas fireplace and watched as the flames licked and danced. "I will never get used to the magic of just pressing a button and having instant fire. The cave people would seek out my friendship if they knew."

"You'd be all over the cave news, I bet."

I took a seat on the couch. "Damn right I would. Sit right here," I said, patting the spot on the floor in front of me.

Her eyes lit up as she anticipated what was on the way. I made a show of interlacing my fingers and stretching my arms in front of my body in warm-up.

"Are you about to do what I think you're about to do?"

"Maybe." I wiggled my fingers like I was Mozart and placed them on the skin of her shoulders, just beneath her sweater.

Kyle let out a quiet moan of pleasure. "I might cry."

I began to rub her shoulders slowly but with moderate pressure, following the muscle and pressing and elongating. "You're really tight right here."

She went still and then her shoulders began to shake. "I'm really sorry, but sometimes I'm a teenage boy."

I laughed with her. "I hear it now, but focus on relaxing."

"With you saying things like that out loud to me?"

I swatted her shoulder. "Let's lose some of this tension." There was a knot just below her trapezoid, which I worked on slowly and with repetition.

"That's amazing. Have I told you how awesome you are because— Oh, wow. Yes, right there. Exactly there. Yes."

Now it was my turn to laugh. "Okay, this massage is inspiring a sex response. Massages are sneaky."

"The more you know," Kyle deadpanned, and we shared another laugh. I loved laughing with her, and for us, it came easily. I had the best time when it was just her and me. Our alone time made me feel free and alive, as if the stress of the real world was far, far away.

She'd gone quiet once I moved on to her neck, applying the light sweeping strokes I'd once read were the most relaxing forms of touch.

I pulled her dark hair to one side, exposing the column of her neck, which I'd always been a little preoccupied with. In the quiet of my living room, I let my hands dip lower, down the front of her shoulders onto her breastbone, and then beneath the neckline of the knit top. I kissed her neck because I couldn't help myself, not with her so close, with her neck looking *like that*.

She murmured her appreciation, reached around, and slid her fingers into my hair, pulling me closer. It was all the encouragement I needed. I continued kissing her neck, the underside of her jaw, her earlobe. She was my favorite everything, and I was drowning in desire for her. I wanted to touch her. I wanted to tease her. I wanted to run my hands through her hair and grip while I listened to her climax.

"I can never get enough of you," I murmured. My hands dipped lower and palmed her breasts through her bra, prompting Kyle to hitch in a breath. She dropped her head back, resting it partially in my lap. I kissed her lips, upside down and hungry. It wasn't enough for her. She went up on her knees and turned fully to face me, her body between my knees. She pulled me to her for a scorching kiss, held my face in place and explored my mouth with her tongue. Our pace, which began slow, picked up, until it was clear we were desperate for each other. Somewhere along the way, I'd done away with her top entirely. My hand was inside the cup of her bra, cradling her breast and pressing it against her body. I pulled one out and then the other. She sent me a flushed-faced smile. I knew from pillow talk that she loved it when I showed them attention. I bent down and pulled a nipple into my mouth, sucking gently. Then not so gently. I was aware of her hips pressing against my leg.

"You're wet right now, aren't you," I whispered in her ear.

She met my gaze, her eyes dark. All I got was an earnest nod. A request.

Without any more communication, I unbuttoned her jeans. Unzipped them. Finally, I slid my hand down the front of her underwear into warmth as her eyes fluttered closed, and she steadied herself with a hand on the couch cushion.

"Such a good day," she said with her eyes closed.

I grinned and began to play. Soft touches. Long strokes. Slow circles. She began to ride my hand, guiding me. She loved control, but in this vulnerable moment, she handed it to me, and it reaffirmed our bond. She trusted me, and I was learning to trust her again.

"Look at me," I breathed.

She opened her eyes and we connected, holding eye contact as her sounds of pleasure increased in volume and desperation. Her lips parted, and I watched her face change as she broke. Pleasure washed over her features, the most beautiful woman in the world. A bouquet of feelings blossomed in my chest, stealing my voice, robbing me of my words and forcing me to simply live in the experience.

Finally, Kyle took a deep, centering breath and stood up. She lost the bra, left her pants undone, and offered me her hand with a gleam in her eye I knew well. "Let's go to bed. I have such plans for you."

"You don't look tired anymore."

"Second wind. Can you believe it? Turns out I just needed proper inspiration, and let me say, I've more than found it."

I laughed as her lips met mine. "I do declare, this is the happiest Thanksgiving."

"And we're so not done with it."

We fell into bed a short time later, and she delivered on every promise, showing me how well she knew the human body. Several orgasms later, I turned to her. "Where did you learn how to do that? The last thing, with the timing and circles because, whoa."

She grinned against my shoulder and raised her chin. "I guess just a combination of science and intuition."

It was the perfect parallel to her personality, logical yet in tune to others. "I think it's your new signature move. We could take a vote, but I would win."

She propped her head up on her hand. "I had no idea you were so politically driven."

"With the proper motivation, I'm finding I could be a lot of things."

"Come here," she said, pulling me on top. It was her favorite. I nestled in, staggering our thighs. "What are we doing tomorrow?"

"Whatever we want." With Kyle in my life, and being part of an us that was the perfect fit for me, the world seemed boundless. "Let's go shopping."

"Okay. For what?"

"Let's not decide."

"Unspecified goods perusal." She pulled her face back and nodded thoughtfully. "You have good ideas. Aimless shopping it is."

I rested my head on her chest and sighed happily. My limbs felt heavy and my spirit light. The house that just a couple of hours ago had been full of chaos and conversation now hummed with quiet contentment. It had been a wonderful day and a perfect night, and I couldn't help but bask as my eyes slowly closed. This was getting good, really, really good.

CHAPTER TWENTY-ONE

An Unlikely Pair

"But why not delete a few?" I asked Jake over lunch at the Serious Sandwich. The shop had been open just over a year, and because of its proximity to the store, I could pop over easily enough for lunch.

"I just don't see the point. What if I need one?" He shrugged and set down his Turkey O'Toole. It was their specialty.

When I'd discovered he never deleted his email and had over 17,000 just hanging out in his inbox, I went into a type A panic. I turned his phone around and showed him an email from eight years earlier about a sale at a shoe store. "But, see, I don't think they're going to take this coupon anymore. That one could go."

He laughed and gave his head a shake. "I just hit the trash can cartoon there?"

"That's all you gotta do."

He hit the icon, sending the email to the trash, and I broke into a smile. "See? Wasn't so hard. Only 16,999 to go."

"Are we going to argue over each one?" he asked with a laugh.

"Let's play it by ear."

It had been twelve days since he'd come to my place for Thanksgiving. We'd gotten together handful of times, all of them on the fly. The great thing? He'd taken the lead, showing authentic interest in my life and all I had going on. It was, dare I say, nice? There wasn't any kind of pressure to leap into an instant relationship. We hung out casually in short spurts, which made the whole thing feel less threatening.

"So, how's the new branding going? Your whole store is green now."

"You should see my office. They came in and redecorated the

whole thing. There's a fancy L-shaped desk and a gorgeous couch. They had a crew come in and paint, and a woman brought in these beautiful paintings of locations around town. My jaw hit the floor."

"Sounds like an upgrade to me."

"It is." I finished chewing. "The best part is that they're green-lighting so many of my ideas. Even the ones I considered long shots. We're having Santa Claus come in and take pet photos every Tuesday in December right in between the dog and cat aisles. Faber would have died before allowing that to happen."

"Yeah, well, Don has his own troubles now."

"What have you heard?" This was fun.

"That woman he runs after all the time?"

"Harlowe?" I waved him off. "She's a lot. I speak from experience."

"She's in jail."

I had to set down my sandwich entirely. "What? How have I not heard about this?"

"Give it a couple of hours. My buddies booked her this morning on fraud, conspiracy, and embezzlement charges." Sometimes I forgot he was a retired cop. Of course he'd have all the good intel before everyone else.

He looked around to make sure he could speak freely. Even so, he leaned in close. "There was this guy who came through here about a decade ago by the name of Grant Tranton and ripped off a handful of folks with all sorts of big promises. Took off with their investments and broke a lot of hearts. They finally caught up with him a few years back at a Pizza Hut in California. Turns out this Harlowe gal is his kid sister."

"Stop it." Suddenly, everything I knew about Harlowe played back in my brain like a movie on fast forward.

"And she was well-versed in the family business. Faber was a perfect mark for her." He shook his head like this whole thing was a doozy of a con. "She'd been moving funds from his account to her own for years."

This was like a Christmas present in so many ways. Harlowe was a scam artist in custody and Faber was outed as a fool. "Karma exists. It's real," I said out loud. "I mean, I've always wondered, but now I'm feeling pretty damn certain."

"I've always thought so."

I took a moment to bathe in the new knowledge of Faber off licking his wounds. It wasn't like me to wish ill upon others, but I might make an exception and enjoy this for a few hours.

Jake brightened, remembering something. "Hey, Peggy and I like to take the boat out sometimes and thought maybe you'd like to join us. Kyle, too, if you like."

"A boat? I've never had a boat in the family before." I paused because I'd just included myself in his family, which, true or not, felt *forward*.

He didn't seem to mind. "Oh, yeah. We're outdoor kinda folks. Nothing fancy, but it could be a fun afternoon."

"Count us in. Oh! And you need to swing by the BeLeaf booth at the Jingle Jamboree." I marveled at actually having a booth our customers could visit. I'd been hoping for one for years now. I already had a sweater dress, boots, and Santa hat picked out. "Peter is organizing a whole complimentary spread of holiday breads, cheeses, meats, and fruit."

"Oh my," Jake added with a laugh. "I'll definitely make a little plate in that case."

"You have to. And Maya will be offering face painting, but even better, we're entering the cider competition. Buster has been tirelessly perfecting our recipe at home." I pointed at myself. "You might be able to tell I'm excited."

"It's good for a person to have things to look forward to." He got this goofy grin on his face. "Charlie used to count down the days to things he couldn't wait for with these numbered magnets on the fridge."

I sobered a little at the mention of Charlie's name. I had hoped I'd run into him again, or even better, work up the nerve to swing by the liquor store and work on setting things right between us. "How's he doing?"

"He's been busy. He's helping set up a second store in Willow Haven about eighty miles from here, and that project has him on the road a hell of a lot. Jill sometimes rides with him if it's a day when school is out."

"That's great." I hesitated, not wanting to overstep. "Please tell him I said so. I mean, if you think that'd be okay. I'm not sure he'd want to hear it from me just yet."

"I think he might be coming around. Understand, he's more upset with me than anyone else. Just took him a minute to figure that part out 'cause he was all jumbled." He tapped the table and offered a weary smile. "And I can take it. Don't you worry."

I wanted to comfort Jake, but I was also aware of the damage that secrets like this one did. I could see so in my own life. As much as I was trying to focus on the here and now, this whole situation had upended so much of what I thought I knew. "When he's ready, it would be nice to have a conversation. We always got along just fine...before. But now he hates me and the horse I rode in on."

"Charlie's a good levelheaded guy. He doesn't hate you, Savanna. He just needs a minute to get his ducks all lined up nice. And he'll be at the holiday hullabaloo."

"Jingle Jamboree."

"That, too. He goes to all the things with the strange names."

"Well, maybe the holidays will help. They tend to soften my heart."

"You got a good one," he said, balling his wrapper and tossing it into the nearby trash like a pro.

"It's going to be okay, I think," I said, to both of us as, he walked me to my car.

"Up until recently, I wasn't sure." He met my gaze. "You changed that, kid. I don't know how, but you did." He shoved his hands into the pockets of his soft and worn jeans. We shared a smile, and I understood that maybe we'd needed each other. Him, missing a piece of himself, and me, all alone in the world.

I slid into the driver's seat. "What an unlikely pair we are."

"Ha. You can say that again. See you soon, kid." He closed my door for me, offered a wave, and backed up so I could reverse. It was his habit to wait until I was successfully on my way before heading to his own car, a gesture that made me feel safe, like someone was looking out for me. A parent. My parent. Surreal. I wondered what my folks would think. I imagined they'd be happy Jake and I had found each other in this crazy world. I imagined them smiling down on me and wished once again, more than anything, that they were still here. We'd probably have game nights like we did when I was younger. Only instead of Candy Land around the kitchen table, maybe it was poker or Codenames.

Imagine that.

Jake would never be a replacement for either of them, but he was family. My family.

I shook my head as I drove, avoiding Main Street at lunchtime, knowing I'd get stuck at every crosswalk in what I called pedestrian central. I didn't mind the slightly longer drive through the residential side streets. I had a lot to think about and celebrate. A really great lunch with Jake that just seemed to build on other interactions. What was more? Harlowe was heading to jail, the store had a booth at the Jamboree, and I'd see my girlfriend in just a few hours to fill her in on all of it. I relished the days her shift allowed her to make it home for dinner. Plus, she looked incredibly sexy in scrubs. Couldn't leave that part out. I smiled at myself in the rearview, very aware of my blessings and counting them.

❖

I'd been counting the days until this year's Jamboree the way kids count down to Christmas. Beleaf it or not, pun intended again, BeLeaf had agreed to close the store at seven that night to make sure all employees could attend the event. As booth project manager, I would head over by three to set up, meet the delivery drivers, and retrieve the coolers and storage containers for our spread.

"What do you need from me?" Kyle asked, peering over my shoulder in the kitchen.

"It would be great if we could coordinate our schedules."

"Does that mean we can spend a little time at the fair together? Just us."

"If by *fair*, you mean Jamboree, then yes. I want to show you the ins and outs because you do not know what you do not know."

"And you're a professional."

"Don't you know it. You have to try the roasted ears of corn with all the spices."

"I'm intrigued. Keeping talking, Small Town."

I accepted my new nickname as a badge of honor. "Then there are the snowball cookies, the peppermint brownies, and Christmas tree cake pops."

"I can feel the sugar high already."

"You'll need to come hungry, because there's also a hot chocolate bar. I'm not kidding."

"Who would kid about that?"

She was humoring me. It was fine. She'd see the wonders of the Jingle Jamboree for herself soon enough. "And we have to make sure we don't miss the big finale. The choir from the Methodist church assemble themselves on these tiers that make them look like ornaments on a Christmas tree. It's really something to behold."

"Do you know what else is?" She placed a hand on her hip. "You when you get that excited twinkle in your eye."

"Say more." I offered a *keep it coming* gesture.

"The first time I saw it was when you told me about your Airbnb business. You were so fired up, and I thought it might have been the sexiest thing I'd ever seen."

I opened my mouth to speak, but the words evaporated. I was sexy on a first impression? No. I could imagine my sex appeal growing on someone over time, but it didn't arrive first. "I'm not sure I believe that. You thought I was sexy in the hallway of that hotel?"

"One hundred percent. I didn't want to leave but also didn't want to make it weird that I lingered."

I laughed and scrubbed my eyes. "I'm just having a difficult time processing this new take."

"Take all the time you need. It's what happened."

"Mm-hmm," I said, watching her. Her dark hair was down and little untamed, which made me imagine running my fingers through it. Probably my favorite look of hers.

"You affect me to a degree that it's distracting." She moved toward me, almost stalking. "It's awesome but also unnerving."

I stood taller. "Why unnerving?"

"Because I want to make you happy." She raised a shoulder. "I want you to be proud of me. And a little part of me hopes you think about me as much as I think about you."

"Trust me when I say that I do." I grabbed her hand and pulled her close to me. "Even when I didn't want to. So there."

"And now?"

"Now I love it."

"Love?" she proclaimed exuberantly with a smile before sinking into a kiss that left my body humming in happiness.

"I love a lot of things about us," I said.

"You're just throwing that word around willy-nilly now. This is remarkable. I think you might mean it."

"We are spending the holidays together. That's a pretty big deal."

"Not as big a deal as the Jingle Jamboree."

"It's super close. I don't know how I'll break the tie."

"You better stop," she said and kissed me again. Truth be told, I'd miss the next eight Jingle Jamborees for Kyle. I'd walk through fire. My feelings had run away from me and grew exponentially each day. She didn't need to know that…yet.

"I like the life we're cobbling together."

She pressed her face against my cheek a moment and then pulled back, meeting my gaze. "Confession time."

"Oh, no."

"I never imagined myself as a small-town kind of person. I like concrete. I like people everywhere on separate missions. It's one of the reasons I lived close to downtown in Charleston."

"Is there a *but* in there?"

"But since I've been here, I've never been happier." She paused. "I'm surprised by the differences I'm able to make at work. I like running into my patients in line for coffee. The pace has been good for me. Is there another shoe about to drop?"

I gripped the counter behind me. "I don't know." I felt the exact same way, but admitting it felt like inviting trouble. Lately, I'd kept my eyes forward, and it served me well. "I don't know what's ahead for us, but maybe we're not always here. Maybe you want to go back to the city. Maybe I'd like that, too. Doesn't mean the Bay can't be a somewhere we sneak off to."

Her eyes brightened. "Maybe this time, it's *our* house on the beach."

I threaded our fingers. "I could certainly get behind that."

"You're going to try to rent it out when we're not using it, aren't you?"

I laughed. "Well, I am a pro now. Speaking of which, I need to write a welcome card before my new tenants arrive. And leave Jamboree hints and tips."

"You're a busy woman."

"It's not like I'm a doctor or anything."

A pause. "Hey, are you serious? About maybe moving to the city someday, or even splitting our time?"

"I would move to the city with you, Kyle."

"And I'd stay in Dreamer's Bay with you, just so we're clear."

The sentiment landed square in the middle of my chest and spread out, my whole body going warm. "That means a lot."

"Well, so do you. The more time I spend with you, the more I dare to want."

Dare to want.

There were words hovering just beneath our exchange that neither one of us was saying. The big ones. The most important words of all. We'd get there, I told myself, not quite able to vocalize what I already knew to be true. I loved Kyle. I loved her quiet thoughtfulness. I loved the way she walked into a room and affected every person in it. I more than loved her intelligence and the way she saw the world. I loved the way she spoke to me. I loved our quiet talks. I loved our playful side. I loved her presence, her heart, her confidence, her everything. *I love you. I love you. I love you,* I thought with everything in me.

Yet I didn't pronounce the words. I wanted to and couldn't. Investing so fully felt like climbing a mountain in the fog. I wanted desperately to make it to the peak, but the path was obscured and dangerous. I'd lost too many people in my life to trust I wouldn't go tumbling off the side.

"Let's keep daring each other," I said instead. "In fact, I dare you to choose what we're having for dinner, because I'm out of brain cells." I was a coward and knew it.

Kyle opened the door to the fridge, keeping things light. She passed me a sly smile. "Look at me go."

CHAPTER TWENTY-TWO

Leaving the Nest

When it came to Kyle, I was stuck in neutral—engine idling, but not exactly able to move forward just yet, even though I wanted to. Fear was a tricky thing. I couldn't let the same happen when it came to Charlie. It was time to set things right between us, because I didn't like where we stood. That meant a faux liquor run was in order, and as the holidays approached, I decided to embrace the theme entirely.

"Hey," Charlie said as I came through the door, but he raised his eyebrows, which meant he was likely surprised to see me. Because he stood behind the counter near the entrance, I was left with the choice to pause and talk to him, or keep things breezy and go about my shopping. I planted my feet.

"Hi." I nodded a minute, nervous but refusing to acknowledge it. "I'm pretending I'm here for loaded eggnog."

"But you're not?" he asked, giving me very little back.

"No. I don't even like eggnog, which feels like a holiday sin, but alas." I shifted my weight. "I do plan to buy something, so no reason to throw me out."

He scratched the back of his neck, looking less than comfortable. "That's not really my management style."

"If you still hate me, that's okay. But I want you to know that I've always thought you were a great guy. You and Jill are an adorably sweet couple, and if I was ever going to have a brother, you'd be a pretty awesome choice." I held up a hand before he had a chance to respond. "And for what it's worth, your dad and I did submit for a DNA test. I don't want you to think that I'm just grasping at straws. I'm not out for any kind of personal gain from your family."

He nodded, regarding me. "That's good, because we don't come from much. We're not rich people."

"Me neither. And I promise, I'm harmless." I smiled, but he didn't say anything, making this whole exchange feel one-sided and slightly awkward. I looked behind me, trying to fill the space. "Yeah, so…I'm just going to shop now. Just grab a few things for the, uh, season." I backed away, which left me nearly knocking over an entire display of Fireball. His eyes went wide and an arm went out until the swaying stack settled. I turned back to him. "My bad. All's well. I think."

I'd said mostly what I wanted to say, which counted for something. This relationship, if there ever was going to be one, would have to take shape slowly and without me jackhammering it into what I wanted.

"Why don't we all have dinner some night?"

I whirled around to find Charlie standing at the end of the seasonal aisle, hands in the back pockets of his jeans. Facial expression dialed to tolerance.

"Me and Jill. You and Kyle. That's her name, right?"

"Yeah." I swallowed my overt surprise. "No, that'd be great. Dinner." I exhaled, enjoying the relief that washed over me.

"She came in here once."

"I'm sorry." I frowned, trying to follow the thread. "Who did?"

"Um, Dr. Kyle. She had a couple thoughts, so I listened."

"She did?" I blinked, thrown off guard. "Wait, you *did*?"

He shrugged. "I try to be polite when I can."

"Right. I just hadn't realized she'd stopped by." I took a beat, trying to decide whether I'd moved past it. Nope. Couldn't do it. "What did she say?"

"Mainly, she wanted me to know that your heart was in the right place and that you didn't ask for any of this either. That maybe you just wanted a chance to get to know me."

It was all true. "I would like that chance. So, yeah. Dinner. And maybe swing by the BeLeaf booth at the Jamboree."

"We'll make the tail end of it. I'm out at the other location this weekend."

"Jake mentioned something about that."

Charlie met my gaze. "He's been lighter since the two of you have been talking. I've never seen the guy smile with teeth before. But there they are." He paused a moment. "That's cool to see."

"I can definitely identify with that." It was inexplicable, but in the short time I'd spent with Jake, he'd done the same for me. He could never fill the space that Lindy had left, or my parents, but he'd begun to create his own. I truly hadn't anticipated any of this. I didn't know whether to hug Charlie or hold on to the lump in my throat until I could get to the car and cry properly. As confusing as this new family discovery had been, it was also a gift. A second chance at a family. And I was so damn grateful.

"I'll have Jill check her schedule for that dinner. Anything I can help you find?" He gestured to the four shelves in front of me.

"I'll just take these," I said, blindly grabbing for two giant bottles that were complete mysteries to me. It was only alone in my car that I looked down and laughed. "I guess we're doing peppermint bark shots tonight."

Apparently, it was meant to be. A lot of things were.

❖

"Wow. So, you're now planning social outings with your father and mending fences with your brother," Jonathan said, as we waited in the short line at the library. The new Sarah J. Maas novel was on hold for Jonathan, who was next on the wait list. He'd been counting the moments until he made it to the top.

"It's weird to hear you refer to them that way." We stepped forward, two back. "I'm not sure I've thought of them in those terms fully."

"I like to be ahead of all the fads." He laughed. Because we both knew it wasn't true. He was a proud nerd, one of the reasons I adored him.

"You could have knocked me over with a feather when Charlie suggested dinner. I was preparing for a lifelong nemesis."

"I wasn't. That guy is universally loved in this town for simply being nice and neighborly. I had a feeling he'd come around."

"Well, that makes one of us."

His smile dimmed. We stepped forward, second in line, now, to the front desk. "So, I have news."

"Tell me all of it. With the BeLeaf transition and our new, hot significant others, I feel like I'm falling behind."

"Well, the headline is that I'm leaving the nest."

I stared at him, not following the thread but feeling a little uneasy. "I might need some more information."

"Christian asked me to move to Austin with him, and I said yes." His eyes went wide, as if to say *Can you believe it?*

"Got your book right here," Darlene said, grabbing a copy from the circulation cart just as my world slipped into an alternate reality, one without Jonathan, my best friend. We'd been inseparable for two decades, and now we were going to follow each other on social media and wonder how things were going? No. I couldn't accept this.

Jonathan accepted the book in quiet victory, surely feeling the weight of this announcement and its effect on me. "The wait has been torment," he said politely to Darlene. I waited for him to finish checking out his book and followed him in silence to a nearby reading corner. One of the soft bench seats was open, and we snagged it and the privacy it offered. "I was waiting to tell you until we had a quiet moment."

"Is this real?" I asked. "You're honestly leaving?" My voice sounded like a squeak, stripped of all strength and semblance of normalcy.

"It's real." He shook his head as if marveling at all of this. He was a goofy kid at peak happiness.

My moment wasn't going as well. "But you two have only been dating a couple of months. Maybe a little more time should go by before you uproot your whole life. Maybe we could hit pause for a second so I can catch up. Maybe we should scrap this whole idea and rewind the last five minutes."

"I hear you. Yes, it's been quick. But these months have changed everything. Christian just gets me in a way no other guy has." He smiled the silly smile of someone gaga in love. "And he makes me feel like this fucking awesome catch, like *he's* the lucky one to be with *me,* which is just unbelievable."

"He *is* the lucky one," I said without hesitation. "And what about the periods of time when you're not feeling your best? Your support system is *here.*"

"He's been great on my more painful days."

I actually couldn't argue. Christian seemed to take great care of Jonathan when he wasn't at his best. They were a great match. I still didn't understand why they couldn't be a great match *here.* "Fantastic. All of it. But why the move?"

"He's been offered a promotion."

From what I understood, Christian worked in hospitality for Elite Resorts and managed a large beach property twenty miles away.

"It's too good to turn down. He said he couldn't imagine leaving me now, not after everything. Plus, I think it would be pretty cool to live in a city."

"Yeah," I said, dejected. "Pretty cool." The truth was, I couldn't be angry when all I'd ever wanted was for Jonathan to be happy. In fact, I rooted for him daily. And here it was, happiness on a platter. I couldn't make this about me, as much as I wanted to cry right now.

"Hey. We're gonna be just as tight as we always are." The tears in his eyes made mine well up. He was going to miss me, too. "We're just gonna have to live on FaceTime more than we're used to. You're gonna be so sick of my endless calls."

"Never," I said, leaning against him on the bench seat.

"And you're gonna need to rake up some frequent flyer miles."

"Imagine me, a jetsetter." We sighed in unison. Jonathan was leaving me. *My Jonathan.* Surreal. "When?"

"He starts the new job in six weeks, so we'll need to be there by then."

A pause. I looked up at him. "You love him."

"Yeah. I do." Another pause. "Do you love *her?*"

Way to throw it back in my court, I thought. I held on to his question a moment, making sure I gave it full weight. Finally, I turned back to him and nodded. "I do."

"Gonna tell her?"

"When it's right," I said. "Unlike some people, I like taking my time, enjoying the journey."

"That's not what this is," Jonathan said easily. "This is you looking both ways before crossing the very busy street."

"That's the thing about busy streets. They're dangerous. More often than not, you get smashed like a reckless frog. Do I look like a reckless frog to you?"

"I can honestly say I've never once called you that, even in private."

"There ya go. You, however, might be one."

He took a deep breath and pulled his shoulders to his ears, knocking me off him. "If this is what reckless frogs feel like, sentence me to the lily pad."

"When did we get to be so poetic?" I asked. "I'm really proud of us."

"Same. A pecan latte and some reading?"

I stood. "Sold."

The time we spent together that day was slow paced and awesome. We read our books, sipped our warm drinks, and chatted intermittently, as if we had all the time in the world. The only problem was, now I knew that wasn't true. There was an expiration date on our regularly scheduled friendship. I felt the tick-tock of every second that passed, knowing it was one fewer that we had together. I didn't know what I was going to do without Jonathan in my daily life. It was honestly something I never thought I'd have to face. We were supposed to find people to get married to, live next door to each other, raise our kids side by side, and watch them grow into the same caliber of best friends we were. This all felt horribly wrong, but what else was I supposed to do but support this person I loved as he reached for the life he longed for?

I could do this, hard as it was. I could adjust. For him. For my friend.

❖

I woke up the day of the Jamboree with a much-needed excited spring in my step. It felt like a special day, and that's because it was. I looked forward to so many aspects of today, it was hard to dim the smile that accompanied me from room to room as I prepared for work. Even the temperature was perfect. A crisp fifty-six degrees, ideal for a light jacket and warm cider by the bonfire later.

Unfortunately, it wasn't long before everything that could possibly go wrong at the store certainly did. First, the registers all froze at the same time, some sort of system-wide glitch. Then a pallet of cranberries overturned, leaving smashed remains all over aisle two like a scene from a Christmas horror flick. Customers tracked the smashed skins and juices all over the store like the footprints of a killer's hasty retreat. Maya had to go home early because her morning sickness was in full force and the cranberry massacre had triggered a strong bout of nausea.

Down a checker, the checkout lines, now entirely manual, were unusually long and customers were not happy. The general state of the store felt chaotic and unorganized to the point that I wanted to sit on the floor and give up. To help push myself through, I raced to the break room to grab a cup of coffee before heading back into the trenches, only to watch the machine sputter its last breath. *Noooo!* All my fault. I should have replaced the thing when it started acting up months ago.

"We'll get you a newer, fancier model," Peter said, and clapped me on the shoulder. At least he was here today. "I will happily make you a cup from it."

I'd say one thing: Having a boss like Peter had gone a long way. He was knowledgeable, collaborative, and kind. Because he lived a couple of hours away and oversaw a group of stores along the coastline, we only saw him about once a week. However, when he was around, he always found a way to improve our service and the store overall.

He was in town today for the Jamboree and had brought his wife, who also seemed like a down-to-earth, truly easygoing person. I'd promised her my blueberry muffin recipe, which I didn't give out to just anyone. It was all about the butter-salt ratio. "And please tell Maddie that the roasted turkey legs are all the way at the back of the park, near the winter wonderland. And if she wants to see the Dickensian carolers from a good spot, she needs to be near the Christmas tree maze twenty minutes before their start time. This town goes crazy for top hats. It gets rabid. I'm not even making that up. It's like their own personal boy band."

"Will do," Peter said. "And I get it. Top hats bring all the girls to my yard, too. Now, get out of here and set up the coolest booth ever. Feed the people. Make us famous."

"You think I can risk heading over with all this going on still?" I looked around the store that felt anything but calm. Mrs. Rabniki had just let out a little scream as Jim Deavers snatched the last box of cinnamon candy canes. I made a mental note to up the order next week.

Peter cracked his knuckles. "I'll open up register three myself. It's been a while, but I can scan groceries with the best of 'em. Look out, Dreamers."

Peter was honestly an adorable person with his shiny dark hair and glasses. Faber would have died before helping an actual customer. I enjoyed the rumors that Faber was nursing his wounded ego alone in his oversized house, pining for Harlowe while cursing her name at the same time, wandering around his front yard in his bathrobe, muttering curse words at passing pets. He'd rebound. People with money often did. But I planned to take solace in the little bit of karma coming his way in the meantime. Maybe he'd pick up an annoying case of the hiccups, too. Would serve the bastard right.

When I arrived at Bountiful Park, the wind whipped through the trees, which caught me off guard. It didn't feel like holiday wind whipping, and instead came with an undercurrent of foreboding. I paused in concern, wishing I'd checked out a more recent weather report. The BeLeaf booth would require some extra reinforcements to keep the salami slices from spiraling into the air and the cheddar cubes from tumbling into oblivion. I certainly didn't need my charcuterie table heading off to Oz on me. Maya was supposed to come with me to set up for the Jamboree, but it looked like I'd have to make do on my own.

"Need some help?" Elizabeth asked, appearing out of nowhere. She placed a palm square on the tablecloth to help secure it.

"God, yes," I said. I quirked my eyebrow. "You're here early." Elizabeth didn't have a booth to set up, and the hour before the Jamboree was reserved for vendors only. Not that I minded in the slightest.

"What can I say? I live for these seasonal events. Did you know I didn't sleep last night?" Her eyes were wide and happy. While Elizabeth and I were kindred spirits in our love for small-town culture, she did have me by a nose in the obsessed category. "Plus, I'm in charge of the bake sale table benefiting teen runaways."

"Of course you are." Elizabeth Draper had always been our resident saint and do-gooder. She participated in anything and everything there was to join.

"Put me to work." She placed a hand on her hip and quickly studied the early stages of my booth. "What do you need?"

"Any idea on how I can keep the wind from whisking all this away."

"Is that a real question?" she asked with a gleam in her eye. "I'll be right back."

We spent the next fifteen minutes using the Velcro and double-stick tape Elizabeth conveniently kept in her car for her odd jobs gig to secure anything that moved to the table. I dared the wind to attempt even the most modest lifting of our trays once Elizabeth straightened to survey her work. "Yeah, that's definitely going to do it. Now you just need to replenish enough and overlap the snacks so that they act as each other's weight and anchor."

"Food science comes in all forms."

She offered a high five, and I honored it with a hearty smack.

"Hey, there. I'm off early. Where's the people in the old-timey costumes?"

We turned at the sound of Devyn's voice, and without preamble, Elizabeth melted into her arms for a kiss. I should have looked away but was too surprised by their instant heat. Oh, they'd definitely been beneath the sheets a lot lately. Zero doubt in my mind, and good for them. Given the steam in my own relationship, there was no need for envy. These days, there was nothing to do but cheer them on. I knew that level of happiness now and could spot it in others. Speaking of which, I scanned the area for Kyle, wondering when I'd catch a glimpse of those blue eyes. She likely wouldn't make an appearance until an hour into the Jamboree, but I missed her and couldn't wait to experience the event hand in hand. Once the booth was up and running, I had a schedule for a few of my employees who were interested in clocking the hours, which would also allow me time to enjoy the evening. The wind hit hard, and a chill moved through me. That felt kind of ominous.

Devyn and Elizabeth turned to me, looking about as unnerved as I felt. "The weather's weird, right?" Devyn asked. "We weren't scheduled for any kind of storm, but it feels like something's in the air."

"Probably just a blip," I said, moving past it. I focused instead on the heavenly scent of gingerbread, cider, and something smoky on the grill a few yards away. I would definitely need to taste-test whatever it was before the night was over. This could still be fun.

An hour later, I had to retract the sentiment.

The wind had not only amped up but decided to bring its friends: rain, thunder, and lightning. The Jamboree had barely begun when the Christmas trees began to fall. The food that hadn't been blown away was getting rained on, and people were running for their cars chased by large raindrops that fell aggressively all around us.

As I began moving our supplies into the wagons beneath the L-shaped table, I caught sight of the bounce house in the distance sink in on itself. People rushed past with hoods on, clutching their holiday favors to their chests. A strand of gold garland flew by as the sound of holiday music was drowned out by the clap of thunder that rolled through the sky. I was worried about Kyle. I hadn't seen her, yet this was around the time she thought she'd arrive.

"I'm gonna take all this to my truck," Buster called.

"I'll be behind you with the rest in just a few minutes!" I yelled back. That's when I spotted KC Collette and Gray heading past the booth. I shielded my eyes from the rain with one hand. "Hey, KC! Have you seen Kyle anywhere?"

She shook her head, dark hair drenched against her forehead. "And I haven't been able to get ahold of Dan either. They were supposed to drive here together."

"I imagine traffic is a little chaotic. Where did all of this come from?"

"This whole storm was supposed to miss us," she called over the newest clap of thunder. "At least that's what Channel Five said this morning. This is madness! We better get out of this rain."

"Yes, and be safe!" I waved goodbye and spent the next five

minutes loading up the soggy remnants of my booth, heartbroken that the event was not to be and amazed by how much water my clothes were apparently able to absorb. As I pulled the second wagon full of ruined food and decorations to the park entrance, I took a moment to look back. The once festive scene had been replaced with a frantic scramble. Above all else, my brain kept repeating one key phrase: *Where is Kyle?*

CHAPTER TWENTY-THREE

Chain Reaction

Anything yet?

I stared at the text from Elizabeth, my stomach not quite right. I'd poured myself a glass of wine to settle my nerves, but now I didn't have the ability to drink it.

Nothing. It's been two hours.

Cell service had been spotty ever since the storm had rolled in, which could easily be why I hadn't heard from Kyle. The fact that Elizabeth's text had just made it through was encouraging. I took another lap around my kitchen, perched on top of one of the counters, and then jumped down again. I was restless. The downtime was doing nothing to help my brain. I needed to find a way to distract myself and relax, especially when the perfectly logical explanation for Kyle's silence was that she'd been held up at work.

On a mission, I headed to the couch, folded my feet beneath me, and grabbed my laptop from the end table. I could at least use this time to catch up on email and knock one thing off my to-do list. By the time I finished, maybe Kyle would be home or at least answering her phone. But I didn't get as far as my email because the page for the local news was up on my screen and auto-refreshed to a shot of several mangled cars on a highway. The headline glared back at me.

Multiple Vehicles Affected in Chain-Reaction Crash

No. We rarely had big accidents here. But I'd been through this before. I'd lost my entire world because of a car crash, and it was unthinkable to imagine it happening again. My stomach roiled, and I gripped the couch hard enough to break two nails. The weather. That was my next thought. The power of the storm had likely caused as much chaos on the roads as it had at the Jamboree. I didn't know what Dan drove or the model of car I should be looking for, which felt ludicrous, because this was a small town, and I knew what everyone drove! Didn't matter. I grabbed my keys off the counter, slid into my tennis shoes by the door, and sprinted in the rain to my car. Torn between heading to the highway just outside of town or straight to the hospital, I went with my gut. There would be more information available at the hospital, and hopefully, I'd find Kyle at work. All would be just fine. Then this sick feeling in my stomach could disappear forever, and we could get back to life as regularly scheduled.

When I arrived in the entryway of the ER, I found the waiting area more crowded and chaotic than I'd ever seen it. Tasha stood in the midst of the masses, holding a clipboard thick with forms. Hurriedly, she flipped between them as she spoke with the different groups of people. Not sure what to do, I stood off to the side, all the while scanning the nurse's station behind Tasha for any glimpse of Kyle or Dan. My chest ached with worry. My body was cold all over. I tried not to shake like a leaf but was wholly unsuccessful. A moment later, Tasha spotted me and came in my direction.

"Babygirl, what have you heard?" The look on her face was grim, and I didn't want her to say another word. I wanted to live in this space for always, a moment when I could believe that everything was okay. Because whatever Tasha was about to impart would be true forever and ever, and I wasn't sure I could bear it.

"Savanna."

I turned and there she was. Kyle. The relief was overwhelming, and I reached for a chair to steady my shaking legs. She looked drawn, tired, and worried.

"You're okay." I was already crying. My limbs went heavy.

"Are *you*? Are you hurt?" she asked, her forehead creased with concern. We walked toward each other at the same time, meeting in the middle.

"I'm fine," I said, wrapping my arms around her. "I thought…" I blinked, unable to voice the worst words ever. "I saw the news and got so scared. It was like my parents all over again." I sucked in air.

She frowned. "You thought I was in one of the cars."

"I did. I just had this feeling something was horribly wrong. But you're here." I squeezed her. "Thank God you're here."

"I'm fine, but—"

"And now that I've seen your face, I can get air." I pulled in more. "I can breathe again."

She nodded. "Let me just slow you down."

"You can do whatever you want now. You can run up a giant bill on my credit card or refuse to do another dish for the rest of your life." I laughed. "In fact, I'll do the dishes from now on."

"Hey, look at me, okay?" She said it rather forcefully, so I did. "Charlie was involved in the accident. He was working at his store's other location and heading back for the Jamboree."

"Oh." I took a few seconds as the meaning washed over me. "Charlie was involved. Where is he?" I asked quietly. Dread approached as if stalking me from behind. Charlie and I were supposed to have dinner. Our first dinner. He was my brother, and he was hurt. This was hard to fully process, yet I knew it was awful.

"They're working on him. He was alone in the car. I should actually get back but I'll stay in touch. Head home, but keep your phone with you."

"Kyle, is it bad?"

She hesitated.

"No. Don't do that." I refused to let go of her hand. "Tell me the truth."

The blood seemed to drain from her face and she nodded. "I'll do everything I can, but he's in bad shape right now."

"Please, Kyle. Listen to me. You have to save him."

The haunted look on her face was one I knew I'd never forget. She squeezed my hand. "I gotta go."

Alone, I looked around the crowded waiting room. Jake would be there soon. Charlie's mother. Jill. Kyle was right. I should wait at home and not insert myself in a moment where my presence might make anyone uncomfortable.

"You okay, sweetie? You want to sit down?"

I turned. Tasha. "I'm not sure. I'm not sure what I should do."

"It's been an awful night. Your girl is helping a lot of people."

"Is she okay?" I should have asked Kyle. The trauma onslaught might be a lot for her, given her difficult year back in Charleston. But it was like my brain didn't have enough room. I needed her to save Charlie, and we would sort out the rest after.

"I think so." Tasha looked back at the double doors leading to the ER. "But I'm sure this one is hitting them all pretty hard. They've already airlifted two patients to a larger facility. Unfortunately, we've had some fatalities as well." She'd said the last part in a whisper.

My stomach dropped. Sometimes I felt like we were isolated from larger tragedies in our tucked-away spot in the world. This was a grim reminder that we weren't.

I gripped the steering wheel harder than I ever had as I drove home, making deals with God and the angels and whoever else had control over the universe not to take Charlie from me when we hadn't even gotten the chance to get to know each other. I'd never had a sibling before, and I couldn't fathom losing him now. I tuned in to the local radio station searching for information, all the while my wipers working overtime in a monotonous dance. The storm still hadn't moved off us. I had no idea how they'd been so wrong about its trajectory. The news was reporting that six people in a passenger van had not survived what had been a head-on collision between two cars on the highway that ran between the towns. Eight others had been injured and transported as a result of the chain reaction. They were asking the rest of us to stay off the roads until the danger died down.

Once home, I sat on my couch with the lights off and watched the last system of lightning move through the sky in a show I would have thought beautiful if I didn't hold it responsible. I knew I wouldn't be able to sleep if I wanted to, so there I remained for what felt like an eternity. Earlier, I'd checked on my employees at the store, happy to hear that when the power went out, the backup generator had kicked in. I had BeLeaf's bankroll to thank. Next, I'd called my Airbnb guests to hear that they'd made it to Sal's for dinner before racing home when the storm intensified. They were safe and so was the house.

It was well after midnight when I heard from Kyle. "Hey, this is the first chance I've had to call."

"How is he?" I asked automatically.

"His family's here and gave me permission to officially update you on his condition."

"Okay." I exhaled slowly, feeling the need to stand, maybe to prepare myself for whatever was next. But Kyle had just said *his condition*. The fact that he was still with us was a blessing I hadn't overlooked.

"He's intubated and dealing with some bleeding in his abdomen. His left arm and collarbone are broken. He needs surgery, but we have to wait until he's strong enough."

"To survive?" I asked.

"Yes. Unfortunately, he's not stable at this point. His vitals aren't showing the kind of consistency we want and need. I'll be honest with you, tonight will be telling."

I closed my eyes and covered them with my hand. "And Jake? How is he?"

"Holding it together. He said he's going to call you in the morning."

I nodded. "I've taken the morning off. God, I wish you were here. Are you okay? Do you need anything? Food, maybe? I can deliver."

"They ordered some pizzas for everyone. I'll grab a slice at some point. I'm gonna stay here tonight."

"Okay." I was relieved she was there for Charlie and also worried about her, but not quite sure what to do in regard to the latter. "Take care of yourself, okay?"

"I haven't had to. Just staying focused."

She was holding it together. I could tell. But I wondered what would happen when she stopped moving. "Kyle." I didn't have the perfect words, but in the midst of worrying about Charlie, I didn't want her to feel like I wasn't there for *her*. "Please call me if you need anything."

"I'm good. Promise." I could almost see her forcing a smile. "What about you? You hanging in there?"

"I am." It was a helpless feeling, sitting around waiting, but that was literally my job at that point. To support everyone from afar.

"Whatever happens, we're going to get through this," she said. "I can just feel it." And for a moment, I actually believed it.

❖

It was the gnawing in my stomach that woke me up. I was still in my clothes from the night before, lying on my side on my couch. I blinked, taking stock of my surroundings and trying to catch up. It was light outside, and notably, the storm had cleared the way for the bright burst of sunlight that shot through my living room window. That's right. I'd slept out here. When had I last eaten? It was lunch the day before. I'd planned on dinner at the Jamboree, which had never even opened its doors officially before the world went to hell on a thunderclap.

I checked my phone. I had a missed call from Jake. Dammit. I gave my head a shake in search of clarity and called him back. With my hand to my chest, I stood upon his answer.

"Hey, there," he said.

"Hi. I saw you called an hour ago, but I guess I finally drifted off. How are things there?" It was a weird dance of not knowing how involved I was reasonably allowed to sound. I felt a little like a guest star on their TV show. Important, yet only adjacent to the main characters.

"They're holding as steady as they can be. Charlie gave us a bit of a scare a couple of times overnight, but he seems to have leveled off. They're saying he's more stable. His blood pressure is holding and his heart rate is good and strong."

I took a cleansing breath and my hand flew to the top of my head. "That's great news."

"They're looking at surgery in a few hours if he's still improving. He's been sedated, but hopefully they'll wake him up tomorrow if all goes well."

I squeezed the phone in gratitude. Things were trending in the right direction, and it felt like I could breathe.

"And hey, Savanna? Kyle's been just fantastic. Was here all night along with the other doctors."

I was flooded with both warmth and pride. "She's amazing."

He filled in a few more gaps about the accident. Charlie had been on his way back from the store's other location, a familiar commute for him, when he'd been involved in the accident. Jill had been a rock in spite of her own fear of losing him, and Jake was trying his best to keep a positive outlook.

"Thank you for taking the time to update me," I said.

"Well, kid, of course. You're part of us now. Though I admit, we're not at our best right now."

Tears sprang into my eyes. "Well, that means more than you realize."

"I'll let you know when there's more."

We ended the call, and I made myself something to eat before checking in at the store. Peter had taken the reins after we'd talked the night before, and he'd ordered me to take the day, if not more. I appreciated his kindness.

With Charlie doing better, at least for the time being, my focus shifted to Kyle. She'd need my support after the long hours and intense trauma. I decided to put together a little care package and a homemade meal and take it up to the hospital. I wondered if she'd gotten any sleep in the on-call room she'd told me about. After a shower, a meal, and assembling my delivery, it was close to lunchtime when I arrived at the hospital. The busy waiting room was much quieter, with the families either having gone home or moved to the rooms of their loved ones. Tasha was gone, too, and a woman I'd seen before but didn't know nearly as well sat in her place.

"Hi, I have a drop-off for Dr. Remington. Is she by chance available?" I peered behind her to the electronic double doors, but they were closed and quiet.

"I'll check," the woman said. Her name tag read Amelia, and she had kind eyes, not unlike Kyle herself, who I missed more and more by the minute. "She's actually not on this afternoon."

"Oh." That was a surprise. Maybe we'd crossed each other in transit. "Um, I guess I'll head home. I bet she's there."

"They said something about Charleston."

I frowned. It sounded like a mistake except for the fact that Kyle was actually from Charleston. Could it be a coincidence? "Is Dr. Collette available? Can you tell him it's Savanna Potter? I just had a quick question about my girlfriend."

Amelia nodded. "He's here. I'll see if he has a moment to talk."

Dan appeared a few moments later with shadows under his eyes. "Hey, Savanna. I told her to get out of here. She'd clocked so many hours this week, even before all of this. Because of our influx, we had some reinforcements from Billingsley Memorial, so I thought it was best she get some rest."

"What was it I heard about Charleston?"

He looked thoughtful. "I could have sworn she said she was heading back there for a bit. But don't quote me."

"No worries at all. I'll just check in with her." Confused and attempting to piece the puzzles together, I handed him the basket. "Lunch for you."

"Oh, that's very thoughtful. You sure?"

"Of course. Thank you for all you did last night for all of those people. For Charlie. You deserve it."

He nodded and gave my arm a pat. "We're all rooting for him."

I wandered back out to the parking lot, phone in hand, willing a text from Kyle. A call. Hell, I'd accept an owl with a letter to quell the concern that licked at my heels like a hot flame. I tried her phone again and then drove by the house to see if by some chance her car was in the driveway. The beach house also offered no sign. Where the hell had she gone? And why?

I found myself overanalyzing all our conversations for a clue. Did I do or say something that had upset her? I checked my phone again and then another eleven times in the course of the hour. It was only once my brain settled that I could clear away all the doubt and recriminations. Kyle was in distress, and if she left, she was likely in crisis mode from all she'd just been through. She was nervous about facing another big trauma, and this one had likely done a number on her.

I sent another text. This time I made sure my worry, my support, and yes, even my love came through.

I know yesterday had to be awful for you, but I'm so worried that I haven't heard from you. Tell me you're okay. I'm here. Come home.

I added a heart for good measure and sat on my front porch. Waiting. The sunshine and the crisp, cool afternoon didn't match the state of my world in the slightest. Yet here it was. A testament to my small grain of sand–like existence. Life went on all around me as my concern gained momentum.

Finally, two hours later, a reply from Kyle.

Charlie's gonna be okay. I'm rallying but might need space to hit reset. I came home for a bit. I want to be the kind of person you're proud of.

I was gutted but also split in two. On one side, my heart ached for Kyle after being thrown into the deep end before she was ready. On another, I wanted her to see me as a partner, someone to go through hard times with her. And she didn't. I wasn't sure how to process that information, because it felt pretty damn dire that we weren't in this thing together quite yet. What if we never would be?

I closed my eyes and sat back against the brick wall of my home. I would need to busy myself if I wanted to get out of this endless cycle of thoughts. I thought through my to-do list. I had a little time before heading over to the rental property to add my final touches once the cleaning crew finished. Email was always piling up, so I grabbed my laptop and settled in. Two new bookings were in my inbox, and I accepted both.

I clicked automatically on an email from the hospital, likely a bill for my ankle, which was feeling almost as good as new. Unless I overdid it, something Kyle had been staying on top of me about. Only this email contained a chart of some sort. No, a test result. That's when it dawned on me. These were the results of the DNA test Jake and I had both submitted for. My heart rate sped up and I scanned the first few lines. I skimmed past the table of DNA markers to the summary result halfway down the screen.

Probability of paternity: 0%.

What? No. Not possible. I stared at the sentence, the weight of it holding me hostage. It felt like someone had grabbed me by the throat and refused to let go. I couldn't move a muscle, which was a new sensation. I read the damning words again and again, but my brain hadn't yet caught up to their ramifications. And then it did. "He's not my father," I said out loud. "They're not my family." I stood and began to move, as if putting distance between me and the screen would somehow allow me to outrun reality. I looked back at it, lost and confused. I'd been losing people most of my life, but this felt like a cruel new way for the universe to make it happen. I was shaking. I only realized it because the table I gripped from behind now shook, too.

Well, this was certainly a twenty-four-hour period that would be hard to top. I was numb until the sun went down, which was actually a blessing. As evening descended and the darkness of early winter engulfed everything, the tears found their way to me.

I was alone, I realized. Not just physically in this room, but in life. Even Jonathan would soon be gone. And any attempt to remedy that loneliness came back to bite me like a snake hell-bent on teaching me a lesson. Well, I was ready to pay attention this time and throw in the damn towel. No more risk taking. No more reaching out to people asking them to love me. Because how pathetic, right? I was a puppy dog chasing after affection, and what had it gotten me? I'd keep my head down, do my job, and get through this life with as few scrapes as possible. I already carried too many scars.

My phone lit up with an incoming call. Apparently, I couldn't turn off my feelings instantly, because my chest squeezed and hope blossomed that I'd see Kyle's name on the readout. Not helpful. It was Jake. I wanted more than anything to talk to him about the email, or even better, have him tell me it was all a mistake and that he was my dad, after all. Nightmare: undone. If only. I answered the call.

"Hi, kid. Surgery's done and the doc says he came through it with flying colors." He added a relieved laugh. He was celebrating, which was entirely appropriate.

I smiled. "I'm so happy to hear it. What's next?"

He took a moment to update me on the steps they were anticipating for Charlie's recovery, which would certainly include some physical therapy once he had the strength. It wasn't until the end of the call that I quietly told him to maybe check his email, and that I would be thinking about him, and Charlie, and Peggy, and Jill.

"You got it. I'll call you soon," Jake said.

We ended the conversation, and I changed into a pair of shorts and tank top, slipped beneath the covers, and tried to forget that my best friend was moving away. My girlfriend was shutting me out (again), my parents and Lindy were still gone forever, and the new family I was just starting to fall for actually didn't belong to me at all. No biggie.

As I drifted off, I missed the arms that were no longer around me. The watermelon hair. The aquamarine eyes. How badly I longed for Kyle was a red flag. I wasn't allowed to keep the people I loved. I was more convinced of that than ever. Happily ever after was a joke, a convention dreamed up by the ad wizards of Hallmark as they ate low-fat yogurt in a drum circle. I had a mounting pile of evidence to dismiss the power of romantic happy endings handily. What was going to be harder? Convincing my heart.

CHAPTER TWENTY-FOUR

Hard Realizations

I didn't hear from Kyle for two days, and that was helpful. It gave me the opportunity to get good and jaded, and boy, did I ever. From the four walls of my living room, I constructed new ones around myself, keeping my feelings inside, behind lock and key and tucked away from anyone and everything with the propensity to work their way in. I was on guard and ready. Also, I was in bad shape and not quite sure how to rebound.

Kyle, who was apparently back in town, had left two voicemails and knocked once on my door. Sitting in my kitchen as she tried the doorbell a second time, I stared at the woodgrain of the kitchen table I'd inherited from Lindy and sipped the latte I'd had delivered by On the Spot.

"Savanna. I know you're home. Elizabeth told me she just had a coffee sent over."

Traitor, I mouthed.

"Please at least consider coming to the door so we can have a conversation about all of this." A pause. "And I know you can hear me. I lived here for over a month."

I walked to the front door and leaned against it. "Kyle, I can't right now, okay?"

A pause. "Can't or won't?" Her voice was quieter now.

I pressed my face to the door and then remembered myself, straightening. "Both," I answered honestly.

"Give me thirty seconds of your time and then I will walk off this porch and allow you space." Another pause. "I have a shift in twenty-three minutes and you know I like to be early. There's your guarantee. And if you're mad, you can be mad at me with the door open."

I sighed. It might be the only way I was going to get on with my morning. I stood and opened the door in my giving-up joggers, worn-in purple flannel, and bare feet. Not my best look, but I was embracing the hermit shouting *I don't need anyone* from the mountaintop vibe.

"Hi," Kyle said, brightening to a small smile. She also looked nervous and maybe like she hadn't slept. "Thank you for coming to the door. I wanted an opportunity to explain myself. The little disappearing act I'm not exactly proud of."

"Yeah. Okay. We can do that." My voice sounded flat, but there didn't seem to be much I could do about that.

"Okay, and now that I have you here, it's almost as if every thought I wanted to impart to you has flown straight out of my head." She studied me and frowned. "Are you okay? First of all, I mean. You've had a rough few days." And it likely showed.

She was referencing Charlie, who was now awake and working through soft foods. A true improvement, a near miracle if I understood correctly. I wanted to see him, but it seemed like a burden he didn't need at the moment. Someday. I wasn't exactly family anymore. He would know soon enough.

"It was a hard few days. Completely agree. And you weren't here for them." It wasn't an accusation. The time for that, and the anger that came with it, had passed. I was resigned now. Numb. It was what it was.

She nodded. "That's true. I hate myself for it more than you know. I was dealing with my own pain, my own mental health issues, and I fell back into an old pattern."

"Running away."

"Apparently so. It's a defense mechanism that's fairly new, which means I'm learning how to mitigate it." She looked to the side in contemplation and back to me. "But in the time that I was gone, I did some thinking and came to some hard realizations."

I placed a hand on my hip. While I was willing to listen, I couldn't leap back into what we'd been. Everything in me had slammed on the brakes because there was no way I was careening into a brick wall again when every indication said that was exactly what would happen if I continued to play house with Kyle. Temporary happiness was a wonderful thing but still quite, in fact, temporary.

"I have some demons I'm working through, admittedly, and some of the moments I experienced in the ER this week were so similar to what happened last summer." She shook her head. "It was like I was back there all over again."

My heart went heavy. I hated imagining her in any kind of struggle. "I was worried that was the case."

"I stayed focused, though. Calm and clearheaded. I held it together through every moment of patient care. I was proud of my work that night and the work of the whole team." She smiled. "God, Savanna. You should have seen them." She gave her head a shake and then something came over her. Her demeanor shifted. She darkened. "But the second I clocked out, I came undone."

I wanted to wrap my arms around her but instead wrapped them around myself. "That must have been awful." I met her gaze. "I could have been there for you. I would have been."

"I should have let you. I wasn't quite sure how to process my emotions, how to handle the onslaught. Here's where I went wrong." She took a breath. "I forgot to consider that it's not just me anymore. It's us. At least, that's what I want. And if there's an us, it means I have to let you in. I have to let you help, and I have to help you right back."

I didn't say anything, so she pressed on.

"Savanna, I promise you transparency and communication in the future." She swallowed as if to slow down. "Bottom line, I'm committed to being present and working through my own struggles so that I don't hurt you again." She shifted her weight, a move parallel to our own shaky ground. "I have so much more to say, but I think that was more than thirty seconds. I'm sorry I went over." She sent me a small smile that, knowing her, was meant to break the tension hanging, thick and uncomfortable, between us.

Her explanation made sense, and under different circumstances would have been reasoning I could work with. The problem was that I had nothing left to give. I was barely holding on through this conversation. "These are all good words and sentences. And beyond that, I believe that your intentions are good. But I'm at a spot where I can't intertwine myself in the way I could even last week." She blinked. "I need a break from the world, Kyle. It's been too much. In the midst of you taking off, I got the paternity test back. It was only meant to be a formality, but it showed that Jake's not my biological father."

"Oh no," she said, brow dropping. She took a step forward and stopped herself, likely picking up on my stay-back energy.

"You don't have to say all the appropriate platitudes. I promise. It won't do any good, but I appreciate the effort. The reality is that I'm not equipped for this right now," I said, gesturing between us. "I'm not sure if I ever will be, and that's the honest truth. I'm not trying to hurt you or punish you, but I'm instead doing what's right for me."

Her beautiful blue eyes blinked at me helplessly. "I'll wait."

"Kyle."

"No. It's my choice. Take whatever time you need, but just know that I'm here. And I'll be waiting for you because you're worth it." She shrugged. "That's all there is to it." Her eyes filled with tears and she sent me a sweet smile. I could tell she wanted to say more but held herself back. Finally, she sucked in air. She had a shift to get to. A burst of panic rose in my chest because I didn't want her held captive in Dreamer's Bay, especially when I doubted my own ability to give myself over again.

"I'm broken, Kyle," I called after her, as she opened the car door. It was my way of releasing her, letting her know that I'd never be who she needed me to be again.

"You're the most perfect person I've ever met just as you are," she said without hesitation. The way she looked at me in that moment would go on to haunt me for the next few sleepless nights and beyond. She'd headed to her car next, back to the hospital where she would attempt to pick up the pieces of her own life, just as I did mine. Two souls trying to get by. I dove beneath a blanket on my couch, turned on the TV, and stared at the screen, hoping it would whisk me away.

I'd pack the drawer Kyle had been using and return her belongings soon.

I'd go to work the next day and smile at my customers and pour myself into making BeLeaf the most amazing hometown grocery store ever seen.

I'd get by. I would. I'd just do it without the highs and lows this time. It was called surviving, and I planned to get really good at it.

❖

January 2 had always felt like a rest to me. The magic of the holiday season fades away and the transition into something new takes its place. Life returns to normal after the break from work and school, but streets are quieter, offices a little more empty.

This year, on January 2, I was saying goodbye to my very best friend, making the details of everything else seem like a blur. I stood at the end of Jonathan's driveway, hands shoved into my green puffer coat, white knit cap on my head, the one Jonathan always said made me look like a Twinkie, and watched as Christian helped him down the driveway toward the U-Haul they'd rented for the last of their smaller belongings. Christian's buddy would be following them and delivering Christian's car. Jonathan was only using one of his forearm crutches, which meant his pain was mild today.

"You two are going to be the cutest couple in Austin. Not even a contest," I called.

"Wait till they see my purple arm crutches," Jonathan said as he approached. "Do Texans appreciate sassy mobility aids?"

"They do," Christian said automatically. "I called ahead." He flashed me a wink and offered my hand a supportive squeeze before rounding the truck to the driver's side. He was giving us our moment, the moment I still couldn't fathom was here.

"I'll need live texting of the entire drive," I told Jonathan.

"Not something you ever have to ask for. You're getting descriptions of every farm animal and pie shop we encounter. Possibly in combination."

"I hear cows love homemade apple. Fresh tip for ya." I tried to laugh. It didn't work. We stared at each other for a moment. In that span of time, the first moment I'd met Jonathan came rushing back to me. I'd walked into that GSA meeting in high school and seen him alone in the room sitting in the circle of classroom chairs he'd assembled. He'd looked so nervous, wearing his lime green sweater with Davie Bowie on the front. He'd held on to that sweater well past the growth spurt that hit the following year. That was Jonathan, undyingly loyal and a little in love with David Bowie.

"So, are we still FaceTiming from our respective libraries next week?" He was nervous. I could hear the shaky quality of his voice. I very much identified.

"Jon-Bon. Are you kidding? I'm taking you to the pods with me. We'll just have to share one this time." I heard the wobbly quality of my own voice and ignored the ache in my throat. I was doing a pretty good job of holding it together but also didn't know how much longer I could go. "Now get outta here. Texas is waiting. There's chicken fried steak to dig into." Cue the emotion.

On that note, Christian came over and pulled me into a tight hug. "Hey. I've got him. You hear me?" he whispered in my ear. "I'll make sure he has everything he needs. And above all else, I plan to do everything I can to make him happy." He pulled back and met my eyes. "My one and only goal."

"Thank you," I said in a strangled voice and kissed his cheek.

Christian leapt into the driver's seat, and I turned to the person I depended on more than anyone else. The anchor to my storm. "I wish you didn't have to go," I whispered.

He nodded and his eyes filled. Wordlessly he opened his free arm and I moved into it, wrapping my arms around him and holding on tight. In that embrace, I let our full history wash over me. All the laughs we'd shared over chips and queso after school let out, and the quiet moments after a rough day when Jonathan had been bullied—I'd held his hand and we'd sat together on my steps, talking or not talking. We'd helped each other through some pretty difficult times. He was still doing that for me. God, this town wouldn't be the same without him.

"I love you," he said quietly.

"I love you, too," I said, pulling back and saying the last part to his face. I gave his shoulders a little shake. "I want you to take it easy when you get there. You tend to get excited, overdo, and pay for it later."

"Good advice. I promise I will." We shared a final smile, he squeezed my hand, and he made his way to the passenger side of the truck. I stood there watching as the U-Haul pulled away and lumbered down the residential street that would always be Jonathan's to me.

Alone in that driveway, the wash of memories swarmed in a jumble. I was dancing with my parents in the living room on my birthday, my mom singing loudly with Fleetwood Mac. I was making spaghetti with Lindy in her kitchen as I learned about spices and the way they fold into each other. I was having a sandwich on my lunch hour with Jake, shooting the breeze about how easy it was to get a fishing license these days. And then lying in Kyle's arms when the sun slanted across our skin through the large picture windows, happy and peaceful. Jonathan was the last one to leave me, and God, I didn't want to let go.

"Just me now," I mumbled to myself and to no one. I kicked a group of pebbles and began my walk home as they scattered. Fitting.

CHAPTER TWENTY-FIVE

Safety First

January passed in a series of overcast days that made my foot ache and seemed to match my less than sunshiny disposition. I appreciated the weather-driven backup that bolstered my rejection of, well, everything warm and fuzzy. Except at work. There, I still behaved like the belle of the grocery ball because that's what my customers deserved. With clearance from BeLeaf, I'd put a lot of my quirkier ideas into action on the floor, staying late and bringing them to life one at a time. Our store was no traditional BeLeaf Foods. We stood out, carrying a charming, small-town vibe. I pushed back against anything that felt too sophisticated or sleek. It just wasn't us.

My first installation was a partnership with Amazin' Glazin','who provided us with several dozen trays of apple cider donuts to sell throughout the morning. I'd commissioned Henry's Humble Hammer to make me a rustic-looking stand with a gabled roof that we could nestle in the corner of our baked goods section. It was already wildly popular, and we generally ran out of donuts by ten a.m. each day. The tourists absolutely loved our Cider Shack and didn't seem to mind the mark-up over donuts they could buy for a cheaper price just down the road. Amazin' Glazin' loved it, too, and was our new partner and best friend. I loved improving our business-to-business relationships, and so did BeLeaf corporate. They'd told me more than once to continue to cultivate them.

"Listen, they love what you're doing out here," Peter told me one afternoon. "You're also building trust with each successful idea you implement. They also very much value the store's unique personality. In fact, the Carmichael family is now personally encouraging its other stores to find small ways to embrace their own communities more, using your branch as the model."

"Really?" I sat a little taller in the break room, apple cider donut frozen on the way to my mouth. It was the exact opposite of my relationship with Donald Faber. Well, that was something to celebrate. And I was learning to relish the small joys that came my way. I needed them. "I was thinking, next, we could get one of those Chiquita Banana animatronics to sing on the wall above the bananas. People around here would eat that up. So would the tourists. We'd be all over TikTok."

He stopped stirring his coffee and stared at me. "I've learned not to question your instincts, but I can't tell if you're serious or not."

"I'm more serious than a *60 Minutes* reporter interviewing a Republican."

He smiled and sipped the last of his black brew. "Write an email. Plead your banana case. As I said, you have currency these days." He stood. "Good seeing you. Store looks great."

"Why, thank you."

Ten minutes later, I found myself in front of the banana section wondering if it might also benefit from an official name. What if next to the singing animatronic banana, there was a sign that read "The Top Banana" or "The Peel Palace" or even just "Go Bananas!" That last one was growing on me.

"Hey, Savanna. What kind of spell have these bananas cast over you? You been staring at 'em for a good two minutes."

I turned to see Jake pushing a cart with nothing but ice cream gracing its depths. I squinted. "This is what I do when I market. I speak to the product and it speaks back. These are show bananas." I motioned to his cart. "Either you have a function coming up, a really fun one, or you've developed a sweet tooth that might come back to bite you at your next jaunt to the dentist."

"We're doing a little welcome home party for Charlie. He's out of the rehab facility and doing great. Looking at returning to work at the liquor store next month. Wanted to see if you'd join us for the celebration."

It had been some time now since we'd learned the news from the blood test. Jake had given me a call after receiving the results. I'm sure it was a lot for him to process in the midst of his son's recovery, or maybe it wasn't. Maybe it had been a relief. I'd never really know. He'd said all the right things. We'd promised that this didn't have to change much, but of course, it had. We were friends now, though, and exchanged smiles and hugs whenever we ran into each other. We had a unique connection, and though he wasn't my dad in the end, he'd been one to me for a little while. That counted for something.

Shortly after that phone call, Jonathan had turned to me from his spot on my couch and posed an important question, one that I'd asked myself from the moment I'd received the emailed results. "So, if Jake Kielbasa is not your biological father, then who is?"

"I don't know," I told him. "But maybe that's okay, too. In fact, it is. I'd rather live with the wonderful memories I have of my own father than chase down some DNA I know nothing about. I have a feeling no one is going to be able to top him anyway." I sent Jonathan a reassuring smile because there was a divot low on his brow. "Hey. I'm going to be okay. I have a dad, and I'm pretty sure he's with me a lot of the time." It'd taken some sleepless nights to come to that conclusion, but I was honestly feeling good with it. It was time to leave the lineage question right where I'd found it.

I turned to Jake, who was waiting on my answer. "Yeah, I like ice cream. I hope you have some chocolate in there. My mom's favorite."

"More than a little. Saturday at four work for you? You can come by anytime you like, really. Bring Kyle."

I dimmed at the mention of her name. I hadn't rebounded from the loss and thought of her more than I was supposed to, according to the new me. I saw her here and there, always surprised she'd chosen to stick around. She was still out at the beach house and still impressing everyone at the hospital, from what I heard. When Jonathan moved, she gave me a hug in line at Brewed Awakening, and my knees had nearly buckled as the scent of watermelons whisked me back to happier times, like a white-water raft in a fast-moving river.

Returning to Jake, I scanned my schedule, which was empty. Not exactly a surprise. Most of my dates these days were with wine and a murder documentary on my ever-worn couch. "Totally free," I told him. "But it will just be me. Kyle and I are not…" I sent him a grimace that I hoped filled in the blank.

"No? But she's great." He seemed supremely disappointed, which I, of course, understood. Normal people don't take a step back from a woman like Kyle, even when she's not at her best. I was not normal people, but rather, someone cursed with endless amounts of loss who couldn't help but expect more.

"She is. No denying that. We just aren't as compatible as I once thought."

"Well, that's okay, too." He leaned in. "You know Peggy and I once broke up for three months before finding our ride into the sunset. Could be you."

"Yeah, but it won't be," I said as lightheartedly as possible. Giving Jake hope might leave me with some, too, and that wasn't helpful.

I spent the rest of the afternoon on my laptop in the office, putting in orders for next week, when a beautiful bouquet of very expensive-looking flowers was carried into my office by Henrietta, who looked incredibly impressed. "Someone is thinking of you, my sweet girl, and I, for one, am dying to find out who."

I had a feeling I knew. "She shouldn't have done that," I said quietly, wondering how much money these gorgeous things actually cost. Henrietta placed the huge vase of flowers in front of me on the desk and presented the card. When it was clear she had no plans to leave, I reluctantly opened it, afraid of what it might do to my heart.

Heard things didn't work out. Call me sometime?—MJ

I was honestly surprised. Just MJ exploring possibilities, it seemed. I'd let her know that I loved the flowers but was out of the romance game for good.

"From Dr. Kyle?" Henrietta asked with a smolder. "Is she fighting to win you back? Wooing you, as they say? Maybe give her another chance. I'm not sure what went wrong, and that's not my business, but you had a light in your eyes over the holidays that's not there anymore. You're a dark hole now."

"Ouch."

"Not that there's anything wrong with that."

"There's a lot wrong with that." I placed the card back in the envelope, sidestepping the comment. "The flowers are from MJ, actually. I think she's testing the waters. Unfortunately, the waters aren't inhabitable. At least for that kind of company."

"Definitely not." Henrietta frowned as if wishing for a redo on that card. It was clear she was Team Kyle and sorely let down. "But what about Dr. Kyle? The waters might be different for her."

"What about me and water?"

We both turned at the sound of the rich, warm tone. I knew that voice as well as I knew my own. Probably no amount of time would change the dizzying effect it had on me. I sat up straighter, wondering just how much she'd heard.

"She's here!" Henrietta shrieked as if having conjured Kyle personally. She held out a hand to show me in case I was suddenly unable to observe for myself.

"I see that."

A grin erupted across Henrietta's face, because of course it did. She was a woman obsessed with romance novels and seemed to think one was playing out in her midst. It wasn't. She was looking at two mature adults working on navigating the terrain *post-romance*, if anything.

"Hi," Kyle said, offering Henrietta a wave. "That was quite a greeting."

"Hi," Henrietta said in a voice reminiscent of a kid in awe of Santa. Seeming to remember herself, she straightened and headed for the exit. She paused in the doorway and placed a hand on Kyle's biceps. "I knew you'd come."

Kyle turned and watched her leave before swiveling back to me. "What was that about?"

"I'm not even sure I could tell you. Henrietta is an unpredictable character."

"Ah. I see." Her gaze trained on the flowers, which were a third the size of my desk. "Let me guess. MJ?"

"You're astute." I laced my fingers and rested my chin on top. God, it was good to see her. I couldn't deny that part. The room felt entirely different now that she was in it. I offered a soft smile that Kyle returned.

She jutted her chin at the bouquet. "And you're not interested in those flowers." It was a gentle statement.

"Not especially. What brings you by? Not that it's not nice to see you."

"Milk, most predominantly. With a side of dog biscuits. There's this adorable mutt with shaggy brown fur that runs up and down the beach. I've been hitting him up with treats when he comes by so we can be friends. I think he's my neighbor's dog from two doors down."

"I didn't know you were a dog person."

"In a big way. I'd like one, but I don't want him or her to be lonely when I'm pulling twelve-hour shifts."

She was thinking of the imaginary dog and what might be best for them, rather than what she wanted. It went along with everything I knew about her.

"Maybe one day. I think you'd excel at the job of dog mom."

"Best compliment ever." She tapped the doorframe. "Okay. I'll let you work. Just wanted to say hello."

"Good to see you, Kyle." There were so many other words threatening to burst from my chest, but I held them back, remembering my chosen path. Safety first these days. My new motto. "About the flowers? I want you to know something. I won't be sending any of those, but only because what you need right now is space. You've asked for it, so that's what you're going to get. However, just know that I'm here. Your friend if you need one, and I'm not going anywhere. Okay? I'm here because you are, and that's not going to change." She nodded, tapped the doorframe again. "I hope your day is amazing. I'm gonna grab some milk and then sleep for about six hours."

"Okay," I said because I had no other response to offer. Sitting at my desk alone, I was off-kilter, adrift in this new understanding. Kyle hadn't left town because of *me*.

She was still here, for *me*.

That was…a new feeling I wasn't sure how to ward off. So instead, I tucked it away. I'd be lying if I said it hadn't been really nice to see her in the middle of my day. I turned to my screen because a distraction was definitely in order. I was getting good at utilizing those. Plus, the cereal wasn't going to order itself while I sorted through the last ten minutes of my life. I clapped my hands in front of the screen and wiggled my fingers as they descended onto the keyboard. "Let's go, Cap'n Crunch."

CHAPTER TWENTY-SIX

Floppy-Necked

Was it selective perception that I seemed to have short little run-ins with Kyle all over town? Maybe even just coincidence. Or was it more likely that she was consciously keeping an eye out for me?

"I promise I'm not stalking you," Kyle said when I ran into her at the card and stationery store. Well, that was a semi-answer to my question. She seemed to be perusing the small grouping of journals one aisle over. She wore jeans and a brown leather jacket, an outfit that I refused to give too much attention to. *You hear that, brain?*

"Well, we do live in a tiny town," I said around the mountain of heart-shaped pillows that separated us. With Valentine's Day just days away, the store looked like Cupid had moved in and personally decorated, without parental supervision.

"Are you two finding everything you need?" Sariah Bright asked. The name was fitting because this woman was always smiling, even when it looked like it pained her to do so. She had her long dark hair in a ponytail today that swung to and fro when she walked. Sariah could easily be described as very happy Hallmark. Very much appropriate for this store. However, in my less-than-thrilled-with-life era, she came across as very much annoying.

"I am. Thank you," I said, applying extra interest to the *You're Doing Great* greeting card I perused for Charlie. I placed it back in its holder and selected a second one. A tortoise in a bandage with the line *Slow and steady wins the race. Get your rest!*

"Fantastic," Sariah enthused. "Dr. Kyle?" Everyone apparently called her that these days. I couldn't blame them. It worked. Respectful yet personable. Kyle deserved as much.

"So these are two for one?" Kyle asked, holding up the leather-bound journals in a variety of colors.

"Until close of business tomorrow they are," Sariah said in a singsongy voice. She had to stop with the happiness bombing. I'd pen a letter to management, but if I remembered correctly, that was also Sariah.

Once she'd swung her ponytail back to the counter, I peered over the hearts at Kyle. "Taking up writing?"

"Yes, in a way." She came around the corner for a more one-on-one exchange. I had the feeling she didn't want to broadcast what she was about to say. "After my struggles in the ER, I went back to Zoom sessions with my therapist back home."

"Oh, yeah?" That was an interesting development. Something adjusted in my chest, and I softened. "Kyle. I think that's great."

"It has been. She's given me some helpful exercises to work through some of those fight or flight instincts." She held up the short pile in her hands. "I've been journaling on my breaks and thought I'd pick up reinforcements." She flashed a killer grin. "Plus, who doesn't love a good sale?"

"Sariah certainly agrees." My attempt at levity. I touched the journals. "This is a good move. I'm"—I was about to say *proud of you*, but the intimacy attached felt like a step too far, given the barriers I had purposely erected—"thinking that's a good-looking group of journals, too."

She looked down. "I like them, too." She took a step back as if she was about to take off and pay. "How have you been? Good?"

"Me? I'm working a lot." It was about all I had to offer. I wasn't good. I was lost in a loop of trying to forge a new path forward while grieving for the things I'd almost had. I kept myself on a short leash when it came to feeling my own feelings and wondered how much journaling a therapist might prescribe me. Maybe I should pick up one of those things while it was on sale.

"Well, I know it's busy at the store, and the changes are honestly so much fun," she turned her head to the side, her hair cascading over one shoulder, "but find time for some things that make you happy. Grab some ice cream on the boardwalk. That kind of thing."

"I broke up with you and you're still looking out for me?" I had meant that to be an internal thought.

Kyle cradled the journals at her side like a bundle of schoolbooks. "Always. That's what I've been trying to tell you. I'm not going anywhere." She met my gaze and held it. "I hope you find the perfect card."

I looked down at the tortoise candidate in my hand, the pleased grin on his little tortoise face. I allowed myself to enjoy it because just as Kyle had reminded me, it was the little things. Maybe I could make more of those add up. I had a library FaceTime with Jonathan tomorrow. I could maybe even allow myself to look forward to it.

"Someone is dreaming about Valentine's Day," Sariah said as she passed behind me. I realized that I, too, was grinning like my tortoise friend. Just to be nice, I didn't even correct her.

But that certainly wasn't the last time Kyle and I circled each other in this town. I found myself anticipating when the next encounter might be, my skin prickling with goose bumps whenever I even thought I'd catch sight of her. Our exchanges were always short, low pressure, and actually really nice. We checked in on each other, exchanged smiles across rooms, and Kyle, to her credit, was always entirely respectful of my romantic boundaries and never crossed any lines.

I saw her at least once a week at BeLeaf, often in line for coffee in the morning, sometimes on the sidewalk in the heart of town, and more often than not at Ronnie Roo's on the night of key sporting events. I now realized the full extent of her interest in, honestly, all sports. It was the early celebration of MJ's birthday that stretched the limit of our friendly/supportive interactions. MJ, who'd been incredibly understanding when I yet again let her know that romance was not in the cards for us.

"I knew you'd say that," she said, leaning up against her car in front of BeLeaf. "But those flowers were killer. Were they not?" She popped sunglasses on and grinned.

I wondered what it was like to come with that brand of confidence. MJ just might own the world one day, and I looked forward to watching her conquer it. "They were damn beautiful. You know how to send 'em."

"Thank you. Come to my birthday gathering at Ronnie's next week."

"Yeah? I'd love to."

"You can buy me a platonic drink."

"You're on."

The gathering, it turned out, was no small affair. The group of MJ celebrators had taken over half the restaurant. After only being in town less than a year, she'd managed to collect a lot of friends. Even Kyle?

"I'm a little surprised to see you here," I said, forearms on the bar next to hers as we each waited for service.

"Why is that? MJ and I are mature adults. She was pumping gas next to me today and told me to come. I follow orders, especially on my nights off."

The whole time she was talking, I was captivated by the sound of her voice. I realized I missed it and I wanted nothing more than for her to keep speaking. The easiest way to make that happen was a question. "How are things going at work?"

"A lot better. I've found my groove, and use my outlets whenever there's the slightest hiccup."

Before I could answer, Sean was in front of us responding to Kyle's gesture for two. He placed a frosty longneck in front of her and poured a dirty martini from his shaker for me. He knew our orders because of course he did.

"I owe you one," I said, accepting the drink.

"No, you don't," she said over her shoulder with a smile that showed off the dimple that would never not snag my entire focus. As she disappeared with her beer into the throngs, I gave my head a little shake. God, she scared me more than any other human being. She just happened to have a medical degree and my heart. Neither were easy feats.

I spent the rest of the night moving from group to group, chatting my face off. Martinis came and went like celebrity marriages. Time felt strange and so did my balance. I always knew I was drunk because my neck muscles checked out on me. I became floppy-necked and rather ridiculous, which was what was happening to me now.

Elizabeth caught my gaze across the room and crowd-surfed over. "You look worried."

"Is that code for overserved?" I asked. I blinked to clear my wayward vision. "What does Sean put in these things?"

"How many have you had?"

"Enough to dull the pain that decades of loss have dumped on my plate."

Her eyes went wide. This was likely more than Elizabeth Draper had planned to handle on one little birthday party evening.

"You can relax. I'm just wallowing. But maybe five? That might be a lifetime record." All my fault, too. The Kyle feelings and bar conversation had me wishing I was by her side tonight and arguing with myself all over again about why love and lust should be kept separate at all costs, and then to silence that argument, "Another martini, Sean!"

"Would you like to sit down?" Elizabeth asked.

"No. I'd love the love and lust intersection to take a seat, though."

"The intersection?"

"The double whammy. Those are the ones that get ya."

The room was too loud. My stomach was too sideways. I needed a murder doc and my PJs with the blue squigglies on the side. "I'm gonna close out and walk home."

"I'll walk you," Elizabeth said without hesitation.

She was, after all, the town do-gooder. She'd likely never gotten drunk in her life. Wait. Not true. I seemed to remember her singing on top of a roof one New Year's Eve. I was taking back her points.

"I volunteer as tribute," a calm voice said.

I turned to see Kyle standing next to us. "No, no, no," I said. "You're literally a walking intersection and you know it. Just look at you. Where's the caution tape?" I made a circular gesture. "Wrap her up, Draper." Whoa, the circle thing left me spinning.

Kyle frowned and Elizabeth squinted at me. "You keep saying *intersection.*"

"Don't worry about it, Elizabeth." I emphasized her name, unsure why I'd labeled her my enemy but I was running with it. "Only I need to know about intersections."

"Can I know? Since I am one?" Kyle asked, hand raised.

"No."

I looked around, weighing my escort options. Elizabeth Draper, my sworn birthday party enemy, or Dr. Soap Opera from the Land of Dimples.

"Sold," I said and pointed to Kyle. I passed Elizabeth a drunken glare.

"You're in rare form tonight," Elizabeth said.

I squinted, trying to filter out the glare from the track lighting above her head. "I can agree." I swiveled to Kyle. "Ready?"

"I think so?" Kyle said, her look dialed to *What am I getting myself into?*

We skipped saying goodbye to MJ, who was too busy being regaled by her guests to notice anyway. We hit the sidewalk and began our eight-block journey to my house in silence. That was good. Who knew what I might throw at her? My thoughts were leaping the gate to my mouth as if on their way to a Black Friday sale. Every so often, I would feel Kyle's hand on the small of my back, steering me back onto the sidewalk. That part was nice.

"Is it?"

"What?" I asked.

"You just said it was nice after I steered you back on course."

Happened again. "Dammit. You're not supposed to hear that stuff."

"I'll try not to listen." She attempted to smother her smile, but I saw it anyway.

The walk was actually helpful, the cold air filling my lungs. The cleansing effect was welcome and I felt a little of myself—and my logic—returning to me as we neared my place. Thank God.

"You didn't have to walk me," I told Kyle in my driveway.

"Would you have done the same for me?" she asked, hands in the pockets of her leather jacket.

No one could work a jacket like this woman. She had exactly three, all quite similar, a testament to her consistent sense of style. I loved them equally. "Wait. What was the question?" I'd been lost in a leather jacket rabbit hole. "Oh! Right. Yes, I would have walked you."

"Well, there you go. We, apparently, look out for each other, which I think is a good thing."

"Can't argue."

She watched me a moment, and I wondered what she was thinking. She had an active brain. I knew that much. "Let's get you inside safely."

I sighed, sobering by the second—a blessing and a curse. It had been nice to check out of reality for an hour or two, but I was not a fan of rooms that shifted and spun without warning. "Fine. Is this the part where you help me get into my PJs and I fall asleep next to you and wake up surprised when we're cuddling and cute? I feel like I've read that particular book a few times." I let us inside the house and flipped on the hall light.

She followed me into my living room/kitchen combo. Me without alcohol coursing through my bloodstream would have been embarrassed by the less than organized space. My bunny slippers still sat in front of my couch. Kyle rocked leather jackets, but I was queen of the bunnies. But tonight? I barely blinked at the clutter. "Welcome to my chaos."

"I'm still caught up on falling asleep and cuddling. It does sound nice, but again, I'm not ever going to infringe upon your space or your comfort level."

"Right. The whole *I'm here for you but from a distance*."

"Does that upset you?"

I scoffed at the question. Good and *scoffed*. Why did she always have to be so calm and in control? Her emergency training was a little unnerving about now. "No." Something flared in my chest that demanded I be entirely honest. "But it's only a matter of time before that gets old and you're outta here. Everyone always is. You can set a fucking clock." I heard the hard edge in my voice. I was a jaded, bitter person these days.

Apparently, I'd been wrong about the calm thing because I watched as annoyance flared behind her blue eyes. "You're never going to *get old* to me, and eventually you're going to see that. I'm not going anywhere. I will keep showing up, and no matter what happens between us, or doesn't for that matter, dammit, my feelings for you won't change."

Her voice was louder than I was used to hearing it, and she was holding one of her arms out to the side to drive home her point. It was honestly a sight to behold. Yet it was her words that struck me the most. *I will keep showing up.* And you know what? A small part of me believed them.

The room was silent. I didn't know what to say, and I didn't trust myself in that moment not to tell her every last thing I felt for her, because my heart, boarded up or not, had things to impart that maybe my head did not. Instead, I walked to Kyle, held the lapels of her jacket and rested my forehead against her chest. When she placed her arms around me a moment later, tears sprang into my eyes, which meant I had to stay there a few beats longer than was probably wise. The problem was that being held by Kyle in that way was entirely familiar and wonderful. "I'm a mess," I murmured without lifting my face.

"Me, too," she said. "I think everyone is. We just each have our own brand."

I laughed, feeling a tad lighter. "I'm sorry I called you an intersection."

A beat. "I've been called worse."

More laughter. "I've gotta go to bed, and I can't take you with me."

"I had a feeling you were going to say that." She gave my chin the tiniest shake, in a move that felt so natural and loving that I wanted to live in that space, which meant she had to go.

I took a big step back and—oh, look at that. The room lurched, a reminder that the alcohol hadn't fled the scene just yet. I steadied myself, slid my hands into my back pockets, and nodded once, which seemed official enough. "Thank you for seeing me home."

"Oh, that's a dismissal if I've ever heard one."

I winced. "I didn't mean it to come off that way."

"But us alone, together is—"

"Daunting. And I'm drunk."

We stared at each other. There was a lot I wanted to say, and I could see on her face that she, too, was holding in her thoughts. A standoff in my living room. I flashed on the first time we'd met in the hallway of that hotel, my shirt stuck in a door. My heart blossomed with all the excitement, infatuation, and hope meeting Kyle had ushered into my life. I cared more for her now than I ever thought possible. So…how had we landed here? Miles apart from where we should be.

"Well, I'm glad you're home safe." She tossed her head in the direction of the door. "I'll see myself out." With a final smile, she turned.

"Will I see you soon?" I asked, hanging tight to the hope I'd just recounted.

Kyle didn't hesitate, which was everything. "Definitely."

CHAPTER TWENTY-SEVEN

Room 201

Baby showers were like weddings but with less pressure and more onesies. Thereby, I was a fan. Who doesn't like oohing and ahhing over tiny socks? Maya, our mother to-be, wasn't interested in learning the potential gender of her baby, which in my opinion was the most exciting way to go. It also offered those of us who organized the event lots of freedom to decorate as we chose. I looked around the break room on the afternoon of her baby shower, for which we'd closed the store for one full hour at Peter's go-ahead. Instead of any kind of boring pink or blue theming, we'd exploded the room in a circus of every color and palette imaginable. Jewel tones, pastels, neons, and in between shades. Balloons, swans, teddy bears, and a catered spread from BeLeaf Corporate made me feel like I'd fallen down the rabbit hole to newborn central. The gathering, attended by our employees and Maya and Jason's family, was a damn delight. It honestly had turned out more beautiful than I'd hoped. Even Buster smiled sweetly in the corner, consuming his square of cake in a blissful display while Maya opened the last of her presents: the bassinette I'd selected from her registry.

"Savanna, no. This is too generous." I watched as Maya and Jason exchanged an excited look. I knew she'd had her eye on the model. Knowing it was out of their price range, I'd encouraged her to add it to her list just on the off chance that someone decided to nab it. All part of my plan. "It is not. I need this baby sleeping in style when they're not sleeping on me, that is." And why did I have baby fever all of a sudden? That was new.

My phone buzzed, which was annoying because this was the

seventh or eighth call from that number in the past hour. "You know what? I might need to take this," I said quietly to Henrietta as I snuck out of the room, sad to leave the fun.

"This is Savanna," I said once I slid onto the call.

"Ms. Potter, thank you for taking my call. This is Bobby Lehman, from Lehman and Saunders." He paused as if I should know the name. I didn't.

"What can I do for you?" I asked, worried this was some sort of marketing call. "I'm actually right in the middle of a gathering for my coworker."

"And I hate to bother you, but I'm only in town for a short time and have an important matter I need to discuss with you before I go."

I paused, mystified as to what this could be about. "Is this something we can do over the phone? Or can you at least tell me what this pertains to?"

"I think it'd be better if we met in person. I'm camping out in an office at the courthouse. Can you meet me in room 201 upstairs as soon as possible? There's an important matter to discuss."

This was cryptic, and I wondered if it was some sort of prank. Maybe Jonathan was in town and planning to pop out from behind the door when I arrived. Now, that was a surprise I could get behind. I peered through the rectangular window in the door to the break room. People were hugging Maya. The baby shower was winding down. "I suppose if you can give me two hours. I have a store to turn around."

"That sounds great. See you then. Room 201."

It turned out room 201, on the second floor of the courthouse, was sparsely decorated, except for a shelf full of law books and a conference table made of dark brown glossy wood. Two men, one older, one younger, stood as I entered. They were wearing suits and definitely weren't from around here. Interesting.

"Ms. Potter?" the older one said.

"That's me. Hi."

"Hal Hobson, and this is my associate Derek Leary." Derek nodded quietly, and Hal took the lead. "Shall we have a seat?"

I eyed him, still with no clues about why I'd been called there, but now I was starting to wonder if someone I knew had committed a crime. Was I about to be on *Dateline*? Because I'd been training for this my entire life.

"I'm not sure if you've heard, but Donald Faber passed away two days ago."

I blinked, confused. "He did? Wow." That didn't seem possible. That man was as strong as mustard gas. I felt a little sad about all this. Not that I'd liked Faber in the slightest, but I had a heart. "That's too bad. No, I hadn't heard anything."

"He wasn't in town at the time."

"That's probably why."

"On a Jet Ski in Hawaii when his heart just gave out on him," Derek offered, followed by a wide-eyed look. Definite sidekick energy.

"Oh. Well, that is a very Faber way to go, making himself happy and spending his gobs of money."

"That's actually why we're here," Hal said.

"Because he was selfish?" I covered my mouth because this was not the best time for me to blurt my feelings. Someone had died, and I should respect the people who were sad.

"Because of his money. You're listed in his will as his sole beneficiary."

I didn't move a muscle. Neither did either of the two men seated across from me. "But that doesn't make any sense. He didn't like me. I was this gnat he occasionally swatted at."

"Well, you wouldn't be the first family I've represented that didn't get along."

"He's not my family, though. That's what I'm saying."

Derek flipped open a manila folder and consulted his paperwork. "He lists you as his daughter."

"But I'm not." I froze. What was happening? No way. Not remotely possible. The men looked at me and then each other, not exactly sure what they'd just stepped into. I stood up and walked the perimeter of the room at an accelerated pace that matched my racing thoughts. After three passes, I came to a screeching halt and whirled on them. "He says he's my father?"

Another exchanged look. "You didn't know that?" Derek asked.

"No, Derek! I didn't know that Donald Faber thought he was my motherfucking father!" I grabbed one of those chunky law books, good and shook the hell out of it, and placed it back on the shelf. I was the Incredible Hulk, reeling and ready to wage war on room 201 and Derek and Hal and whoever was the great puppet master in the sky.

I slunk into a chair, breathing heavily, and gathering my bearings. Finally, I eased out an exhale, found a glimmer of calm, and explained. "But the wonderful father who raised me is not a blood relative. Bio dad has been a bit of a question mark recently."

"So, maybe this is the answer to your question," Hal said gently. "Once his affairs have been handled, most everything he has is going to you."

I hadn't let myself acknowledge that portion yet. "You're saying I'm rich now?" My voice sounded flat. I couldn't make myself care about anything other than the bad news that it was very likely Donald Faber, that tool of a human, who was my paternal contributor. Dad was not a word I'd be using. He barely deserved former boss.

"It depends on your definition."

"No, you're rich," Derek corrected. I had a feeling these two would be having a talk in the car.

Hal slid me a very detailed sheet, only I had no idea what I was looking at. "In addition to the properties he owns, and there are many, this number at the bottom is a rough estimate of what will be left once we settle everything."

"Shut up." I looked down at all of the zeroes. "That's real."

"It is."

"And it's coming to me? I manage a grocery store."

"I'm sure you're great at it, but you probably don't have to anymore."

That seemed like a ludicrous thing to say. "I love my job."

Hal held up a logical hand. How was he so calm right now? "You don't have to make any decisions right now. Today is about letting you know of Donald's passing and what he asked us to do with his estate."

I looked back down at the zeroes, and something interesting happened. I thought of all the taking Faber had done while on this Earth. All the days he'd ruined, the feelings he'd hurt, and the air he'd sucked up all for himself. This money was a chance to cancel out all of it. I could use his fortune to make a difference for other people in a way he never did. And maybe I was one of those people. "You say he has houses?"

"Several."

"I'm a pretty good Airbnb host." Maybe my side hustle could sprout wings and grow. But I was getting ahead of myself. I decided to take Hal's sage advice and not make any decisions or moves.

We made plans to talk the next week, and still in a daze, I headed for the elevator.

"Ms. Potter?"

"Savanna," I said, as I turned around to see Derek approach. "You were just a part of one of the weirdest moments of my life. I think we can work with first names."

"Savanna." He shrugged. "I just wanted to say that for what it's worth, this man has no bearing on who you are. You said you had a wonderful father growing up? Nothing has changed."

His words touched me in a manner I didn't know I needed. "Thank you," I said. "You sound like you speak from experience."

He dropped his tone to *just between us*. "I'm raising a little girl who is not related to me by blood and never will be. But she's one hundred percent my family. I'm her dad. She's my kid. You know?"

I exhaled and smiled. "I do know. Sometimes I need reminding. Thanks, Derek."

I left the office in a daze. I'd walked in one person and walked out quite another. I needed the world to slow down, I needed either a warm beverage or an alcoholic one, and I desperately needed Jonathan.

First things first. I found a bench down the sidewalk and took a seat. He answered his FaceTime almost immediately. "Did you know that all they eat in Texas is tacos and barbecue? Seriously. Austin takes these two items very seriously." Then he saw my face. "What's wrong? You look pale, or is it just your redheaded fairness again?"

"I'm rich, and I'm a Faber." My mind raced while, at the same time, I was operating in a daze. A strange combination.

He squinted. "I don't know which of those to tackle first. What do you mean you're a Faber?" Then it seemed to hit him. "Oh, God. No. Are you sure?"

"Fairly. He left me all his money."

"Faber died?"

"Right. Should have led with that. He died in Hawaii and sent his attorneys to tell me that the money is all coming to me, his *daughter*."

"Stop that right now!" he yelled. "This is amazing!"

"It is not." Was Jonathan drunk? "I don't want to be a Faber."

"Well, you're not. And you never could be. That asshole's not even around anymore for you to have to deal with. Do you know what is around? All his selfish money that you'll turn into good money."

I softened because it was like he was reading my mind. Apparently, distance hadn't dulled our connection. "I was thinking the same thing earlier. I don't know. Maybe I could find a way to put it to good use? There are so many fantastic causes out there that are underfunded. Even some in this very town." Talking about all of the financial potential helped soften the news. "I could set up a scholarship through the GSA at the high school. And what about a donation to the Arthritis Foundation for research? Maybe even in your name. Hell, maybe we even start a nonprofit."

"I love that. And I'm sure it's just the start of the wonderful things you'll make happen. Focus on the silver lining." He looked into the camera. "This is what I know about you, my best friend in life. You're going to take every wrong turn he made and *right it*."

I nodded along, absorbing his words. I liked the plan, and right now I very much needed one.

"The opposite of everything he did."

The concept was already taking root.

"You hear me?"

"I think so," I said.

He leaned into the screen. "I think this is your new mission in life. You're the Anti-Faber, and the world is about to be bathed in glitter."

"Glitter is so messy, though."

Jonathan closed his eyes. "It's a metaphor, Savvy. You're going to leave this place better than you found it."

"Yeah. That I can get behind. But first? I think I have to figure out how this all happened. Lindy had to have known something. She and my mom weren't just sisters, they were best friends."

"Then you know where you have to start."

CHAPTER TWENTY-EIGHT

The Key to It All

My guests that week had checked out two hours earlier, which meant I had the all-clear to head up to the attic of the Airbnb, where two boxes belonging to my aunt remained. With the attic mostly cleared out, I hadn't been in a rush to go through them because, as best as I could tell, they simply contained old playbills from shows she'd seen and trophies and artwork from when she was a kid. It was a hail Mary that I'd find the information I was looking for, but I planned to turn every damn stone I could.

With a deep breath, I sank to my knees and opened the first box and then the second, finding much of what I expected. Odds, ends, sketches from her artist phase, and mementos. I smiled at the little reminders of Lindy but sighed as I sifted to the bottom of the final box. I texted Jonathan.

Nothing but dead ends. The attic was a bust.

As I awaited his reply, I looked down at the last piece of artwork in my hand. A sketch of a winding pathway through a serene landscape. Honestly, Lindy had been a fairly decent artist, having taken multiple classes at the local library. The shading was quite good. Next to her penciled-in signature was the name she'd given to the work: *Find Your Key to Happiness*. It was an interesting title, and when I looked closer at the sketch, I could see that there were actually tiny gold keys hanging from many of the branches on the trees along the path. How unique. I sat back on my heels. *I might just have to frame this one*, I thought, gently running my hand across the paper in reverence. That's when the smile fell right off my face.

The jumble of keys.

For as long as I'd known Lindy, she'd always had a key ring in the drawer near the fridge. Four or five keys on a tiny keychain that said *Eat More Cake*. I'd allocated all but the smallest key in the bunch to things like the shed out back, Lindy's bike lock, and several spare keys for her house and car. The little one's destination had eluded me, and I figured I'd get around to figuring it out someday. Yet I remembered right where I'd stashed those keys and headed down to grab them, then rushed out the door.

On pure adrenaline and with the jumble of keys burning a hole in my pocket, I stood in line at the bank.

"Hey, Savanna, you got a deposit for me?"

I don't know why I felt the need to keep my voice low, but I did. "I actually just had a question. I think my Aunt Lindy, um, Lindsay Bright had one of those locked boxes. Here is the key. Would you be able to check for me?"

After a round of typing, she smiled. "Right this way."

I was in absolute shock. I was escorted to a vault-like room I'd never seen before with an entire wall of safety deposit boxes.

"This one is Lindy's. You're listed as an authorized accessor as well. I'll just need you to sign in and we'll each use our keys."

This was astounding. I actually couldn't believe the series of events that had led me here, but I managed my expectations until I knew what might be inside that box. Two minutes later, Michelle placed the long rectangular box on the table in front of me. "I'll give you some privacy."

"Thank you," I said, and slid it open.

I peered inside and my breath caught. Goose bumps erupted on my arms. There was an envelope inside with my name written in those recognizable swoops. My mother's handwriting. I lifted it reverently and opened the flap. Her words rose off the page, and for a minute, it felt very much like she was right there in that room with me. In fact, I knew she was.

Savanna Rose,

> *If you're reading this letter, it means you're all grown up. I plan to hand over this letter to you once you're eighteen. Maybe not on your birthday, though. No seriousness at all on my girl's special day. The precocious two-year-old playing*

at my feet as I write these words is already on her way to being a kind and smart human being. I can only imagine what you're like now at eighteen! I have no doubt that you're my very best friend.

I have so many hopes for you that are ready to burst from my chest at any given moment, which is why I've decided to put pen to paper now. This letter is as much an outlet for me as it is sentiment I want to communicate to you.

First you should know that your father and I love you more than I ever realized was possible. We talk nightly about what an amazing little baby you are and how we were blessed "with a good one."

I worry a lot, however. I stay up late, tossing and turning, because I want to protect you from the world while also being as open and transparent as possible. I'm not sure how to make both exist. Because your start in this world, Savanna, and our journey together wasn't exactly the cookie cutter model. I don't want my journey to motherhood to in any way interfere with your sense of self-worth. I've done what I can to shield you from the choices that I've made, but I will always wonder if it was enough.

By now you've known for years that your father isn't related to you by blood but, in my firm belief, is a true soul connection instead. You two were meant to be together, two peas in a silly pod. I can feel it as much as I can the rays of sun on my skin each day. Our family is a perfect one, just the way it is.

That brings me to how I came to have you. While you're the best thing that ever happened to me, the man who you are biologically related to wasn't someone I was in love with. We met at a party and I was dazzled by things that were designed to dazzle. It was clear to me that he wouldn't be a positive influence in your life, so I made the choice to ask him to stay out of it, which he agreed to. Up until now, you've been aware of his existence but not his name. I have it for you now because as an adult, you have every right to explore that part of you. His name is Don Faber, and last I heard, he was living in Dreamer's Bay, South Carolina, where I grew up.

I sucked in air because my mother's words just confirmed it. Donald Faber was my biological father. I took a moment with the full realization, holding it in my hands and coming to terms with the truth. And then an important understanding clicked into place. I stared at the wall, and it was almost as if I could feel my mother's hand on my shoulder. I closed my eyes and let the feeling wash over me. At the very same time, something else washed over me as well. Strength. The will to overcome all of this. If my mother could fight so hard for me and my well-being, I could fight for me also. In fact, I felt like I owed it to her. She'd be devastated to see me roll over and give in. I wasn't alone. She was with me, and so was my dad.

In case anything should ever happen to me, I'll be handing this letter over to my sister for safekeeping. Though I imagine I'm not that easy to get rid of. I love you, Savanna. You're the best damn thing that could have ever happened to me.

With all the love in my heart,
Your Mom

I didn't move for a long time, and I had the room to myself to marinate on what I'd learned and to fully absorb my mother's words. I owed the bank a debt of thanks for that. When I did stand up and return the box, keeping the letter, I knew I'd been given a gift. While my goals for myself floundered, my mother's goals for me took over. They were now mine, too. Not only that, but everything in me wanted to live my life like my parents had, in love and light, the opposite of how Faber had lived his.

Instead of going home, I drove in silence through the streets of Dreamer's Bay, following the thread of my thoughts, which seemed to be moving at a million miles an hour.

Donald Faber didn't have love in his life. At most, he had lust. And the hot young thing he'd been so infatuated with had used him for a cash grab. That's what a loveless life looked like. No, thank you. I refused that destiny. It was as if a light had been turned on in a dark room. My parents, my true parents, against all obstacles had reached for each other and filled every room of our house with love. I looked up to them. I treasured the life they made for all of us, and in a contest, I'd choose them over the Donald Fucking Fabers of the world, time and time again. I gave myself my marching orders, and they involved ending my pity party and taking control of my life the way my mother once had when she was young, pregnant, and likely afraid. Nothing in life was easy, but if my parents could overcome difficult obstacles, so could I.

I needed to find Kyle, and it had to be right now. No sitting around and thinking or planning or trying to make sure everything was neat and tidy. I was done with that. Life was *messy*, and that was okay.

As I made a right hand turn toward town center, my phone rang. Seeing it was Elizabeth, I slid onto the call and placed it on hands free. "Hey," I said, only a little surprised by the newfound energy in my voice. "Everything okay?" Elizabeth and I only ever called each other about the turnovers at the Airbnb. All friendship communication was relegated to text.

"Yeah, I'm great! I just had this intense feeling that I needed to check in on you. Shake your tree a little."

I didn't hesitate. "It's been a day I can't quite describe. And I'm not surprised you were nudged. Today is full of all the nudging. Wait till you hear about a sketch of my aunt's that sent me to the bank, which wound up being, honestly, one of the most intense and important moments I've ever experienced."

"I can't say I've ever had an intense experience at the bank. I'm jealous."

"Rightfully. But I'm okay. Actually, things got really awful earlier. The worst ever. Then I rebounded to a high. I have a new perspective on things. Also, I'm rich now."

A pause. "Savanna, it's sounding like you might have robbed the bank."

I laughed. "It does, doesn't it? I promise that no laws were broken. But I do have updates for you soon. And I want to get a list of some of your favorite causes. But before all that, have you seen Kyle around anywhere?"

"Oh, I'm heading to the bowling alley to see her now. She's subbing in on the Ballbusters. Did you know she used to bowl?"

"I do remember. I think I'll swing by."

"Fabulous! Does this happen to mean anything significant?"

"I think it just might." I said goodbye to the sound of Elizabeth squealing, clicked off the call, and turned my car right around. I'd never wanted to see someone so badly in my life as I did Kyle Remington in that moment. Bridges were fine, but I heard bowling alleys were where it's at. If Faber was my surprise past, Kyle was my future, and it was truly time to turn the page.

"Thank you," I said quietly to my mother, as I squeezed the steering wheel. I wasn't alone, and never would be again.

CHAPTER TWENTY-NINE

An Important Announcement

The sound of music and bowling balls colliding with pins greeted me when I stepped through the sliding doors into the slightly too cold bowling alley. They always kept the air conditioning on even in the colder months. I was also smacked in the face with the mingling aromas of nachos and pizza. I'd never realized how chaotic this giant room was or just how awesome.

I scanned the lanes, each one occupied by teams of people, some of them high-fiving each other. Children walked by, lugging balls under their arms, en route to the few lanes not being used by the Tuesday night adult league. One guy carried not one but two pitchers of beer.

I spotted Elizabeth first. The Ballbusters wore their blue and canary yellow bowling shirts tonight. With them, you never knew what you were going to get in the way of fashion. Like professional franchises, the Busters had multiple versions of their uniform, which made me smile. A moment later, I saw her. Kyle had her hair in a ponytail tonight and wore scrubs beneath her bowling shirt, which meant she'd likely just finished a shift. She was laughing at something someone on the next lane had said. My stomach went tight, my chest warm. All the feelings I'd kept tamped down for months moved through me in a burst. I loved this woman with every fiber of my being, and it was time I put my longtime fear of abandonment in a headlock and left it in a closet for all time.

I realized I was clutching my phone extra tightly, one part excitement, the other part nerves. I approached the counter where a bored-looking teenager was doling out shoes and waited until there was a lull in traffic. Finally, I leaned in.

"Hi, there. Could I possibly make a brief announcement?"
His eyebrows shot up.

"I promise it's for good and not evil."

That seemed to help. He relaxed into a grin. "My manager's not here tonight, go for it." He slid the mic on a stand my way.

"Not to bother anyone, but I need the attention of Dr. Kyle Remington for one moment. I suppose the rest of you can listen, too." I watched. Kyle swiveled in my direction, her eyebrows pulled in curiosity, her lips pulled into a small smile. Elizabeth spotted me immediately and beamed like a lit-up Christmas tree. When Kyle's eyes found mine, I saw everything in her soften, as it so often did when we connected. I would never get tired of that effect.

"Hi, Kyle." Around her, bowling balls continued to be thrown down the lanes. Pins flew into each other in a blur. People tossed a glance or two my way, but for the most part we were alone. She raised a hand back to me with questioning eyes.

"So, I recently thought love was more likely to explode in my face before ever making me happy for a lifetime." Okay, maybe not the strongest start. My voice shook and there was a slight echo on the speaker that I hadn't been expecting. The teenager quirked his head in critique. "But that's not why I'm on this loudspeaker. Bear with me."

"Get it, Savanna!" someone yelled from across the room. Kyle folded her arms, waiting with her lips slightly parted in surprise, which made sense. "Thank you," I said to the random voice. "Uh, I've learned a few things since then that I'd like to share. I've learned the kind of life I want to live and the kind of legacy I want to leave behind for my children one day." That pulled in a few more audience members. The buzz of conversation in the room dipped. "And when I think of who I want to spend my days with, there's literally no one but you, Kyle. You're the first person I think of when I wake up in the morning and the last person on my mind when I fall asleep. I love you so much, Kyle, and I don't just want you to know it, I want the world to." I looked around to see all eyes now on me. "I give it about an hour until the rest of town does." I heard a few folks laugh. "We're gonna make mistakes and screw up all over the place. That's part of life, but can we please move into the phase of life where we screw up together? Because I want nothing more in this world than to make you happy and call you mine."

That seemed to have done it. Kyle began to walk in my direction, and the slightly tipsy bowlers she passed gave her a knock on the shoulder here or there while calling out things out like "Go get your girl."

She arrived in front of me and smiled. "I don't think I will ever forget you declaring yourself on the loudspeaker of a bowling alley."

I laughed, my heart hammering. "I wanted you to know how seriously I take this." I swallowed, searching her eyes for any sign of how she was feeling. For all I knew, I'd waited too long, and she'd embraced our newfound friendship. "I've had a lot happen today, and I'm going to tell you every detail. But there was no way I could go to sleep tonight without you being a part of all of it. I'm supposed to be here with you right now. I feel like we were meant to be together."

"We were," she said simply. "I've always known that. It's why I never left town. That's why I wasn't in any hurry. Because something told me that the ending was always you and me together."

My arms were around her neck in a burst. I needed to feel her pressed to me. All eyes were on us, and that was fine. I'd gone and made us into a spectacle and had no problem with every person in town knowing how much I loved Kyle. It was time that she knew it as well. Before I tugged her away, I leaned into the microphone. "And number twenty-six, your fries are ready."

The teenager shot me a thank-you wink, and I laced my fingers through Kyle's. "Follow me a minute."

"Anywhere," Kyle said, trailing behind me as I wound us through the whirs and pings of the small arcade section until we were alone in a sea of pinball machines. I didn't mind the whimsical underscore because my heart soared with whimsy and a healthy dose of relief to be back where I'd always wanted to be. I went up on my toes and kissed Kyle slow and long, reveling in the feel of doing exactly what I'd longed to for too many ridiculous months.

"I have missed these lips," she murmured. Next, she locked her gaze to mine. "And you're sure?"

"I'm just as sure about us as I am about salad not being a romantic meal."

Kyle laughed. "I love you. I don't know if you know that or not, but it's the biggest, most prominent thing I've ever experienced in my life. I'm head over heels for you, and tonight just confirms it once again."

My eyes filled. I was planning to say the words myself, but

hearing them from Kyle's lips made me feel like the luckiest person alive. I wasn't alone in this life, and I knew that now. Kyle wouldn't be leaving me. I don't know how I knew, but the confidence I had in us overflowed.

"I love you, too," I said, trying to impart every ounce of that love. She smiled, gave my chin the tiniest victory shake, and kissed me again. Nearby, a pinball machine offered a fireworks show that was the most fitting finale I could imagine.

"Go finish crushing the other team. I'll be here."

She grinned, and the skin around her eyes crinkled. "Yeah? Me, too. For always." She began walking back toward her lane before turning over her shoulder. "I forgot how much I like bowling. Maybe I should join one of these things."

"I could buy you a bowling alley now."

"What?"

"I'll explain after your match."

❖

There were so many things I had to tell Kyle, so many ways in which I wanted to show her I loved her. The sheer number of items on my to-do list when it came to her and me practically overwhelmed me to paralysis.

In order to keep it simple, we decided on a peaceful evening at the beach house that night, in which we could talk, enjoy each other, and catch our breath. We had plenty of time to settle back in at my place, but tonight I wanted to hear the waves roll in and the seagulls overhead as I held Kyle in my arms again. And while every moment I spent with Kyle mattered, this one felt extra important: a promise that things were different now. We were no longer a question mark or a couple hoping to make it. Kyle Remington, savior of women trapped in doors, was the love of my life, and I wouldn't forget it ever again. No matter what conflicts, obstacles, or salad disagreements came our way. And I fully expected some, too.

"I'm in shock right now," Kyle said from our spot on her front deck. Spring had only just begun peeking its head around the corner, leaving the Bay with a moderate chill at night. "This is like something out of a movie. Your asshole of a boss winds up being your father, but he dies before telling you. But, oh wait, he leaves you his riches."

"Yes. My life is quite cinematic."

"And how are you doing with all of this?"

"Obviously, it's not how I would have wanted it, but it's my story now. The only thing I'll never fully know is why Lindy didn't give me that letter when I turned eighteen."

Kyle paused. "Because she saw firsthand how awful he was and was trying to shield you from further trauma?"

I nodded. "I think so, too. It wasn't the right decision, but I can try and put myself in her shoes. She was raising a child who'd lost her whole world. If I'd taken the information in that letter and run off to start a relationship with Faber, I would have been crushed by who he turned out to be."

"Her heart was in the right place, at least."

I laughed. "Lindy wanted me to leave my job so badly. She must have suggested it twice a week. Now it all makes sense."

"I'm glad the pieces are finally assembling themselves."

"Me, too. It feels like I can finally breathe again."

We stared out at the darkened shoreline, listening to the sounds of the quiet beach. I snuggled closer to Kyle under the blanket. "And how are you these days?" I looked up and placed a kiss on her neck. "We've talked in passing, but I want to know everything."

"Well, the headline is, I like it here. People know my name at the grocery store!"

"Imagine that!" We shared a laugh.

"It's such a great fit at the hospital. I love the slower pace, but we have also faced a lot of trauma that, I'm happy to report, has been just fine. Even so, I'm continuing talking with my therapist back home once a week. She's helped a lot with the little bit of PTSD I occasionally battle."

"I'm glad to hear that." I met her gaze and kissed her softly. "I'm here, too. Utilize the hell out of me if you ever need to talk, or not talk, or decompress with a glass of wine or some ocean staring. If you've had a hard day. Say so." I popped up. "Did I tell you Charlie is up and around? He came into the store and gave me a great big hug. Jill wants to do a game night soon."

She shook her head. "His recovery has been remarkable."

"Thanks to you."

"I'm just a piece of the puzzle."

I looked up at her and lost myself in those eyes that never stopped.

"You're everything." And that's when it tipped, the lust scale. I'd fought it off as long as I could, but my hand was now making its way beneath the blanket to the hem of her top.

"You're attempting to seduce me," Kyle said with a raised eyebrow.

"Maybe."

The smile dimmed. "You don't have to. I'm so there."

"Yeah?"

She shook her head, eyes dark. "You have no idea."

We were making out like sixteen-year-olds on top of her covers in less than two minutes. One of the things I loved about scrubs was how easy they were to take off her. In fact, I brushed her hands away several times when she tried to help. "Uh-uh," I said, catching her lips and devouring them. I had her beneath me in her bra and underwear, a matching set I'd yet to see, in record time. We kissed in long spurts, short gaspy ones, and my favorite of all, the ones where our lips sought and clung. Her mouth tasted just as sweet as it always had. The murmurs and moans of appreciation with each little thing I did made me feel strong and appreciated. I stroked her through her underwear as she gasped and pushed into me for more. "Savanna," she pleaded.

"Right here," I said. I removed her underwear completely just as she dropped her bra, and shortly thereafter mine, to the floor. We certainly had no time for the clothes tonight. I had one goal in mind, and that was to watch *her* come.

"You're doing so many things to me," she said at one point. "What are you doing to me? What?"

"Making up for lost time," I said around the nipple in my mouth. If that wasn't the damned truth. How had I been so foolish as to let so much of it go by when all the while we should have been kissing, touching, or anything without our clothes? We were so good together.

As I continued to stroke, my fingers moving through wet folds, Kyle arched her back and pumped her hips in the sexiest hypnotic rhythm. I wanted to taste her. I closed my mouth over her most sensitive spot and sucked softly and then not, until she cried out loudly, gripping the quilt beneath her like a lifeline to Earth. I hadn't yet entered her and did so then, doubling her cry as I pushed her to greater and greater heights. Finally, she came back down in a whoosh, falling back against the pillow and searching for air. Still inside her, I continued to move to short little kicks of her hips.

"Are you trying to kill me?" she asked in a weak voice.

I continued my mission, pushing in and retreating slowly. To my surprise, she parted her legs further and began to move in tandem with me. First slowly and then very rapidly until she called out a second time, her head turning sideways on the pillow. "You are a menace," she said finally.

"I think that was a compliment."

"You're also so hot when you get that determined look in your eyes. I swear I get there faster just watching you."

"I happen to know from experience that you put on quite the show yourself."

"What's that?" she asked. "It's time for my show now?"

I grinned as her mouth found my throat, sending sparks of heat. Her hips settled between my legs, and holy fuck, the world tilted on its axis. Kyle rocked into me, a move she knew I couldn't resist. My hands were in her hair because it was too luxurious for them not to be. Her mouth was everywhere and also very focused, which was impressive in its duality. I didn't know if it was how badly I wanted her or how amazing she was in bed—probably both—but I was already skittering close to the edge. The pressure between my legs rose and caused an ache I could scarcely handle. Kyle knew my signals and was right there for me, moving down the bed like naked Wonder Woman about to save my day. She settled between my legs and began to trace circles with her tongue that grew more precise by the moment until I broke and careened down the roller coaster in a wash of pleasure that shook my entire being. I exhaled, slow and shaky. It had been one hell of a ride.

I looked up at Kyle, who'd settled on top of me, and touched her cheek. "I love you."

She smiled, and instead of answering right away, it seemed like she was soaking in the moment, memorizing my face. She intertwined her fingers with mine. "I love you, too. I will spend every day showing you how much. In fact, I can't wait to get started."

I pulled her down to me and held on, burying my face in her watermelon-scented hair as the waves rolled in nearby. Kyle was mine, and I was hers, and I knew without a single doubt that this was what forever felt like.

EPILOGUE

Pact Number Two

One year later

I was nearing the end of my romance novel (I had forgiven Parker Bristow at long last) when I looked up to see Kyle approaching in the distance, surfboard under her arm, bathing suit outlining her athletic form and more quite nicely.

Wailea Beach in Maui had proven itself to be one of the most beautiful places I'd ever visited. Beyond the lavish resorts and amazing restaurants, the island served up the most breathtaking sunsets I could ever imagine, and I now had the opportunity to enjoy them with my wife. Happy sigh. I was a doctor's wife. Even better, I was Kyle's.

"How was your shred session? Isn't that what all the cool kids call it?"

"Why don't you hop on a board and find out?"

"You know, I've tried and am awful at it. I much prefer to drink fruity cocktails and watch you out there. Objectifying you in a swimsuit on a board might be the favorite thing that I've ever done. Want to move here?"

She laughed wryly because the topic of where we'd reside had been a key discussion lately. Kyle had been offered a position at MUSC Health Hospital back in Charleston, which was too prestigious to pass up. We'd decided to divide our time between the city and Dreamer's Bay, especially since my new job offered me flexibility. I could work from almost anywhere for the nonprofit organization I'd set up to reach out to people dealing with chronic pain, find little ways to make their lives easier. It was all new, but I was passionately invested. None of it would have been possible without the money from Faber's estate. My vow to put as much good into the world as Faber had bad was still at the top of my goal sheet. In a surprise to no one, Jonathan was handling the financials and doing so pro bono.

"I don't know about moving permanently, but you could certainly open up one of your fabulous Airbnbs here." I had five now and worked hard to be the best host in the land. The little thrill I got from a positive online review kept me going the rest of the week, almost like the high from finding out Chipotle didn't charge me for my guac upgrade. The little things mattered.

I lit up. "You know, that's not an awful idea. That would give us a very solid reason to come back. The water is so blue here. It's like the gorgeous color of your eyes."

She placed a hand on her hip. "Look at you, the smooth talker today."

"I just happen to love you more than even parking spots that open up right in front of the store."

"Wow. And I love you more than a lull in ER admits."

"I really feel that one." I enjoyed this game we played and the constants we'd established in our relationship. I especially loved how I never could get enough of Kyle, and that didn't just extend to sex. I loved her mind, her patience, her humor, and the long talks we had after work each day. I took her hand and pulled her down to me in my chair.

"Careful. You're about to get wet," Kyle said, laughing. She wasn't wrong. She was still dripping. "But I do like the idea of you that way," she said with a wink.

I leveled her a pretend glare. "You never behave."

She nuzzled my neck. "Do you want me to?"

"Not in the slightest." She found my lips and kissed me, doing just as she'd warned, getting my dry suit all wet. I didn't mind. We were on our official honeymoon and had certainly spent a lot of it in our oversized king at the resort. It was shaping up to be a sexy honeymoon to remember. I'd never been happier or more myself.

I wrapped my arms around her waist. "You want to take a walk at sunset to that section of the beach that's supposed to have the most beautiful view?"

"If you're going, yes, I definitely do. Sold."

"Speaking of sunsets, I also want to show you the preliminary shots the photographer sent over from the wedding. There's one of us exchanging vows as the sun is setting between us."

"Really?" Her mouth fell open. "They're here already?"

"Mm-hmm. Some framers in there."

"Because you were the most beautiful bride ever."

"We're going to continue arguing that point until the end of time because I know of another." Our wedding day had honestly been the best day of my life. We'd gotten married in Bountiful Park in an outdoor ceremony attended by half the town. Kyle's parents, who are too smart and quiet and sweet to be believed, flew in for the week. Jonathan walked me down the aisle, and I even snuck in a dance with Jake, who'd beamed with pride, always asserting that we were still family. He was a keeper.

Early that evening, I put on a red sundress with little yellow flowers and waited for Kyle to join me for our sunset walk to dinner. She'd selected a royal blue strappy dress, slightly longer than mine. Her hair was down and full of sexy beach waves. How did I get so lucky? I asked myself this daily. But according to Kyle, she asked herself the same thing about me, which was...baffling, but awesome.

When we got to the stretch of beach known for its gorgeous views, we slipped out of our shoes and went barefoot. Our feet sank into the soft, warm sand. I took a deep breath of the salty air mixed with the sweet scent of the tropical flowers.

"Look at her," Kyle said reverently, as she studied the sky that very much resembled a painting in which the artist had swirled the oranges, pinks, and purples. "Sometimes I can't believe any of this is real." Her voice was soft, almost lost in the gentle rush of waves. "You know, I didn't realize anything was fully missing from my life. Until I met you."

"For me, it was different. I think I was always searching for this person who I just knew was out there somewhere, who would step into my life and make everything finally feel complete."

"And?" she asked with a beautiful smile and hopeful arch of her brow.

I squeezed her hand. "When you walked into my life, or rather down that hotel hallway, it was like someone turned the lights on. I thank God for you every day, and that's not an exaggeration. You're my dream come true, my answered prayer." We shared a quiet smile, so much love passing between us. Just days ago, we'd been married in front of our family and friends, but this felt like the true celebration. Just the two of us in our own little paradise.

I released her hand and stepped into the water, the coolness of the ocean enveloping my ankles. I reached for Kyle, who'd been silhouetted by the waning sun. "Come here."

She took my hand and joined me in the water, just in time for a wave to crash too close to the shoreline, splashing us aggressively. We laughed and looked down, our legs now soaked. "Well, this is not ideal," I said, shaking my head while still enjoying every second. "Do you think they'll still let us into dinner?"

"We have time to dry off first," Kyle said, wiping her eyes from laughter. Once we'd moved a safe distance away, she wrapped her arms around my waist from behind and rested her chin on my shoulder. I leaned back into her warmth, realizing I could stay right there in that spot forever.

"You're my greatest adventure," she murmured as we watched the sun dip lower in the sky, staying right where we were until the last sliver disappeared. They'd been right about that view. I'd never watched a more breathtaking display.

I turned in her arms. "Before we go, let's make a promise. No matter what obstacles life tosses on our path, we'll always do our best to get back to this feeling—this moment, this love. To right here."

"You have my word," Kyle said, her eyes sparkling with sincerity. "You have mine, too."

She leaned down and kissed me, and in that instant, I knew that whatever came next for us, we would take it on together. Our future was full of so many possibilities, boundless and stretched out before us like the endless sea. "Let's go," I said, giving her hand a tug. "I hear a fancy dinner awaits, and I want to stare at my wife some more."

Kyle tilted her head and grinned. "Well, your wish is my command."

The stars twinkled overhead as we stepped off of that beach and into the next chapter. Together.

About the Author

Melissa Brayden (http://www.melissabrayden.com) is a multi-award-winning romance author, embracing the full-time writer's life in San Antonio, Texas, and enjoying every minute of it.

Melissa is married and working really hard at remembering to do the dishes. For personal enjoyment, she spends time with her Jack Russell terriers and checks out the NYC theatre scene as often as possible. She considers herself a reluctant patron of spin class, but would much rather be sipping merlot and staring off into space. Bring her coffee, wine, or doughnuts and you'll have a friend for life.

Books Available From Bold Strokes Books

Discovering Gold by Sam Ledel. In 1920s Colorado, a single mother and a rowdy cowgirl must set aside their fears and initial reservations about one another if they want to find love in the mining town each of them calls home. (978-1-63679-786-1)

Dream a Little Dream by Melissa Brayden. Savanna can't believe it when Dr. Kyle Remington, the woman who left her feeling like a fool, shows up in Dreamer's Bay. Life is too complicated for second chances. Or is it? (978-1-63679-839-4)

Emma by the Sea by Sarah G. Levine. A delightful modern-day romance inspired by *Emma*, one of Jane Austen's most beloved novels. (978-1-63679-879-0)

Goodbye Hello by Heather K O'Malley. With so much time apart and the challenges of a long-distance relationship, Kelly and Teresa's second chance at love may end just as awkwardly as the first. (978-1-63679-790-8)

One Measure of Love by Annie McDonald. Vancouver's hit competitive cooking show *Recipe for Success* has begun filming its second season, and two talented young chefs are desperate for more than a winning dish. (978-1-63679-827-1)

The Smallest Day by J.M. Redmann. The first bullet missed—can Micky Knight stop the second bullet from finding its target? (978-1-63679-854-7)

To Please Her by Elena Abbott. A spilled coffee leads Sabrina into a world of erotic BDSM that may just land her the love of her life. (978-1-63679-849-3)

Two Weddings and a Funeral by Claudia Parr. Stella and Theo have spent the last thirteen years pretending they can be just friends, but surely "just friends" don't make out every chance they get. (978-1-63679-820-2)

Coming Up Clutch by Anna Gram. College softball star Kelly "Razor" Mitchell hung up her cleats early, but when former crush, now coach Ashton Sharpe shows up on her doorstep seven years later, beautiful as ever, Razor hopes the longing in her gaze has nothing to do with softball. (978-1-63679-817-2)

Firecamp by Jaycie Morrison. Going their separate ways seemed inevitable for two people as different as Fallon and Nora, while meeting up again is strictly coincidental. (978-1-63679-753-3)

Fixed Up by Aurora Rey. When electrician Jack Barrow and artist Ellie Lancaster get stuck on a job site during a blizzard, close quarters send all sorts of sparks flying. (978-1-63679-788-5)

Stranded by Ronica Black. Can Abigail and Whitley overcome their personal hang-ups and stubbornness to survive not only Alaska but a dangerous stalker as well? (978-1-63679-761-8)

Whisk Me Away by Georgia Beers. Regan's a gorgeous flake. Ava, a beautiful untouchable ice queen. When they meet again at a retreat for up-and-coming pastry chefs, the competition, and the ovens, heat up. (978-1-63679-796-0)

Across the Enchanted Border by Crin Claxton. Magic, telepathy, swordsmanship, tyranny, and tenderness abound in a tale of two lands separated by the enchanted border. (978-1-63679-804-2)

Deep Cover by Kara A. McLeod. Running from your problems by pretending to be someone else only works if the person you're pretending to be doesn't have even bigger problems. (978-1-63679-808-0)

Good Game by Suzanne Lenoir. Even though Lauren has sworn off dating gamers, it's becoming hard to resist the multifaceted Sam. An opposites attract lesbian romance. (978-1-63679-764-9)

Innocence of the Maiden by Ileandra Young. Three powerful women. Two covens at war. One horrifying murder. When mighty and powerful witches begin to butt heads, who out there is strong enough to mediate? (978-1-63679-765-6)

Protection in Paradise by Julia Underwood. When arson forces them together, the flames between chief of police Eve Maguire and librarian Shaye Hayden aren't that easy to extinguish. (978-1-63679-847-9)

Too Forward by Krystina Rivers. Just as professional basketball player Jane May's career finally starts heating up, a new relationship with her team's brand consultant could derail the success and happiness she's struggled so long to find. (978-1-63679-717-5)

Worth Waiting For by Kristin Keppler. For Peyton and Hanna, reliving the past is painful, but looking back might be the only way to move forward. (978-1-63679-773-1)